BLUE
ANGEL DAYS

Also in this series

BLUE ANGEL NIGHTS

BLUE
ANGEL DAYS

Margarete von Falkensee

Translated from the German by Egon Haas

W.H. ALLEN · LONDON
1987

Copyright © Egon Haas, 1987

Printed and bound in Great Britain by
Adlard & Son Ltd The Garden City Press,
Letchworth, Herts.
for the Publishers, W.H. Allen & Co, Plc
44 Hill Street, London W1X 8LB

ISBN 0 491 03125 4

Foreword by the translator

Margarete von Falkensee's first novel of Berlin in the late 1920s, forgotten for nearly sixty years, was translated and published in English in 1986 as *Blue Angel Nights*. It was a satirical view of the politics of the collapsing Weimar Republic in which she lived, presented in terms of sexual activity among a group of people broadly representative of the times.

Her second novel was accepted by the same publisher, OBUS Verlag, but the firm went out of business before the book was published and the author left Germany for America in 1933 when the Nazi Party took office. What has survived is a set of uncorrected proofs, now edited and translated into English under the title of *Blue Angel Days*, to make the connection with the earlier novel apparent. The author's own original title for this novel was simply *Friends*.

Blue Angel Days is also satire to the point of indecency and beyond, in the established German tradition of social comment, but unlike *Nights*, this has no optimistic ending. It is very evident from a comparison of the two works that the author's outlook had changed very considerably in the few years between them. Looking back, the reason is plain; the moderate centre in politics was fast eclipsed in these years by the rise of the Nazi Party, fuelled by the widespread unemployment and social unrest brought about by the Stock Market crash of 1929. The old Germany that lived on as a shadow of its former self in the Weimar Republic is here represented by the General, old, forgotten and impotent, while his successors are waiting for his death and planning a very different society for themselves.

This is a novel of relationships between people, and the most

5

obvious thing about them is that every relationship has been corrupted, particularly that of the two leading characters. The comedy has become more vicious and the relationships are obsessively self-destructive in this fable of a society in disintegration.

Egon Haas,
Munich, 1986

Chapter 1

Gerhart attends a public exhibition of skill and strength

The first time Gerhart von Rautenberg met Lotte was on an evening when he had been invited to accompany a party of his friends on an outing to a poor district of Berlin. He went because he was curious to see what Heinrich, who had arranged it, had in mind as entertainment. When he arrived at Heinrich's apartment he found that there were six of them, four young men and two girls, all in their twenties like himself. Besides Heinrich, there was Heinz Graunach, the comedian of the party, and Bertolt Heller, whom Gerhart hardly knew at all, a very tall man with his hair cut so short that he looked as if he had come straight from either an army barracks or a prison. One of the girls he knew well, Clara von Nimitz, a cousin of Heinrich, but Lotte Furer-Diest was a stranger to him.

To make her acquaintance was a pleasure. She was tall and shapely and her hair was so raven-black that it must have owed as much to the art of her hairdresser as to nature. She wore it in a long bob that framed her face dramatically, and her short evening frock was also chosen to be dramatic. It was of sheer black chiffon, cut square across the front and back, and held up by narrow straps over her powdered shoulders, so that it half-covered her breasts. She was, it could be stated without fear of contradiction, a woman who intended to be noticed and admired. Gerhart took note that she was wearing a gold wedding-ring, but that there was no husband present.

After a glass or two of champagne they set off in two cars, Heinrich leading the way with Lotte and Bertolt. Gerhart sat in the back of Heinz' car alone, Clara in the front with Heinz, a disappointing arrangement. They followed Heinrich, with much high-spirited tooting of horns, to Alexander-platz and turned up towards Prenzlauer Berg, a part of the city which Gerhart had never visited before. Nor would he willingly visit it again, he decided, as they left the well-lit and broad streets behind and drove through very shabby surroundings. They arrived at the public hall which was their destination and parked, with jokes from Heinz that the cars would be stolen inside ten minutes. The hall, when they entered, was packed full and smelled strongly of old clothes, unwashed bodies, boiled cabbage and stale cigar smoke. Heinrich had reserved ring-side seats and, as they sat down, there was no mistaking the unfriendly stares of the people about them at the sight of their evening clothes.

'Filthy brutes,' Heinrich commented loudly, 'half of them are drunk!'

'Frightful,' Bertolt agreed, glaring fiercely at a fat man in a threadbare blue suit sitting next to him, 'given half a chance they'd knock us down and rob us. Watch out for your hand-bags, ladies – there are some hardened criminals in a place like this. They'd steal from their own mothers – if they knew who their mothers were.'

Lotte was sitting next to Heinrich, and Gerhart had managed to get the seat next to her. She slid her fur wrap from her shoulders and sat with bare arms, ignoring the whistles from the rows behind her.

'It's not my hand-bag they want to grab,' she said with a smile, 'nor Clara's. They want to get their paws on something else.'

'Pigs!' said Gerhart, squaring his shoulders and sticking out his chin pugnaciously.

'Ah, you'll protect me, Gerhart, won't you?' she teased him. 'You won't let anyone touch my valuables, will you?'

'Your treasures will be safe with me,' he told her with a grin, 'though I suppose that Heinrich will want to keep them secure if he has a claim on them.'

'My valuables are entirely my own to dispose of,' she answered.

During these pleasant exchanges the house-lights were

dimmed and the master of ceremonies, a burly man in an old and badly-fitting tail-suit, made his appearance at the ring-side and was picked out by a spotlight.

'Ladies and gentlemen,' he bawled into a microphone, at which point the amplification system broke into screeches and then went silent, leaving him to mouth inaudibly until a rising din of jeering and whistling persuaded him to abandon his opening announcement. He sat down, and the contestants for the first bout climbed through the ropes and stood facing each other across the thick black mud of the ring.

They were both big women, brawny of shoulder and solid of thigh, wearing tight black bathing-costumes. Gerhart stared in astonishment at melon-sized breasts rolling under the thick material as the women raised their arms above their heads and showed off to the wildly cheering crowd.

'My God, look at those legs!' he said to Heinz, who was sitting on his left, 'if they were round your waist you'd be cracked like a walnut!'

'Fantastic!' said Heinz, 'I wonder what it feels like to be crushed in the embrace of a woman like that?'

The referee was small and thin and he wore a white shirt and spotted bowtie. He stayed outside the ring while he addressed the contestants, from which safe position he evidently intended to regulate the match. The time-keeper's bell clanged sharply and the wrestlers advanced slowly towards each other.

With a mighty thump they went down together and rolled over and over in a tangle of black-smeared arms and legs. They became a large and indistinguishable mud-ball from which, now and then, a limb rose into the air and was jerked down again as grips slipped and changed. But however long they wallowed in the mud, the action was totally inconclusive and eventually they responded to the referee's shouts and broke free. They stood up, bedaubed from hair to feet, and backed off a step or two. One of them hitched the strap of her bathing-costume up her shoulder and the other used both hands to tug hers down at the join of her thighs.

'Look!' said Heinz, jabbing his elbow into Gerhart's side.

'What?'

'Are you blind? You can see their nipples poking through now they're wet. And the one on the right pulling her costume down – she's got something as big and hairy as a coconut between her legs!'

'You can't possibly find that great cart-horse attractive!'

As if at an agreed signal the wrestlers hurled themselves at each other again, their bellies meeting with a loud squelch, to resume their clumsy battle. One of them dropped like a sack of mud onto one sturdy knee, thrust her head between the splayed legs of the other, held her by the thighs and jerked herself upright to throw her opponent over her head.

'My God!' Lotte gasped and seized Gerhart's hand as the thrown woman somersaulted in the air to land on her back and send a fountain of mud gushing upwards. Gerhart held Lotte's hand tightly, as if to reassure her, though his motives were plainly otherwise and he and she knew it. The standing wrestler turned faster than might be expected of someone her size and threw herself bodily on her fallen foe. She landed with a smacking thud, her broad belly across the other's breasts and shoulders and Gerhart distinctly heard Heinz moan. The pinned woman's legs kicked in the air, almost as if she were riding a bicycle upside down, but she could not break loose, it seemed. Her opponent held her while the referee, who showed great reluctance to spoil the fun, took at least ten seconds to count to three.

'I wonder they don't kill each other,' said Lotte, her hand still in Gerhart's, 'think of all that weight falling on you!'

'They are well padded, of course.'

'Padded? That's impossible! You can see that they have nothing under their bathing-costumes.'

'Well padded with flesh, I mean. Each of them weighs twice as much as I do and it's not all muscle.'

'Neither would win a beauty contest,' she agreed. 'Do you find this interesting?'

'Interesting, yes,' he answered as the wrestlers came to grips with each other again, 'I had no idea what to expect when Heinrich suggested we should come here. What do you think of it?'

'I've seen it before. My husband finds this sort of thing amusing and I have accompanied him a few times.'

The bout ended at last in victory for one of the contestants, by which time both were so thickly smeared with mud that it was utterly impossible to tell them apart. Heinrich passed a silver hip-flask along the row and Lotte took a sip before handing it to Gerhart. After a long swallow of good brandy Gerhart offered it to Heinz, who refused, and then leaned across Lotte to give it back to Heinrich, the back of his hand brushing across her bosom as if by accident. Lotte's only reaction was to blink.

'Now comes the moment we are waiting for,' Heinrich announced, his face flushed, 'the main bout of the evening. You've seen these two before, Lotte – aren't they astounding?'

'If you like female clowns,' she answered.

The first contestants had been big, but the women now entering the ring were giantesses. Gerhart stared in awe at their breadth of shoulder and biceps and asked himself how it could be possible for anyone, man or woman, planted on such tree-trunk legs to be ever thrown off balance. The master of ceremonies, his microphone now in order again, announced Fraulein Gretchen and Fraulein Lenchen and their unbelievable weights. Both were blonde and had their hair cut very short. The only way to tell them apart was by the colour of their bathing-costumes, one bright red and plain, the other with black and white stripes.

Gerhart turned to look at Heinz and saw that he was open-mouthed and round-eyed with disbelief at the sight of these battling Valkyries. The bell clanged and the giant women moved ponderously towards each other. It became apparent quite quickly that they were in a different class from the previous fighters whose only ambition had been to knock each other down and roll about in the sludge. Gretchen and Lenchen were entertainers and their struggle was, in its slow way, as carefully planned and rehearsed as a ballet. The huge feet churned the mud and spattered their bare legs, but neither threw the other. After a time Lenchen had Gretchen in a head-lock, her cropped blonde head under her arm, and hauled her round the ring two or three times. The purpose was to display to the spectators Gretchen's massive bent-over bottom under the tight-stretched material of her costume. Hold followed hold, each designed to throw into prominence some part of one body or the other. The crowd loved it, they cheered, whistled and stamped their feet and even through that noise Gerhart could hear Heinz gasping loudly beside him.

'Hot stuff, eh?' he asked with a grin.

'Incredible!' Heinz panted, 'I've got to have one of them! I don't care what it costs!'

Indeed, though he had treated it as a joke in speaking to Heinz, Gerhart had to admit secretly to himself that the spectacle in the ring was having an effect on him. The plain truth was that he was becoming aroused and he had to wriggle his bottom on the hard seat to let his stiffening part find more comfortable accommodation in his underwear.

By some curious move the wrestlers were back to back, their arms entwined. Gretchen bent forward and heaved Lenchen in the red costume off her feet, as if to tip her over her head. But the move was not completed, Gretchen stopped halfway, bearing the full weight of her opponent on her back and dragging her shoulders down tight to her own, so that Lenchen's colossal breasts were pushed up high. Her legs, well off the mud, opened and closed like scissors, bringing roars of approval from the spectators as they stared up between her massive thighs. This continued for ten or fifteen seconds and, as if unable to complete the throw, Gretchen released the other's arms and let her roll off her back, to land as firmly on her feet as ever.

Their bare arms and shoulders were shiny with sweat, but neither woman was splashed above the knee with mud yet. Gerhart realised that the outcome of the bout was arranged in advance and he wondered how it would be brought about. After so provocative a display of skill and strength, a quick trip and a scramble in the mud would be most disappointing.

'Have you seen these two before?' he asked Lotte as the wrestlers circled each other warily.

'Oh yes, they are famous.'

'Which do you think will win?'

'It is a question of whose turn it is tonight.'

The spirit of the contest underwent a change, as if Gretchen and Lenchen had decided that they had been through the preliminaries to the satisfaction of the spectators. The time had come to give them something different and raise the already heated mood even higher. The crowd sensed the change and started to shout again, urging the contestants into action. As if in response, the one in the black and white costume lunged forward, brought her blacksmith's arm up shoulder-high and struck the other woman a resounding blow across the jaw with her forearm. The crowd screamed as Lenchen staggered backwards, her head hanging down as if dazed by the mighty blow. Gretchen followed up at once, smashing her forearm again and again into the other's jaw and neck, until she stood swaying on bent legs and splayed feet, her arms dangling loosely by her sides, and the crowd roared for the kill. Gretchen moved in, hands clutching to grip and throw, but Lenchen was by no means dazed and ducked under the outstretched arms. In a second she had Gretchen from behind, an arm round her throat to choke her into submission and a brawny knee up in the small of her back to bend her over until she lost her balance. But that point was never reached. Gretchen teetered, almost falling over backwards, but never actually doing so, and Lenchen reached round with her free hand and smacked Gretchen's out-thrust breasts resoundingly with her open palm. The crowd roared its approval and she did it again, the sound of the slaps clearly audible in the front rows, even through so much noise.

'I'm dying!' Heinz screamed, his fingers tugging at his white collar to loosen it and let him breathe.

Urged on by the roaring approval of the spectators, Lenchen took hold of the top of her helpless opponent's costume and ripped it open right down to her belly. The clamour of the crowd was truly deafening when Gretchen's huge and heavy breasts burst out into plain view and Lenchen smacked them again with her flat hand.

'Monstrous!' Heinz croaked. 'Undeniably and magnificently and gloriously monstrous! I can't stand any more – do it again!'

The referee had been waving his arms and screaming

unregarded for some time and it was only now that Lenchen appeared to hear him. She released Gretchen, whirled her clumsily round and gave her a great smack on the backside which sent her reeling across the ring, breasts flopping and rolling through the torn costume, towards that side of the hall where the spectators had not yet had the pleasure of viewing these bouncing balloons.

'You'd like them for pillows!' Gerhart shouted at Heinz to make himself heard.

'Oh my God – it's too much!'

Gretchen was on the ropes, breasts hanging over the top one, as if summoning up her reserves of strength. When the spectators on that side had been treated to an adequate view, she turned to face her tormentor, showing every sign of cold fury, exposed breasts heaving, fists clenched and teeth bared in a snarl. She slipped the shoulder-straps of her torn costume down to her waist and tied them together in front. Thus prepared, she plodded back purposefully through the mud, naked to the waist, towards Lenchen.

'I want them both!' Heinz gasped, 'I must have them!'

Lenchen was crouching defensively and sidling away from her advancing foe. But not for long. Gretchen had hold of her and the two were using their weight against each other, straining to win. For long seconds they swayed and shuffled backwards and forwards, until in a sudden move Gretchen went down on one knee and toppled Lenchen so that she fell on her back across the out-thrust thigh. She clamped a hand round Lenchen's thick throat to hold her head down near the mud while she returned the earlier compliment by ripping the front of her costume open and smacking her bare breasts.

The spectators were up on their feet, bellowing at Gretchen to finish Lenchen off. Lotte was shouting and waving her bare arms while she hopped up and down on her high-heeled shoes. Gerhart was shouting himself, staring glassy-eyed at the big floppy breasts being maltreated in the ring. Without completely knowing what he was doing, he clapped a hand to Lotte's silk-covered bottom and squeezed hard. She flashed him a quick look over her shoulder and looked back to the extraordinary events taking place in the mud-ring. Gerhart held on to her bottom, sinking his fingers deep into the warm flesh.

If Gretchen heard the cries of the referee running round outside the ropes, she ignored them. She took hold of Lenchen's red bathing-costume between the legs and, in a fearful display of strength, broke the material and tore it upwards. Everyone, Gerhart included, stood and screamed themselves hoarse as Lenchen's costume was ripped up to her belly-button and the thick mat of brown hair between her legs was revealed. Heinz was beyond shouting, he clung to Gerhart's shoulder as if he could no longer stand without assistance, and uttered shrill whining sounds. Gerhart had forgotten that his hand was still clenched on Lotte's bottom and only partly aware that she had hold of his upright stem through his trousers and was squeezing it unmercifully in her delirium.

Gretchen scooped up a big handful of mud and held it up for all to see. The roaring of the crowd rose to an impossible din as she smacked the thick mud firmly between Lenchen's parted thighs and rubbed it in. The hand on Gerhart's shoulder slid away and Heinz, totally overcome, collapsed into his seat and missed seeing the second and third handfuls rubbed into the door-mat of thick hair which Lenchen boasted. As if satisfied with her triumph, Gretchen rolled Lenchen off her knee, face down in the mud, and stood up, arms raised above her head in a gesture of victory, and shuffled round in a complete circle to make sure every side of the hall had a proper view of her dangling breasts. For good measure she kicked her prostrate opponent's massive behind and set one bare and mud-caked foot on her back.

This was at last too much for the non-intervening referee. For the first time that evening he climbed over the ropes and squelched miserably across to Gretchen, much like a dwarf approaching a mountain. He pummelled her vast belly and shouted at her until he drove her back into a corner. By that time Lenchen had climbed slowly to her feet, her face and front smeared with black mud and one big hand clasped modestly between her legs to cover what the spectators had already seen. The little referee paddled back to her, spoke briefly and went to the ropes to confer with the master of ceremonies.

The crowd was silent, waiting for his announcement. Gerhart realised that Lotte had been gripping his stiff part only when she took her hand away and he let go of her bottom.

'Ladies and gentlemen! Fraulein Lenchen is unable to continue the match in her present condition of indecency and she concedes it. The winner is – Fraulein Gretchen!'

It was not a universally popular decision. Mixed with the cheering were cat-calls and hisses from those who thought that the bout should continue, whether Fraulein Lenchen was indecent or not.

'Come on,' said Heinrich along the row, 'let's get out of here before a riot breaks out.'

Chapter 2

Sieglinde is entertained by the General

While Gerhart was studying the skills of female wrestlers, his sister Sieglinde was concerning herself with family obligations by dining with the General in the old-fashioned splendours of his apartment. Old he may have been, so old that he had fought in battles everyone else had long forgotten, but he retained his air of command. His iron-grey hair was cut short in the old Prussian military style and brushed upright from a square and powerful head set on a solid body, without any sign of a neck between. His thick and curved moustache was as hopelessly out of date as the monocle screwed tightly into his left eye. There was no chance that anyone in the world, however stupid or unobservant, could have mistaken him for anything other than what he was. Even in civilian evening clothes, he gave an impression of wearing uniform and a casual visitor would have looked automatically for the row of medals that were nowhere to be seen.

He sat straight-backed on his uncomfortably hard sofa, a glass of brandy in his hand, and opposite him there hung on the wall a large oil-painting of which he was very proud. It showed the former Kaiser Wilhelm riding in an open state carriage through the Brandenburg Gate, surrounded by his mounted bodyguard, while respectful Berliners lined the pavements to cheer. It was at least a quarter of a century old, this painting, and it proclaimed unambiguously the theme of the General's life before the collapse of the German Empire and the abdication. In a sense, it was an epitaph.

The picture's antiquated look gave it a certain interest historically, if not artistically, which could certainly not be said of the painting on the wall behind the sofa. That one showed a troop of booted and helmeted lancers riding down and skewering ten or twelve routed enemy foot-soldiers. This too was an echo from the old man's past and it expressed, in however romantic a form, the reality on which the vanished Empire had been based.

But the past is the past, and what is done is done. The pictures were merely part of the furniture now. The General was in a cheerful mood, as might be seen from the absence of the usual hard glare in his pale blue eyes, even the one behind the monocle. The reason for his good humour was the presence of his dinner guest, Sieglinde, twenty-two years old and very pretty. She sat beside him on the hard sofa, reclining gracefully, her legs crossed and the skirt of her short plum-coloured evening frock hitched almost up to her knees, she being a very modern young lady and casual about such matters.

The General smiled fondly at her and asked her to bring him a cigar. This gave him an opportunity to watch in appreciation the way the cheeks of her bottom slid under the thin silk of her frock while she walked across the room to fetch the silver box in which the cigars were kept. When she turned quickly, holding the heavy box in both hands, her breasts swayed inside her frock and she pouted in amusement at the brief grin she saw on her host's face. When she offered him the box, its domed lid raised to display two ranks of short and thick cigars, she stood close to him, to let him catch the fragrance of her expensive perfume. The General made his selection without hurrying over it and handed the cigar to her. All this was a little game they played on these occasions and they were both aware of what they were doing. After the silver box was back on the table it always stood on, Sieglinde returned to stand close to the General again, to stage a little performance for his benefit. She raised her plum-coloured skirt slowly up her legs until the lace edge of her underwear could be seen, then set one foot in its high-heeled evening shoe on the edge of the sofa by the General's knee. He stared at her legs with close attention, and they deserved it. They were long and well-shaped from thigh to ankle and her black silk stockings, gartered above the knee, contrasted most provocatively, as they were intended to, with the pale and smooth skin of her thighs. She had thighs such as every woman wants, but few have, not thick and clumsy, not thin and lacking in charm, but exactly right. And on the fine skin of the inside of her raised thigh she rolled the cigar under her palm, from the lacy edge of her knickers to her stocking-top and back again.

'What memories it brings back to see you doing that,' said the General, his voice tinged with wonder.

'I am sure that your memories are scandalous beyond belief,' she flattered him gently.

'They say that this is how cigars used to be rolled in Cuba,' he told her, not for the first time, 'they say that scores of dark-skinned young senoritas sat on stools in the tobacco sheds and rolled the leaf on their bare thighs to make the perfect cigar. Perhaps it was true once. I've never been to Cuba, more's the pity, so I cannot speak of this from my own experience. But I am sure that the cigars are made by machine now, even there, exactly as they are made here in Germany. I do not regard this as progress. Only a fool would exchange a pretty young girl for a machine, but the world is full of fools and tight-fisted businessmen snatching at profits.'

Sieglinde put the end of the cigar in her mouth and leaned forward, her foot still up on the sofa to display her legs, while the General fished in his waistcoat pocket for his gold lighter and flicked it into flame. She put her hands on her hips in the Spanish gypsy way and leaned further towards him to touch the cigar to the flame and inhale, knowing that his eyes were on her breasts, almost entirely visible down the low-cut bodice of her frock. She puffed out clouds of fragrant blue smoke until the cigar was properly lit before handing it to him. The General drew in a long breath, savoured the smoke and exhaled it slowly.

'It tastes of you, my dear, a wonderfully sensual taste.'

Sieglinde put her foot on the floor at last, ending the display of her legs and underwear, and stood as if in thought, hands still on her hips and her head tilted to one side.

'What am I to do with you?' she asked in mock disapproval.

19

'There is something I would like to do with you,' he answered, 'but as that is no longer possible for an old ruin like me, I can only ask you to humour me.'

'You are shameless,' she teased him, 'your thoughts should be turning towards higher things.'

He blew a smoke-ring and watched it drift slowly away.

'I have always been on excellent terms with my Maker and He has never begrudged me the simple pleasure to be found with pretty women. The pastors put sour looks on their faces over these little matters, but that's what they are paid for, I suppose, though to the best of my knowledge no one of any importance has ever taken the least notice of what pastors say.'

'But I thought that the Kaiser was a pious man! At least, that's what they told us at school.'

'Your teachers got it wrong. How would they know? They never talked to him. It was his wife who was the pious one. She built some of the most stupendous churches in Berlin. I took you to see them when you were a little girl, though I doubt if you've ever visited any of them since.'

'Do you think I should be religious? If I were, I would never roll a cigar for you on my thigh. Think what you'd miss!'

'It was always my intention that you should grow up to have confidence in yourself and have the courage to do what you want to do without looking for approval to others.'

'And have you succeeded?'

'I am proud that you are no simpering idiot. You are as bold as a man and you will make your own way in life. That's how it should be. If you'd turned out differently I would have had to marry you off two or three years ago to some decent and dull young man from an acceptable family. He would have made you pregnant every year until you were middle-aged and fat as a barrel.'

'Thank heaven I was spared that!'

'Then you will indulge my elderly fancies a little?'

Sieglinde laughed at that and undid the fastening of her frock over one hip so that she could take it by the hem in both hands and pull it up over her head. The General grinned briefly and appreciatively at the sight of her standing before him in only her black silk knickers and stockings. Indeed, she was a sight any man would have appreciated, being well-made, round-breasted and with elegantly curving hips, the bloom of youth and health on her skin.

'Black underwear for a funeral and a brothel,' he said. 'At least, it was so once.'

'They're new. I bought them especially to wear this evening.'

'You did well,' and he patted the sofa beside him to indicate that she should sit down.

Sieglinde stretched herself along the sofa, her back propped by the end away from him, one foot on the floor still and the other leg tucked under her. The General puffed slowly at his cigar as he surveyed his obliging guest, approving what he saw, from her straw-blonde head down to her legs, leaving out nothing in between. He put a hand on her knee and then stroked the satin skin above her garter.

'We must enjoy our little pleasures to the full while we still can,' he said, 'this is something we all learn eventually. When we are young we do not understand it. We are always in a hurry and so we experience much and enjoy little. Isn't that so?'

'Perhaps. But times have changed. This is 1930, not 1910. Things move faster now.'

'And you think that the change is for the better? I tell you that it is not. In 1910 we knew where we were and what we wanted. Today everything moves so fast that it is out of control. Germany is on the brink of a revolution that will finish people like us. We must make the most of what we have in the time left to us.'

'I can't imagine anything that is going to finish people like us. Why should it?'

'You will see,' he answered darkly. 'For me the end will be quick and not without dignity. When the Bolsheviks break down my door they will find me ready for them, in full dress uniform, on my feet and with a revolver in my hand. I shall kill as many of the swine as I can before they down me. If God is good to me it will be six of them first.'

'Oh, politics! Why do you upset yourself with such boring

stuff? It's all nonsense, this talk of revolution. The newspapers invent it so they have something to print.'

The General's broad hand had eased itself further up her thigh and lay in the warmth where the lace edging of her knickers crossed her skin.

'Newspapers!' he snorted, 'I can tell you a story about newspapers. Back in 1919 the Reds tried to drown us in Bolshevism with their dirty uprising. You were only a child then. It was the day after your eleventh birthday, I think. I left you and your brother here with the servants to look after you while I put on my uniform for the last time and went to do my duty. The mob had seized the railway stations and government offices and put up their red flags. They were armed, though God only knows where they got their weapons from. I marched towards the sound of the firing and found a group of the swine barricaded in a newspaper office. They'd hung a banner out of the windows with one of their stupid slogans on it, some rubbish about *Bread and Freedom*. By good fortune the army was ready for them and there was a detachment of infantry surrounding the building. I found the Colonel in charge and offered my services. I out-ranked him, of course, but I was already on the retired list and there is an etiquette to be observed. He was a great patriot, that Colonel, even though today his name is reviled by the so-called liberals. He thanked me and asked me to take cover and observe the overall action while he directed the first attack. Do you know, even though he was dealing with revolutionaries, he was punctilious in his respect for the military code. He gave the rabble in the newspaper building a chance to lay down their weapons and come out with their hands up. I admired him for that. When they refused, he ordered his men to open up on them with machine-guns and mortars.'

His fingers had found their way under the lace and were combing through the curls between Sieglinde's legs. She was not really listening to his story, a tale she had heard many times before. Perhaps it was true, perhaps not, perhaps memory had exaggerated what had happened. In any case, it was a long time ago and of no importance or interest to her.

'By the time we'd downed a few of the scum there were white flags waving at the windows – shirts and handkerchiefs. The machine-gunners stopped firing. I said to the Colonel *Why let these swine escape and cause more trouble later? Why not finish them now and be done with it?* So he sent in his men with the flame-throwers and grenades and that was the end of that little revolution.'

'Dreadful,' said Sieglinde, stifling a yawn.

'It did no good. We got rid of twenty or thirty that day but now there are thousands of them, millions perhaps, and this stupid government of ours does nothing about it. My God, they're even allowed to vote to elect Communists to the Reichstag.'

'You are a terrible man!'

'What, for killing a few Bolsheviks?'

'For what you are doing to my new knickers. They will be ruined beyond repair if you force your hand in like that. Wait a moment.'

He removed his hand while she slipped the knickers over her hips and down to her knees. The General put his cigar down carefully on an ashtray and helped her to take her knickers off completely. He removed her shoes, dropped them on the carpet and stared at her pleasurably. The curls between her legs were somewhat darker than her straw-coloured hair but still authentic blonde. He stroked her flat belly and put a finger-tip into her round little belly-button.

'My grandfather was born in the year 1815,' he told her, 'That was the year we smashed the French.'

'Napoleon, you mean?'

'An upstart little captain of artillery who called himself an Emperor! Well, von Blucher put paid to him at Waterloo. There was a true German hero – seventy years old and still riding into battle at the head of his army.'

The General's musings on the past came to an end as his fingers found their way gently into the tender little pocket half-hidden by Sieglinde's curls.

'You are very beautiful, though not in the way that the women were beautiful when I was young. They had what we used to call the hour-glass figure, with a broad behind for a man to get hold of and a round belly to lie on like a cushion.'

'They were fat, you mean.'

'Comfortably plump. It is good to see that the fashion among young women now is to have breasts and hips again, not that thin and half-starved look of a few years ago. I never understood how men could find that attractive.'

'But you find *me* attractive, don't you?'

'If I were younger I would ask you to marry me, even though your breasts are barely a handful each. When I was a young Captain the girls I knew had breasts big and soft enough to push up until they could lick their own nipples. You couldn't possibly do that.'

Sieglinde had become aroused by the caress of his fingers inside her.

'I can do this,' she said, her eyes half-closed.

She put the middle finger of both hands to her mouth to wet them, then touched the pink tips of her breasts and stroked them lightly.

'So!' the General exclaimed, his pale blue eyes bulging and the veins standing out on his temples. 'Where did you first learn this little trick?'

'At school, of course,' she murmured, 'the other girls showed me what to do. We often used to play with each other.'

'I remember now,' he said, his voice hoarse with emotion, 'you told me about your friend Maria. You used to bring her here – a pretty girl with a round face and plaits. You used to tell me you had to study and took her into your room. You were both innocent little virgins to my way of thinking.'

'Virgins but not very innocent,' Sieglinde breathed, smiling at the recollection.

'Not innocent at all! Instead of studying your books you were playing with each other's breasts, weren't you? And I was out here in the sitting-room with my newspaper, totally ignorant of what was going on. Isn't that so?'

'Oh, yes, yes!'

'What else did you do to each other?' he demanded, his face flushed dark-red.

24

This too was a game they had played many times together, he handling her and pretending to force confessions from her of her school-girl pranks. He knew all her tales as well as she knew his military tales, but it still excited him to hear them.

'We used to pull our knickers down and see who had most hair between her legs.'

'And who did?'

'Maria's hair was darker than mine and showed more. But mine was prettier.'

'Did you touch each other?'

'We felt each other's slits and put a finger in and tickled to make it feel nice. Just like you are doing to me now!'

'And could either of you reach a climax when you stroked each other?'

'Yes, both of us . . . sometimes we played at who could make the other do it first.'

'If only I had known!'

'What would you have done – watched us through the key-hole? That would have been very exciting if I'd known you were watching.'

'Then you would have lost your game every time!'

'I always did!'

Sieglinde was breathing fast through her open mouth. She rolled her buds hard between thumb and forefinger, her head went back and the combined sensations of her own fingers and the General's between her legs brought her to a climax of pleasure.

'Ah, ah!' she murmured, her black-stockinged legs twitching uncontrollably.

It was over very quickly. She breathed out in a long sigh of satisfaction and lay still. The General's hand cupped her furry mound, covering it protectively.

'Good!' he said, 'The greatest pleasure of my life is to see your beautiful body and touch it.'

'I owe you everything. I am glad if I can give you pleasure.'

The General picked up his cigar, tapped off the long grey ash and drew in a mouthful of smoke.

'I am sure you know younger men who can give you more

25

pleasure than I can,' he said calmly. 'At least, I hope that you do.'

'Young men think only of themselves. They want to use my body for their own enjoyment.'

'I knew a woman once, a long time ago. A Baroness she was and very lively. She had much the same objection to men and she devised a way to remedy matters.'

'And how did she do that?'

'She refused to let any lover enter her before he had first made her enjoy at least three complete thrills with his hands and mouth. Sometimes it was more, it depended on her mood. A night of love with her was hard work, believe me.'

Sieglinde giggled.

'And when you eventually got inside her, was it worth it?'

'It was unbelievable! Her legs gripped you round the waist and pulled you deeper and deeper into her, as if she wanted your whole body in her belly. And when she was near her moment, she raked her finger-nails down the length of your back until the blood ran. She was like a tiger.'

'Did you love her?'

'It's too long ago to remember things like that. I still have the marks of her nails on my flesh, honourable scars in the battle of love, if it was love,' he answered, giving her one of his rare smiles.

But now that the excitement of playing with Sieglinde was over, it was not long before his thoughts drifted back to his earlier preoccupation with the doom he foresaw.

'You and your brother are grown up now and no longer my wards under the law. You were only children when your father sacrificed his life for Germany at Verdun and your poor mother died of a broken heart. You had no other family but me and although the connection was a remote one, I felt it my duty to take care of you as best I could. I still feel a sense of responsibility towards you both, more than ever in these dangerous times.'

'Why are these dangerous times? I don't understand that.'

'You have already told me that you find politics boring. I must talk about this to Gerhart and he will understand me. The

26

fact is that this damnable Republic of ours is about to collapse, that is what I mean by dangerous. We are ruled by corrupt and traitorous politicians, all intriguing for their own advantage or working secretly for foreign powers.'

'How can you say such a thing!'

'Because it is true. This is what democracy means – a ragbag of dirty swine fighting each other to get their snouts into the trough. Communists. Social Democrats, People's Party, Nationalists and the National Socialists led by their mad Corporal. This is anarchy and it cannot last. Mark my words, a revolution is in the making that will sweep all this filth away.'

To distract him from another tedious exposition of the state of politics as he saw it, Sieglinde changed her position on the sofa so that she could lean against his shoulder and stroke his face and bristling moustache.

'How fierce you are! I'm sure you were just as much a tiger in bed as your Baroness was. Did you bite and claw the women you made love to?'

'A strong back and legs, that's what a man needs. There were times when women fainted away with pleasure when I lay on them and drove hard.'

He stubbed out his cigar and used both hands to caress her bare breasts.

'I know that you think they're too small,' she said with a grin, 'but you have to admit that they are well-shaped. I know lots of men who think they're pretty. At least, they try to get their hands on them.'

'There was a girl in Dresden . . . I think it was Dresden. She had pretty little breasts like yours and she liked them to be played with. She was a train-driver's daughter, as I recall. She must be a great-grandmother by now, but she was only sixteen then.'

'You are a terrible and wicked man. Even while you are caressing me you are thinking about somebody else. That is not polite.'

'I think of you and your future constantly, believe me. And your brother's, of course. I made my will a long time ago and when I'm gone everything I have will be shared equally between you.'

'You mustn't say such things!' she exclaimed, putting her palms over his hands to make him squeeze her breasts.

'A man must take thought for these matters and make his arrangements. That is the correct thing to do.'

'I refuse to listen.'

'No matter. The day will come when you receive your inheritance.'

Chapter 3

Gerhart engages in a duel for a young lady's favours

Sometime after midnight Gerhart found himself in Bertolt
Heller's apartment with Bertolt and Clara von Nimitz. After
the wrestling the party had moved on for supper and dancing
and at some stage Gerhart could not now remember, Heinrich
had slipped away with Lotte. Heinz had also disappeared,
though whether that was before or after Heinrich, there was no
way of telling. It had been Gerhart's intention to say goodnight
and leave the remaining couple to themselves, but Bertolt had
got so amazingly drunk that he was incapable of driving his car
– at least, not without danger of death to himself, Clara and
anyone who might be on the street at the time. The outcome
was that Gerhart had driven the car and when they arrived,
Bertolt had insisted that he came into the apartment for a final
drink.

Not, of course, that Gerhart was entirely sober. Nor was
Clara. But neither of them was as far gone as Bertolt. There was
a fixed and foolish smile on Clara's very plain face, her brown
hair was mussed and she sat on the sofa in Bertolt's sitting-room
with her legs sprawled out in front of her in an inelegant
manner.

Bertolt, a glass of brandy in his hand, was searching round
the room in the vaguest of ways for an ash-tray, a long and unlit
cigar in his mouth.

'It was a fraud, that wrestling,' he announced, as if he had
just made an important discovery. 'Did you realise that,
Gerhart? Or were you deceived into believing that those enormous women were trying to beat each other?'

'The thought never crossed my mind,' Gerhart answered

with a sarcasm that was entirely lost on his host.

'Ah! They deceived you! But not me – I am an expert boxer and I know by instinct when two contestants are really trying or just fooling around. That's the difference between us.'

'I've seen Bertolt boxing,' said Clara, 'he's so big and brutal in the ring!'

'Is that why you have your hair cut so short?' Gerhart asked.

'Naturally.'

'But you are not a professional – you only box for sport.'

'That's neither here nor there. I want to look the part. Besides, if I wanted to become a professional, I could.'

He had given up his search for the ash-tray because he had forgotten what it was that he was looking for. He had even forgotten the cigar in his mouth and it waggled up and down as he talked. He stood in the middle of the room, swaying slightly.

'If you become a professional boxer your father will disown you,' said Gerhart, 'And then you'll have nothing to live on and you'll lose this apartment and your car and everything else he pays for.'

'That's where you're wrong! I could soon earn enough by boxing to replace the pittance I get from the old man. I'm a potential champion – world champion, I mean.'

'You are!' Clara breathed in adoration, 'you are so huge and strong.'

On that note, Gerhart thought it best to take his leave, so that Bertolt could demonstrate to Clara how huge and brutal he could be, out of the ring as well as in it. He rose unsteadily to his feet, but Bertolt put a hand on his shoulder and stopped him from leaving.

'Out of the question,' he said, squinting as he tried to focus his eyes on Gerhart's face, 'we haven't resolved the problem.'

'I didn't know that we had a problem. Do we have a problem, Clara?'

'If Bertolt says so.'

'Well, what is this problem then?'

'The problem of the missing girl, of course,' said Bertolt, 'you don't have to be polite and pretend that there is no problem. Roma was going to be with us this evening, but she developed a head-ache and so we are one short. Heinrich has Lotte and you and I are left with dear Clara between us.'

'If you intend to be logical, then we were two girls short, because Heinz was with us. But he's gone home and if I now do the same, the problem vanishes, leaving you with Clara.'

'Out of the question,' Bertolt insisted, his face flushed red from the drinks he had consumed, 'this is a matter of honour and it cannot be made to disappear like that. You and I must fight for Clara. I will get my boxing-gloves from the bedroom.'

'Not a good idea,' said Gerhart quickly, 'you might get hurt and then I would blame myself.'

'Me hurt? What nonsense! I shall knock you out with the first punch.'

'At this moment you are not very steady on your feet. There is no prospect of knocking me out.'

'What an insult! Are you suggesting that I cannot hold my liquor? I shall beat you black and blue for that!'

Clara smiled foolishly from the sofa, her dark blue eyes switching from Bertolt to Gerhart and back.

'You must fight each other,' she exclaimed, 'I am the prize for the winner!'

Gerhart shrugged Bertolt's heavy hand off his shoulder and took a short step back from him.

'Punch me on the nose,' he suggested, 'if you manage to hit me, we'll fight for Clara.'

Bertolt screwed his face into a ferocious mask, drew back his arm and swung a slow and uncertain punch at Gerhart's face, oblivious of the fact that he had a half-full glass in his hand. Gerhart swayed backwards out of harm's way, the brandy left the glass and splashed down Clara's legs, while Bertolt stumbled foward off-balance, tripped over a chair and collapsed against the wall.

'He's knocked himself out,' said Gerhart, when his fallen opponent did not stir.

'Oh Gerhart!' Clara exclaimed. 'You are so strong and brutal – you've knocked Bertolt out! I'm yours! Take me!'

He turned to stare at her plain face and wondered why this well-brought-up daughter of an important family was offering

31

herself as a prize to two drunks. More to the point, did he want her prize?

'I may be down but I'm not out,' came a voice from the floor, and Bertolt hauled himself up on to his hands and knees and crawled to the sofa. He collapsed beside Clara, a dark red mark on his temple where he had hit the wall.

'You were right,' he said to Gerhart, 'I am not in form for boxing this evening. We must settle this in some other way.'

'We are both reasonable men, Bertolt. What do you suggest?'

'It is your turn to make a suggestion.'

'We could flip a coin.'

'Certainly not! In affairs of honour the decision is not left to mere chance. It must be a contest of skill and strength between us.'

'You could wrestle with each other,' Clara suggested, 'it would be wonderful to see two such big and brutal men wrestling for me.'

'Impossible!' said Gerhart and Bertolt together. 'Wrestling is for low-class professionals,' Bertolt added.

'Let's have another drink while we give our fullest consideration to how we can settle the question,' said Gerhart, hoping that if Bertolt drank much more he would fall asleep.

'I'll get it,' Clara offered, levering herself up from the sofa to find the brandy bottle.

Gerhart sat down beside Bertolt and looked closely at the mark on his temple.

'You've given yourself a nasty knock. Does it hurt?'

'Does what hurt?'

'That's all right then. But you'll have a big bruise in the morning.'

Bertolt was staring across the room at Clara as she filled three fresh glasses.

'She is very beautiful,' he said with an air of judicious solemnity, 'And very desirable. I can say that without fear of contradiction because I have enjoyed the privilege of being admitted to her . . . damnation, what's the word I mean?'

'Her bed?'

'No, no! That's not what I was going to say. It is not polite to refer to a lady's bed in that sort of way.'

'I apologise. Did you mean her favours?'

'That's it! Her favours. Thank you, my dear Gerhart. Have you also been privileged to enjoy Fraulein von Nimitz' favours, may I ask?'

'Naturally. We have known each other for some time.'

'Excellent. Then we are old comrades in sharing this delightful experience, if I may express myself with a degree of freedom.'

His speech was becoming slurred and difficult, and to compensate he was becoming increasingly pompous.

'Clara, my dear,' he called across the room, 'you may remove your clothes and allow us to appreciate the magnificent prize we are competing for.'

By then Clara had three glasses on a tray and was about to walk very carefully towards them, concentrating very hard on not spilling a drop. At Bertolt's words she giggled and her hands shook so that she slopped brandy over the tray. She wobbled towards the sofa and bent forward unsteadily to offer the drinks, showing the curve of her breasts down the front of her frock.

'I drink to your beautiful body,' said Bertolt, taking a glass in each hand and half-emptying one in a single gulp. 'We must see it at once before we risk our lives fighting each other for the honour of closer acquaintance with it.'

There was no time for Gerhart to take the other glass. Clara stood upright and dropped the tray to free her hands to wriggle out of her close-fitting crimson frock. The tray bounced and rolled away, the glass lay on its side, the brandy seeping into the carpet.

Gerhart and Bertolt stared at her, as well they might, for she had an exceptionally well-developed body, with big round breasts and strong thighs. If only nature had formed her face in a more classical mould, she could have played the role of Storm-maiden in any Wagnerian opera.

'Black underwear is sensational on a beautiful woman,' said Bertolt, 'don't you agree?'

'Fantastic,' said Gerhart, interested at last in her and the comforts she might provide.

Clara's heavy breasts were half-hidden in a black lace brassiere that pushed them upwards.

'Such bouncers!' said Bertolt, his admiration causing him to forget his deliberation of speech.

The two men's gaze travelled downwards simultaneously to Clara's black silk knickers and then to the bare thighs between them and her black silk stockings.

'No danger is too great for a prize like this,' said Bertolt, back to his previous formality. 'we will fight each other with sabres.'

'No,' said Gerhart hurriedly, afraid that Bertolt actually had a couple of sabres somewhere about his apartment, 'that would be unfair to you.'

'Why? I am a skilled swordsman.'

'But I am left-handed. That would give me an enormous advantage over you. What about pistols?'

Pistols seemed reasonably safe. It was improbable that even sport-mad Bertolt would have two in his possession.

'Good!' Bertolt said, to his dismay, 'I'll go and get my revolvers.'

Before he could do any such thing, Clara's eyes rolled up to show the whites and she sank down on folding legs until she was sitting on the floor. Both men lurched to their feet at once, took her under the arms and lifted her on to the sofa, where she lay with her head back and her eyes closed.

'Clara – what is it?' Bertolt exclaimed in alarm. 'Are you ill?'

All that was wrong with her was that she had far too much to drink, but so simple an explanation did not cross Bertolt's fuddled mind.

'Her pulse! We must check her pulse!' he gurgled, taking her wrist between his fingers.

They sat down, one on either side of her, staring at her sleeping face and open mouth.

'I can't find her pulse, she must be dying!' Bertolt wailed.

'Nonsense,' said Gerhart, reaching round the unconscious girl to undo her black brassiere and pull it away from her magnificent breasts.

'What are you doing?' Bertolt screamed. 'This is no time for that!'

'I am feeling her heart to make sure that it is beating normally,' Gerhart explained.

And indeed, it was beating very normally, a slow and regular thump that spoke of sturdy good health.

'Is she all right?' Bertolt demanded, as Gerhart's hand moved away from its medical investigation and fondled her big and warm breast.

'She is perfectly all right, but she is tired and needs to sleep. Feel for yourself – her heart is perfectly normal.'

In his confusion Bertolt was evidently not at all sure where to locate Clara's heart. His large hand spread itself over the breast nearest to him and felt it very thoroughly.

'You're right,' he said after a while, 'her heart-beat is normal. There is nothing for us to worry about.'

'Nor do we have a problem any more,' Gerhart pointed out.

'What do you mean?'

'Since Clara is fast asleep, there is no longer a prize to contend for between us. We do not have to shoot at each other.'

They sat there, each playing with a breast, while Bertolt pondered what Gerhart had said.

'I cannot agree with you,' he said eventually, 'honour requires that we should continue with the duel, whatever state Clara is in. I shall go and load my revolvers.'

'Before you do – one thing!'

'What?'

'Before Clara fell asleep she was responding to your proposal that we should be allowed to see the prize we are about to fight each other for.'

'You're right! And there is no doubt at all that we are entitled to view the prize before we endanger our lives to win it.'

Between them they got Clara's black silk knickers over her bottom and down her legs. She lay sprawled with open thighs, snoring slightly, as her two suitors surveyed her closely.

'A fine broad belly,' said Gerhart, running his hand over it.

'And strong thighs to grip a man with,' Bertolt added, running his palm up the one closest to him until he had his hand over her brown-haired mound. 'And as for *this* – what can I say about it? My experience of it has been heavenly. I'm sure you found the same.'

'Oh, very pleasant,' Gerhart agreed, 'if she has a failing, it is not in her body.'

'A failing? What do you mean? She is beautiful?'

35

'She has a beautiful body,' said Gerhart, thinking it unkind to mention her plainness of face, 'but she is not very intelligent.'

'I don't understand you at all,' Bertolt complained, stroking Clara between her legs, 'what the devil does intelligence have to do with it? Who wants intelligence in a beautiful woman? That's like putting mustard on chocolate-cake.'

'Perhaps I'm being foolish, but I like clever women.'

With a final squeeze of Clara's big soft breast, Gerhart stood up to leave.

'The prize is yours, Bertolt.'

'Sit down! I refuse to let you back away from a matter of honour, especially now that you have seen Clara naked.'

'But there is no prize,' Gerhart pointed out. 'Let's arrange to meet tomorrow or the next day and start all over again, when Clara is available.'

Not that he had any intention of making the arrangement, once he was clear of the apartment.

'You are not being logical,' said Bertolt with ponderous and slow speech. 'Did not Clara say of her own free will that she was the prize for whichever of us won the contest for her – you heard her say it!'

'Yes.'

'So what has changed? Here she is, ready for the victor. All we need to do is decide which of us it is to be.'

'But she's unconscious!'

'What of it? Whether she consciously enjoys being the prize is neither here nor there. She is still the prize and one of us must have her to prove that he is the winner. How did we decide to settle the matter?'

'We didn't,' said Gerhart, thankful that Bertolt seemed to have forgotten about pistols, 'we were still discussing it when Clara went to sleep.'

'This has become very difficult. Haven't you any suggestions at all?'

'Yes, but you may not like it.'

Bertolt's eyes were almost closed and his hand was still between Clara's thighs. He began to nod slowly.

'Anything you suggest,' he slurred, 'anything at all, so that we can settle things and go to bed.'

'Do I have your word that you will accept my suggestion?'

Bertolt nodded, half-asleep already.

'Then what I suggest is this – that we share the prize between us, as two old comrades should.'

'Old comrades . . . yes, that's right. All for one and one for all and . . . share Clara . . . I like that.'

'Then it's settled. Would you like to go first?'

'Why should I have the advantage? Old comrades share.'

'Then let it be decided by seniority. How old are you?'

'Twenty-three. How about you?'

'The same. Which month is your birthday?'

'March.'

'So is mine.'

'Are we twins?' Bertolt asked drowsily. 'No, that can't be right. What date in March?'

'The fifth,' said Gerhart, his heart sinking.

'I've beaten you! Mine's the second!'

'Well done! Congratulations! Your turn first with this wonderful prize.'

Bertolt lumbered to his feet, almost fell on his face, and shuffled round to face the sofa.

'Watch,' he said, his words hard to distinguish, 'Now you'll see how an expert gets to grips with a beautiful woman.'

With great difficulty he took off his dinner-jacket and dropped it, the sleeves inside-out. He rocked backwards and forwards on his heels, trying to remember what he should do next.

'How expert are you?' Gerhart asked.

'Expert boxer . . . expert swordsman . . . expert swimmer . . . expert shot . . .'

'With women, I mean.'

'A world champion . . . everybody knows that.'

'How many women have you made love to – fifty, a hundred?'

'Thousands,' said Bertolt vaguely, 'thousands and thousands.'

His glance fell on Clara's limp and naked body and, with this reminder of what he was attempting to do, he unbuttoned his trousers and hauled out his limp tail.

'Now we're getting somewhere,' he slurred.

37

He sat down with a bump on the floor and tried to reach his foot with both hands.

'What are you doing?' asked Gerhart.

'I'm taking my shoes off . . . it's out of the question to make love to a lady with your shoes on . . . surely you know that.'

He succeeded in removing one of his black patent leather shoes and then fell over sideways and lay still.

'Bertolt – are you all right?'

The answer was a bubbling snore. Bertolt had passed out.

'You've given up,' said Gerhart to no one in particular, 'you're out of the contest. I declare myself the winner.'

He fondled Clara's breasts again and tried to make their pink tips go hard, but nothing happened.

'The question is,' he said aloud, 'do I want the prize I've won? It's not as if this was new territory. I've played with her bundles plenty of times before, when she was awake. Some people might say that it's better when she's unconscious, because she doesn't say all those silly things she comes out with when she's awake.'

He stroked the smooth insides of the thighs and the soft-haired lips between them.

'It's nice enough. And very accommodating, as I recall. There was one afternoon when I did it to her three times in a row and she said I'd ruined her – what was it she called it? I know, her *little mousy*. Only there's nothing little about Clara – big bundles, big backside, big mousy. If she was awake at this minute she'd be going on about her *little mousy* being hungry and grabbing at my tail to stuff it in. Which is fine when you're in the right mood and your tail is as hard as a broom-handle.'

He took his hand away from her and felt between his own thighs.

'To be absolutely and ruthlessly honest,' he announced aloud, 'Clara is having no effect on me at all, Mine's as limp as poor Bertolt's.'

He took the carnation from his lapel and, with meticulous care and attention, inserted its short stalk between the lips of *little mousy*, so that the white blossom adorned it. With an effort he got to his feet and gestured with one hand at each of his sleeping companions.

'Goodnight, dear Clara, sleep well. You will find a small token of my esteem where you least expect it when you wake up. And goodnight, Bertolt, old comrade. My token of esteem will prove to you that I won the prize, not you. And now I'm going home to bed.'

Chapter 4

Breakfast in bed

Gerhart and Sieglinde shared an apartment in Tauenzienstrasse, not large perhaps, but pleasant. They had furnished it
in the most modern style, all bright colours and angular furniture, as different as it was possible to be from the dark
and heavy style of the General's home. Gerhart awoke when
Sieglinde came into his room carrying a silver tray with two
large cups of coffee and a plate of bread-rolls. She set it down
while she drew back the curtains to let in the sun and Gerhart
rolled on to his back and looked at her. Her yellow hair was
brushed out and fluffy and she wore a long dressing-gown in
rose-pink, with a frilly collar.

'Good morning,' she greeted him cheerfully, 'It's nine
o'clock. I heard you come in alone last night.'

He heaved himself into a sitting position, propped his back
with the pillows and took the cup she handed him. His hair was
the same straw colour as hers and tousled from sleeping but
he was a handsome sight. His blue silk pyjamas matched the
blue in the tapestry of dark red and blue which he used as a
bed-cover over daffodil-yellow sheets. Sieglinde sat on the
bed facing him, the tray between them, and sipped her own
coffee.

'Did you have a nice evening?' she asked.

'Comical! Would you believe it, Heinrich took us to watch
women wrestling in mud! Afterwards we went to the Excelsior
for supper and danced for a while. I was home by two o'clock.
Did I wake you?'

He munched a soft bread-roll and washed it down with
coffee.

40

'I wasn't really asleep,' she said, 'who else was there?'

'Do you know someone called Lotte Furer-Diest? Very pretty, with black hair and a good figure.'

'No, I don't think so. Who was she with?'

'Heinrich invited her. She's married and separated.'

'I can see that you liked her.'

He grinned and took another roll from the tray.

'You wouldn't have been here at two in the morning if she'd asked you to take her home, that's certain. Didn't she find you interesting enough?'

'She went off with Heinrich. I think she's been out of things for a while, being married, and she's making use of him to introduce her around.'

'She's probably penniless if she left her husband and looking for someone who can afford her.'

'Maybe. She made a point of telling me her telephone number when we were dancing.'

'That's no surprise. You're a hundred times better looking than Heinrich. Did she look as if she'd be nice to make love to?'

'That was the impression I got. We were so carried away by the wrestling that I grabbed hold of her bottom and she grabbed me in a way Heinrich would have objected to if he'd known about it. It's just as well he was shouting his head off at the wrestlers and saw nothing.'

'What was this mud-wrestling like? It sounds squalid.'

'Squalid, yes, and grotesque, but amusing in its way. Two of the fighters ripped each other's bathing-costumes off and gave us a look at parts of themselves so huge and unattractive that I couldn't believe my eyes. Heinz was tremendously affected by it. I was afraid he was having a heart-attack.'

Sieglinde laughed and cleared the tray off the bed now that breakfast was finished. She settled comfortably beside her brother, leaning against the pillows.

'Poor Heinz is so susceptible. Did I tell you what Clara did to him once?'

'What?' he asked.

'He took her to the Winter Garden and it was the usual sort

41

of show they have there with singers and lots of chorus-girls prancing about practically nude. They were going to eat somewhere afterwards and in the taxi Heinz was so steamed up from the show that he wouldn't stop kissing her, so she pulled her skirt up and pushed his hand up her knickers. He was so overcome that he did it in his trousers then and there.'

'Which was more embarrassed – Heinz or Clara?'

'How do I know? Since she told me that I've always turned down his invitations.'

'I've told you about my evening. How was yours?'

'The General sends you his warmest regards and hopes that he will see you soon. In fact, he suggested that we should both go there to have lunch with him on Sunday. I said I'd let him know, but I suppose we have to go.'

'How is he?'

'The same as ever. He went on about politics a lot. Sometimes he sounds quite frightened when he talks about what he thinks is going to happen. But I suppose all old people get like that eventually.'

'And what is going to happen?'

'The usual thing – the revolution, the end of civilisation and all that. All the same, he wanted me to take my clothes off after dinner and let him have a good feel.'

'Naughty old thing! If he were still up to it he'd have you on your back with your legs in the air.'

'If he were still up to it he'd ask me to marry him, he said. Just think of that – if I accepted I'd be your stepmother.'

'No you wouldn't. Did you tell him about my work?'

'I told him over dinner that you're doing very well selling your drawings to magazines now, but I don't think he understands properly. If he ever looks at a magazine he probably thinks that the illustrations are drawn by the editor. You can tell him again on Sunday and perhaps he'll understand.'

'It won't do any good. For him the world is divided into soldiers, politicians and civilians. He loves soldiers, hates politicians and despises the rest. He thinks I'm wasting my time.'

42

'You mustn't take it too seriously. It's just the way he is. He mentioned his will again.'

'He mentions it every time we see him. Are we still his joint heirs or is he going to leave his money to a home for retired army officers?'

'You know we are. He'd never go back on his word. But why we should get equal shares when I'm the one who looks after our interests, I don't know.'

Gerhart put an arm round her shoulders.

'Because you're beautiful, that's why. He thinks I'm a waster and if I went to see him on my own it would do more harm than good. The retired officers home would get the lot. Anyway, it's not so bad when you go to see him, is it? He gives you a good dinner and a bottle or two of first-rate wine. And if he wants to fondle you after that, where's the harm? In his place I'd do exactly the same.'

'You would, would you?'

He turned on his elbow to face her and slipped a hand into the front of her frilly dressing-gown to cup a breast affectionately through her thin silk night-dress.

'They're very pretty, your little bundles. Any man between nineteen and ninety who isn't tempted to get his hands on them is either mad or lilac.'

'But don't I have any say in the matter?'

'Naturally you do. It's entirely up to you to decide which are allowed to do so.'

'And you're one of the privileged, are you?'

'I'm an exception, you know that. You and I have no secrets from each other, not since you moved out of the old man's apartment and came to live here with me.'

Sieglinde unbuttoned his pyjama jacket and stroked his chest. The hair on it was so fair as to be almost invisible against his skin.

'There's something else you haven't mentioned,' she said.

'What is that?'

'That we're both so beautiful that we can't help being attracted to each other.'

'That's true,' he said in all seriousness, his fingers playing

43

delicately over the firm little tips of her breasts inside her nightdress, 'I have never known anyone as beautiful as you.'

'And I don't know any man half as beautiful as you are.'

'How lucky we are,' he said in a contented tone.

She put her hand into the bed and tugged at the string of his pyjama trousers to undo it.

'Your monkey-tail is standing up. Is that because you were dreaming about the girl you met last night?'

'No, I wasn't dreaming about her, not that I remember.'

'Then why is this stiff?' she asked, trailing her fingers along it.

'It must be because I'm playing with your little bundles.'

'Show me.'

The tapestry covering and sheet were thrown aside and he lay beside her with his body exposed from throat to groins.

'Am I beautiful?' he asked softly.

'You know you are.'

'And so are you,' and he opened her pink dressing-gown and pulled up her night-dress to clasp her lightly between the legs. Her hand moved up and down on his hard stem and Gerhart cuddled close to her, his head on her shoulder, enjoying what she was doing to him without a thought for the consequences. It was by no means the first time that he and she had played this little game together.

'When are you going to have this Lotte?' she asked him.

'Soon maybe. I don't know.'

'Is she as beautiful as I am?'

'No,' he murmured, 'she is as dark as night and you are a wonderful golden child of the sun. She hasn't got your high cheek-bones and blue eyes.'

'I wonder if she knows how to play with a monkey-tail.'

'Not like you . . .'

'You like it when I play with yours?'

'It's as exciting as having it between another woman's legs . . . more exciting even!'

'I feel that you are going to tell me something important soon.'

'Oh yes, something very important.'

'What is it that you're trying to say – is it a secret?'

'A big secret . . . something we never tell anyone else . . .'

'So important?' she asked, her hand moving fast. 'Tell me then!'

'Oh, yes, yes!'

His hand in the cleft of her thighs clenched tightly, his body jerked against her and his ecstatic outpouring spattered across her uncovered thighs.

'That's what you wanted to tell me!' she exclaimed, her clasped hand pumping busily, 'that's what I wanted to hear!'

She waited until he was calm again before she asked him if he wanted to hear what she had to tell him.

'Of course I want to know!' and his fingers parted the warm folds of flesh between her thighs and felt for her slippery bud.

'Perhaps I shouldn't tell you,' she teased him.

'I insist that you tell me! I shall not let you leave this bed until I know what it is that you are hiding from me.'

'I never hide anything from *you*,' she murmured, her legs parting wider as sensations of pleasure coursed through her from his stroking finger tips. 'Can't you guess what it is?'

'Guessing is not the same as knowing. I want to be sure.'

'Sure that I love you?'

'I know that already. The question is – how much do you love me?'

'Then kiss me and you'll find out,' she breathed.

Gerhart rolled over to lie between her outstretched legs and his thumbs opened her wide to expose her secrets. His wet tongue licked at her little bud and her bottom lifted off the bed in climactic throes.

'I love you, I love you!' she moaned, her fingers twining in his hair.

When it was over they lay side by side, his arm round her and her head resting on his bare chest.

'Nice?' he asked.

'It's always nice when we play Secrets together. Do you love me?'

'You and no one else. That's why we play Little Secrets together.'

45

'We play Big Secrets with other people,' she said, 'shall we ever play it together?'

'I don't know. One day, perhaps.'

'When?'

'I don't know that either. One day we shall look at each other and know that the time has come.'

Chapter 5

Gerhart is taught how to appear in a circus

Even though he had no need to work, Gerhart had been trying for some time to establish himself as an illustrator of books and magazines. His efforts were not held in high esteem by the General, but the fact of the matter was that he had a certain talent and was developing it with some success. There was a continuous demand from the popular magazines for well-drawn and amusing little pictures, in colour and in black and white, and this he could well meet. Needless to say, the range of subjects was limited, and so was the artistic treatment. Every picture had to show a pretty girl engaged in some interesting action, within a narrow range of possibilities. She could be painting her lips or finger-nails, or dressing to go out to meet a boy-friend, and this gave the illustrator scope to show her partly clothed, most frequently in a slip and stockings so that her bare thighs could be shown.

If the boy-friend appeared in the picture, then he must be kissing the girl's hand as he greeted her, or she could be getting out of his car and displaying her legs up beyond her garters. Or they could be dancing together, which allowed the artist to use his imagination on a suitable frock which left her shoulders and back bare. They could be taking the sun together beside a lake, a situation which called for a tight-fitting bathing costume. None of this presented any difficulty to Gerhart. He was skilled in figure-drawing of this kind and the only problem was to think of new situations.

It was not the type of cultural endeavour which attracts the attention or the praise of art critics and other guardians of the national heritage, but Gerhart was content to go along with it

47

for the time being. He was hoping that he would eventually become well enough known to be commissioned to illustrate a book – any book – where he would be free of the constraints of popular magazine taste and have an opportunity to display to the full his creative talent. One of the people he wanted to meet was Rudolf Knuppel, a publisher of expensive illustrated books, and he succeeded in persuading a friend to introduce him to Knuppel at the Café des Westens.

This regular meeting-place of those who saw themselves as the artistic and intellectual elite of Berlin was nicknamed the Café Megalomania by those unconvinced of the importance of the regulars, but that was neither here nor there. On the day after his visit to the wrestling-match, Gerhart made his way to the Café soon after six o'clock, for the meeting arranged by Roma von Gloeden. About two-thirds of the tables were already taken by groups of people arguing vociferously, everyone talking and no one listening. Roma, who evidently had recovered from the head-ache which prevented her from attending the exhibition of skill and strength in the mud, was at a table towards the back and with her was not only the publisher Knuppel but two other men and another woman. Roma effected the introductions and more drinks were called for.

One of the men, Bruno, was involved in film-making out at Tempelhof studios, which Gerhart thought sounded interesting, though it gave him much to say on the abstractions of composition of scenes and sets to suggest mood, which sounded far from interesting. The other youngish man in the party, Fritz Kindermann, had a doctorate in philosophy, but had found no particular role in life so far, it seemed. He made it very apparent that he was a devoted disciple of such profound modern thinkers as Edmund Husserl and others Gerhart had never heard of, and he claimed to be writing a book which would demonstrate that the essence of objects is correlative to states of mind. The book would be finished in about four years time, he said, a delay which Gerhart thought not long enough.

Rudolf Knuppel, the only person present he wanted to talk to, was older than the two geniuses. He was in his mid-forties, smoothly shaven, his dark-brown hair smoothed back over his round head without a parting. His plump body was encased in an expensive suit of midnight-blue and he wore a blue and white spotted bow-tie. He was very sure of himself and had not the slightest hesitation in expressing scepticism of Fritz' philosophical theories.

'There is too much theorising about uncertainties,' he said firmly. 'It is all lost endeavour and a waste of time. Take, for instance, the astrologers of the Middle Ages. They drew diagrams to show how the signs of the Zodiac corresponded to different parts of the human body and influenced them. They believed there was a correspondence between Virgo and the belly, and between Scorpio and the sexual organs. I have a copy of one of these pictures printed at Strasbourg in 1484 – an enchanting and valuable piece of work. But it is all nonsense.'

'But that was hundreds of years ago,' Fritz objected.

Knuppel swept the object aside.

'Today we are equally foolish,' he said, 'instead of astrologers we have the Viennese school of Psychology, founded by Dr Freud, who publishes long and tedious books to explain things about ourselves which need no explanation. Solemn idiots who have never felt any emotion more powerful than mild fear or faint anger or lukewarm lust are impressed by this boring speculation. But it is still astrology under a new name.'

Gerhart's attention was not entirely directed towards what Rudolf Knuppel was saying. He was looking at Erna Klemt and considering whether it would be more or less than averagely pleasant to make love to her. About Roma von Gloeden he knew all that he wanted to know – in bed she was adequate, but not inspiring. She participated cheerfully and responded well enough, but afterwards she became unnecessarily grateful, and Gerhart found that mildly irritating. Her friend Erna, or more accurately, Knuppel's friend Erna, was a different proposition, to judge by appearances. She had dark brown eyes and had completely removed her eyebrows and drawn in thin curving lines with some dark cosmetic. But it was the expression of her face that set Gerhart's train of thought in motion. She could not be more than a year or so older than himself, and yet her face was as expressive of experience as if she were twice that age. He concluded that it was impossible to guess whether she was very enthusiastic in bed or whether she had already exhausted the possibilities of love-making and now found it boring. Whether this speculation was psychological or astrological, he was undecided, but he thought that Rudolf's statement should not pass unchallenged.

'That's all very well,' he said, 'but those who give way to overpowering anger or lust commit criminal acts and end up in prison, or worse.'

'Those who commit criminal acts to test the strength of their emotions are the unintelligent ones,' Rudolf answered at once. 'We read of their antics in the newspapers, the so-called lust-murderers. They drag young girls up dark alleys and stab them in the belly with knives. Many of them do not even rape their victims. What these miserable creatures are doing is acting out in violent drama their own frustrations. They are incapable of releasing their deep emotions and so achieving a true understanding of their own nature. And so they keep on repeating the same dreary acts until they are caught.'

'I'm not sure that I know what you mean.'

'I know what he means,' said Erna, her eyes bright.

'And you can bear me out,' said Rudolf, patting her hand on the table. 'Be truthful now – has anything ever changed your understanding of yourself so fundamentally as taking part in one of my dramas of the spirit?'

'Nothing,' she answered at once.

'Drama of the spirit?' Gerhart repeated slowly. 'What does that mean?'

'It means the total release of the deepest and most secret emotions in the company of a small group of friends,' Erna explained.

'You mean an orgy? But that is a drama of the body and hardly involves the spirit at all.'

'Orgy!' Rudolf said scornfully. 'What a vulgar interpretation of Erna's words! It amazes me that a person of your creative ability and sensitivity should be so imperceptive.'

Gerhart was dismayed to think that an ill-chosen remark might have offended the man he hoped would give him a commission to illustrate a book. Happily for him, Erna came to his rescue.

'He's never been present,' she said. 'You can't expect him to understand so profound an experience without knowing anything about it. Perhaps you should invite him.'

'Perhaps,' said Rudolf, 'we shall see. Tell me something about your work, Gerhart. According to Roma you are the best illustrator in Berlin, but I am sure she is exaggerating because she is fond of you.'

Gerhart was only too pleased to have the opportunity to talk about his work. Eventually this led on to a wider discussion of the importance of the visual arts, on which Bruno had a great deal to say. Rounds of drinks were brought to the table at regular intervals and, by nine o'clock, the whole company was more than half drunk.

'It is time to go,' Rudolf announced, waving to a waiter to bring the bill. 'You are welcome to come with us, Gerhart.'

They went to Rudolf's apartment, not very far away. It was large and impressive, redolent of money and taste. The sitting-room had stark white walls, one whole side being covered by black-painted shelves crammed with books, the others displaying large and brightly-coloured paintings which were no more than geometric designs. A beautiful leopard-skin, complete with head, lay on the polished wooden floor.

'Fill the glasses, Fritz,' said Rudolf, his face already flushed from drink. '*In vino veritas*. Alcohol dissolves the veils we drape over ourselves to conceal our true nature. Drink enough and the truth will emerge. Do you dispute that, Gerhart?'

'What you say is true. But is it a good idea? It may be that we need to keep some part of ourselves veiled.'

'But the truth makes us free! Self-discovery, my dear boy, that is the all-important thing. Don't you want to be free of all the deceptions and compromises of ordinary half-asleep people?'

'I don't know,' Gerhart said truthfully.

'Then it's time you found out.'

Fritz handed round large glasses of brandy. Roma and Erna were side by side on a white satin sofa, giggling and pink-faced. Rudolf raised his glass to Gerhart.

51

'After tonight you will see the world in a way you cannot yet imagine.'

Gerhart nodded, his head swirling from the amount he had consumed in the past hour or two in the Café.

'So be it,' he said, and grinned.

'Roma – show our new friend round and explain our system to him. Bruno, help Fritz move the furniture.'

Roma struggled up off the sofa and took Gerhart's hand. She had a foolish smile on her broad face and weaved slightly from side to side as she led him round the apartment and explained to him that he had to dress up as an animal to take part in the drama. The idea struck Gerhart as ludicrous.

'An animal! But what animal?'

'Whatever you like. It's very interesting – you'll see. Everyone is dressing up, so you have to join in if you want to stay.'

'Rudolf said it was some sort of tremendous experience, but it sounds more like a fancy-dress party.'

'He's a very strange man.'

They were in one of the bedrooms and, by way of a cover, the bed had a whole sheepskin on it, fluffy and white.

'There you are,' said Roma. 'You can be a sheep. Just put that round you.'

'I cannot imagine myself disguised as a sheep.'

'Please yourself,' and she led him out of the bedroom, or tried to, but Gerhart had another idea. He put his arms round her, kissed her and took her to the bed and pulled her down onto the sheepskin, his hand up her bottle-green pullover to fondle her breasts.

'I have a better plan,' he said, 'you be a sheep and I'll be a ram. They're all so drunk out there that they'll never miss us.'

But Roma pulled away from him and stood up, swaying a little.

'We'll have plenty of time for that later. We mustn't upset Rudolf by not joining in his drama. Come on.'

Certainly Gerhart did not want to annoy Rudolf, however silly his games, and he let Roma lead him into the dining-room. His attention was caught by a carved wooden mask hanging on the white wall.

'I like that,' he said, 'is it African, do you think?'

'I don't know. Will it suit you?'

She took it down from the wall and handed it to him. It was black and highly polished, with jaws set with real fangs.

'What do you think it is?' he asked. 'It looks like a wolf, but there are no wolves in Africa, are there?'

'How do I know what animals they have in Africa? Try it on.'

It fitted over his face without difficulty, the eye-holes in more or less the right places to let him see out. There were braided strings attached to the sides of the mask and Roma tied them at the back of his head and neck to keep it in place.

'Let me see you – yes, that's terrifying,' she said with a giggle.

Wearing the mask produced a strange sensation of being cut off from the rest of the world and this, combined with Gerhart's semi-drunken state, give rise to feelings he found impossible to make sense of. Roma took his hand again and led him back to the bedroom with the sheepskin. But the sheepskin was gone, and a man's clothes lay strewn across the bed.

'Strip off,' she said, 'And hurry up – they'll be waiting for us.'

'Take my clothes off?' he asked in surprise, his voice sounding muffled through the wooden mask.

'Animals don't wear clothes. You have to be naked.'

'Will you be naked?'

'Everybody will be.'

'This is the maddest party I've ever been to. But why not?'

He undressed and threw his clothes on the bed alongside the others. Roma helped him get his shirt over his masked head and undid his trousers for him.

'You can manage on your own now,' she said, 'I'll leave you to it or I won't be ready in time myself.'

Gerhart took his trousers off, asking himself how idiotic he would feel when he walked naked into the sitting-room.

'Hurry up,' said a man's voice, 'we're waiting for you.'

It was Fritz. He was wearing the sheepskin down his back, but otherwise he was naked. Gerhart grinned inside his mask at the strange sight, and followed Fritz back to the sitting-room.

The furniture had been pushed back to the walls, to leave as large an open space as possible. The main lights were turned off and a table-lamp, with a red scarf draped over it, lit the room dimly. A leopard lay curled up on the parquet, and when it stirred, Gerhart saw that it was Rudolf, wrapped in his own leopard-skin.

Bruno, the film-expert, lay full-length on the white sofa, asleep from too much to drink. He had got as far as removing his jacket and trousers before sliding into unconsciousness, and presented a comical sight with his dangler on show.

'So!' said Rudolf. 'The menagerie is assembled. Fritz the bold thinker has turned himself into a sheep. As for you, my young friend, you demonstrate either great ambition or great stupidity in wearing the mask of a god.'

'I thought it was supposed to be a wolf.'

'It is a representation of the hyaena-god of an African tribe and is worn by the witch-doctors. Why did you choose it?'

'I liked the look of it.'

'Your choice was guided by some unacknowledged force within you. It will be interesting to see what happens when that force is released. Tell the girls we are ready, Fritz, my little sheep.'

Gerhart sat down on a chair, wondering what was going to happen. It was very important to him to make a good impression on Rudolf Knuppel, and for that reason alone he was prepared to go along with his nonsense. Besides, he told himself, if the girls were going to appear naked as well, the party could get lively and he might have a chance to get Erna Klemt into one of the bedrooms. Or if Rudolf wanted her himself, there was always Roma.

At this moment Erna and Roma made their appearance and he began to understand the point of the animal disguises. Both women had stripped to their knickers and shoes, and had rouged their nipples to make them as bright red as their lips. Roma had tall ostrich plumes sticking up from her hair, and Erna was wearing a glossy black top-hat. Both of them carried the long and springy whips which are used in circus acts to control animals.

54

Roma closed the door behind her and leaned against it, while Erna strode into the centre of the floor and started the proceedings.

'*Hopla!*' she said sharply. 'Take your places! Move!'

Fritz at once sank down on to his hands and knees, almost covered in that position by the sheepskin, with only his head sticking out towards Erna. Rudolf squatted like a cat, his fists on the floor and his bent knees outside his arms. Gerhart was slow to grasp what was required of him, and the end of Erna's long switch stung his bare thigh to urge him into the same posture as Rudolf.

'This beast is badly trained,' she said loudly.

There had been a transformation in her personality since she had taken off her clothes and put on the ring-master's top-hat. Gone was the friendly conversationalist of the Café and instead she presented an appearance of hard determination. Even her face looked different, flushed red and set in severe lines.

It was to Rudolf that she first directed her attention.

'Up!' she cried, flicking at him with the whip.

He snarled and pawed at the air, as Gerhart had seen lions do in circuses.

'Up, I said!' she repeated harshly, and Rudolf in his leopard-skin sat back on his haunches, raising his bent arms and growling in his throat.

'Good! Stay now!' and she half-turned to face Gerhart.

At once Rudolf, thoroughly into the spirit of his drama, dropped to his hands and knees and started to glide stealthily towards Erna's back. But she had played this game before, if it was a game. She turned quickly on her high heels to slash at him with her whip and drive him back.

Then it was Gerhart's turn, and through the eye-holes of his mask he saw her face him again. She seemed to be a long way off and not entirely real, but perhaps that was the effect of drinking so much. He stared at her bare and widely separated breasts, trying to understand in his befuddled state why their reddish-brown tips pointed not forwards but away from each other. And slowly the thought that came uppermost in his mind was that he wanted to pull her down on the floor and ravage her.

55

Her whip stung his chest and he heard her say '*Up!*' but evidently he responded too slowly and the whip stung him again and he howled. The sound that emerged through the mask had an extraordinary animal quality. Again she flicked at him, and at last he understood and rose on his haunches to paw the air. He felt the end of her switch rest against his chest and then trail down his belly to tickle his stiff stem.

'I must watch this animal,' Erna said over her shoulder to Roma. 'He's exhibiting signs of tension.'

Gerhart growled and swayed forward, his intention to seize hold of Erna's legs and bowl her over. He was rewarded by a stinging cut across his outstretched arms and then, when he jerked them back, with another hard slash across his bare chest.

'Ah, I thought so!' she said. 'This one is dangerous. Get back!'

Gerhart grumbled wordlessly. He had forgotten that he was involved in someone else'e ridiculous game. As Rudolf had predicted, the alcohol had temporarily checked his power of reason and was allowing deep instincts to surge up from within him. Erna was his enemy, but she had the power to hurt him. He must wait his chance and use his cunning. He watched her closely as she moved towards Fritz in his sheepskin. Her slack little breasts bounced with her movement and, without knowing it, Gerhart slobbered inside the mask.

'Silly sheep!' he heard her say. 'What can I do? Roma, come here!'

Roma came to her side, the ostrich plumes nodding above her head.

'Ride this stupid animal round the room,' Erna ordered.

Roma laughed and threw a leg over Fritz to seat herself on his back. Her knees clamped his sides and her fingers gripped his hair.

'Show me what you can make him do, Roma!'

Fritz set off round the cleared space on hands and knees. After one circuit, Roma got her knees up on his back and knelt upright, her arms raised above her head.

'Faster!' Erna cried, flicking at the uncovered backs of his thighs with her switch.

56

He speeded up his awkward shuffle, Roma lost her precarious balance and screamed, grabbed at his hair, and both of them toppled over sideways. At once Fritz curled up tight into a ball to protect his thighs and belly from the whip, but his unseated rider rolled over on to her back, laughing drunkenly. At once the leopard that was Rudolf hurled himself at her, his hands scrabbling for her breasts. Erna sprang forward to slash at him with her whip, shouting hoarsely. Rudolf howled and twisted away from the blows, but tried to hold onto his prey. A short and noisy battle of wills ensued, until Rudolf was forced to back away on his hands and knees, Erna pursuing him with repeated blows until he was back at his starting-point. He screamed shrilly as she gave him a final flick across his now upright part.

'Stay put or I'll flog the skin right off it!' she said menacingly.

Fritz had taken advantage of the scuffle to crawl back to his place, and Roma still lay on her back, giggling. It was the moment Gerhart had been waiting for – Erna standing with her back to him while she threatened Rudolf. He launched himself at her with a great bound, hooked his hands in the back of her knickers and dragged them down her legs. Before she had time to react, he swung his legs round to catch her below the knees and knock her down sideways, the whip flying from her hand. As she fell he caught her by the waist and rolled her over, and flung himself on top of her, to pin her to the floor. She fought him like a wild-cat, twisting and screaming, her fingernails raking down the polished wooden mask, while trying at the same time to use her knees on his tender parts to disable him. Her shiny top-hat had fallen off and it was crushed beneath them as they rolled over and over, legs flailing and arms flying. She half-winded him with a knee in the belly and, as his grip loosened, broke away and scrambled free. But Gerhart caught her by an ankle while she was still on her hands and knees and pulled her back towards him. With his other hand he grabbed the green knickers round her thighs and tore the flimsy silk free. Her arms came round behind her to try and get hold of whatever would hurt him most, but by then he had her by the hips with both hands and heaved himself up and over her bare bottom. He gripped her tightly by the back of her neck and pressed her face down to the parquet and she was helpless.

From the rear he stabbed into her hairy split, ignoring her wailing, and lunged furiously, not even aware of whether it was pleasurable or not, and discharged his red rage into her with a howl of triumph.

When he was finished, he pulled away from her and sat back on his haunches. As soon as he let go of her, Erna collapsed slowly on to the parquet and lay still. He looked dazedly round the room and saw that Roma had still not moved from where she had rolled from the sheep's back, but that Rudolf had. He was lying on top of her, the beautiful leopard-skin covering them both, and heaving up and down in time with his movements. Fritz sat nearby, his legs crossed and his tail stiff, patiently awaiting his turn.

In another minute or so Rudolf moaned and twitched in convulsions under the leopard-skin. He lay breathing heavily for a time before he freed himself from Roma, to kneel up between her legs, his chest and belly shiny with sweat. Roma lay unmoving on her back, staring at the ceiling, her twisted knickers round one ankle. Rudolf was muttering to himself as he stared at the tuft of brown hair between her splayed legs, and he ran his clawed fingers down her belly, evidently still in his leopard mood, before he shuffled away backwards on his knees. He lay down, curled up on his side, his eyes still on Roma. He growled, but made no move when Fritz spread himself over her, the sheepskin fastened round his neck slipping away sideways to expose his heavy bottom jerking up and down. Roma received him passively, her arms and legs spread wide, and after a time she began to giggle mindlessly. The giggling continued, though after a while it was interspersed with gasps, and the curious sound plucked at Gerhart's nerves and roused him again.

He went scurrying across the floor towards Erna. She had recovered sufficiently to move from where he had left her, and was slumped in one of the white arm-chairs, her face expressionless as she watched Fritz having his way with Roma. But as Gerhart approached her, she drew up one leg and kicked out at him, aiming between his legs. He jerked sideways and took the kick on his hip, and got hold of her ankle. Her other foot, still with a shoe on it, kicked upwards and this time he took the blow on his shin. The pain made him gasp with anger and, before she could do any more damage, he had closed in and was kneeling between her thighs, gripping her by both ankles to force her legs outward so widely that it was her turn to screech. Her red-painted finger-nails scraped down his belly towards his vulnerable stem, making him release her ankles and grab her wrists just in time.

Her mouth was open in a grimace that showed her teeth and her dark eyes were glaring murderously at his masked face. But for all that, with her arms pulled up and held behind her neck, she could do no more than squirm about on the chair as Gerhart shuffled in ever closer until his fleshy spike touched the hair between her legs. Wriggle as she might, it was only a question of time before a lunge of his body sank him into her slippery depths. Her rouge-tipped breasts flopped up and down to the strength of his attack, her mouth pulled back to show her pink gums as well as her teeth, and she was making a strange hissing sound, almost like a snake. The conclusion was not long in coming, and it was like a whirlwind that shook their joined bodies like rag-dolls.

Gerhart slid out of her warily, ready to block a sudden kick, but she lay panting loudly, no more resistance in her just then. He sat on the floor and put an arm over one of her thighs and rested his head on it, and she let him. His face was burning hot inside the mask and he was panting like an animal after a life-and-death struggle.

In the middle of the room Fritz had finished with Roma and crawled away from her, to lie on the parquet with his sheepskin pulled over him like a blanket. Roma still lay without moving, as she had through the assaults of Rudolf and Fritz, on her back with her arms and legs spread, an easy and willing victim. Gerhart's appetite was satisfied, but something in him made him unable to leave so tempting a prey, and he crawled across the room to her. Her eyes turned towards him and stared blankly at the hyaena-masked face above her. Her chubby breasts were lolling slackly outwards, and they looked as exhausted as she did. Gerhart put his head down to nuzzle them and was thwarted by the wooden mask. He tugged at the strings behind his head and threw the mask away from him, then put his cheek against the warm skin between Roma's breasts, sniffing at her hot smell, before he put his hand between her thighs to feel her wetness.

'Gerhart,' she whispered.

His mood changed, perhaps at the sound of his name, and perhaps with the removal of the hideous mask that had denied his humanity. Or maybe it was no more than that the alcohol fumes were leaving his brain and he was sinking into lassitude after his strenous ravaging of Erna. Whatever the reason, he lay down beside Roma and gathered her into his arms.

'I want to sleep,' she murmured.

'Then go to sleep while I hold you.'

'Not here. It's not safe.'

'Why not?'

'Rudolf.'

He helped her to her feet and, an arm round her waist, led her to the bedroom where he had left his clothes.

'Lock the door,' she said.

He turned the key in the door, got into the bed with her and took her in his arms. She held his limp tail in her hand, but it did not respond, and in another minute or two they were both fast asleep. Sometime in the night her handclasp roused him and he climbed on top of her and satisfied them both, though in his half-asleep state and in pitch darkness, he had no idea who he was doing it to.

Chapter 6

Gerhart meets Lotte's brother-in-law

An invitation as promising as that hinted at by Lotte Furer-Diest could not be left for too long without a response. Gerhart gave himself twenty-four hours to recover from the excesses of Rudolf's masquerade and telephoned Lotte to arrange to take her out for the evening. He suggested a visit to the theatre, having no wish to repeat the coarser entertainment arranged by Heinrich. In fact, after the unusual events of his meeting with Rudolf Knuppel, he was looking forward to a civilised evening with a beautiful young lady of normal inclinations.

His ring at the door-bell was answered by an elderly maid in black, who led him to the sitting-room and announced him without enthusiasm. Lotte had explained to him that she was staying temporarily with her married sister, since leaving her husband.

'My brother-in-law Maximilian Glotz,' she introduced him, 'and my sister Kathe.'

Glotz was fifteen years older than Gerhart and gave the impression of being even older. He was a tall and thin man with a long face and a nervous manner. His short and gingery hair was retreating from his forehead to leave a large and shining patch. Frau Glotz greatly resembled her sister Lotte, being a few years older, but plumper and more matronly in her ways.

'Please sit down,' said Glotz, 'you have time to take a glass of wine with us before you go. I have checked on the time that the play begins.'

Gerhart sat beside Frau Glotz and took the offered glass. He had an uncomfortable feeling that he was being inspected – almost as if Glotz was Lotte's father – to make sure

61

that he was a suitable person to be entrusted with her for the evening.

'Lotte has told us very little about you,' said Glotz. 'Where did you meet?'

'We were introduced by a mutual friend.'

'Ah, that will be Heinrich Preuss, I suppose. A frivolous young man.'

'Frivolous? I've never thought of him as that.'

'But not a serious person, you agree?'

'Offhand, I can't think of any of my friends that are serious persons. It would make them very boring.'

Maximilian Glotz shook his head sadly.

'Herr von Rautenberg is right,' Lotte's sister said unexpectedly. 'Young people should enjoy themselves. There's time enough to be serious when they marry and settle down.'

'Not all accept their responsibilities even then,' said Glotz, staring at Lotte in what Gerhart considered an offensive way.

'I can't see where all this seriousness gets anyone,' he said, 'old or young – who wants to be miserable?'

'This insatiable desire for enjoyment can lead the young to disgraceful lengths,' Glotz answered darkly. 'Many a life has been ruined by the actions of a few thoughtless moments. Do your parents live in Berlin?'

'They died when I was a child. I was brought up by a distant relation.'

'A lack of parental guidance is usually calamitous,' said Glotz, shaking his head, but when Gerhart told him the General's name, his melancholy tune changed and he became friendly in a way that was almost ingratiating.

Gerhart was glad to escape from the household with Lotte.

'How long are you going to live there?' he asked her.

'I'm waiting for things to be settled with my husband. Until they are I can't afford a proper place of my own. I know most people think that Maximilian is awful, but he's being very helpful to me. He's a very clever lawyer, which is what I need if I'm to get a decent settlement. I can't pay him, but he's willing to wait until I have my own money.'

The play for which Gerhart had reserved seats was the latest comedy, light, frothy and amusing. Glotz would have disapproved. Afterwards they went for supper and they danced and drank champagne until well after one in the morning. Gerhart found Lotte a delightful companion, full of natural charm and good humour, and he enjoyed the evening immensely. As they rode back to the Glotz apartment in a taxi he held her hand affectionately and she made him laugh by telling him that after their visit to the mud-wrestling she'd had a bruise on her bottom that was only now fading.

'First it was purple, now it's greenish,' she said, 'you must have strong fingers.'

'My humble apologies! I was carried away by the spectacle and didn't know what I was doing. Not that I was the only one.'

'What do you mean?'

'I seem to recall that you too were carried away and grabbed hold of me.'

'Did I? I don't remember that,' she said so innocently that it made him laugh again.

'I really can't remember squeezing your bottom,' she insisted.

'Of course not. You grabbed my door-knocker.'

'I did no such thing! However, if I did touch you at all, it was entirely by accident.'

'Naturally.'

'What must you have thought of me!' she exclaimed.

'I thought that you were one of the most beautiful girls I've ever met and that I would like you to put your hand there again as often as possible.'

'To give you an excuse to bruise my bottom, I suppose!'

'No, to stroke it and kiss it.'

'Kiss my bottom?' she asked demurely. 'Are you serious?'

'To kiss it and then bite it very gently, before turning you over to play with your front.'

'Maximilian was right – you are not a serious person. Is this how you talk to women you hardly know?'

'Only if they are as beautiful as you – which is not very often.'

Lotte laughed and squeezed his hand.

63

'So now that you have decided that you want to kiss my bottom and turn me over – what are you proposing to do to my front?'

'The most delicious things! First I would kiss your little bundles until their buds were standing up hard. And then . . .'

But before he had time to continue his description of all the things he would like to do to her, the taxi arrived at her temporary home. Gerhart paid off the driver and stood with Lotte on the pavement.

'I want to kiss you,' he said.

'So you were saying. Which part of me do you want to kiss?'

'All of you! But at this moment I want to kiss your lips.'

'This is hardly the place for that, at two in the morning in the street.'

'But there's no one about.'

She took the street-door key from her hand-bag and let him into the entrance hall of the building. The light had been turned off long ago, but there was illumination enough from the street-lamps. Gerhart put his hands on her hips and held her against the wall, his belly pressed against hers, while he kissed her so long and passionately that the tip of her tongue emerged between her parted lips to touch his tongue. He wanted to feel her breasts, but she was wearing a high-fronted evening frock that made his fumbling very unsatisfactory.

He reached down to get a hand under the hem of her frock and up between her legs to the warm and bare flesh above her stocking-tops. Her hand brushed against his thigh and then found the bulge in his trousers.

'If only we could!' she whispered, 'but I can't ask you in, you know that.'

'No problem – come home with me.'

'I can't! The last time I was out all night there was a tremendous row.'

'But your awful brother-in-law can't expect you to live like a nun!'

'I can't afford to upset him, believe me.'

'This is ridiculous! We can't just stop now.'

'Be sensible,' she said, 'we can't do it here in the hall – someone might come in and see us.'

Lotte's words and her actions were not in accord. Even while she was denying the possibility of proceeding any further with their intimate exploration of each other's body, she was undoing the buttons of his trousers. Her hand slid inside, under his shirt and into his underwear, to find and hold his stiffness. Perhaps it was because by then Gerhart had two fingers between the curly-haired lips between her thighs and was teasing her wet button.

'No, no more!' she exclaimed. 'We must say *Goodnight* now!'

Her hand was still sliding up and down under his shirt and Gerhart felt that the culmination of his excitement was not far off.

'Goodnight, then' he murmured, his face pressed into her perfumed black hair while his fingers fluttered between her legs, 'goodnight, dear beautiful Lotte, goodnight, good-night . . .'

He gasped at the sudden warm squirt up his belly and his fingers ravished her and she too gasped and shook in the ecstasy of release. It was some time before she became aware of the surroundings again and glanced nervously round the dark and empty hall.

'This is crazy,' she said, 'I must be out of my mind to let you do that to me here.'

Gerhart put his arms round her and kissed her. Her hand was still in his open trousers, holding his sticky peg.

'I can't let you go now that we've started,' she whispered, 'I want you too much. You must promise to be very quiet.'

He followed her up two flights of stairs to the Glotz apartment door. She unlocked it silently and they were inside in the dark.

'Take your shoes off,' she whispered.

He took them off and she led him by the hand past several closed and dimly-discerned doors, moving very slowly and quietly. Gerhart hardly dared to breath, appalled by the prospect of being confronted by an irate Maximilian Glotz roused from his sleep. At that point he remembered that his trousers were still unbuttoned and almost laughed aloud at the thought of what Glotz would have to say about that. Lotte opened a door and they were in her room, and one of his shoes slipped from Gerhart's hand. Fortunately it landed on his foot and made very little noise.

The curtains were not drawn across the windows and there was enough light to move across the room without bumping into anything, towards the bed by the far wall. Gerhart undressed, glad to be rid of the clammy shirt clinging to his belly, but Lotte was quicker and lay on the bed waiting for him, her long body a pale glow in the darkness. His stem was limp after the little adventure in the hallway, and he lay beside her to kiss her mouth and breasts, his hands stroking her soft-skinned belly.

'You will be quiet, won't you?' Lotte murmured. 'We mustn't wake the children.'

'What children – yours?'

'Of course not! My sister's – they sleep in the next room.'

'Does the bed squeak?'

'I don't think so, but be careful.'

She pulled his hand down from her belly to between her legs and he played with her secret bud, slowly and lightly, to give himself time to recover his strength before she became aroused enough to want him to lie on her and use more than his fingers. In the event, he need not have worried on that score. Lotte was in a mood to be played with very thoroughly indeed and was in no hurry for him to do anything which might put a stop, even a temporary one, to her pleasure. It was not the bed that squeaked, he found, it was Lotte – little squeaks of delight she tried to suppress.

She was squeezing her own breasts and one of her elbows was uncomfortable against his ribs, but he did not complain. It took some time before it dawned on him that the long and continuous spasms of her belly did not indicate that she was approaching her golden moments – but that she was actually enjoying them, and that they were not moments but minutes. His wonder grew and became amazement at how long she could sustain this long drawn out ecstasy and the thought of it excited him even more than the feel of her hot body and wet split. His fingers slid over her little trigger and it was as if he was handling

66

a machine-gun that fired a continuing burst of delight deep inside her belly. How long this went on he had no way of telling, but eventually her hands moved from her breasts to take his wrist and pull his hand away.

'Stop for a while,' she gasped, 'I have to rest and cool down.'

'You were fantastic, Lotte.'

'I'm like that – once I get going I can't stop.'

'But that's amazing. I mean, with most women it's over in a few seconds.'

'Not with me. When it starts, it keeps coming in waves. It doesn't build up and then stop, and it doesn't get fainter as it goes on. It's wave after wave going through me, till I have to stop it myself.'

'And if you don't stop it?'

'It goes on until I practically pass out.'

'Were you near that just now?'

'Oh no, I made you stop long before that. When I've calmed down a bit you can start again.'

Gerhart reflected, not for the first time, on the astonishing variations to be found in the way women were affected by sexual passion. Erna, as he had discovered, liked to be treated roughly and then produced a short and devastating explosion. Or take Roma, eager for the feel of a man's pointer inside her, but her crisis was so undetectable that Gerhart wondered whether she actually experienced one at all. Both of them were very unlike Lotte, whose pretty face gave away nothing of her inner fire, but who could be aroused to these marathon climactic feats.

From this biological and philosophical musing he was drawn by Lotte's hand taking firm hold of his peg, now returned to a usefully stiff condition. She pushed him over onto his back and sat over him with her knees up. He thought she intended to steer him into her and ride him until the natural event took place, but she did no such thing. The soft flesh between her thighs pressed his stiffness flat against his belly and she rocked herself backwards and forwards slowly.

'Ah, do you know what that's doing to me?' she whispered.

'Tell me.'

'It's driving me wild – I'm starting again!'

It was doing very little for Gerhart, but if he had wanted any confirmation of what she said, he had it when she began to mewl quietly. He saw her hands creep up her body from her thighs to her breasts, and she rubbed them and squeezed them. Gerhart felt as if he was a passenger on an express train, being rattled about by its long rush over the rails, and unable to exert any degree of control over it. He was cut off from what was happening to Lotte. He was not sure if she even knew that he was there on the bed with her. To her he was, perhaps, only a length of hard flesh against which to rub herself to maintain her train-like rush through ecstatic sensations.

It was annoying to be reduced to a mere object for her gratification, no matter how spectacular that gratification might be. He reached up and pulled her hands away from her breasts, took possession of them himself, and held them firmly. He squeezed them full-handed, in time with the spasms that were shaking her, as she had been doing herself, but all that achieved was to keep her long climax going, he realised. He wanted to be more than a minor player in her heroic drama. He took her stiff buds between his fingers and thumbs and rolled them, gently at first, but then with increasing pressure. The rhythm of her spasms became faster and her squeaking grew louder, until he was afraid that she might awaken the entire household. He groped about on the floor by the bed for anything which might serve as a gag, and found one of her silk stockings. He rolled it up quickly and reached up to stuff it into Lotte's open and panting mouth.

By then her hands were back on her breasts, and again he pried them loose and replaced them with his own. Her teeth had closed on the gag, for when he rolled the tips of her breasts again, hard and fast, and her throes became more intense, the only sound he heard was a muffled gasping.

Lotte was not like a train now – she was more like a car and Gerhart was the driver with his foot on the accelerator. He plucked at her buds, he stretched them and treated them roughly, speeding her up into a headlong rush that was completely out of control. The wet lips between her thighs rubbed against his stiffness with frantic rapidity that Gerhart waited breathlessly for the crash he thought imminent, his hands manipulating her cruelly. But what happened disappointed him. Instead of crashing violently, Lotte's car ran out of petrol and coasted to a standstill. She sat swaying on his belly for a few seconds, gulping through the wadded silk stocking, and then slid sideways and lay still on the bed alongside him.

He removed the gag from her mouth and put his arms round her while he waited for her to recover from her strenuous pleasure. It took a long time and, just when he was beginning to think that she had fallen asleep, she rolled away from him and lay face down.

'I'm done for,' she said slowly, 'that was wonderful.'

'So there is a limit for you?'

'I usually need three or four bouts to finish me off. You've done it in only two. I like you.'

Gerhart fondled the upturned cheeks of her bottom, enjoying the feel of her smooth skin.

'Poor dear!' said Lotte, 'You never did get a chance to bite it.'

'We'll see about that!' and he twisted round on the bed so that he could nip at the soft flesh with his teeth. He was greatly aroused but, while Lotte let him do what he pleased to her bottom, she showed no sign of responding.

'Lotte – you can't go to sleep and leave me like this!'

'I'm past it,' she said with a little yawn.

Her indifference to his plight after the tumultuous pleasure he had given her annoyed him so much that, without being aware of it, he growled in his throat, as he had on the memorable occasion when he had become a hyaena. In a moment he was on Lotte's bare back, his legs between hers and his hands under her hips to drag them upwards from the bed.

'No!' she cried out, 'I won't !'

'Shout and you'll wake everybody up,' he muttered, pulling her rump close up against his belly so that he could jab at her wet opening with his pointer. Her fatigue had slackened her muscles and he sank into her with a single push and used her briskly. He heard her moan and sob as she bit the pillow, and he paid not the least attention to her feelings. Just as he had been no more than a length of stiff flesh to her, so now she was no more than a slippery opening for him. And very soon he heard nothing of the noise she was making, all his attention taken by the overpowering physical pleasure he felt, and seconds later there was a burst of golden sensation in his belly as he sent his sap jolting into her.

He rolled off her and lay breathing heavily.

'You beast!' she said, her voice angry. 'That was a rotten thing to do. I never want to see you again.'

'That goes for me too. You invited me to bed to make love – and then suddenly you've had enough and I'm lying here frustrated. What did you expect would happen?'

'I told you I was done for.'

'You can't get a man going like that and turn away and leave him with his clapper standing up and nowhere to put it. Or do you treat all your friends like that? Is that why you and your husband parted?'

'That's none of your business. You've had your fun – it's time you went.'

'Believe me, I'm going,' and he got off the bed to fumble around on the floor for his clothes. He was dressed and ready to leave before Lotte spoke again.

'Gerhart, I'm sorry. I don't know what happened to me tonight – I've never folded up as fast as that before. You have every right to be annoyed with me and I don't blame you for doing what you did.'

'That's all right,' he said, pacified by her change of tone, 'we got our timing wrong. It happens sometimes.'

'Was it all right?'

'What?'

'What you did to me. I mean, did you enjoy it?'

'I've known worse.'

'I just thought that it might have been awful in the circumstances. Shall I see you again?'

The truthful answer, in the mood that possessed him, would have been *No*, but not wanting a scene he answered, 'Why not?'

'Kiss me before you go,' she said anxiously.

He leaned over the bed to kiss her a brief goodbye, but Lotte had other ideas. Her arm encircled his neck and held his lips pressed to hers, while her other hand felt for his wrist and rubbed his palm lightly over her bare breasts.

'It will be different next time,' she promised when she released him, 'I'll have you inside me till you can't make it stand up any more. I'll come to your apartment and you can do it to me as many times as you like.'

'I'll telephone you,' said Gerhart, doubting whether he would.

'*Auf wiedersehen*, then. Ring about twelve. Be careful not to bump into anything as you go out – we don't want a row with Maximilian.

Chapter 7

Gerhart and Clara reach a satisfactory arrangement

It was very obvious to Gerhart, when they met at the Hotel Excelsior, that Bertolt had been drinking heavily, though it was only three in the afternoon. His face was red and shiny, his collar seemed to inconvenience him, and his tie was crooked. Nevertheless, he rose and bowed formally to Gerhart before shaking his hand warmly and offering him a seat.

'Champagne – and be quick about it!' he said to a hovering waiter, and then to Gerhart, 'I am most grateful to you for agreeing to meet me at such short notice.'

'Bertolt – why on earth are we sitting in this stuffy place on a fine summer day? You said that you had something of importance to discuss.'

'All in good time. Where the devil has that waiter got to? Really, the service here is not as good as it should be!'

'Have you been here for some time?'

'An hour, perhaps,' said Bertolt vaguely. 'Since lunch, that is. I brought Clara here for lunch.'

Before Gerhart could ask what had become of her, the waiter arrived with a bottle in a silver bucket of ice-water and popped the cork. He filled two glasses and Bertolt handed one to Gerhart with a flourish that slopped some of the champagne on to the carpet. The other glass he raised in salute.

'To you, Gerhart,' he said, 'I know how to accept defeat with a good grace. It grieves me to say it, but the best man won. I am glad that it was you and not someone I don't like.'

'To you, Bertolt,' Gerhart responded, 'though I am not at all sure what you are talking about.'

'There's no need for modesty or reticence between

us – we're old comrades. You beat me fairly and won the prize.'

'Ah, you mean dear Clara.'

'Naturally I mean dear Clara! What did you think I was talking about?' Bertolt said with sudden belligerence. 'Be serious – we are discussing a wonderful lady. This is a matter of honour!'

Gerhart's heart sank when he heard those words. He emptied his glass and stared at Bertolt, wondering what utter nonsense was about to be perpetrated. The fact was, that Bertolt drunk was stupid, and Bertolt sober was not much better.

'Honour, yes,' he said, trying not to smile at the pomposity of his friend.

'You were the victor, as in other circumstances I might have been. Clara was the prize for which we fought. You won her. She was yours. There she was, naked on the sofa, while I lay unconscious on the floor. The spoils were yours and woe to the vanquished, as the saying is. You asserted the right of conquest and enjoyed her on the sofa.'

Gerhart decided to play along and see how far the joke would go.

'Should we be talking of a lady like this?' he asked sternly.

'Quite right! We should not be talking like this if it were any other lady. But the circumstances are extraordinary. We have both been privileged in the past to enjoy the favours of this particular lady. There is a bond of comradeship between us. You are aware of that, of course, and will understand why we can permit ourselves to speak more freely than would be correct in other circumstances.'

There were beads of sweat trickling down Bertolt's flushed forehead, though whether this was the result of being indoors, or drunk, or some strong emotion played a part in it, Gerhart was unable to decide. He nodded, fascinated by Bertolt's stupidity.

'You are a man of honour,' said Bertolt, 'your breeding guarantees that. And you demonstrated it beyond any possible doubt by the courteous way in which you informed me of my defeat. I am not acquainted with anyone who would have

73

behaved with such courtesy. The flower you left as a token of your triumph was a stroke of genius. I salute you!'

He refilled the glasses and they drank again.

'About this flower . . .' Gerhart began, but an imperious gesture that almost upset the bucket and bottle silenced him.

'I will not attempt to make light of my disappointment,' Bertolt went on, 'I confess to you without reservation that I am deeply in love with Clara. It was my intention to ask her to do me the honour of marrying me. But that is now out of the question.'

'But why?' Gerhart asked in surprise.

'That must be obvious. We fought for her and you won. She is yours.'

'Bertolt – Clara will lie on her back for half a dozen of the people you and I know.'

'Enough!' Bertolt shouted, his face turning purple. 'What the lady in question may or may not have done in the past has no bearing on the present situation.'

His outburst brought a worried looking waiter to the table. He filled the glasses and gave Gerhart an imploring look, as if pleading with him to either keep his companion quiet or take him somewhere else. He kept his eyes averted from Bertolt as he fussed about the table, and the truth was that Bertolt looked dangerous.

'Very well, Bertolt, this is between you and me. I must ask you to lower your voice – there are other people here and it would be improper for them to overhear a discussion of a lady's honour.'

'Damned right,' said Bertolt, 'I apologise.'

'Things being as they are, what do you want me to do?'

'Good – now we are reaching the point! I have said my good-byes to Clara. It was painful, but I had no choice. She is upstairs in a room I have reserved, and she is waiting for you.'

'But I don't want to marry Clara!' said Gerhart in alarm.

'That is not my business. She is yours to do as you wish with. I have no more to say.'

'This is going too far! Let me explain about that carnation . . .'

'Not another word! Clara is waiting for you.'

'But how does she feel about this suggestion of yours? Have you asked her? She's not a parcel to be handed about, you know.'

'We have discussed the matter at great length. She understands that in an affair of honour she has no choice but to accept the verdict.'

'Honour again! I can't believe my ears!'

Bertolt fished a key out of his pocket and pressed it into Gerhart's hand.

'Go and make her happy,' he said, 'it is your duty.'

His pale blue eyes were staring out of his head and he looked as if he was about to commit murder. Gerhart decided that it would be safer to leave him alone, and stood up hurriedly. Bertolt also lumbered to his feet, holding himself upright with both hands on the table. He bowed to Gerhart and clicked his heels before collapsing back on to his chair. It went over backwards with a crash, and Bertolt's flailing feet kicked the table over, sending the glasses and ice-bucket sliding to the floor.

Instantly there were three waiters on the scene, one of them glaring accusingly at Gerhart.

'The gentleman is drunk,' said Gerhart, 'it would be better if you put him in a taxi and sent him home.'

'Perhaps you will accompany him,' said the waiter in charge. 'The gentleman is a friend of yours.'

'An acquaintance,' said Gerhart quickly, bringing out his wallet to pay for the champagne and bribe the waiters into following his suggestion. He told them Bertolt's address and left them to the unenviable task of helping the confused Bertolt to his feet and steering him to the hotel entrance.

The number of the key was 217. He found his way to it, tapped on the door and heard Clara's voice saying, 'Come in.'

Bertolt had reserved a large and pleasant room for the culminating scene of the comical drama he had staged, with himself as tragic hero and Gerhart as villain. On one side there was a double bed and on the other two comfortable chairs and a glass-topped table. Clara was sitting in one of the chairs, wearing only a peach-coloured slip, and eating a wedge of double-cream gateau with a silver fork. She looked up and smiled at Gerhart in a very friendly way as he closed the door behind him.

'Clara, what is going on?' he asked, taking the other chair. 'That idiot Bertolt gave me the key to this room and told me that you were waiting for me. Is this some sort of joke the two of you are playing?'

'It's a very serious matter,' she told him, 'Bertolt says that I am yours now and since you didn't come to claim me, he's arranged this handing-over.'

'That's all very well, but you've been mine before. Or have you forgotten that?'

'Certainly not. It was always very nice with you, Gerhart. Why did we split up?'

'I can't remember now. I suppose we both found someone else. Why are you eating that – I thought you had lunch downstairs in the restaurant with Bertolt.'

'I like to eat. Are you angry with me?'

'No,' he said, knowing how pointless it would be to lose his temper with Clara, 'but I am puzzled. You and I were never in love when we were together, but Bertolt says that *he* is in love with you and then sends me up here. Is it true?'

'He says he is.'

'And he wants to marry you?'

She nodded, with a satisfied little smile.

'Do you want to marry him?' Gerhart enquired.

Clara reached forward to put her empty plate on the small table. Her heavy breasts rolled under the silk of her slip, almost distracting Gerhart from his intention of staying away from her. She had a little smear of cream at the corner of her mouth as she looked up to smile at him.

'I don't know,' she said, 'I'm very fond of him. My parents like him – they would approve. He's well-connected, they always say, and he's got lots of money. And he's so strong and brutal when he makes love . . . it's very exciting.'

'What more could anyone ask? Why don't you marry him and stop this nonsense with me?'

'Well . . . he won't ask me now. Not after the other evening when you knocked him out and raped me while I was asleep.'

76

'I knocked him out? What makes you think that?'

'He woke up on the floor with a big bruise on his face, so you must have knocked him out.'

'Did he say so?'

'He can't remember. But he's sure that's what must have happened. So you were the winner.'

'And what makes you think that I raped you while you were drunk?'

Clara giggled and crossed her bare legs.

'I know you did. You left me a white flower to prove it. That was a very nice idea – it made me feel sentimental when I woke up and found it.'

'Dear God, the complications that can arise from a little joke!' said Gerhart, dismayed by what he had let himself in for with Clara and Bertolt through one unthinking and half-drunk act.

'It was a loving joke,' said Clara, smiling fondly at him, 'look!'

She uncrossed her legs and pulled up her slip, opened her knees and there, displayed on her brown-curled mound was a white carnation, its petals somewhat crushed and flattened.

'It can't possibly be the same flower!'

'No, silly – it's one I bought from the flower-seller outside, specially for you. That's how you left me, that's how you find me.'

'Are you telling me that Bertolt and you haven't made love since that night?'

'Bertolt has behaved very honourably,' she said solemnly.

'Clara dear – this is me you are talking to, not a stranger. You couldn't go more than a day without making love. I refuse to believe that you haven't parted your legs for Bertolt since the last time I saw you.'

'Well . . . I let him do it for the sake of friendship, but it didn't mean anything. You don't mind, do you?'

Gerhart laughed and reached forward to remove the flower from its unusual resting-place. He tucked it into his button-hole and laughed again.

'Why should I mind? The fact is, you and Bertolt are well-suited to each other. I think you should stay together.'

'But that's impossible. We've agreed that this is the correct thing to do – for me to go with you.'

Gerhart stared thoughtfully at the plump mound that Clara was still displaying between her fleshy thighs. She saw his interest and spread her legs wider.

'You used to love my *little mousey*,' she said softly. 'Why don't you want it any more? Are you in love with another woman?'

'I'm not in love with anyone. Tell me something, for the sake of old friendship – how soon after I left you was it before you and Bertolt gave *little mousey* some brisk exercise?'

'If you must know, it was when we woke up, about five in the morning, I think. I had a dreadful hangover and Bertolt had a headache because you'd knocked him out. But that didn't stop him – he plucked your flower and threw it on the floor and stamped on it like a madman. And then he jumped on me on the sofa. But afterwards he had a bad conscience.'

'A what?'

'He said he'd deceived you by making love to me like that after you'd won me in a fair fight. And he burst into tears.'

'Maybe that was the headache, not his conscience. What on earth did you do?'

'I went to bed with him, of course, and made him feel better.'

'All this with a hangover?'

'Oh, that vanished as soon as he jumped on me the first time. And I soon cured him of his headache. But his conscience has bothered him so much since then that he made his mind up to hand me over to you once and for all. And here we are.'

She was stroking the brown curls between her legs with her finger-tips and Gerhart's tail was reacting.

'How often has Bertolt deceived me since then?' he asked with a grin.

'I don't know – six or seven times maybe. Does it matter now that he's doing the correct thing? I know it was wrong of him, but you ought to be able to forgive him now you've got me back.'

'I forgive him,' said Gerhart, still grinning.

78

He stood up and held out his hand for Clara to take, pulled her to her feet and led her to the bed.

'Shall I take my slip off?' she asked breathlessly.

'If you would be so good . . . I would like to examine my prize from head to foot. There was no proper opportunity the other evening, when you were unconscious.'

'But you've seen me naked lots of times,' she said archly, pulling the peach-coloured slip over her head.

'Never in circumstances like these. You were my girl-friend then, not my prize. It makes a difference, you know.'

Clara lay naked on her back, her legs apart, to watch him undress, and a look of appreciation appeared on her face when she saw his pointer standing up. When he got on to the bed with her she took hold of it in a decidedly possessive way.

'I know that it did lovely things to my *little mousey* on Bertolt's sofa,' she said, 'but I was fast asleep and so I missed the fun. I was cheated, now I come to think of it – why didn't you wake me up so I could enjoy the naughty things too?'

'It would have taken an earthquake to wake you up,' he answered as pleasurable sensations spread through him from her massage of his spike.

'It's just like an earthquake inside me when it happens,' she sighed. 'You know, like the earthquakes you read about when the buildings come crashing down and everything is destroyed in a few seconds. I don't know how I could have slept through that.'

Her strong thighs were well apart as Gerhart ran his palm down her belly to stroke the plump prize between them.

'I simply don't understand why the earthquake didn't wake me up . . . it always has before . . .' she murmured.

Gerhart eased himself on to her broad belly and impaled her *little mousey* with a quick stab.

'Oh, that's wonderful!' she said, all other thoughts forgotten.

'This is for the sake of friendship,' he told her, using her own words, 'it doesn't mean anything.'

Clara's arms clasped him to her big soft breasts and her legs twined over the back of his thighs.

'Friendship is so nice,' she whispered as Gerhart rode her

79

fast and hard to make her feel that she was being used brutally.

'We all need friends,' he gasped.

'Yes! Lots of friends! Close friends! Strong friends!'

Her babbling turned into a long cry of ecstasy and her bottom heaved up off the bed as the final delirium of sensation seized them both.

'Friends, friends, friends!' Gerhart moaned as he jolted into her in long spasms.

He lay resting on the comfortable cushion of her body while he got his breath back. When he raised himself on his elbows he was surprised to see a frown of concentration on Clara's face instead of the contentment he had expected.

'Didn't you enjoy it, Clara? It sounded as if you did.'

'It was nice – but it's made me realise something.'

'And what is that?' he asked, amused by the seriousness of her tone in such circumstances and after so obviously gratifying an experience.

'I've just realised that you couldn't possibly have made love to me on Bertolt's sofa. If you had, there would have been an earth-quake inside me that would have woken me up. You deceived me with that carnation – and you deceived Bertolt too.'

'Dear Clara, what can I say?' said Gerhart, thinking furiously. 'You were lying there naked and you were so desirable that I wanted with all my heart to make love to you. I sat beside you and stroked your beautiful big bundles, wrestling with my conscience. I was so desperate for you that my desire very nearly overcame my conscience – I played with your *little mousey* and I remembered how wonderful it felt to be inside it.'

'Oh, how romantic!' Clara sighed. 'But how did you find the strength to control yourself after that?'

'I knew that Bertolt was deeply in love with you, and you with him. How could I betray the affection and loyalty I feel for both of you? Never! I kissed your forehead tenderly and went home, so that the two of you would be together when you woke up.'

'But the flower!' said Clara, her plain face still puzzled. 'I thought that it could mean only one thing – and so did Bertolt when he saw where you left it.'

'A complete misunderstanding,' said Gerhart, telling the

truth at last, still warmly ensconced in Clara, 'I left it as a token of my esteem for you and as a tribute to your beautiful body.'

'Then why didn't you say so before? Bertolt has been frantic for days.'

'There has been no opportunity until today. Not that I thought any explanation was necessary. I assumed that my floral tribute would be understood.'

'But why didn't you tell this to Bertolt half an hour ago?'

'When I saw that he had misunderstood my intention, I tried to explain it to him, but he was upset and didn't want to listen to anything I said.'

Clara rolled him off her body and sat up, her chin on her knees, obviously thinking very hard – a proceeding which caused her some problems. Her face was a picture of concentration, and if Gerhart had a sketch-pad with him, he would have recorded her expression for future use.

'So,' Clara said, 'if you didn't make love to me, you didn't really win me.'

'That's right,' Gerhart answered with enthusiasm, sitting up beside her and putting an arm round her broad shoulders, 'Bertolt won you – he was the one who removed the carnation and replaced it with something more solid as a sign of victory.'

'Then he hasn't been deceiving you at all, by making love to me?'

'Absolutely not! It was his right.'

'In fact,' said Clara, her brow wrinkled in thought, 'you've just deceived *him* by making love to me.'

'Ah, no!' Gerhart said quickly. 'The question of deception does not arise at all, either way. We all misled ourselves, even though we have all acted in good faith. That is what you must keep firmly in mind – whatever the three of us have done, we were acting in good faith.'

'That's true – I see that. But what is not clear to me is that you said you held yourself back from making love to me when I was asleep because you knew Bertolt was in love with me. How did you know that?'

'Everyone with the least claim to sensitivity can see that he adores you,' Gerhart answered untruthfully. 'His eyes shine

81

when he looks at you. He speaks of you with all the tenderness of a devoted lover. He wants to be with you all the time, to kiss you and embrace you.'

'I think that's wonderful! No one has ever been in love with me before – at least, not like that. You had your hand between my legs and played with me and you still controlled yourself because of what you knew of Bertolt's love!'

'Love like that is rare,' said Gerhart, anxious to convince her, 'you must not let it slip through your fingers.'

'But do I love him?'

'Do you want to be crushed in his arms night and day?'

'Yes!'

'Do you want him to rip your clothes off and throw you on your back and make love to you passionately?'

'Yes, yes!'

'Do you long for him when you are alone at night, and wish he was with you in bed with his hands on your lovely big bundles?'

'You're right – I love him!'

'And he wants to marry you.'

'Not now,' she said, her joy disappearing as quickly as it had come.

'He was unwilling to ask you to marry him because he believed that he had lost the duel for you, and he is a man of honour. But when he knows that he won it . . .'

Clara threw her arms round him with such vigour that he was rolled over sideways and lay pinned to the bed by her body across his chest.

'Gerhart – you're a genius,' she said happily, 'the moment you tell him the truth everything will be all right again. I shall like being married to Bertolt – he's so strong and brutal in bed! Get dressed and go and tell him right away – and I'll wait here for him. We'll have a wonderful reunion!'

'Let's just think about this for a moment,' said Gerhart, worried by the prospect of explaining so delicate a matter to a drunken Bertolt.

'What is there to think about?'

'Bertolt is a proud man. He may think that I am lying to him, out of pity for his suffering at losing you. That would make the situation worse.'

'A proud, strong man,' Clara agreed. 'That's why I love him.'

'It will not be easy to get him to see the truth without offending that pride of his. We must be careful how we go about it. You know him best – would he believe *you*?'

'Of course he would. We trust each other completely.'

'Even in something that affects him as deeply as this?'

'Silly question! That's the answer – I explain to him that there was a misunderstanding. It's as simple as that! Why didn't I think of it!'

'And you must impress upon him that we have all acted in good faith towards each other.'

'Good faith – yes, I'll remember that. Then he'll make love to me and afterwards he can ask me to marry him. Oh, I've just thought of something!'

'What?' Gerhart asked anxiously.

'What am I going to tell him about this afternoon? I mean, you've just made love to me when you had no right to do so because you knew very well that you didn't win the duel.'

'No problem,' Gerhart said with difficulty, hardly able to breathe for Clara's weight on his chest, 'there is no need to tell him that we made love. Say nothing about it. Tell him that we sat and talked – you on one chair and I on another – both of us fully clothed.'

'But what did we talk about?'

'I was explaining to you at great length that the flower did not mean what you took it to mean.'

'Of course! You *are* a genius, Gerhart!'

She kissed him and he put an arm round her waist to pat her plump bottom with affection now that she seemed to have grasped what she had to do. They deserve each other, he was thinking; they're both such idiots that they'll make each other very happy.

'Then everything is settled,' he said, 'off you go and take the happy news to the man you love.'

'Yes! Did he say where he was going when you left him?'

'He was going home. I saw the doorman calling a taxi for him,' said Gerhart, thinking it better to leave out the more distressing details of Bertolt's departure from the hotel.

'He'll get drunk to drown his sorrow,' said Clara, 'poor Bertolt!'

'That is possible.'

'It's better if I let him sleep for an hour or two before I wake him up and tell him the wonderful news. He's wonderful when he wakes up from being drunk – he makes love so savagely!'

'It should be a very successful marriage, then.'

'Yes – I shall get him drunk every evening at dinner and he'll make love to me before he falls asleep – and then he'll wake up in the night with a hangover and love me brutally!'

'Marriage is a wonderful thing,' said Gerhart, not meaning a word of it.

'I was thinking,' she said hesitantly.

'Thinking, Clara?'

'You know how you explained to me that I'm not going to tell Bertolt that you and I made love this afternoon? I was thinking that it won't make any difference if I don't tell him that we made love twice.'

She rolled off him and lay on her side, her big breasts hanging close to his face. Her hand smoothed its way down his body to play with his limp tail.

'What you say does have a certain logic,' Gerhart admitted, nuzzling his face between her soft bundles.

'After all, we're very good friends,' she reminded him.

'We are dear friends,' he agreed.

His tail was stiffening in her hand as she fondled it.

'Only if you *want* to, of course,' she said.

'And only if *you* want to, dear Clara.'

'It's not as if we'd be upsetting Bertolt,' she said, clasping his stem full-handed now that it was hard. 'He can't be upset if he doesn't know, can he? And it would be wrong for me to tell him when he's going to ask me to marry him. Don't you agree?'

Gerhart slid a hand between her warm thighs.

'It would be wrong of you to upset him, Clara. Fiancés and

husbands must never be made unhappy by being told things which would upset them.'

'That's very good advice,' she sighed as his fingers parted the wet lips of her *little mousey*, 'I shall remember that all my life. It will be my duty to keep dear Bertolt very happy.'

'And I'm sure that you'll succeed admirably,' said Gerhart.

'I want to be a good wife for him,' she murmured, little quivers of sensation running along her belly as his fingers teased her hidden bud, 'Oh Gerhart, I love it when you do naughty things like that to my *little mousey!*'

'I'm going to do some very naughty and exceptionally brutal things to it,' he gasped, pushing her on to her back.

'Poor little mousey . . .' she sighed, her parted legs trembling as his fingers ravished her bud.

'I'm going to turn your *little mousey* inside-out,' Gerhart promised.

Chapter 8

Gerhart paints a picture

Lunch on Sunday with the General proved to be a trying occasion for Gerhart, even though Sieglinde did her best to keep up a flow of cheerful conversation. The old man listened in polite silence when Gerhart told him about his work and what he hoped that it might eventually lead to, but there was no word of approval or encouragement. As soon as they could after the meal, Gerhart and Sieglinde took their leave and went back to their own apartment. In the taxi he sat huddled and despondent and Sieglinde did not try to talk to him.

As soon as they were in their home, the threatened outburst took place. Gerhart ripped off his jacket and tie and threw them on the floor.

'Damn it to hell! Why must he treat me like that?'

'Like what?' Sieglinde asked, picking up the discarded garments.

'As if I'm some stupid, useless delinquent! Can't he see that the world has moved on since he was young?'

'He knows that, but he can't accept it.'

Gerhart pulled his shoes off and threw them at the sitting-room wall.

'It never fails!' he said indignantly. 'He always manages to make me feel small and insignificant.'

'But you're not! What does it matter what he thinks? You and I know that you are going to do great and important things. He's the one who has become insignificant. You should feel sorry for him.'

'How can I feel sorry for someone who makes me feel useless just by the way he looks at me?'

'My poor Gerhart! I'll get you a glass of brandy.'

'I don't want any brandy!'

'I'll run the bath for you. A good long soak always makes you feel better.'

When she returned to announce that the bath was filling, she found him slumped in an arm-chair, looking very miserable.

'Come on,' she said, holding out her hands to him.

'I don't want to.'

'Come on,' she insisted and, with reluctance, he took her hands and let her pull him to his feet.

She put an arm round him to lead him to the bath-room, where the hot water was gushing into the big tub.

'I've put half a bottle of bath-essence into it. Doesn't it smell nice?'

He said nothing, and stood listlessly while she unbuttoned his shirt and trousers and helped him out of his clothes.

'In you go. I'll turn the water off.'

Gerhart lay in the scented water, only his head above the surface. His eyes were closed and he looked wretched. Sieglinde stood looking thoughtfully at him.

'This won't do,' she said, 'you and I must have a serious talk.'

'There's nothing to talk about. Just leave me alone.'

She took off the electric-blue frock she had worn for the lunch and perched on the side of the bath to remove her shoes and roll down her silk stockings. Gerhart's eyes stayed closed, his forehead wrinkled and the corners of his mouth pulled down, even when she stood up again and slid her frilly knickers down her long and slim legs. He did not move or look at her when she got into the bath facing him.

'Pull your knees up,' she said, 'I need a little room too, you know.'

His knees emerged above the water and Sieglinde fitted her legs between his. She sat more upright than he did, her pretty little breasts in plain view, but Gerhart paid no attention at all.

'So your feelings are hurt,' she said. 'that I understand. But be truthful now – in all the years since he became our guardian has he ever stopped you doing anything you wanted to do?'

Gerhart shook his head grudgingly.

'Suppose he hadn't been there to look after us when we lost our parents – what would have become of us?' she asked.

'It would have been better.'

'You don't really believe that, and you're not being truthful. Did he forbid you to go to art school?'

'He looked at me as if I'd taken leave of my senses when I told him. I'll never forget that look – it was worse than if he'd hit me.'

'But did he try to talk you out of it?'

'No.'

'That proves my point. What you always forget is that he has always let you go the way you wanted to go, even when he thought it was the wrong way.'

'He still thinks it's the wrong way.'

'He's never said so.'

'He doesn't have to say it in words. It's that damned blank stare of his when I talk about my work. That says it all.'

'You're not being reasonable. Whether he approves of what you're doing or not, he's always made it possible for you to do it. And he's going to leave you half of his money in his will.'

'Not because he likes me. It's that awful sense of duty of his.'

'He doesn't dislike you, or you'd get nothing,' Sieglinde pointed out. 'He doesn't understand you, but you don't understand him, so that makes you equal. Not that it's important. The main thing is that you and I are going to have a lot of money one day. What are you going to do with yours?'

Gerhart's blue eyes opened at last and he looked at her.

'I think he'll live forever,' he said.

'But he won't. And then what?'

'I've never stopped to think about it. What will you do with yours?' he asked, a note of interest in his voice at last.

'I shall buy the most beautiful and expensive clothes I can find in the whole of Berlin. And something I've always wanted – a fur-coat of black Russian sable. After that I'm not sure. We could find a better apartment.'

'Yes, and buy some fantastic modern furniture for it! We'll give wonderful parties.'

'And we must travel,' Sieglinde added, 'I want to see Paris.'

Under the water her foot slid forward between Gerhart's parted legs until her toes touched his limp part. She had long experience of bringing him out of the black moods into which his dutiful meetings with the General plunged him. She had found that a hot bath took the tension out of his body and that did much to ease his mind, to the point where a little frolic with his monkey-tail would return him to his usual good nature.

'Travel! Yes – there are so many places we must see. Paris for you, then we'll go to Madrid and Rome and Venice and Naples. We'll have a wonderful time and I'll come back with enough drawings for a whole travel-book.'

Under the touch of Sieglinde's toes what had been limp before was growing hard and strong. She stretched out her other leg so that she could press his peg between the soles of both feet.

'Your own travel-book,' she said, 'that's a very good idea, But not all about buildings and museums and things they have in ordinary travel-books. Yours must be about the things we enjoy – pictures of restaurants and dinner on the terrace overlooking a beautiful bay. And dancing under the moon by the Mediterranean. And scenes in expensive shops, with me trying on beautiful clothes. What else can go in it?'

She was massaging his upright stem with her feet. The first time she had done this to him in the bath, on a sudden whim, it had brought about so rapid and remarkable an outburst that his violent throes had slopped half the bath-water over the side and onto the floor. On subsequent occasions the results were a little less dramatic, but no less gratifying.

'I shall put pictures of you in it,' he said.

'Of me? Doing what?'

'Not doing anything, necessarily. Pictures of you, looking absolutely beautiful, against different backgrounds that we visit.'

'But will that be interesting to anyone except us?'

'What I have in mind will stun people. For example, when we are in Paris we'll go to the Louvre and I'll sketch in some of the building so that everyone recognises it, and then afterwards I'll add a picture of you in the foreground, wearing silk knickers

89

and with a parasol, and the rest of you naked. And in Rome I'll draw the Spanish Steps and then add you to the picture, walking down towards the viewer, completely naked except for a hat and high-heeled shoes.'

'Oh Gerhart, that sounds fantastic! What else?'

'We'll find the places people recognise wherever we go – Vesuvius at Naples and the Greek temples in Sicily, things like that – this will be a travel-book to astonish the world!'

'And how about Berlin – are there any scenes here you might include? How about the Brandenburg Gate?'

His stem felt very hard and solid between the soft soles of her feet and his bad humour had long gone.

'The Brandenburg Gate,' he said, 'you walking through it in a long skirt with your little bundles uncovered – not a bit like the General's dreary old painting. My God, I've got it!'

To her surprise, he scrambled out of the water and wrapped himself in a towel, his pointer sticking out like a flag-pole.

'What on earth are you doing?' Sieglinde asked, startled by his sudden activity.

'I've had a flash of inspiration! I must paint it while I can see it clearly.'

He left the bath-room at a fast trot. Sieglinde settled back comfortably in the scented water and closed her eyes. He would be busy for some time in the little room he used as a studio, she guessed. In his creative mood he was best left alone. But how strange that he had rushed away when he must have been close to his moment of release, she thought. Whatever it was that had come into his mind must have a powerful appeal for him.

She soaked until the water began to cool, then dried herself and went to her bedroom to put on a dressing-gown and brush out her pale yellow hair. She lay on the bed and dozed for a while, and when she woke up it was after six o'clock. Gerhart was not in his own room or the sitting-room. She tapped on the studio-room door and went in to find him sitting on the tall stool before his drawing-board. The bath-towel had slipped unnoticed from his waist and he was naked and so absorbed in what he was doing that he was unaware of it. He looked up and grinned at her when she came into the room.

'Can I see what you're doing, Gerhart?'

'Yes, come and look. It isn't finished, but most of it is there.'

She stood beside him, a hand on his bare shoulder, to look at his large water-colour. The subject was familiar to her. He had painted a version of one of the pictures in the General's apartment – the one showing the former Kaiser riding in his carriage by the Brandenburg Gate. It was not a copy, but a different interpretation of the scene. The mounted bodyguard round the carriage were not men at all, but skeletons in uniform, with eyeless skulls under their helmets and bony fingers holding the reins of their skeleton horses.

'Oh!' Sieglinde exclaimed.

The Kaiser was shown as a living man, with the points of his moustache turned up and a stupid expression on his face, but he had not escaped Gerhart's attentions. The point of view of the picture had been raised so that the inside of the carriage could be seen, and the Kaiser's breeches were missing, revealing fat and hairy thighs between his military tunic and his black riding-boots. A fat, ugly and big-bottomed woman crouched between his knees, sucking the Imperial spike. The loyal Berliners lining the pavements were depicted with sheep's heads.

'But . . . but . . .' Sieglinde stammered.

Gerhart put his arm round her waist and pulled her onto his lap.

'Well, what do you think?'

'I shall never be able to look at the General's picture again without giggling. You've ruined it for me!'

'It's good, isn't it?' he said happily.

'It's clever and you're thoroughly wicked to even think of it.'

Gerhart slipped a hand into her rose-pink dressing-gown and stroked her breast slowly.

'If the General ever sees it,' she said, 'you can say goodbye to your inheritance, you know that.'

'He'll never see it. No one else will ever see it. It's enough for me that I've painted it.'

'It's made you feel better?'

91

'The next time that we visit him he won't be able to make me feel miserable now I've done this. I see now that his world of Kaiser and soldiers was a big sham and I've exposed it.'

He had also exposed Sieglinde's breasts by opening her dressing-gown down to the waist and he was playing with them without even thinking what he was doing.

'The old man is only a ghost,' he said, 'he's been haunting me, but he can't anymore. You and I are real, he's not.'

'Am I a real person to you, Gerhart? Sometimes I think that I'm only a doll you play with when the mood takes you.'

'But you're the one person in the whole world I love!' he said, worried by her words, his hand cupping a bare breast. 'Why do you say such a thing – have I upset you in some way?'

'Are you sure that you love me, or do you say that because you like to play with me?'

'I play with you because I love you – surely you know that?'

'You play with lots of girls, but you don't love them.'

'That's different.'

'Maybe. Will you always love me, or will you fall in love with someone else and go off with her and leave me?'

Gerhart slid his hand deeper down her pink dressing-gown to stroke her belly.

'I shall never fall in love with anyone else,' he assured her, 'How could I? You and I have been in love all our lives.'

'So far,' she whispered, kissing his cheek.

'And so it will always be – unless you fall in love with someone and decide to leave me.'

'I'd never do that – there's no one in the world like you.'

His hand was between her slim thighs, stroking the golden curls there with a delicate touch.

'Do you have a little secret to tell me?' he murmured as she pressed herself closer to him.

'Do you really want to hear my little secret or would you rather finish your painting?'

'Your little secret is the most important thing in the world to me. Of course I want to hear it – if you want to tell it to me, that is.'

Her legs had moved apart on his lap to let his fingers probe gently for her little bud and tease it.

'Oh yes, I want to tell it to you,' she sighed.

'And then, because I love you dearly, I shall tell you my own little secret – if you're not too bored to hear it, that is.'

'I'm never bored when I'm with you, Gerhart.'

Her pale blue eyes were half-closed with pleasure. Gerhart turned his head to kiss her mouth tenderly while his fingers fluttered between her thighs to persuade her body to produce its loving response.

Chapter 9

A business discussion with Rudolf Knuppel
and his assistant

Rudolf Knuppel's office was on the first floor of a building in Friedrichstrasse and was even more modern in style than his apartment. It was very obviously designed less as a place for work than as a theatrical setting for its occupant. The side of the room that overlooked the street was mainly windows, half-hidden behind white venetian blinds; two sides of the room were lined with bookshelves, and the fourth, behind Rudolf, was covered from floor to ceiling by a black and white mural of couples dancing to the music of a saxophonist and drummer. Rudolf's desk was like nothing Gerhart had ever seen before – an oblong sheet of thick glass supported on two chromium-plated metal trestles.

He greeted Gerhart warmly, shook his hand, sat him in an extraordinary chair of crimson leather with a high back and no sides, and told him that the reason he had asked him to this meeting was to discuss the possibility of commissioning him to illustrate a book he intended to publish. In anticipation of this happy news Gerhart had brought with him a portfolio of his published work and some other drawings and paintings. He opened the portfolio and showed what he considered to be his best drawings from several popular magazines.

'Yes, yes, very nice,' said Rudolf in a dismissive tone, 'put it away. You are wasting your talent on this kind of thing. I know that you are capable of much more – of really exceptional work.'

'It is good of you to say so.'

Gerhart was finding that it was not the easiest thing in the world to have a serious discussion with a man he had last seen naked and draped in a leopard-skin, pounding away on top of a girl he had known from his days at art school. In his mind's eye Rudolf's handsome black silk suit would keep disappearing to show him as he had been when he crouched on the floor of his sitting-room and snarled like a big cat at Erna Klemt. Nevertheless, while such thoughts were amusing, they had to be resisted firmly so that a proper discussion could take place.

'It is good of you to have such a high opinion of my skill,' Gerhart continued, 'though all I can offer by way of proof is what you see here.'

'Not at all! Your magazine pictures tell me that you are very competent in figure-drawing, but they are facile and uninteresting because they are drawn for a particular market which wants nothing more. But I know from my observation that you are capable of an intensity of emotion that is beyond all but a few. If I put these two considerations together – competence and emotional depth – what do I have? A strong probability that you can create really outstanding pictures for me.'

'You must mean your observation of what took place at your party.'

'Party! There is no need to use such evasive words with me. The animal force you released from inside yourself during my drama of the spirit was very impressive – and even frightening.'

It seemed best to say nothing in reply to that.

'Do you know the work of Leopold von Sacher-Masoch?' Rudolf went on.

'No, who is he?'

'He died about forty years ago. This is his *Venus in Furs*,' and Rudolf picked up an old-fashioned looking book from his glass-topped desk, 'I intend to produce a very special edition of it – for collectors only.'

'I like the title. What's it about?'

'It is presented as fiction, but in reality it is autobiography. It is a story about a man who enjoys being ill-treated by the woman he loves. I'll read you a few lines to give you the flavour of it:

She tied my feet together and then my hands, behind my back, as if I were a criminal.

'There! Can you move?'

'No.'

'Good.'

She looped one of the ropes, put it over my head and slipped it down to my waist and tied me to the bed-post. An uneasy shiver ran through me.

'I feel like a victim.'

'Yes, you're going to be whipped hard today.'

'I want to see you in your fur coat.'

'I'll put it on for you,' she said.'

'Can you visualise the scene?' Rudolf asked, looking up from the book to stare at Gerhart. 'There he is, bound hand and foot against one of the corner-posts of an old-fashioned bed. And the woman – her name is Wanda – puts on a long fur coat before he is whipped. Does that stir your imagination?'

'It certainly does!' said Gerhart, letting his fancy roam. 'The man is naked and totally exposed, the woman's fur coat is open so that her breasts and thighs can be seen. It should be a dark fur, to contrast with her body – I would make her very pale-skinned, with her mouth painted a bright red.'

'I like the sound of that.'

'I see her with long thin fingers which reach out to touch the man's bare chest in mockery before he is whipped.'

'Excellent – but her caress should be lower down, since she is mocking his manhood by subjecting him to this cruelty.'

'She touches his tail, you mean?'

'That's it. And she has a little dark fur coat of her own, glimpsed between her legs – you get the idea? Now, imagine Severin's face – that's the hero tied to the bed-post – his expression one of terror and adoration as he looks at this beautiful and cruel woman. Can you draw such an expression?'

'Not easy to achieve – I shall have to experiment to get it right. What about the woman's face?'

'It should be very beautiful and delicate, but cold and cruel. Soon she will hear his screams as he is whipped and she will take pleasure in his torment. Her red lips will curl in merciless enjoyment when she sees the scarlet marks of the lash on his flesh.'

'My word – what a challenge to draw that!' said Gerhart, amused by Rudolf's rising emotion as he talked about his vision.

'But there is more,' Rudolf continued, 'her face must also show her shuddering anticipation as she waits for the high moment of his agony.'

'When he dies, you mean?'

'No, no – when he ejaculates!'

'So it's not exactly a torture-scene. I misunderstood.'

'It is a scene of refined sexual torture,' said Rudolf, raising his dark eyebrows in surprise at the remark, 'I thought you knew that.'

'You must give me the book to read.'

'If your illustrations are to be any good you must grasp that Severin is sexually stimulated by being humiliated by the woman he loves. That is the whole point of the book.'

'I see. Then in this particular scene his clapper should be standing up?'

'Naturally. Wanda has put on the luxurious fur coat which excites him. She has humiliated him by tying him up so that he is helpless. Everything must be shown in detail – this is a limited edition at a very special price for connoisseurs. The pictures must show what the text is silent about – and with powerful emotion. Are you clear about this?'

'About this scene, yes, now that you have explained it to me. There is Wanda in a long fur coat using a whip on – whatever his name is.'

'Severin. But she does not whip him herself. She submits him to more degradation by watching him flogged by another lover of hers. Listen:

He flogged me without mercy, so brutally that I shook with pain from head to foot at each blow. Tears trickled down my cheeks and Wanda, reclining on the sofa, watched with savage curiosity and laughed.'

'Now that would make a good illustration,' said Gerhart, 'Wanda lolling on a sofa and showing her body through her unfastened fur coat. She is excited by the whipping she is watching and her hand is between her thighs to caress herself. Perhaps she will reach her climax when Severin does under the lash. What do you think?'

'Yes!' said Rudolf, his smooth face red with enthusiasm, or some other emotion, 'You understand what I am trying to achieve with this book and the illustrations. Tell me more.'

'I need to think carefully about the positioning of the three people to get it right and achieve the maximum effect – we have Wanda on a sofa playing with herself, Severin tied upright to a post with his tail standing up in full view, and another man with a whip.'

'A little experiment in aesthetics may help you,' said Rudolf huskily, and he picked up the telephone on his desk and spoke into it.

'Ask Fraulein Klemt to come to my office, please. And I am not to be disturbed until further notice.'

'Erna is here?' Gerhart asked, somewhat surprised.

'She works for me. I thought you knew that.'

'What does she do?'

'She is my assistant.'

While Gerhart was considering this unexpected information, Erna Klemt came into the office. He stood up politely and said 'Good morning' to her, not at all certain how to behave towards someone he had treated roughly the last time they met. Erna smiled and answered without any indication of her feelings towards him after what he had subjected her to in Rudolf's apartment. Her calmness made him nervous and he guessed that it would be out of place to try to make any sort of apology.

She was dressed in a businesslike manner, in a long-sleeved and plain white blouse and a close-fitting dark grey skirt. The only concession to vanity was a black patent leather belt pulled in very tightly round her waist to emphasise the curve of her hips.

'Erna, we are discussing illustrations for *Venus in Furs*,' said

98

Rudolf, 'and we are trying to make up our minds about one scene in particular.'

'Yes?'

'You remember the part where Wanda is reclining on a sofa, watching Severin being whipped?'

She nodded.

'A question of perspective has arisen. It will help us to settle this little matter if you will recline on my desk, as if it were a sofa.'

Her face was totally impassive as she complied with his request, as if it was an ordinary part of the routine of the office. Rudolf came round from behind his desk and stood by Gerhart's chair to watch Erna sit on the glass top of his desk, take her shoes off and swing her legs up until she could lie full-length on her side, propped on one elbow.

'What do you think?' Rudolf asked.

'Interesting,' said Gerhart, 'especially the long top line from her head to her feet. You see how it slopes downward from the shoulder to the waist, then curves up over the hip and then down again in a long line along her leg to the ankle. Have you got a pencil?'

On the back of one of the pictures from his portfolio Gerhart made a quick outline sketch to demonstrate what he meant.

'Yes,' said Rudolf, 'very artistic. But what you have drawn is lifeless – it could be a wax dummy of a woman from a shop window.'

'This is only a rough sketch to show you how the pose creates its own balance. But to be truthful, Erna does not look very comfortable on your desk – after all, it is not the same as being on a sofa with support for the back and shoulders.'

'That may be, but your sketch has no warmth, no life – it arouses no emotion.'

'You can hardly expect Gerhart to get emotional while I'm fully dressed,' said Erna, with her lop-sided grin, 'I can't see his sketch from here but all he's drawn is my clothes, I suppose.'

'True,' Rudolf answered, 'it was unfair of me to blame him. Perhaps you would remove your clothes and resume your position on the desk. Then we shall see what he makes of the scene.'

Erna got off the desk, her face impassive. She unbuckled her tight belt and undid the buttons down the front of her white blouse before tugging it out of her skirt. The blouse came off to display an uncomfortable-looking brassiere of white satin and, when that was removed, she shook herself a little to make her breasts roll from side to side, as if pleased to have them unconfined.

'Yes,' said Rudolf, his face flushed, 'now our artist has a scene with more emotion – perhaps his inspiration will now make itself felt.'

Apart from his emotion, something else was making itself felt in Gerhart's trousers as it grew hard and upright. Erna stepped out of her grey skirt and took off her magenta-coloured knickers.

'And the stockings?' she asked, raising one dark-painted eyebrow.

'What do you think?' Rudolf asked Gerhart.

'Keep them on, please,' he said, 'a naked woman looks even more naked if she is wearing silk stockings and garters.'

Erna put her bare bottom on the glass-topped desk and drew her legs up to lie along it again, facing them, one elbow propping her up. Gerhart busied himself with another quick outline sketch, Rudolf peering over his shoulder at it.

'Better,' he said, 'but not yet full of emotion to stir the viewer. Look at her breasts, for example – I am sure you have noticed that they hang in a provocative way, but in your sketch they do not invite the hands to reach out to touch them.'

'I am not trying to give you a finished work,' Gerhart answered patiently, 'This is only an outline to get the proportions right. I have shown Fraulein Erna's breasts in the right place and the right shape and size. But obviously breasts of a different shape and size would hang differently – it is a question of the model and the pose.'

Rudolf was staring at Erna and not really listening.

'Your legs are too close together,' he told her, 'all that we can see is a little patch of brown hair. Bend your top knee upwards and open your thighs so that we can see between them.'

She pouted at him and rearranged herself on the desk to his suggestion.

'A great improvement,' he said, 'Don't you agree, Gerhart?'

Gerhart stopped drawing and looked at Erna. He saw her now not as a model for a picture but as a naked young woman, and her sideways grin stirred his fantasy.

'The question is, Rudolf, how do *you* visualise Wanda in the book? That will determine what I do. Do you see Fraulein Erna in the role – brown-haired, with smallish breasts and bottom? Or is your Wanda taller, blonde, big-bosomed? Or black-haired and white-skinned, with a figure like a boy?'

Rudolf had one hand thrust deep into his trouser-pocket and was stroking himself slowly, evidently in the same condition as Gerhart.

'I don't know,' he said, 'I suppose that every time I've read the book my imagination has been limited to Wanda's cruel smile and her fur coat. Now that it comes down to a question of detail I don't know if she should have big breasts or small breasts or what colour her hair should be. The fur coat has always prevented me from seeing her properly. I don't know what would be best.'

'But I can tell you what would be best,' said Erna.

'And what is that?'

'I shall be the model for Wanda.'

'But ought you to be seen in the book?'

'No buts,' she said firmly, 'Wanda makes a speciality of taming lovers – where will you find anyone who knows more about taming men than I do?'

'You have a point,' Rudolf conceded, 'But I cannot agree to having my professional colleague and assistant shown in this light.'

'Why not? You know how expert I am at taming men. You were so thoroughly tamed on the night you invited Gerhart to be with us that you scuttled away while he took what he wanted,' she reminded him, her faint smile thin and cruel.

'I held myself back so that he could express himself with complete freedom. But the leopard was not tamed, as Roma can tell you,' he said, his face very red.

'Roma! She was so drunk that a one-armed cripple could have had her. She lay helpless on her back with her legs wide open and let you climb on top of her.'

Gerhart found this exchange embarrassing, as if he were listening to a private dispute between a married couple. He was also worried that if Erna annoyed Rudolf too much the commission might be cancelled. But he had not yet learned how expertly Erna could dominate her employer, in his apartment and in his office.

'Roma was not helpless,' Rudolf protested, though without much conviction, 'she resisted me fiercely. She even bit my shoulder.'

'She certainly was helpless – for the simple reason that you were so drunk yourself that a six year old girl could have fought you off,' Erna retorted.

She was trailing her finger-tips up and down her belly, from its round little button to the tuft of hair between her parted legs. Gerhart glanced at Rudolf and saw that he was fascinated by the gesture, his eyes bright and fixed, his hand still moving slowly in his trouser pocket.

'I was not too drunk to have you after Roma,' said Rudolf, almost in a whisper.

'Is that so, my little leopard?' and she laughed briefly in a way that was almost a snort of contempt.

'You cannot deny it,' he insisted.

'You've forgotten something,' she told him, mockingly, 'you've forgotten that I had to roll you on your back and squat over you. The leopard turned into an old tabby-cat after its little pounce on Roma, didn't it? The truth is that I had *you*, not you me. Do you know how long it took me to make your tail hard again?'

'It was hard in seconds,' said Rudolf, 'you are merely saying these things to make me look small in front of Gerhart.'

'Excuse me,' said Gerhart, 'perhaps we should talk about the book illustrations at some other time.'

'Not until you have heard my side of the story,' said Rudolf thickly, 'I will not let you leave thinking that Erna is telling the truth. In fact, you were there and so you know that I had her.'

'I regret that I did not observe you in action with Erna,' Gerhart said with reluctance, 'I took Roma into another room.'

'There you are!' said Erna. 'You were too drunk to notice

102

when Gerhart took Roma into the bedroom after you'd finished with her. Bruno was unconscious on the sofa with his trousers down and Fritz was snoring on the floor under the sheepskin. There was only you and me for the final act of the drama. And you were so tamed by then that it was hard work to get any response from you.'

'But I did respond!' Rudolf exclaimed, pleased by the admission.

'I must have been riding up and down on you for half an hour – I don't know why I even bothered.'

'Because you enjoyed it,' said Rudolf quickly.

'It's agreed then – Gerhart is to draw the pictures and I shall be the model for Wanda?'

Gerhart was fascinated by her smile as she imposed her will on Rudolf.

'Your expression is perfect!' he said. 'Exactly what you said you wanted, Rudolf – a smile of delicate cruelty!'

'Yes,' Rudolf mumbled, 'I agree, Erna will model for you.'

'And you will pay me the proper modelling fee, won't you?' Erna asked, and Rudolf nodded.

'I am most grateful for the commission,' said Gerhart, 'but we haven't discussed my fee.'

'Leave that to me,' Erna answered for her employer.

'We will discuss it later,' said Rudolf, his face flushed dark red as he stared at Erna's tantalising fingers stroking her belly. 'At present I have another urgent appointment and I must ask you to excuse me. *Auf wiedersehen.*'

'*Auf wiedersehen*,' said Gerhart, taking the hint, 'May I take the book to read?'

'Take it!'

The book was on the desk near Erna's elbow. Portfolio under his arm Gerhart went to get it, his back to Rudolf still standing by the red chair. At close range he winked at Erna and, when she gave him her lop-sided and lascivious grin, he deliberately brushed his hand across her bare breasts as he reached for *Venus in Furs.*

'*Auf wiedersehen*, Fraulein Erna,' he said, and her grin grew wider.

103

At the office door he turned for a moment to look over his shoulder before leaving. He saw Rudolf lurching towards the desk, unbuttoning his trousers as he went. Erna turned to meet his rush, swivelling her bare bottom on the glass, her legs opening wide and then closing round Rudolf's waist. Gerhart closed the door silently and left.

Chapter 10

The art of wrestling

No one who knew Heinz Graunach took him very seriously, perhaps because he was always affable and inclined to fall in with the suggestions of others very readily. His rhapsodies over the spectacle of the colossal women wrestling in mud had been dismissed as a joke by his friends, including Gerhart. It came as something of a shock when Heinz confided in him that he had been in earnest. They were drinking coffee together in the Café Schon when Heinz told him that he had sought out the manager of the wrestling couple and made private arrangements to meet them. Gerhart was not sure whether to believe him or not, but a close look at the round and honest face of his friend convinced him that this was no laughing matter.

'But Heinz, they're too big for you! They're even too big for me. In fact they're too big for anyone except a heavy-weight boxer.'

Heinz was not in the least put out.

'I've been having dreams about them,' he said, smiling. 'Such dreams! Dreams you wouldn't believe. I've woken up with sticky pyjamas three times since we went to see Gretchen and Lenchen in the ring. What do you think of that?'

'I'm astonished. If I'd dreamed about them I'd have woken up screaming from a nightmare of being squashed to a pulp.'

'But you felt the animal attraction of their huge bodies struggling together, whatever you say now. There's no point in denying it. You were shouting as loud as everyone else when the bathing costumes were torn and the big melons came bouncing out.'

'I was carried away by the hysteria of the crowd. We all were.'

'I suppose it was only hysteria when you groped Lotte?'

105

'You saw that, did you? I thought you were too far gone to see anything except balloons and bottoms in the ring.'

'Have you made love to her yet?'

'Maybe.'

'I see,' said Heinz with a grin. 'She was no good in bed. She'd be no good to me either.'

'Why do you say that?'

'I can never do it right with our sort of girl. The women who really get me going are the rough ones.'

Heinz' difficulty was common gossip among his friends, but Gerhart had never heard him say anything about it himself.

'Whores, you mean?' he asked.

'They don't have to be whores. They can be factory-girls or market-women, or even middle-aged wives from the poor districts. As soon as I get on top of a woman like that I turn into a human steam-engine and I can't get enough.'

'What are you saying – that you have to despise a woman before you can perform with her?'

'You don't understand. I adore them. That's why I can keep going for hours with women like that.'

'But what's so different about them?'

'It's hard to say,' said Heinz. 'At first I thought it might be the poor clothes and underwear that got me going. But it's not, because when I get them stripped naked and see their bodies, I can't hold myself back.'

'Aren't most of them a bit . . . well, plain?'

'Outright ugly, some of them,' said Heinz cheerfully, 'and it doesn't make any difference – thick ankles, pot bellies, sagging bouncers, missing teeth, straggly hair – all I know is that I want to get on top of them and hump away.'

'Well, either of the wrestlers should suit you well, if that's what you prefer. They're both huge and they've got bouncers that sag to their waists.'

'Not either, *both*,' said Heinz, 'I'm going to have them both. It's all been arranged, that's why I asked you to meet me. I want you to come with me.'

'Heinz! I'm not going to sit and watch you belting away at your mud-wrestlers!'

'You don't have to watch. You can join in. We'll swap them between us.'

Gerhart stared at him in amazement. Heinz gave every appearance of being sane, and more purposeful than usual, but his suggestion was ludicrous.

'Thank you for the offer, but no. Why ask me?'

'To be truthful, I'm almost afraid to go on my own. And that's very strange – you see, I've been into some dismal back-streets with women I've picked up and it's never bothered me before.'

'Are you afraid of being robbed and beaten up?'

Heinz shook his head.

'This time is different,' he said, 'Will you come with me?'

'Ask Heinrich. He's as strong as an ox and afraid of nothing. Or that great idiot Bertolt – he's a champion boxer, he says.'

'They'd laugh at me. I know I can trust you.'

'The answer is still no.'

'This is very important to me. I've told you how the mere thought of those gigantic women affects me, even when I'm asleep. And to grapple with them in the flesh! I have this tremendous and portentous feeling that this is a spiritual experience that will shake me to the soul. It's so overwhelming that I can't face it alone. Will you stand by me?'

'If it means that much to you,' said Gerhart with reluctance, 'I'll hold your hand till you jump off the diving-board. When is this big adventure arranged for?'

'Now,' said Heinz eagerly, 'We'll get a taxi outside.'

If Gretchen and Lenchen made much money from their performances in the mud-ring, they did not spend it on their apartment. They lived together on the second floor of a ten-ement block, and the apartment was dingy and uncared for. Lenchen opened the door, wearing a tent-like man's shirt with no collar, her massive legs and feet bare. Not that Gerhart knew it was Lenchen until Heinz greeted her by name. Without a word she led them through the apartment to a frowsty bedroom that had neither curtains at the window nor carpet on the stained wooden floor. The other wrestler, Gretchen, was push-ing two iron-framed beds together to make a larger area of

107

operations for whatever was planned. The big eiderdowns in plain covers on the beds looked none too clean to Gerhart.

Gretchen finished heaving the beds together and straightened her back, to stand a head taller than Heinz and no shorter than Gerhart himself. Like her partner she was dressed informally, which is to say sloppily, in a shabby green dressing-gown that had evidently been made for a big man in the distant past. It was tied round her middle with a thick cord with frayed ends, and she resembled an untidy parcel. Gerhart was taken aback by what he saw and wished he'd never agreed to come, but Heinz' face was wreathed in smiles of pure delight.

'So you've come to do your exercises,' said Gretchen, brushing back her short-cropped fair hair. 'Who's this you've brought? We only expected one.'

'A good friend,' said Heinz, 'he too was struck by your charms in the ring. I hope you don't mind that he's here – after all, there are two of you.'

Gretchen yawned and stretched and then scratched at her ribs through her dressing-gown. Gerhart's impression was that the two women had only just got up, though it was after eleven in the morning.

'He can stay,' she answered indifferently, 'the more the merrier. Do you want a cup of coffee?'

'Later,' said Heinz quickly, 'we are keen to make a start on the exercises. And since we are both amateurs, you must teach us everything you know.'

Lenchen poked him in the side with a forefinger as big as a sausage and chuckled in her throat.

'You're a bit underweight for our kind of fun. Your friend looks tougher, but he won't last long either.'

'You are mistaken, Fraulein Lenchen,' said Gerhart, 'that is, if you mean what I hope you mean. I am sure that you can easily overpower me in wrestling, but when it comes to the sort of contest in which the woman lies on her back and the man lies on top of her – that's another story. In that sort of contest I have great endurance.'

'Boasting, are you?' Lenchen asked, not in the least impressed. 'You've had your tail up a slack-muscled rich girl or

108

two and think you know all about it – you're in for a surprise, my lad!'

'I hope that we're all in for a pleasant surprise,' said Heinz, 'why don't you strip for action, ladies, and give us the pleasure of watching you, for a start?'

'That won't take long,' said Gretchen.

She unknotted the frayed cord round her middle and shrugged herself out of her ancient dressing-gown. Underneath it she wore a knee-length night-dress of pink flannelette, crumpled and none too fresh-looking. Meanwhile Lenchen pulled her striped shirt over her head to uncover short knickers of sky-blue artificial silk. While her arms were raised, Gerhart noticed what had escaped his attention when he had seen her in the mud-ring, tufts of coarse light-brown hair in her armpits. He grinned when she waggled her chest to make her big balloons roll about.

'Get a good eyeful,' she said, 'you'll never see another pair like mine, not if you live to be a hundred.'

'Except for Fraulein Gretchen's,' he replied, still grinning at the sight of her rolling bouncers.

'Not even then – I'm four centimetres bigger round the chest than she is.'

She turned away from him and bent over double to stick out her barrel of a backside at Heinz, the thin material of her knickers stretched almost to breaking-point over her vast and fleshy cheeks.

'How do you like that?' she asked.

'My God!' Heinz exclaimed, 'What a truly monumental sight!'

Lenchen reached back to pull her knickers down over her hips and thighs. Heinz stretched out a trembling hand to lay his palm on one huge cheek while he stared at the split mound between her legs.

'Awesome!' he declared. 'I feel that I am in the presence of some cosmic force!'

Gretchen was stirred into action by her friend's exposure of her bottom to the visitors.

'Don't listen to *her*,' she said, 'Compared with me she's got nothing. I've seen ninety year old market-women with better backsides on them than that. And she's only bragging about her chest – she has to hold her melons up with both hands to make them measure more round than mine.'

'Show me,' Heinz pleaded.

She moved Lenchen out of the way with a push that would have sent a person of normal size reeling across the room.

'You want to see, do you?'

'Fraulein Gretchen, I am shaking with anticipation,' said Heinz.

She took off her pink night-dress and stood naked, her huge dumplings pushed out proudly in front of her, and struck herself a resounding slap across her broad belly.

'Solid muscle,' she boasted, 'I can take a punch there that would kill you. Want to try?'

Heinz could hardly believe his ears. He stepped forward to within a short distance of her, his eyes glowing at the sight of her melons.

'Go on,' she urged him, 'you can't hurt me.'

He yelped in delight, drew back his arm and smashed a fist into her belly. She didn't even flinch.

'Harder,' she said with a grin, 'I didn't feel that at all.'

Heinz punched her again, this time with all his strength, and the impact of fist on flesh resounded through the bedroom. Gretchen grinned and grabbed him by the wrist and throat. Before he knew what was happening, she was down on one knee and had him helpless, face-up across her out-thrust thigh, exactly as she had held Lenchen in the ring.

'You're not much of a puncher,' she told him, 'If I hadn't known it was you I'd have thought a flea jumped off Lenchen and landed on my belly. It wasn't one of your fleas, Lenchen, was it?'

'You're the one with fleas,' said Lenchen, 'not me. Still, it didn't look much more than a tap he gave you.'

'If he can't punch, then he can't take a punch either,' said Gretchen, 'Let's have a look at *his* belly and see if it's muscle or fat.'

Heinz gurgled and wriggled in delicious terror, but could do nothing to help himself when Gretchen undid his jacket and

110

trousers and pulled up his shirt to uncover his pale and soft belly. Her enormous hand almost covered it when she gripped the flesh and squeezed hard.

'Nothing but fat,' she chuckled, 'you'd be dead if I gave you a thump – wouldn't he, Lenchen?'

Lenchen had removed her blue knickers. She squatted on her haunches on the other side of Heinz and prodded his belly.

'They're all soft, rich people,' she said. 'If you left them out for a night in the rain they'd be dead the next morning. Half of them can't even get it to stand up – you remember the young Baron who gave us all that money to strip off for him? His little tassle wouldn't stand up, whatever we did to him.'

'All the same, he got his money's worth,' said Gretchen, 'he wrote from Munich to say so – I've still got his letter somewhere.'

'This one will be the same, you see,' said Lenchen, 'let's pull his trousers down and see what he's got.'

Between them they stripped off Heinz' trousers and under-pants and inspected their find. Whatever else was soft about him, what they had bared was not. It stood up and waved about stiffly as he squirmed uncomfortably across Gretchen's thigh.

'Not bad,' Lenchen admitted, 'but whether it's any use for anything is another matter. They usually shrivel up when you least want them to. Why don't you put him on the bed, so we can find out?'

She moved away, and with remarkable speed Gretchen changed her grip on Heinz and heaved upwards. He flew through the air, squealing in fright, and landed flat on his back on the bed. And while Gerhart was distracted by the sight of his friend casually thrown about, Lenchen reached out with easy skill, took him by the ankles and jerked him off his feet. He landed on his bottom with a painful jar and, before he recovered from the shock, Lenchen was kneeling behind him, her heavy breasts squashed against his back. She had an arm under his left armpit and the hand flat on the back of his head. He was held very securely and, though she was not hurting him, he guessed that she could exert excruciating pressure if he resisted.

'You've been very quiet so far, whatever your name is,' she

111

said. 'What are you – one of the perverts who gets a thrill out of watching other people do it?'

'Fraulein Lenchen . . . I can assure you that I am normal in every respect.'

'They all say that. Have you come here to watch your friend, or are you going to join in?'

Until this moment Gerhart had not the slightest intention of having anything to do with the giant wrestlers, but a casual pressure of her hand to force his head forward persuaded him to change his plans.

'Naturally to join in! But as this is my friend's party and I am his guest I thought it would be best to let him go first.'

'Does that mean he's paying the lot?'

'We haven't talked about that yet.'

'You'd better start thinking about it now. Anyone we like the look of gets in here free, but it costs a lot of money to get out again. Unless you want broken bones and torn muscles, that is. I could cripple you for life in two seconds if I wanted to.'

'Dear Fraulein Lenchen, put such aggressive thoughts from your mind. Money is no problem for Heinz or for me. We came here as admirers of your skill and strength, in search of an interesting experience.'

'Your friend's having his interesting experience now – look!'

On the joined beds Gretchen had stripped Heinz off his clothes and was dealing with him as if he were an opponent in the ring. She twisted him about in arm-locks, leg-locks and head-locks, her huge bulk of flesh rolling over him and under him in a virtuoso exhibition of the wrestler's art. Immobilised by Lenchen's grip, Gerhart stared and wondered at the ease with which Gretchen was mauling Heinz and eliciting cries, moans and shrieks of pleasure from him. At least, it sounded like pleasure, but who could be sure? The display ended with Heinz on his back, shiny with sweat and exhausted, and Gretchen astride his chest, her bent knees beside his ears and the big brown door-mat of hair between her legs only a hand's-breadth from his face. She sat up straight, her hands joined behind her back, and her immense breasts pushed out like a balcony above Heinz' face.

112

'Your friend's down for the count,' Lenchen observed, 'your turn now to show what you've got. Get your trousers off.'

'Let me get up then.'

'Do it!' and she put just enough pressure on his neck to make him grunt.

It was not easy, with only one hand and sitting down, and it took Gerhart some time to struggle out of his lower garments. Lenchen's arm released his neck but, before he could move, both her arms were round his waist, her hands between his legs and she had hold of his fragile parts. She held them just firmly enough to warn him not to resist.

'Now the rest of your clothes,' she said, and he slowly got rid of his jacket, tie and shirt.

'Are you sure you're normal?' she asked unkindly. 'Your friend's tail was as stiff as a barge-pole before Gretchen laid a hand on him, and your's is still dangling. Even though you've been staring at Gretchen naked. Not to mention the fact that I'm holding it in my hand. Are you another one like the Baron who can't get it to stand up?'

'Having my head twisted off is not very exciting,' Gerhart answered. 'Just let me get my hands on your bouncers and you'll see something to your advantage.'

'It'll take more than you've got to do me any good,' she retorted.

All the same, she released her dangerous grip and spun him round on his bottom to face her.

'Go on then,' she said, 'You wanted a feel – now's your chance. You'll never get your hands on anything like mine again.'

'Not even if I live to be a hundred and one,' said Gerhart, grinning at her as he fondled her grossly oversized breasts.

They had grown to the point where the pink halo around their buds had been stretched to discs the size of Gerhart's palms, though the buds themselves were small and flattened. Gerhart's previous experience with women had led him to think of their breasts as a pleasant handful each, but Lenchen's were of other dimensions – each an armful in itself. Playing with them soon brought him to a condition that had her

113

approval, and she demonstrated how to take hold of her tiny buds and stretch them out several centimetres.

'Were they big when you were a young girl, or did they grow this size later?' he asked.

'They were bigger than most grown women's when I was twelve,' she said with pride. 'And they've kept on growing bigger all my life. Have you ever seen a bigger pair?'

'Never! How old are you, Fraulein Lenchen?'

'Twenty-four – and you must be about the same.'

Her enormous hands were stroking along the insides of his thighs, up towards his stiff tail. He hoped that she would treat it with consideration when she got that far.

'What are you fiddling about at down there?' Gretchen demanded from the bed, 'bring him up here!'

'Up you go!' said Lenchen.

She grasped his now prominent handle and rose to her feet. Gerhart rose hastily with her, afraid of having it torn out by the root. Her upward pull continued until he was standing on tip-toes and beginning to panic. Judging her moment exactly, she released him and, with a push against his chest, sent him reeling backwards, off-balance, towards the bed. It caught him behind the thighs and he fell backwards. As his legs came up, Lenchen had him by the ankles to twist him over, so that he landed face-down, with his chin on Gretchen's massive thigh.

'Would you!' she laughed. 'Trying to get your face between my legs and nibble me, are you? I enjoy a bit of that, but I'll decide when I'm ready for it.'

Lenchen still had his ankles. She dragged him away from Gretchen and arranged him parallel to Heinz, before settling her crushing weight on the small of his back.

'I'll let you off your exercises because you were nice about my melons,' she said.

Gerhart turned his head to see what was happening to Heinz. He too had been rolled over face-down, and Gretchen was sitting astride his back. His face was towards Gerhart and his eyes were half-closed.

'Heinz! Are you all right?'

'I'm dead and in Heaven,' Heinz murmured, 'such absolute

114

bliss is beyond all earthly experience. Promise me that on my tomb-stone you'll put that I died in ecstasy.'

Before Gerhart could reply, hard fingers dug into the muscles of his shoulders.

'You're nearly as flabby as your friend,' he heard Lenchen say, 'you need toning up, both of you. A good massage will help.'

Her fingers probed, pushed and prodded into muscles, sinews and nerves until Gerhart thought that his whole back was on fire. The sensation was agonising, and yet at the same time it excited him. Heinz must have felt the same, for he was squealing happily. Lenchen's fingers moved down Gerhart's spine, her weight slid to the back of his thighs, the mat of hair between her legs rubbing over his skin in a way that made him gasp. But the gasp became a groan when she sank her fingers into the cheeks of his bottom. Then, after what seemed an eternity of torture, her weight was off him. The ordeal was not yet over – she wrenched his legs widely apart, knelt between his thighs and her finger-tips probed between the cheeks of his bottom.

'No!' he said loudly, starting to get up off his face, but at once a heavy hand was on the small of his back, pinning him to the bed.

Lenchen's finger-tip was rubbing the little knot of muscle between the cheeks of his backside and, wriggle as he might, he could not get away from it. What she was doing to him aroused in him a mixture of emotions so strong that he lay as if paralysed – shame, fear, disgust – and sexual excitement that added to his shame and fear.

'No!' he moaned, afraid that he would burst into tears if she didn't stop.

Her finger-tip forced open his little knot. In desperation Gerhart got his hands under his chest and heaved himself up off the bed to drag his body away from Lenchen. But it was too late – her hand on the small of his back held his belly pinned to the bed and her hard finger slid into him. His body jerked in climactic spasms and he collapsed weakly back on to his face as his elixir squirted out on to the eiderdown beneath him.

'Now you know what real massage is like,' he heard Lenchen say from somewhere behind and above him. 'How's yours, Gretchen?'

'I think he's fainted.'

Even through his unspeakable turmoil of emotion at what had been done to him against his will, Gerhart turned his head in concern to look at Heinz. He saw Gretchen roll him over and slap his face lightly until his eyes opened.

'Too much for you?' she asked.

'Unbelievable!' Heinz croaked, 'I passed out from sheer pleasure! Do it again, Gretchen!'

'Get your breath back, little man. You'll need it before I'm finished with you.'

Gerhart yelped as Lenchen gave him a hard smack on the bottom, before turning him over face-up and kneeling astride his hips, her door-mat of hair harsh against his shrinking spike.

'That took you by surprise, didn't it?' she asked, grinning at him.

'Why did you do that?'

'I do believe I've shocked you,' she said, her grin broader.

Her steely fingers sank into his shoulders and around his collar-bones, then worked their way painfully down his ribs to his belly.

'Soft body!' she said contemptuously. 'What a waste! You're well-built – you could be an athlete if you trained properly. You'd make a middle-weight boxer if you've got a punch.'

'I don't want to be a boxer!' Gerhart gasped.

'Your sort never do. All you want is to drift about spending your daddy's money and getting on top of silly young girls.'

Her fingers kneaded his belly deeply, churning up his inner organs. With blurred vision he saw her looming over him, her mighty breasts swinging, and a trickle of sweat between them. Eventually she moved her weight down to his thighs and he stared at the thick tuft of mouse-brown hair between her straddled legs, marvelling at the heavy texture of her curls. She held his stem in a hand so broad that it completely enclosed it.

'It's woken up again,' she said.

To Gerhart's surprise, not only had it woken up but it was at

116

full-stretch and ready for anything. There was a glowing feeling throughout his body and the aches Lenchen had aroused in his muscles seemed to have transferred themselves and become a concentrated throb in the part she held.

'Are you going to finish the massage?' he asked.

'A few rubs and it would be all over,' she said, 'you don't get off that easy. I've done all the work so far – now it's my turn to lie on my back and let you sweat. Look at your friend – he's on top of Gretchen already!'

And indeed, Heinz was lying on the other enormous woman, huffing and puffing like a train while he pounded away between her spread thighs.

'He means to have you both,' said Gerhart, 'he'll be on top of you when he's done with her.'

'If he's the one who's paying he can do anything he likes to either of us, front, back, sideways, up, down or whatever he fancies. Maybe he'd like to have both of us at the same time.'

With her wrestler's agility she moved quickly to spread herself over Heinz' back, her drum of a belly thumping against his backside, reinforcing his thrusts into Gretchen, her breasts bouncing up and down on his shoulder-blades. Gerhart stared in disbelief at this human sandwich as it heaved and shook, and he wondered if the bed was strong enough to survive the pounding it was taking. He heard Heinz screech in ecstasy as his ambition was fulfilled.

'Don't stop!' Gretchen howled from the bottom of the stack. 'Don't stop now!'

Heinz was not allowed to stop. Lenchen's belly slammed at his bottom in double-time and kept him going for the benefit of Gretchen below, until at last she wailed in paroxysms of delight. At once Lenchen slid off Heinz, wrapped her arms round Gerhart and dragged him by brute force on top of her. Her legs were locked over his thighs and her brawny arms crushed him to her breasts in a bear-like hug. Gerhart had no choice but to do what she wanted. He stabbed hard between her open legs and felt himself sink into her depths. Her response was immediate – her back arched off the bed, lifting him as if he weighed nothing, and her mouth gaped wide in a howl of climactic release. Her internal muscles gripped Gerhart's stem tightly and pulled at it so fiercely that she drained him of his essence at once.

Before he could get his breath back, Lenchen freed him and gave him a smart smack on the bottom.

'That's what I like!' she declared. 'A man who doesn't mess about when he gets it in! I never thought you were up to it, but you did that well. I'll have you again in a minute.'

She rolled him off her with a casual push of one hand. Gerhart sat up on the crumpled and stained eiderdown to make sure that Heinz was still alive after what he had been through. He was lying half over Gretchen, stroking her bulging breasts with great respect, a foolish smile on his face.

'Heinz, I thought you'd been squashed flat!'

'The sensations!' Heinz answered dreamily. 'One under me and the other on top of me! All that weight of female flesh just for me! I never thought that anything could be as fantastic as that.'

'Not even in your dreams about them?'

'My dreams were pale and weak visions of the reality. This experience has opened up amazing new perspectives for me.'

'You've certainly opened up one perspective. Are you going to stay and do the same for the other one?'

'Stupid question! I'm going to stay here all day, and perhaps all week. Aren't you?'

'I have to go.'

'You must be out of your mind to leave! This apartment is Heaven and there are two angels to supply needs I never knew I had. I'm going to stay right here and explore my needs until I die of exhaustion. Don't forget the words for my tomb-stone.'

'Telephone me when you get back to the ordinary world from Heaven.'

Gerhart climbed off the bed and picked up his scattered clothes. He was half-afraid that either Lenchen or Gretchen would grab him and haul him back into the ring for the second round. For that he had no taste at all – once through the exercise with either of the battling Amazons was more than enough for him. But he need not have worried. Heinz had an arm round

118

each of his massive playmates, as far as it would go, and was whispering happily to them. Hands as big as dinner-plates were stroking his thighs and belly, as if preparing him for the next bout.

Chapter 11

Perhaps old friends are the best after all

To be brutally mauled by hulking female wrestlers may have seemed heavenly to Heinz, but to Gerhart it had more a touch of Hell about it. He left the apartment in an unsettled state of mind, profoundly unsatisfied in spite of his involuntary climaxes, unhappy and exceptionally displeased that he had allowed himself to be talked into so grotesque an adventure. He found his way to the main street and caught a tram, wondering what he should do. He had a great desire to talk to someone about what he had endured and the effect it had on him, thinking that this would purge him of the memory of Lenchen's prying fingers. She had robbed him of his self-confidence by precipitating in him two crises with no better reason than to gratify herself.

In other circumstances he would have turned to his sister to pour out his distressed feelings, but not this time. What had been done to him made him feel so demeaned that he could not bring himself to take the risk of lowering himself in Sieglinde's esteem. Eventually an idea came to him and he got off the tram and found a taxi to take him to Roma von Gloeden's home. There was no certainty that she would be in, of course, but if she were then Gerhart intended to take her to a café and get her to listen to his troubles. He thought of her as a sympathetic person who would listen without reproach and help him put his miseries behind him.

Roma lived with her widowed mother, just off Potsdamerstrasse. An elderly maidservant opened the door and, in answer to his question, informed him that Fraulein von Gloeden was having lunch.

'At this time of day!' Gerhart exclaimed.

He glanced at his wrist-watch, expecting it to show that it was late afternoon. In disbelief he saw that it was not yet one o'clock. The episode with the wrestlers had taken no more than an hour from start to finish.

'Who is it?' he heard Roma's voice call from inside the apartment.

'Herr von Rautenberg,' the maid answered over her shoulder.

'Ask him to come in.'

Roma was in the dining-room, sitting alone at one end of a long table, with a plate of cold meats and a glass of beer before her. Although she and her mother were by no means poor, she had never taken the trouble to dress fashionably. Today she presented a very plain appearance in a knitted frock of beige wool.

She greeted Gerhart warmly, asked him to sit down and told the maid to bring another plate.

'It's nice to see you,' she said, 'how are things going with Rudolf?'

'Very well. He's asked me to illustrate a book for him. I haven't thanked you properly for introducing me to him. Why don't you come out to dinner with me tomorrow or the next day? We'll have a little celebration.'

'Anyone could have introduced you to him. He hasn't commissioned you because of me. You owe it entirely to your own ability.'

'There must be hundreds of illustrators as good as me that he could have chosen. It's because of what happened at his party, when we all took . . .'

He broke off as the maid returned to set a place for him. For the rest of the meal they changed the subject and talked of friends and other neutral matters, while the maid fussed about them. Gerhart ate little, his appetite depressed by his state of mind. After they had finished eating they moved into the sitting-room and the maid asked Roma if anything else was required.

'No, thank you, Lisa. Have a nice time.'

'She's gone out?' Gerhart asked when the door closed behind her.

'It's her afternoon off.'

'And your dear mother?'

'She's out visiting for the day. If you've come here to make love to me you've picked a good time for it.'

'No, not that. I want to talk to you privately, as a friend. In complete confidence, that is.'

'That sounds very serious, for you. What do you want to talk about?'

It was a struggle to begin, even with so undemanding a companion as Roma, but Gerhart forced himself to relate his meeting that morning in the cafe with Heinz and all that had followed. Roma listened in silence, but with round eyes in her chubby face.

'Well, well!' she said at the end of his tale of woe, 'I know what you need right away.'

'What?'

'A scrub in hot water to get the smell of those women off you.'

It was almost as if she were Sieglinde. He followed her without a word to the bath-room, big, old-fashioned, with a tub that stood on lion's-paw feet and with a shower rosette over it.

'Off with your clothes! Don't just stand there with a long face.'

He undressed slowly, slightly embarrassed to be doing so, even though she had seen him naked enough times in the past.

'You don't have to be shy with me,' she said, noticing his hesitation, 'we're friends, after all.'

She coaxed him out of his clothes and under the shower. He felt exposed and vulnerable again, but he gritted his teeth and let the hot and soothing water cascade down his body. Roma sat on a cork-topped stool and smoked a cigarette, hardly looking at him.

'Try to explain to me how you feel about what happened,' she suggested.

Gerhart summoned up his courage and tried to make her understand.

'I know it sounds stupid, but I feel as if I've been raped,' he said, trying to grin at her.

'Do you know, I think that you have,' she said in a sympathetic tone, 'It's strange – I've never heard of a man being raped by a woman before.'

'It's as unpleasant as the other way round, believe me!'

'But there must have been some pleasure in it when you reached your climax.'

'It was over so fast that it was like sneezing. There was no time for any sensation of pleasure, and all I could think of was that she'd tricked me out of it twice. I must sound like an outraged girl who's been seduced and didn't enjoy it.'

'That's better – you're beginning to see the comical side of it.'

'Comical is right! We must have looked like a couple of clowns rolling about on the bed . . . I wonder if I could draw it and make it look awful and comical at the same time?'

'As for being seduced,' said Roma, 'You seduced me when we were both sixteen.'

'That's not true,' said Gerhart, grinning at her, 'it was you who seduced me. You wanted to find out what it was like.'

'Only because you told me it was wonderful. How did you know that if you hadn't done it to a girl before?'

'Because everybody said so. That was the first time for me.'

'And for me. I was a virgin till then.'

'Technically, perhaps. But you let me play with you for weeks before. And there must have been other boys before me who'd felt your little bundles and had a hand up your skirt.'

'Maybe, but I was still a virgin until you did something about it.'

'We were both so nervous that it was only luck that we managed to do it at all,' said Gerhart, smiling at her with affection, 'but it was fantastic. When it was all over I lay on you kissing your face and thinking to myself *I've done it!* And then I got worried that you might have a baby.'

'You certainly did! You kept telling me to run home and wash so that nothing would happen. But it *was* nice, and I had a crush on you.'

'And I had a crush on you.'

'Not in the same way. I was just a girl who'd let you do it to her. The most important thing for you was to be able to say that you'd had a girl. Admit it – it doesn't make any difference now.'

'Boys are like that, I suppose. But I really did like you, Roma. You had a sweet nature and those plump little dumplings of yours were irresistible. And they still are, now they've got plumper still.'

123

'You're beginning to sound more like yourself. Turn the water off and I'll scrub you.'

She pushed the sleeves of her frock up above her elbows and used scented soap and a big bath-sponge on his shoulders and back.

'Arms up,' she said, 'I don't know if it's your sweat or the woman who raped you, but it isn't very nice.'

He held his arms high above his head while she washed under them and round his chest.

'At least Heinz seems to see the comical side of the visit,' she said, 'I always thought he wasn't quite right in the head.'

'He loved being pulled about and flattened. I thought I knew him well, but I was wrong. I've learned something about him today – that he understands his own nature and accepts it.'

'And do you?'

'There are times when I don't understand myself at all,' he confessed. 'It makes me confused and unhappy. But you – you understand yourself, I'm sure about that.'

'Oh yes, I understand myself well enough,' said Roma sponging his belly and bottom and between his legs, 'The problem for me is that I don't like myself much.'

She lifted his limp tail on the soapy sponge and looked at it.

'The poor little thing has got the miseries,' she said. 'Doesn't it want to stand up for me?'

'There's not a flicker of life in it!' Gerhart said, aghast.

'After where it's been this morning it needs a good wash,' and she dropped the sponge so that she could clasp his limpness in her hand and soap it thoroughly. Its total lack of response to her manipulation depressed Gerhart.

'My God – I'm impotent!' he exclaimed mournfully. 'That fat bitch has ruined me!'

'You're exhausted, that's all,' Roma reassured him. 'You've been drained emotionally rather than physically by a bad experience. You need to rest.'

She turned on the shower and washed the soap from his body carefully, then put a big towel round him and rubbed him dry all over.

'Poor little thing,' she said, using the towel very gently on his

124

dangling tail. 'It's not often as meek as it is now.'

She took him into her own room and made him get naked into bed while she pulled the curtains over the windows to dim the light. Gerhart lay wrapped in disconsolate thoughts, hardly noticing that she was taking off her shoes and stockings and her far from elegant frock.

'Close your eyes and rest,' she said, 'I'll have a nap too. I won't disturb you, I promise.'

She hung her frock over the back of a chair and got into bed beside him wearing a peach-coloured silk slip. Gerhart made room for her and she put her arms around him loosely and cradled his head on her shoulder.

'Go to sleep,' she soothed him, 'everything will be better when you've had a good rest.'

Her nearness was comforting and undemanding. In truth, he was emotionally fatigued from his disagreeable bout with Lenchen and wanted nothing more than to be able to forget it. After a while he slipped into a light sleep and in this state there arose from his memory the most grotesque image of his morning's adventure – Heinz sandwiched naked between massive Gretchen and equally massive Lenchen, the three of them heaving up and down together. In the dream Heinz turned his head to grin at Gerhart and called out *This is the tenth time!*

In spite of the repulsion the dream aroused in him, this monstrous coupling also excited Gerhart. He wanted to climb on top of the human heap, spread himself over Lenchen's huge backside and stab into her from behind. Then he would be in control of the pace and rhythm, not her, and it would be his discharge that sent a shock-wave rippling through the stack to trigger off not only Lenchen's climax but also Heinz' and Gretchen's down at the bottom of the heaving heap. *You'll do it when I want you to, you bitch*, he said to her, *Not when you want to – and I'm going to keep you hanging on for it till you're screaming for mercy!*

He woke with a start, to find that Roma had turned on her side away from him, and that he was rubbing his hard spike against her bottom through her thin slip. He reached over her hip to get his hand under the slip and stroke her warm belly.

125

She too had been dozing, but she woke up slowly with a sigh of pleasure as he handled her. After a while she rolled over on to her back and let him pull her slip up so that he could play with her chubby breasts.

'Oh, Gerhart!' she murmured, 'I could lie here like this forever with you.'

She lay still, letting him do whatever he pleased, not touching him or trying to arouse him further. He was thankful for that, for he was still slightly unsure about the return of his strength, even though his tail was hard. When the buds of her breasts were firm, he slid his hand down her body and into her knickers, to stroke her between her parted thighs very softly. Roma's little sighs and quivers reinforced the pleasure that was starting to grow inside him and her abandonment of herself to him to do what he chose was soothing to his bruised ego. He made this pleasure last as long as he could, but it could not be protracted indefinitely. The moment came when her loins jerked upwards and he savoured the triumph of making her respond, however quietly, to his will.

Afterwards she sat up to wriggle out of her slip and knickers and to throw the bedcovers off.

'That *was* nice,' she said, with a smile of pure affection, 'Thank you, Gerhart. Your rest has done you good.'

He was on his side, facing her, his stem sticking out towards her, but she sat cross-legged on the bed near him and looked at it without touching it.

'And there's another old friend of mine who's more cheerful now than an hour ago,' she said.

'Tell me something,' said Gerhart, troubled by another memory.

'Anything.'

'That party of Rudolf's, when we played at being animals – was that the first time for you?'

'First time for what? The very first time for me was with you, years ago – you know that!'

'I mean was it the first time you had played that game with him?'

'Does it matter?'

'No, but you seemed to know all about it and what was going on. You lay on the floor and let Rudolf and Fritz make love to you without even moving. Just as you were lying on your back for me a minute ago.'

'What of it? I like it to be like that.'

'I know, but it all seemed so unlikely. How did it all get started – do you know?'

'It was about eighteen months ago, or a bit more, when I was going out with Bruno – you met him that evening.'

'The one who works in films?'

'Yes, he invited Rudolf to see a film he'd made, and Rudolf brought Erna with him.'

'Bruno makes films? I didn't realise he was that important.'

'He's not. He'd been working on a film about Madame Pompadour or some other French king's mistress. It came out last year but I've forgotten what it was called.'

'I think I saw it. It wasn't very good. In fact, it was silly.'

'They all knew that at the time, when they were making it. Bruno persuaded some of the extras and technicians to stay on secretly one night after the director and stars had gone, and he used the sets and the costumes to make a little film of his own – it only ran for about fifteen minutes.'

'What was it about?'

'It was a sort of parody of the ball-room scene they'd shot for the real film. You know – men in long silk jackets and knee-breeches and women in tall white wigs and belled-out skirts. They were doing one of those slow and stately eighteenth century dances where they walk up and down in lines, just touching each other's finger-tips and bowing and curtseying to each other. They were all wearing black velvet masks.'

'I remember the scene.'

'Bruno put the extras in the same costumes and masks and did the same dance-scene. Only in his version the women pulled their bundles out of the top of their low-cut frocks, one after the other, all down the line of dancers. The men bowed in turn and got their tails out of their knee-breeches – all standing up stiff, of course.'

'It must have been very funny!' said Gerhart, reaching up to touch Roma's breasts, 'I wish I'd seen that.'

'Oh, we laughed! You have to imagine the contrast between the slow dance, with two lines of people just touching hands as they parade up and down the ball-room, and what they were showing each other. At the end of the dance the men made deep bows, their things sticking out like truncheons, and the women picked up their skirts at the front and held them up round their waists.'

'No underwear, I'm certain. A line of hairy little slots – what a sight!'

'That wasn't the end of it. The men went down on one knee and kissed their partners between the legs.'

Roma's hand was resting timidly on Gerhart's shoulder.

'He's clever, that Bruno!' said Gerhart. 'Was that the end of the film?'

'No, but after that it was just an orgy on the ball-room floor. All you could see was men's bottoms thumping up and down and women's legs waving in the air. The thing was though, it gave Rudolf his idea about liberating the hidden emotions.'

'I don't see the connection at all.'

Roma's fingers were caressing the skin of Gerhart's chest and it felt pleasant to him. He moved his own hand down from her breasts to her thigh and squeezed gently.

'He explained it to us,' she went on. 'He said that the costumes and the masks made the people in the film feel anonymous and so they were able to do things which they wanted to do but had never dared.'

'Maybe.'

'It made sense to Rudolf. So the next evening the four of us tried it out. He hired the costumes and wigs and we dressed up and had a few drinks and did the dance ourselves to a gramophone record.'

'Did it work out as he expected?'

'It made me giggle when Rudolf and Bruno pulled their tails out while we were walking up and down the room, but Erna took it as seriously as Rudolf. When the record stopped we got down on the floor and that was fine. Bruno made love to me, both of us in the costumes and masks. Rudolf did it to Erna, and then we changed partners and did it again. Rudolf was very pleased and since then he's been experimenting with different costumes. He thought of the circus animal act a month or so ago and it's become his favourite ever since.'

'Always the same four of you. But what about – what was his name – Fritz something with the sheepskin?'

Her finger-tips teased his nipples and Gerhart's stem quivered.

'The original four, yes, but Rudolf invites others sometimes if he thinks they'll join in properly. I can make your tail jump by tickling you here with my nails – did you know that?'

'Don't stop, then – make it jump!'

'Like that?'

Gerhart nodded and smiled happily and asked her if she was still a close friend of Bruno.

'He fell asleep at the party before we started,' he added.

'Bruno is bored with Rudolf's games. And he's been bored with me for a long time,' she answered.

'Then why does he go there?'

Roma's hand was sliding over his belly in a slow circular motion.

'He goes there because he's in love with Erna,' she explained. 'He wants to make love to her, but he gets drunk and passes out before he gets the chance because he can't stand the sight of Rudolf or anyone else making love to her.'

'What an idiot! Why doesn't he meet her on her own if that's what he wants?'

'She doesn't like him much. His only chance of making love to her is in Rudolf's games, when she's there for everyone who wants her.'

'Everyone who's strong enough to take her!' said Gerhart. 'She doesn't play as gently as you do. She gave me a few bruises that evening.'

'But you had her, all the same. I saw you ramming this naughty thing of yours into her,' and at last Roma's fingers touched his stiff tail and trailed along it very lightly. 'The reason why she doesn't care for Bruno is because the first time we played the circus game and she was a lion-tamer she fought him so hard that he gave up and made love to me instead.'

'Dear Roma . . .' Gerhart murmured, 'if you keep on doing that to me you'll make me squirt all over your hand.'

'And why not?' she asked. 'If that's what you want, that's what you shall have.'

She clasped his trembling stem and played with it.

'You can have Erna any time you like, you know that. She likes you because you were strong enough to hold her down and make her do what you wanted.'

'What you mean is that she was able to make me do what *she* wanted.'

'It comes to the same thing, doesn't it?'

Gerhart sat up and pushed Roma on to her back. He spread her plump legs wide and mounted her, his belly on hers while he pushed deeply into her. He felt no urgent necessity to prove anything to her or to himself any more and so he rode her slowly and enjoyed it intensely. Roma lay passive, arms lying loosely out from her sides and legs splayed. This, more than any words she could have used at that moment, said to him *Do whatever you want to me*. A murmuring grew in his ears, like the faint murmur of the sea in a shell, and the final lingering memory of his humiliation earlier that day was washed away by the rising tide of his desire. His belly clenched in spasms of pleasure and he cried out in exultation.

Later on, when they were lying side by side, his hand resting comfortably between her thighs in a way that was almost pro-prietorial, he returned to the subject of Rudolf and his games.

'What I don't understand is, Rudolf built his circus game up as some kind of exploration of the self, but it was only an orgy, like the one in the film you told me about. And yet he's an intel-ligent man – why does he want to deceive himself?'

'Oh Gerhart – didn't you learn anything from it?'

'There was nothing to learn. We all got drunk and I jumped on your friend Erna.'

'You are blind about yourself if you think that. Rudolf wanted to tame her himself, but he hadn't the courage to knock the whip out of her hand and do it.'

'So he made love to you instead. What is so significant about that?'

'It was a defeat for him. It wasn't me he wanted, not the first time.'

'At least he didn't have to fight you.'

'It's not my nature to fight. I was excited and I wanted him to do it – and Fritz. And Bruno if he'd been awake. And you, of course.'

'You and I made love later, in the bedroom.'

'You still don't understand. You like to win and I like to surrender. This morning you felt that you'd lost, and it made you unhappy. But with me you won again, and I surrendered, and that made us both happy.'

'At least *you* understand yourself.'

'I understand myself very well. My problem is that I don't like myself,' she said.

'All this philosophising about making love!' said Gerhart. 'It makes my head spin. Why don't we forget about it and lie here and make each other happy?'

Chapter 12

Erna offers a contract for signature

Now that Gerhart had seen for himself in Rudolf's office that the relations between him and his assistant were not those that usually existed between an employer and an employee, it did not seem out of the way to be asked by Erna to meet her at her apartment to sign the agreement for the book illustrations. From the conversation he had with her on the telephone he had the impression that it was Erna who took care of the financial side of Rudolf's business, while he devoted himself to the choice of books to be published.

Her apartment was so very different from Rudolf's that Gerhart hardly knew what to make of it when he arrived. It was not even an apartment – she lived in a large room in someone else's apartment, he discovered when he presented himself at the address she had given him. A thin woman of about thirty-five, in a white frock and big gold ear-rings, let him in, told him that Fraulein Klemt was expecting him and showed him to a large room overlooking the street below. The room was adequately furnished, with two arm-chairs and a divan-bed that served during the day as a sofa – but what struck Gerhart like a blow to the face was the vivid colour of everything. The chairs were upholstered in bright scarlet, and there was a cover of the same material on the divan. The walls and ceiling were painted a brilliant blue, and much of the floor was taken up by a lurid green rug.

In the midst of this gaudy clash of colour Erna's tobacco-brown linen frock seemed positively restrained. She cleared away a stack of new books from one of the chairs and asked him to sit down. They talked about the illustrations for *Venus in*

132

Furs and Gerhart found himself agreeing to produce ten original pictures in water-colour within three months, for what appeared to him to be a reasonable sum of money. Erna agreed to have his name properly credited as the artist on the book-cover.

'That's settled then,' said Erna, producing a typed document, 'it's all in here. Sign it for me and we'll drink to our collaboration. If this book sells well, Rudolf will want you to illustrate others for him.'

A bottle of white wine and glasses were ready on a small side-table. While she was pouring the drinks, Gerhart read carefully through the document and signed. it. She handed him a glass and he said *Prosit!* and drank it in one long swallow.

'About last week,' he said, 'I was very rough with you. I didn't mean to be, but I was very drunk and didn't know what I was doing.'

'There's no need to apologise. You did what was in you to do. That's exactly what is supposed to happen.'

She filled their glasses again and perched on the arm of his chair.

'Did I hurt you?' Gerhart asked.

'Yes, and it was very exciting,' she answered, with a laugh.

'That game of Rudolf's is dangerous – surely you realise that?'

'Things can get wonderfully dangerous when people really let themselves go. There was an evening when I beat Fritz so hard that he bled on the carpet. And Rudolf nearly throttled me another time – my throat was so sore that I couldn't speak for two days.'

'You enjoy danger, I see.'

'I enjoy anything that causes strong emotions.'

Erna went to fetch the bottle from the table to fill up their glasses. Gerhart stared at her and her brown frock against the blue wall made him think that she had turned into a tree against the sky. He blinked hard, wondering what was going on, and there was Erna again, standing at his elbow and pouring wine into the glass he held. For a moment the pale wine glowed like a rainbow as it cascaded into his glass.

'I feel very strange,' he said slowly.

'In what way?'

133

'As if everything has suddenly become unreal. A minute ago I thought you were a tree . . . now you're wearing a white wig . . . what's happening?'

'I put a few drops of something special in the wine, that's all. There are things you must experience before you can release your talents fully, and this is the quickest way.'

'I feel quite drunk!'

'That will wear off in a minute. This is much better than getting drunk.'

To Gerhart the walls of the room were the open sky and he saw clouds drifting slowly across his field of vision, stately and slow.

'The clouds!' he said, pointing to them.

He was still staring at them when Erna sat on his lap. She had taken all her clothes off and her breasts were close to his face, soft-skinned bundles that jiggled. He brought up his hand to touch them and laughed when he saw that he was still holding his glass and had spilled wine down her belly. It seemed important for some reason that was obscure to him to fit the nearest breast into his wine glass. He tried to do it, and more wine ran down Erna's body and into his lap as he put the glass over the russet tip and pressed firmly. Erna laughed with him and used her hands to squeeze more of her soft flesh into the glass.

'Look,' she said, 'I've filled it with my milk for you.'

Gerhart smiled beatifically and raised the empty glass to his lips to drink. What happened after that was inexplicable – there was a gap in time and when he next became aware of himself he found that he was sitting on bright green grass, his back propped against something hard and his legs stretched out in front of him. There was something odd about his legs, he saw. They were too long for him, those legs, two or three metres long at least. Longer even, for his feet were so far away that he couldn't see whether he had his shoes on or not. He tried to settle the question by wriggling his toes, but that was no help – his toes were too remote from him to feel whether he had shoes on or not.

A woman was kneeling beside him. He didn't recognise her but he knew it was a woman because she was naked and he could see her breasts. She was undoing his trousers, though he couldn't remember asking her to. She pulled his pink tail out and stared at it as it poked up stiffly.

'My feet,' he said, still uncertain about his shoes, and hoping that she could settle the question for him.

She moved away from his side and his attention became fixed on the pink stem standing up from his trousers. The longer he stared, the thicker and taller it seemed to grow, until it was as long as his fore-arm and twice as thick. It was very impressive and he began to chuckle.

There were bare feet moving towards his column and he guessed that they were not his own feet because they had toe-nails that were painted scarlet. And they were on the ends of long bare legs that lay between his own trousered legs. One of the feet touched his stalk and the toes curled to rub themselves against its smoothness.

'Have you seen how peasants make wine?' a woman's voice asked. 'They tread the grapes with their bare feet to squeeze the juice out. Do you like wine?'

Gerhart was so engrossed in watching how the scarlet-nailed feet held the pink obelisk between them that it was some time before he understood that he had been asked a question. *Wine*, he repeated, and the sound of the word set him off reciting a catalogue of the names of all the wines he could remember. At the end of it he tried to see the woman's face to ascertain whether she approved. He started at the slowly rubbing feet and looked along the pale legs to which they were attached, but it was such a tremendously long way to the knees that his eyes became tired and he had to close them for a rest before he could continue along the elongated thighs beyond the knees. Where they met he could make out a dark and fuzzy patch, but his eyes would not focus properly at so enormous a distance, so he closed them again and thought about wine and how good it tasted and how well he felt after a bottle or two. He decided to explain his thoughts and opened his eyes slowly, to see bare feet gently treading grapes between his thighs. The warmth in his body was so pleasant that he knew it must be a fine summer day, and the bright green grass was springy beneath him.

135

'The sun is so hot!' he said. 'Why don't we go swimming?'

The trodden grapes gave up their juice and it splashed over the red-nailed feet. Gerhart's senses slipped away and he let himself sink into sleep.

When the daylight returned he was lying on something soft and scarlet, and he was naked. There was a woman lying on her back next to him, and she too was naked. She was propped up on her elbows and staring fixedly down at her own body. It took Gerhart some little time to orient himself and understand that he was lying on his side between the woman's parted knees. She spoke from what seemed to him a long way off.

'Look at me,' he heard, and he looked at her face and saw that she had dark eyebrows drawn in over half-closed eyes.

His gaze travelled slowly downwards, over her pointed chin and her short neck, to the smooth skin between breasts whose red-brown tips pointed slightly outwards, away from each other. Her belly was a pale and steppe-like plain to travel across, its only feature the button that stared back at him as if it were a little round eye. And at last his uncomprehending gaze reached the curls at the join of her splayed thighs.

'Yes, there!' she said unhurriedly. 'What do you see?'

'A big chrysanthemum . . . with golden-brown petals,' he answered, trying to make sense of what he saw.

'Do you like flowers?'

'Sometimes I paint them.'

'Will you paint mine?'

'Flowers and women are the same,' he said, amazed by his own sudden insight, 'there are chrysanthemums and roses and lilies. Did you know that?'

'Who is a rose?'

'Sieglinde.'

'Who is she?'

Bemused though he was, the inner restraint on revealing his secret attachment to his sister was so strong that Gerhart clenched his fist and brought it down as hard as he could on the bare thigh near him. The blow was not hard at all, for his movements were as slow as if he were swimming underwater, but it ended that line of questioning and set his companion off in another direction.

'Yes – beat me!' she said, 'I want to be beaten all over!'

He struggled to a half-sitting position and used both fists to rain feeble blows on the thighs on each side of him. They began to shake and he could hear faint moans. The brown-petalled chrysanthemum opened down the middle and changed into a pink rose, wet with dew, as the woman's hands pulled at it. Gerhart was enchanted by the transformation and stopped his beating to stare at this new wonder.

'I shall paint this flower,' he said, more for his own benefit than hers, 'A big painting for exhibition . . . everyone must see it!'

The rose fluttered up and down, as if caught in a summer breeze. He put a hand to it to hold it still and found that it was not set on a stem, as flowers usually are. He felt where the stem should have been and it was so wet that he guessed there had been a rain-shower. From afar there was a long-drawn mewling noise that reminded him of something, but he was not sure what. When the sound ended, the wet rose-petals closed themselves and the flower was a chrysanthemum again. Gerhart rested his head on it and drifted away into nothingness.

When next he awoke he was in the half-light of dusk. He was on his back and something heavy lay across his legs. It took several attempts to get himself up on an elbow, from which position he saw that there was a naked woman lying face-down across his legs. He wondered who she was and why she was in so inconvenient a position. Not only inconvenient, but uncomfortable. He tried to pull himself from under her and found that either she was too heavy or he was too weak to free himself. He lay back again to consider what was the best thing to do, and perhaps he slept, or perhaps he only closed his eyes briefly, until a touch on his chest made him look up. A woman was standing near him. Not the one who had been lying across his legs – he was certain about that, because this one wore a white frock and gold ear-rings and the other one had been naked.

'Do you know how long you two have been at it?' the woman asked, grinning at him in a familiar sort of way.

'I've met you before,' said Gerhart, 'but I can't remember your name.'

137

'Why are you wearing Erna's knickers?' she asked.

He raised his head to look down his body and saw something that was totally inexplicable. He was wearing lace-edged knickers. His bewilderment evidently showed in his face and the woman standing by him laughed.

'You don't even know where you are, do you?' she said. 'Can you remember your own name?'

After a little reflection he came up with it.

'Gerhart von Rautenberg. Who do I have the pleasure of addressing?'

'I'm Ruth. So what are you doing here, Gerhart?'

He thought about that for so long that she laughed again. Her fingers touched the thin silk of the knickers he was wearing and stroked over his limp tail.

'You're here because Erna wanted to sample this,' she told him, 'and she's certainly done that. She's out cold.'

It was very pleasant, thought Gerhart, to lie there and let her stroke him through the silk. It was far too much of a bother to ask who she was and why she was there.

'Erna,' he said thoughtfully, 'I know a girl named Erna. She works for a publisher.'

'You certainly do know Erna! After what you've been doing to her for the last eight hours there can't be any of her you don't know. Where is she now?'

'How should I know? Either at work or at home, I suppose. The last time we met we talked about chrysanthemums.'

'She hasn't managed to finish you off,' said the persistent woman in the white frock. 'You've gone hard.'

'Finish me off?' said Gerhart, not sure what she meant.

The woman dragged the lacy knickers down over his hips to inspect the result of her fondling.

'I'm talking about *this*,' she said, grinning broadly and taking hold of it.

'I don't understand what you mean,' said Gerhart, 'did you say that Erna is at home or at work?'

'Never mind. She's overdone the happy-drops again. I'm always telling her to be careful, but she doesn't listen. One of these days I'll find her dead with a man on top of her.'

'Murdering her, you mean?'

'Murdering her with *this*,' she answered, rubbing it quickly, 'she'd love that! I came in to make sure you were both all right – you've been quiet for so long after the noise you were making before. And there's Erna, snoring her head off, and a nice young man all ready and willing and with nowhere to put it. Some people have all the luck! She gets more than she can cope with and some of us never get enough.'

'Enough what? Money?'

'This!' she said, squeezing his tail hard.

'I like you,' said Gerhart, 'lie down here with me.'

'Much good that would do either of us! You're so doped that if I let you get on top of me you'd forget what you were doing halfway through. You're only awake now because I'm playing with you.'

'Do I know our name?'

'I've told you – it's Ruth. Not that you'll remember it five minutes from now. Or me either, for that matter.'

She let go of him and used both hands to lift her skirt and get on to the scarlet divan with him.

'Erna doesn't want it, so I'll have it,' she said, 'she'll never know.'

She straddled Gerhart on her knees, her feet jammed against Erna's body across his legs.

'And you won't remember either,' she said.

She undid the buttons between the loose legs of her camiknickers and pulled up the front to show him a broad triangle of brown curls beneath a pale-skinned belly.

'After all, we don't want it to go to waste,' she said.

'Oh!' said Gerhart, a warm and pleasant sensation spreading through him as she impaled herself on his spike, 'I like that!'

'I'm sure you do! So do I!'

She rocked herself backwards and forwards on him, stroking the insides of her own thighs above her stocking-tops.

'My God, that feels good!' she exclaimed jerkily.

'I had a strange dream about Erna,' said Gerhart, 'we changed clothes with each other so that she was the man and I was the girl.'

'Stop talking and let me enjoy myself,' said the woman in the white frock above him.

He closed his eyes and was soon adrift in a colourful hallucination. He was soaring up high into the blue sky in a huge scarlet zeppelin and he knew that when it reached a certain height the pressure of the gas would burst it wide open. He'd be flung out into space and the sensation would be fantastic.

Chapter 13

Lotte apologises in full for her behaviour

For two days after his visit to Erna's room Gerhart was sick and wretched. He was confused from the after-effects of the drug she had given him and totally exhausted from something, though he could only guess what. He stayed in bed, half-sleeping, woken from time to time with violent fits of shivering and nausea. When he dozed he was haunted by dreams so fantastic that he knew they must be unreal, though he was afraid that they might be partly memories. By evening he managed to eat the soup Sieglinde made for him and talk to her a little – enough to persuade her not to send for a doctor. In the night the strange dreams woke him again and again, colourful and grotesque for the most part, and the next day he was still too weary to get up before evening. He told Sieglinde some of what had happened – as much as he could remember – and she saw that he was almost better.

That night he slept calmly, and it was nearly noon when he woke up, feeling hungry. Sieglinde was out and had left a note for him in the kitchen to say that she would be back by six. He made himself a meal of frankfurters with sweet mustard and washed the lot down with beer, by which time he was beginning to feel human again. Erna was a dangerous person to know, he decided.

He was thinking of going out for a stroll in the sunshine when the door-bell rang. He opened the door to find Lotte Furer-Diest standing there, looking very pretty in a light blue linen costume and a broad-brimmed hat. Gerhart, still in pyjamas and without even a dressing-gown on, unwashed and unshaven still, felt suddenly scruffy.

141

'Can I come in?' Lotte asked, 'I telephoned earlier and your sister said you were not well. So I thought I'd bring you these flowers to cheer you up. Did I get you out of bed? I *am* sorry!'

'Come in, please. I'm feeling much better and I was up, anyway. Thank you for the flowers.'

He took her to the sitting-room and she made herself comfortable while he found a vase for the pink roses she had brought. He was not overjoyed to see her, after the curious hour in her bed, but he thought it kind of her to call.

'What was the matter with you, Gerhart? Nothing serious?'

'I don't know exactly. Something upset me, but a couple of days in bed cured it. How are you?'

'To be truthful, I've been feeling rather ashamed of myself.'

'Why?'

'I mean, after what happened the other night, when you took me home. I've been hoping you would call me so that I could apologise. But as you didn't, here I am.'

'There's no need to apologise.'

'But there is. I didn't behave at all well, and you had every right to be angry with me. There, now I've said it! Are we friends again?'

She had taken one of the arm-chairs and Gerhart was sitting opposite her on the sofa. She leaned forward to clasp both his hands during her apology and, to do so, she had to lean so far towards him that he caught a glimpse down the top of her blouse, her jacket being unbuttoned.

'Of course we're friends, Lotte. I lost my temper and treated you very roughly. I was ashamed of myself afterwards.'

She saw that he was looking at her breasts down her blouse and smiled happily, rubbing his hands slowly between her own.

'You had every right to lose your temper with me. I was very selfish.'

'And you were very tired,' he said with a grin.

'Exhausted,' she sighed in contented reminiscence, 'But that's no excuse for behaving as I did.'

'I think you had every right to be exhausted, in the circumstances.'

142

Lotte left her chair and seated herself by him on the sofa, smoothing her blue linen skirt under her in a way that displayed her knees. She touched Gerhart's cheek to feel his blonde whiskers.

'Well, you did wear me out, that's true,' she said softly.

Gerhart laughed at her version of the truth.

'I didn't do anything,' he said, 'you wore yourself out, my dear.'

'But you did,' she insisted, 'you let me make use of *this*.'

And to demonstrate what she meant beyond the possibility of misunderstanding, she slipped a hand through the slit of his pyjama trousers and took hold of his tail.

'Judging by the effect it had on you, it served you well on that occasion. I must offer my regrets that it is not very serviceable at present.'

'Your illness *has* made it weak! What a pity! I hoped that I could make up for last time. It was very hard and frustrated then. Can I just hold it while we talk?'

'On condition that you do not blame me if you are frustrated this time. How are your family – well, I hope.'

'I'm having problems with Maximilian,' Lotte confided, 'he's crazy about me and it makes life very complicated.'

'I guessed that when I met him. Does your sister know?'

'My God, I hope not! I'd never do anything to hurt her. It's not as if I felt anything for Max, but he won't leave me alone.'

'He looked a perfect image of self-restraint to me. What does he do – try to kiss you?'

'You'd be surprised what he gets up to. He's not nearly as restrained as you think.'

The feel of her hand inside his pyjamas was very pleasant and Gerhart's wariness of her was thawing.

'Really?' he said. 'He tries to stroke your little bundles, does he?'

'He's like an octopus! Wherever I go in the apartment, you can be sure he's there. Before I can get away from him he's got an arm round my waist, two hands squeezing my bottom, two more down the front of my frock and another up my skirt.'

Gerhart laughed at the thought of Glotz with so many hands, all in use at the same time.

'You may laugh, but it's not at all amusing for me! I'm terrified that Kathe will find him and me together and blame me. Or the maid might spot us and tell her.'

'He sounds like a determined fellow. Is he always like that with pretty women, or is it just you?'

'It's me he's after. I don't believe he's ever made love to anyone in his life except Kathe. He keeps on about being desperately in love with me and if I refuse him he'll have a nervous break-down – things like that. He makes *me* feel guilty for the state he's in.'

'He sounds a bit of a nuisance.'

'He's more than a nuisance. You wouldn't believe how jealous he gets when I go out for the evening. He was so rude to Heinrich that they were shouting at each other and I thought Heinrich would punch him. And after I went out with you he questioned me for hours the next day – where we'd been, who we'd met, what we did – as if I were a child.'

'He had something to be jealous of that night,' said Gerhart.

'If he ever found out that I'd let you come to my room, I think he'd kill me!'

'Can't you find anywhere else to live while the business with your husband is settled? You must have friends, surely.'

'Yes, but the trouble is that Max has been looking after the arrangements from the beginning with my husband's lawyer. If I move out now he'll be so furious that he'll spoil everything. I simply have to stay on the right side of him for the time being. You're nice and hard now, you know – shall I stroke you slowly?'

'You're the perfect cure for whatever it was that upset me! But don't expect too much – I doubt if I'm completely recovered yet.'

'Nothing strenuous, I promise,' she said, smiling at him while her hand move lightly up and down the length of his stem.

'I can't think of any solution to your problem with Maximilian,' he said. 'But you seem to be coping well. You're

144

getting his legal services and all it's costing you is a quick feel now and then when your sister's not looking.'

'Beast! I have to put up with more than that.'

'Do you? That sounds very interesting – tell me about it, Lotte.'

'Why should I tell you? You think it's all a joke.'

'No, I have every sympathy for you.'

'Sympathy is no use to me.'

'You have my friendship and you can rely on me for any support I can give you.'

'Are you being sincere?'

'The proof is in your hand.'

She chuckled at that.

'Swear to me that you are sincere, Gerhart.'

'I swear it to you by what I treasure most in this life,' he murmured.

'And what's that?'

'You are stroking it.'

'I believe you. So I'll let you into a secret – just between us. When Max gets me cornered on my own and I can't get away from him without screaming for help . . .'

'Yes?'

'And his hands are all over me and I'm afraid that he might make me give in to him . . .'

'Yes, his hand up your knickers – what do you do?'

'I feel down inside the front of his trousers and give him a quick thrill. He's very sensitive and it's all over in a few seconds,' she said in a matter-of-fact way.

'Like you're doing to me now?'

'No, nothing like it. I'm give you a slow and tender massage to make you feel better, because you've been ill and you're my friend. With Max I grab hold tight and flick it hard, and that's it. He goes red in the face and rushes off to wipe himself. I make sure he doesn't enjoy it.'

'I'm glad I'm not Max,' Gerhart sighed, remembering how he felt cheated when Lenchen handled him roughly.

That particular memory wiped out his excitement completely. To his shame he felt his tail wilting in Lotte's hand.

145

'Oh dear,' she said, 'you really are weak after your illness. I'd better go and let you sleep until you are better.'

'No, don't leave now. I feel so much better already.'

'If you say so. I'll just sit here quietly and hold your little tail. I have a lot to make up to you for the last time we met, and I want you to truly forgive me. I like you very much and I want you to feel the same about me – do you understand? There's nothing I wouldn't do to make you happy.'

'Darling Lotte!' Gerhart murmured, his head resting on her shoulder, 'it's so comforting to have you here and listen to your voice. Don't stop.'

'Where was I? Oh, yes – coping with Max. The first time he tried anything with me I was dumbfounded – I mean, everyone thinks he is such a correct and restrained person. But one afternoon when Kathe had taken the children to the park I was sitting with him while he explained how the legal business was going on – and before I knew what he was up to he'd got me on the sofa with my frock up round my waist and his hand between my legs! I didn't know what to do – in another two seconds he'd have my knickers down and if I screamed the maid would come running in and Kathe would know everything.'

'What on earth did you do?'

'I had no choice. While he was kissing me and fumbling about in my knickers I ripped his trousers open and grabbed his tail and rubbed it so fast that he gasped out *No!* and soaked his shirt-front straight away. And that was that. It was pure self-defence – I didn't want to touch him.'

'But you do want to touch me?' he said. 'Even if it doesn't have the same effect on me.'

'Of course I want to touch you – and it is having some effect, isn't it?'

'Yes,' he said happily, 'it's not a weak little tail anymore, it's a big strong one!'

'After that first time with Max I thought about things and it seemed to me that if it was that easy to stop him in his tracks – why not? And that's where we stand now – whenever he gets over-anxious and starts to paw me, I see him off with

146

a few sharp flicks. Do you think I'm doing the right thing, Gerhart?'

'He might not be satisfied with that forever . . . sooner or later he'll find a way to get you on your back. From what you say, it will be a very brief experience.'

'I don't care how brief it is – I'm not going to let him do it to me. I'm too fond of Kathe to risk breaking up her marriage by playing games with her husband.'

'It's not a game for him, is it?' said Gerhart, his body aglow with pleasure as Lotte stroked his quivering spike. 'He sounds demented to me – and that can be dangerous . . . a friend of mine got into a state like that once over a girl . . . oh!'

'What did he do?' she asked softly.

'Oh, Lotte, Lotte!'

'You can tell me later,' she said, her nails pinching his stem sharply to slow down his rush towards release, 'something nice is going to happen to you first. But I won't let you get there so fast that you don't even know what's going on. Not like silly Max who's lost it before he knows he's got it.'

With her free hand she opened his pyjama jacket and pulled the cord of his trousers loose so that she could bare him from neck to groin. His head rolled on her shoulder and he stared wildly at his distended stem in her hand.

'Your big moment is arriving, Gerhart,' she whispered, 'are you ready for it?'

'Lotte, Lotte!' he moaned.

'Yes, you're going to do it for Lotte.'

In the last few moments of her hand moving up and down in its steady rhythm the sensations of pleasure became so acute that they were almost painful. Delirium seized Gerhart and he cried out loudly as he fountained his torrent up into the air, his body shuddering violently. When he collapsed against Lotte she put an arm round his shoulders and held him close until he recovered.

'That was spectacular,' she said, admiration in her voice.

Gerhart drew a deep breath and stayed close to her.

'I shall return the compliment in a minute or two,' he promised.

147

'You're not obliged to do anything of the sort. I came here to repay my debt to you.'

'The debt is repaid, with interest. Come into the bedroom with me.'

'Give yourself time to get your breath back,' she answered, 'Tell me about your friend.'

'What friend?'

The one that got into a bad state over a girl – like Max with me.'

'Adalbert, you mean. He met a girl and he fell in love with her. But after a month or two she didn't want him any more. She told him, and he became obsessed and started to act like a lunatic.'

'What did he do?'

'He kept calling her on the telephone – a dozen times a day. And when she wouldn't speak to him he wrote her two or three letters every day. He followed her about and sat staring at her in cafés and restaurants. It was all very stupid, but he wouldn't listen to anyone. More than once he started fights with men she was dancing with and got himself thrown out. He was even arrested once for causing trouble – I think that was at the Excelsior. None of it did any good.'

'The poor man!' said Lotte.

'He followed her home one night – I don't know where from – and the man she had been out with went up to her apartment with her. That finally drove Adalbert over the edge, standing in the street and seeing the light go off in her window and torturing himself with the thought that she was in bed with another man. He tried to break into the house and get up to her floor. God knows what he would have done – killed her perhaps. Anyway, the people on the ground floor were woken up by the banging and shouting and they called the police. Adalbert saw them coming and ran away, and the police chased him through the streets. They almost had him, but he jumped into the Spree to drown himself.'

'Did he die?'

'No, they fished him out in time. After that his family sent him to a clinic in Switzerland to get his scrambled brain cured.'

148

'And were they able to cure him?'

'I don't know. They let him out after about a year, and he married one of the women patients he'd met. His family won't let him come back to Berlin, which is probably just as well. He lives in Zurich and he and his wife can be as crazy together as they like.'

'That's terrible! I wouldn't want to see Max locked up in a Swiss clinic. He's not that bad! I don't think he's off his head – he's just a bit too keen on me.'

'And why not? You're very beautiful,' said Gerhart.

He sat up and pulled Lotte across his lap, so that she lay full-length on the sofa.

'Am I?' she whispered.

He tugged her white blouse out of her skirt-band to uncover her breasts and fondle them.

'Very beautiful. You'd be too much for Maximilian.'

'I know. He'd be worse than Harald in bed, and he wasn't much good.'

'Your husband?'

She nodded and smiled as he played with her breasts delicately.

'You are a special person, Lotte. Poor Max would fire his little shot and sag before you even got going. If you want my opinion, you won't find many men who can keep up with you – to judge by the other evening, that is.'

'You think I don't know that? I'll tell you something – I've only ever met one until now. You're the second.'

'I'm flattered. Who was the first?'

'No one worth mentioning.'

'That sounds interesting – what was he like?'

'He was uneducated, boring and poor. The only thing he was any good at was making love. But he was looking for a rich woman to keep him.'

Gerhart put his hand on her knee and slid it under her linen skirt, along her bare thigh above her garter and into her loose silk knickers. Her legs moved apart when his fingers touched her curls.

'Was that here or in the country?'

'In the country, on Harald's estate.'

'And he was good at making love to you?'

'He was rough and clumsy at first. What he had was a truly amazing stamina.'

The fleshy lips between her thighs parted under Gerhart's fingers.

'Naturally, you taught him to be more expert,' he said. 'You showed him how to put his stamina to the best use?'

'Dear Gerhart, you understand me so well!'

'No, but I'm beginning to understand you a little.'

'Ah!' she gasped when his fingers probed her wet and smooth interior, 'I'm starting already, Gerhart! Don't spoil it!'

'My dear, after you did me the honour of pleasuring me so thoroughly a few minutes ago, courtesy requires that I repay the compliment in full. Trust yourself to me.'

He played carefully with her little secret bud, making her tremble and cry out in her long ecstasy.

'There is no need for restraint here,' he said, 'scream as loud as you like – no one will interrupt us. I'm going to see how long I can make your pleasure last.'

'Forever!' she moaned, her body shaking across his lap.

Forever was, of course, a gross exaggeration, but while Gerhart's stroking fingers kept her in continuous convulsions of delight he glanced occasionally away from her face to his gold wrist-watch. He was fascinated by the way in which her beautiful face was contorted with passion, lips drawn back to show her teeth, and her eyes staring wildly. Her shrill cries went on without a pause for nearly six minutes, the longest paroxysm Gerhart had ever witnessed or heard of.

It ended in the way that, as before, disappointed him. Instead of a final cataclysmic outburst, she ran down slowly like a clock, her shuddering throes diminishing away to nothing. Eventually she lay silent, quivering faintly, her eyes closed and her face pale under her make-up. His watch said seven minutes.

'Wonderful,' he said, 'I've never known anyone like you, Lotte.'

'Really wonderful,' she answered, with a long sigh of

150

contentment, 'Most men are frightened when they see me do that the first time. But I don't frighten you, do I – you were enjoying watching and making me do it. I knew you were the right man for me the moment we met.'

'When I bruised your bottom at the wrestling-match? Has it faded now?'

'It's very nearly gone. First it was purple, and then it turned green, and then it faded to yellow, and now you can hardly see where it was. But suppose Max had seen it – think of the row he would have made!'

'Why should you show your bottom to him?'

'I don't! But I was in my room reading a magazine and eating an apple and he crept in without my realising that he was there. I was on the bed face-down, and all I had on was my underwear and stockings. And then suddenly there was a hand between my legs and I knew it was him!'

'That must have been before I marked your bottom.'

'No, it was after. It was the day before yesterday. But he couldn't see the bruise while I had my knickers on.'

'How did you stop him from pulling them down and discovering it?'

'It was dreadful! I rolled over to get away from his hand – and what a sight! He'd opened his trousers wide before he sneaked up to the bed, and his thing was sticking out. I hardly knew what I was doing – I grabbed it and pulled him down beside me.'

'He must have thought it was his lucky day! Was it?'

'No it was not, you beast! He tried to get hold of my bundles and by then I'd handled him so roughly that it was all over and he'd done it on the front of my knickers. After that he left me alone.'

'He's going to cause a lot of trouble, that man,' said Gerhart, 'the sooner you can get away from there the better.'

'Another month or so should see everything settled, and I'll be independent.'

'My poor Lotte! I wish I could do something to help you.

'Would you let me move in here with you – only till I get a place of my own, of course.'

The suggestion was far from welcome to Gerhart.

'When you're ready to move out of your sister's apartment I'll talk to Sieglinde about it,' he said cautiously, 'this is as much her apartment as mine.'

'Thank you,' she said effusively, taking the result for granted, 'there's something else you can do to help me, if you really want to.'

'All you have to do is name it.'

'Do I? I thought you knew already,' and she touched his bare chest.

'Of course! Let me show you my bedroom.'

In spite of what had passed between them, Gerhart had so far had little opportunity of familiarising himself with Lotte in any detail. The first time they were together had been in Glotz's apartment, and she had taken off her clothes in an unlit room, so that she was no more than a pale shape in the dark. In his own sitting-room she had been fully clothed throughout. It was therefore with a keen sense of anticipation that Gerhart took her to his room and stripped her naked.

His fingers traced the outline of her face, long rather than broad, with prominent cheek-bones under smooth skin and face-powder. Her nose was long and straight, her chin small and round, but when he felt under her mass of jet-black hair he found that the corners of her jaw were angular and strong. She had a long neck, set on shoulders that were squarer than was to be expected in a woman. Gerhart kissed her mouth and face, her eyes and chin, his hands moving slowly on her breasts.

'Can we do it my way?' she whispered.

'Why not? I'm sure we shall both enjoy it.'

He took off his pyjamas and lay on his back on the bed. Lotte straddled his hips on her knees and lowered herself down on to his stiff tail. A faint memory stirred in Gerhart's mind, a memory of some other woman who had done the same to him, but he couldn't recall who she was or when. Perhaps it had been Erna during the hours he had been with her, most of which was still a blank to him. But he wasn't sure it was Erna, and there was a white frock in the memory that was hard to account for.

The moment of half-memory passed and was lost as Lotte swayed very slowly back and forth on him.

'We have to find a way of compromise,' she said, her face pink with emotion, 'If I let myself go, it will be all over for you very quickly. And then you'll go soft and that will spoil it for me.'

'I can use my fingers to take you all the way.'

'Not this time . . . I want us to really make love to each other.'

Gerhart lay still, smiling with pleasure at her slow rocking, and he stared at her body fully for the first time. Her breasts were exceptionally pretty, he thought, set wide apart, perfectly round, with pink-brown tips that tilted slightly upwards. And yet, pretty as they were, in relation to the size of her body he considered them to be somewhat too small. Not that this artistic consideration of proportion detracted from the pleasure of reaching up to fondle them.

Lotte's cheeks were bright red and she was breathing heavily, struggling to prevent herself from plunging headlong into her extended climactic passion. Her belly was shuddering with sensation and it was, Gerhart thought, as nice a belly as he had ever seen, being broad and delicately rounded, with a button round and shallow as a dimple. He took his hands from her breasts and stroked her thighs. For the purposes of love-making they were extremely well-formed – a dream of warm and pliant flesh and satin skin. Yet even while he fondled them, Gerhart's artistic eye insisted that they were just a little too plump to conform to the elegance of her breasts and the length of her legs.

For all her good intentions, Lotte was unable to hold herself back any longer. A piercing wail announced to Gerhart that her ecstatic throes had begun. It was as if a velvet-gloved hand was massaging his upright part and he stared in fascination at the soft flesh and black curls between her thighs, where he was so well embedded. Lotte's curls grew in an unusual pattern – on most women he had known they formed a triangle, starting in a fairly straight line across the belly and tapering down between the thighs to a concealed point. But not Lotte's – hers grew in

153

an oval that framed the fleshy slot into which he was plunged. At first he thought that perhaps she shaved herself to produce this striking conformation, but when his fingers explored the skin, he found it soft and smooth everywhere. Her sable muff was natural, he concluded, and gasped aloud as the squeeze of her internal muscles carried him towards the inevitable conclusion.

Lotte's rhythmic cries set the pace for what was happening to him. Without being aware of it, at the start of each cry his loins thrust upwards off the bed to pierce her to the limit. Then as the cry trailed away, he sank slowly down again, to thrust up at the next outcry – and so it continued, a slow-motion love-making that maintained Lotte's ecstasy unbroken and kept Gerhart trembling for what seemed an impossibly long time on the knife-edge of release. His mind had long ceased to function, and he was aware of nothing, not even Lotte, only the tremendous sensations that shook him like a leaf.

His passion culminated in an explosion of sensation that short-circuited Gerhart's nervous system at the moment he discharged. He fainted.

When he became aware of his surroundings again, Lotte was lying beside him and rubbing his cheeks to bring him round.

'It's all right,' she said when she saw his eyes open slowly, 'I'm here.'

'What happened?' he asked tremulously.

'Oh, Gerhart – it was incredible! You took me to the absolute limit of love-making – you were wonderful! But the effort was too much, so soon after your illness. How do you feel now?'

'Exhausted . . . nothing like that has ever happened to me before.'

'You need a few days to get your strength back,' she said, stroking his face.

'Yes, being unwell has weakened me . . . I hope I didn't spoil it for you.'

'Spoil it? It was marvellous! We were really together all the time!'

'Good,' he sighed, 'but I'm so tired, Lotte.'

'Yes, you must rest,' and she cradled him in her arms.

As he drifted off to sleep he thought he heard her whisper *I love you, Gerhart,* but when he woke up it was evening and she was gone.

Chapter 14

The artist at work

Lotte telephoned the morning after her visit and talked to Gerhart for a long time, in terms of warm affection. It was not until she suggested that she should come round to see him after lunch that Gerhart understood that her sudden attachment to him might prove inconvenient. He told her that he was so far behind on his commission for the book illustrations that he must make an effort to catch up, even if it meant slaving at his drawing-board without a break for the next few days. Lotte was disappointed – so much was apparent in her voice – but she said bravely that she understood. She promised to telephone again the next day.

Gerhart went back to the breakfast-table, where Sieglinde in her rose-pink dressing-gown was spreading cherry-jam on a buttered roll.

'Your coffee has gone cold,' she said. 'Who was that?'

'Lotte – the girl I told you about. The one I met with Heinrich.'

'The one you took out to the theatre?'

'That's her.'

'The one who was here yesterday, while I was out?'

'How did you know that?'

'Silly question!' she said with a smile, 'I got back about six and found your slippers abandoned in the sitting-room and the sofa cushions crumpled up as if someone had been lying on them. So I peeped into your room and you were fast asleep and stark naked. Your bed looked as if a herd of elephants had stampeded over it. So I drew the obvious conclusion – that you'd had a visitor and that it was a girl. I didn't know what to make of the fresh roses in the vase, but when someone calling herself Frau Furer-Diest had already been on the phone that morning before you woke up, she seemed to be the best candidate.'

'What a detective you are! She turned up unexpected after lunch. I wasn't all that pleased to see her, but one thing led to another – you know how it is.'

'I know how it is with *you* – you can't resist anything in skirts. I hope you didn't over-tire yourself. You looked so awful the day before. Is she coming here again?'

'No, no! I've put her off for the rest of the week, I hope. I must get on with the pictures for Rudolf's book. This is the first big chance I've had to show what I can do. From now on, if anyone phones for me, say I'm working and can't be disturbed. Or say I'm ill – or out and you don't know when I'll be back. Say anything that will keep people away, especially Lotte.'

'That means you'll be in all day?'

'And tomorrow. After that, we'll see.'

Gerhart's resolution was fixed and firm. But when he was in his little studio-room and sketching rough outlines of the pictures he had in mind for *Venus in Furs*, he found it increasingly difficult to concentrate on them. He persisted, but after a time he discovered that he was drawing something completely different. He threw his pencil down and sat back with folded arms to stare at his drawing-board.

'*Flowers!*' he said aloud, in his surprise. 'Why am I drawing flowers?'

In fact, they were very strange flowers that he had sketched, and far from realistic. There was one that looked something like a chrysanthemum, and another like a half-open rose. And one other that was unrecognisable. Deep down in Gerhart's memory some image was struggling to free itself and rise to the surface, something that would make sense of his drawings. Or so he thought. Without knowing why, he felt it would help things along if he took his water-colours and painted the flowers again, larger and bolder. He chose a sunny golden-brown for the petals of the chrysanthemum, and a rich blue-black for the unidentified flower. The opening rose needed a most delicate

157

shade of blush pink and was not easy to achieve.

The whole morning slipped away as he painted the three flowers again and again, making changes that suggested themselves to him. He was convinced that there was a correct version of what he was trying to achieve and that it was somewhere in his mind. The problem was to bring it out and capture it on paper. In the course of successive transformations the flowers looked less and less like the simple blossoms he had started with. At the same time they became more exciting to look at, almost as if they contained a hidden meaning. The excitement was more than merely artistic or intellectual – Gerhart became aware that his tail was stiff and uncomfortable in his trousers. And at last he recognised what he was painting.

'That's Erna's chrysanthemum!' he exclaimed, astonished by his own work, 'And that's Lotte and that's Sieglinde! Where in the world did I get an idea like that from?'

He finished his final versions easily after that, and pinned them to the studio wall. He was standing admiring his work when Sieglinde tapped at the door and announced that lunch was ready. He decided not to call her in to see his pictures just then – he needed more time to think about what he had produced. The pictures were very private, after all, and he was not sure what Sieglinde's response would be if she saw her hidden flower alongside two others.

After lunch he went back to work, and was able to make a proper start on the book pictures. Now that he had read *Venus in Furs* he knew that it was not very forthcoming in the scenes of maximum interest and he must therefore use his imagination to interpret the spirit of the novel in whatever way appealed to him most. He sketched away happily, accumulating a stack of sketches of possible pictures.

About three o'clock Sieglinde interrupted him again.

'There's someone here to see you, Gerhart. I told her you were working and she says that's what she's come about. Her name is Klemt – what do you want me to do?'

'That's all right – she works for Rudolf Knuppel. Bring her in.'

Erna's summer frock of red and yellow stripes accentuated

the fact that she looked pale and not in robust health. She shook hands with Gerhart in a most businesslike manner and took a seat in the little studio.

'Rudolf asked me to drop in and see how you're getting on with the illustrations,' she said brightly, pulling off her white gloves.

'Yes?' said Gerhart doubtfully, 'I'm in the very early stages. There's nothing to see yet.'

Sieglinde brought in coffee and told Gerhart she was going out to meet Heinrich for five o'clock tea at the Adlon. She might not be back for dinner, she added pointedly.

The moment that she had gone, Erna smiled her lop-sided grin.

'Rudolf didn't send me to see you. I came to make sure you are all right after your little adventure with me. No ill effects, I hope?'

'I was half-dead for two days,' Gerhart complained, 'and you look as if you're still suffering from it. What you did was crazy!'

'But it was fantastic at the time,' she answered.

She leaned back in her chair and crossed her legs. They were well-shaped legs, Gerhart was compelled to admit to himself.

'You look pale,' he said, his voice more friendly.

Erna brushed her hair back from her face with a hand that shook slightly.

'Admit that it was fantastic!' she said.

'I don't know if it was. I can't remember what happened.'

'Yes, you can,' and she pointed to the flower pictures on the wall.

Gerhart realised with a start that Sieglinde had seen his pictures when she brought in the coffee. But she had said nothing, so perhaps she hadn't understood what they were.

'That's me,' said Erna, 'you saw a chrysanthemum when you were staring between my legs – you said so.'

At once the recollection of that moment was vivid in Gerhart's mind.

'So that's where the idea came from!'

'Where else? A little of that stuff in your wine and you understand things which no one else can. It illuminates you and you experience things which change you.'

'It's a dangerous way of inspiring three water-colours,' said Gerhart.

'It will inspire more than that. It was your first time, and your brain was overloaded with visions. So your memory switched off. But everything will come back slowly, and you'll be astonished by what you remember.'

'Most of what I eventually remember will turn out to be making love to you in unusual ways.'

'That too,' she said, grinning at him, 'but there'll be much more than that. The proof is there on your wall – the flowers. I shall look to see what else is on the wall the next time I'm here. I'm certain that some of what you remember and paint will amaze even me.'

She stood up, and Gerhart thought she was about to take her leave so that he could get on with his work. But that was not her intention at all. She casually unbuttoned her striped frock from neck to waist, unbuckled her narrow white belt and put both hands into her open bodice to pull out her breasts.

'It's time I earned my fee,' she said.

'What fee?'

'Don't tell me you've forgotten! I'm the model for Wanda in the book.'

Her breasts were cupped in her hands and she was squeezing them.

'But I haven't reached the point where I need a model. I'm still trying to make my mind up what each picture will show.'

Erna was running her thumbs over the red-brown tips of her breasts. She yawned.

'I slept nearly all day yesterday and I'm still tired,' she said. 'Why do you say you're not ready for a model yet? I don't know much about painting but surely you look at the model's body and that inspires you to invent ways of showing it in your pictures.'

'Perhaps some work like that,' said Gerhart, unable to look away from her exposed breasts and her slowly moving thumbs.

'But you don't?'

Gerhart shook his head.

'Then it's time you did!'

160

She stripped off her frock and sat down to take off her white shoes and roll down her silk stockings.

'You go out in the street like that?' Gerhart asked in surprise, 'With nothing on at all under your frock? Don't people stare at you?'

'Men stare at me,' she said, with some pride.

'I'm sure they do! Do you always do this?'

'When I'm in the mood to be stared at. The men who pass me can see my bundles swinging under the frock. Then they look down and see how the silk clings against my thighs and round my bottom. They want to grab me and do things to me – and I laugh at the look of frustration on their faces.'

'Don't they try to talk to you and get to know you?'

'Sometimes I get on a tram that's crowded when I'm in the right mood,' said Erna, trailing her fingers up and down her belly, 'men press themselves against me. I feel something hard squeezed against my bottom and the man in front of me pushes himself so close that my bundles are flattened and I can feel a hand touching me between my legs. When I get off the tram I can't stop myself bursting into laughter at the thought of all the hard tails I've left behind. Has your sister got a fur coat?'

'What?'

'Wanda wears a fur coat to excite Severin – surely you've read the book by now.'

'She has a fur jacket, but that wouldn't do at all.'

He had decided to make the best of the situation by drawing a few pencil-sketches of Erna which he could use later on as references. He certainly had no use for a model, but by giving Wanda a facial and bodily resemblance to Erna, he would keep her in a good humour and allow her to claim her fee from Rudolf.

'Sit there,' he said, 'cross your legs and lean back with your hands behind your head.'

He sketched away, pad in hand, moving from time to time to get a slightly different view and drawing again – not all of her, but the portions he would use for his paintings. He took care to record the shape and size of her breasts, seen from in front and from each side, the curve of her hips and the shape of her legs.

161

In ten minutes he had as many little sketches and after that he concentrated on getting her face right. That would be most important if Wanda was to look like Erna.

'You told me that Sieglinde was a rose,' Erna remarked nonchalantly.

'Did I?' he said, his mind on his work.

'You've painted mine like a chrysanthemum. And that rose-bud must be hers. Does that mean that she shaves it bare?'

Gerhart was not listening to what she was saying. He was intent on getting her pointed chin and narrow face right. And the curve of her drawn-in eyebrows.

'I'm sorry – what did you say?'

'Sieglinde's pink rose – does she let you look at it?'

'What!' he exclaimed, in sudden dread that his secret had been guessed.

Erna smiled knowingly and shook her body to make her breasts sway from side to side.

'There's no need to be alarmed,' she said, 'you're not the only one.'

'I don't know what you mean.'

'Your painting says that you do. Still, if you tell me that the rose is a work of imagination, I'll take your word for it that you've never played with it.'

This was said in a slightly mocking tone that indicated clearly that Erna knew what she knew. Gerhart was sweating slightly. He put down his sketch-pad and pencil and wiped his palms on his trousers.

'Let's have a change of position,' he said, meaning *let's have a change of subject*, 'stand up and put one hand on the chair-back and the other on your hip.'

'How boring,' said Erna, and she positioned herself with one knee on the chair to open her legs, a hand on the chair-back and the other hand flat across her belly so that her crimson-painted finger-nails just reached to her golden-brown curls.

'Who's the third flower?' she asked. 'The one that looks something like a black peony, if there is such a thing.'

'A friend,' said Gerhart shortly, getting the jutting curve of her bottom on his pad, 'no one you know.'

'Why are you so secretive? It doesn't matter to me who you make love to. If she asks about the chrysanthemum, tell her it's me. What's her name?'

'Lotte.'

'Does she really have hair that black between her legs?'

'It's about right, just as the golden-brown is about right for you.'

Erna glanced down at her curls and then up to the picture on the wall and back down again.

'Near enough,' she agreed, 'for someone who says he can't remember what happened to him, you've made it look very pretty. When was the last time you saw hers?'

'Oh, not long ago,' Gerhart answered with deliberate vagueness.

Erna changed her pose without waiting to be asked. She sat on the chair cross-legged and put her hands on her hips.

'You're being evasive again. What does *not long ago* mean? Last week, last night, last year?'

'If you must know, yesterday afternoon.'

Gerhart was sketching the long lines of her thighs. They were increasingly attractive to him.

'So! You were playing with the black peony yesterday! And there was I in bed feeling wretched and in need of someone to comfort me.'

'It was your idea to put that stuff in the wine. If you were ill, you have no one to blame but yourself.'

'To be honest with you, I wasn't alone all day,' said Erna, her hands moving up her body to cup her breasts, 'Rudolf turned up to see why I wasn't at the office. He worries when I'm ill.'

'I'm sure he comforted you.'

'He got into bed with me and did his best. But I wasn't up to it – I got a wave of sickness when he put his weight on me. All I could manage was to comfort him with my hand. It's a pity Wanda doesn't do that to Severin in the book when she's got him tied up. It would make an interesting picture. Maybe I could persuade Rudolf to come here with me and model for it.'

'You're a wicked girl!' said Gerhart, grinning at the thought.

'These art school poses you're working at are useless,' said

163

Erna suddenly, 'Rudolf will tear them up and throw them in the waste-paper basket. Shall I show you what Wanda's style is?'

'If you think you know.'

Erna put her feet on the floor, spread her legs widely apart to display her chrysanthemum fully, and put her index fingers to the tips of her breasts to tickle them.

'But she doesn't do that in the book,' Gerhart objected.

'A good illustrator goes far beyond the author's words. You have to invent scenes that will make readers gasp when they turn the page and see them. Like this one – that will cause a few gasps.'

'Not to mention a few stiff tails! But is it allowed to depart so far from the text?'

'Rudolf expects you to. If you offer him conventional little pictures of me naked and say that's his Wanda, he'll throw them in your face.'

Gerhart watched her fingers leave her stiff buds and travel slowly down her body to her parted thighs. She pulled open her brown-petalled flower to display its pink inside.

'Draw me like this,' she suggested.

'I can't!'

'Why not?'

'Because I can't concentrate while you're doing that to yourself.'

'But your pictures have to make the men who see them as excited as you are now,' she told him, grinning her lop-sided grin, 'how can you hope to achieve that if you can't draw from life?'

Gerhart put his pad and pencil down, knowing that the inevitable was going to happen and quite sure now that Erna had come to visit him for the purpose of provoking it.

'What sort of artist are you?' she teased him. 'Would you prefer to work from photographs? I've got dozens of photographs of me doing interesting things with men. Shall I bring them here for you to copy?'

When he made no reply, her expression turned hard.

'I can see that Rudolf made a mistake,' she said, 'you're not up to it.'

In two strides Gerhart was close enough to seize her shoulders and drag her off the chair. She fell with a bump on to the polished parquet floor and at once brought her knees up to defend herself. Gerhart threw himself on her and got his weight between her legs to pin her to the floor. He tugged at his trouser buttons while she bucked and squirmed under him and freed his stem just in time to use both hands to catch her wrists as she clawed at his face. Her violent movements made it difficult to penetrate her without the use of his hands, but he dare not release her wrists. It took some time, but eventually he found the entrance he was seeking and sank his stem into her.

She rolled from side to side in an effort to tip him off her body, but he was too heavy for her, and through her heaving and writhing he rode her hard, determined to have his way. Her head came up off the floor and she bit at his nose and chin and, when that failed, screamed piercingly. Gerhart thrust sharply, nearing his goal, panting with the effort of taming this demented girl. She stopped screaming and spat in his face – at the very moment when he reached his climactic victory and spat into her belly. At that she screamed again, but in a very different one, and the heaving of her naked body beneath him became the convulsions of ecstasy.

'You bitch!' Gerhart panted, when he could speak again.

There was a look of content on her narrow face as she stared up at him.

'So I'm a bitch,' she said, 'but it's a lot more exciting to rape a bitch than to play about with a little girl's rose-bud.'

'I don't want to talk about that.'

'Not now, because it embarrasses you. But one day you'll tell me all about it. And I'll tell you about when I was a girl and played games with my brothers.'

'Bitch,' Gerhart repeated, but this time he said it with a kind of affection.

Chapter 15

Some pictures are more interesting than others

Gerhart had not seen Heinz since the occasion of their visit to the female mud-wrestlers, and so when Heinz invited him to lunch he cheerfully abandoned his illustrations and went to meet him at the Café Kranzler. They sat on the terrace to drink an aperitif, Heinz wearing a new brown suit with a pink carnation in his button-hole, and looking very pleased with himself. The reason, he explained, was that he had a new girl-friend.

'Please! I don't even want to hear about her,' said Gerhart at once.

'Why not?'

'The last time I listened to you I let you talk me into going to meet those two dreadful women.'

'What's wrong with Gretchen and Lenchen?' Heinz demanded, puzzled by Gerhart's lack of interest, 'I've had some wonderful times with them.'

'Good for you,' Gerhart said with no enthusiasm.

'The last time I was there they both sat on me. Can you imagine the combined weight of those huge bodies crushing you into the mattress? I nearly died of sheer joy.'

'Of suffocation, more likely.'

'I don't understand you at all. It was a unique and cosmic experience.'

'They've both got behinds like beer-barrels – I don't see how there would be room on you for both of them at the same time.'

'Lenchen sat on my face,' Heinz explained, his voice hushed in reverence at the memory, 'and Gretchen was across my belly with my clapper wedged in her. They were so close that they could rub their bouncers together.'

166

'If your head was under Lenchen's bottom you couldn't possibly see any such thing. You're making it up.'

'No, I'm not! I couldn't see it but they told me about it afterwards. My God, I love those two women!'

'Then why have you left them for someone else?'

'I haven't left them. They've gone on tour for three months. I can't go chasing all round the country after them, so I'm filling in the time till they get back in the autumn.'

'So what monstrous female have you found this time?'

Heinz smiled happily.

'She's not monstrous,' he said proudly, 'she's beautiful.'

'Yes?' said Gerhart in total disbelief.

'What you don't seem to realise is that Lenchen and Gretchen are very nice persons. All you see is their size and weight, but if you got to know them as well as I have, you'd find that there's a lot more to them than their appearance, exciting as it is. They're not freaks, they're women – big, strong women with kind hearts.'

Gerhart shrugged.

'Tell me about your new conquest. Where did you find her?'

'You said you didn't want to hear about her.'

'After the mud-wrestlers, anyone must be an improvement.'

'I'll prove to you that Gretchen and Lenchen are warm-hearted – they introduced me to Mina before they went on tour, so that I wouldn't be lonely while they're away. That's real friendship.'

'Another wrestler?'

'No, a friend of theirs from when they worked in a circus, before they took up professional wrestling.'

'She works in a circus?'

'No, she left it when she got married. But she's still a friend of the girls.'

Girls seemed a very inappropriate word for the wrestling pair and it made Gerhart laugh.

'I'm almost afraid to ask, but what did this one do in the circus – train elephants?'

'She's tattooed all over. People used to pay to look at her.'

Heinz' round face beamed with pride as he revealed this astonishing item of information about his girl-friend.

'But surely that must make her very ugly,' said Gerhart, in wonder.

'You wouldn't say that if you'd seen her. You'd want to paint a portrait of her.'

'I doubt it. What did you say her name was – Mina?'

'Mina Bucholz. She's twenty-eight and beautiful.'

'And married, you said. Isn't that risky? Husbands who marry circus people can be violent if they find someone else helping himself to what they regard as theirs.'

'Her husband went off with another woman last year. You must come and see her for yourself.'

'I don't think so.'

'But I mean it,' said Heinz, a most serious expression on his face, 'Mina is a sight not to be missed. I want you to paint her.'

'Is she really tattooed all over?'

'Everywhere, except for her face. When she takes her clothes off it's a sight to make your eyes bulge! One look at her and my tail stands up like a ram-rod.'

'Heinz – the oddest things excite you!' said Gerhart, chuckling. 'You are unique.'

'No, I'm not. People pretend that all they're interested in is a pretty young girl with her clothes off because they think that's normal. But when you get to know them better, you discover all sorts of things get them going, though they never admit it. I bet you've been with some unlikely women and done some unlikely things with them.'

'Not me. I'm so normal that I'm boring,' said Gerhart quickly.

'There's no such thing as normal. You just don't want to tell me.'

'Well . . .'

'I thought so! Out with it – what's your dark secret?'

'There's a girl I know who likes to pretend that she's being raped. She puts up a tremendous fight, right up to the last minute.'

'A real fight? Or just wriggling about?'

168

'She uses her nails and knees on you. If you don't get on top of her fast she'd do you real damage.'

'She wouldn't suit me,' said Heinz, 'I'm lazy by nature and I like the women to do the hard work. But you've proved my point about normality.'

'Nonsense! One example doesn't prove anything much except that this girl enjoys fantasies about being raped.'

'And from the sound of it, you enjoy fantasies of raping her. Listen – maybe middle-aged men lie on top of their fat wives and chuff away, but I'm not even sure about that any more. Mina's husband was well over forty when they married and she told me that he used to make her get down on her hands and knees, so that he could use her back door.'

'Why did she marry him if she knew that?'

'To get out of the circus, of course. He owns a butcher's shop and makes more money than she'd ever seen.'

'Does he still keep her, now that he's got another woman down on her hands and knees?'

'He pays the rent and lets her have free meat from his shop. Only when she goes there, he tries to drag her into the back room. She's very grateful to have me around.'

'You're paying her, just like your wrestlers?'

'I don't think of it as paying her,' said Heinz. 'She makes me happy and as she's poor and I'm not, it's the most natural thing in the world to help her out financially.'

'Are you the only one who is helping her out?' Gerhart asked, grinning.

'What does it matter? Are the girls you make love to faithful to you?'

'I'm sure they're not. But I don't pay them to be my girl-friends.'

'You spend money on them. You take them to theatres and restaurants and night-clubs. It comes to the same thing. Who's your girl at the moment?'

'Lotte Furer-Diest,' Gerhart answered at once, to end this line of enquiry.

'The last time we met you said she wasn't any good in bed.'

'I said no such thing.'

169

'You weren't very keen on her. And you don't sound very keen now. That's the difference between you and me – I'm a simple and emotional person. I jump into things with enormous enthusiasm. They never last long, but while they do I have a wonderful time. With you it's all caution and second thoughts.'

Gerhart laughed and agreed.

'Well then,' said Heinz, 'who's enjoying himself most – you or me?'

'That's a different question altogether. Maybe neither of us is really enjoying himself, or maybe we're both enjoying ourselves in our own curious ways.'

'That's too complicated for me. Let's order another drink before lunch. When would you like to meet Mina?'

'The thought of a tattooed lady from a circus doesn't appeal to me at all. Is she really tattooed all over?'

'Everywhere. She has pictures from her ankles right the way up to her neck.'

'But not *everywhere*?'

'Especially there. I didn't believe it when the girls told me about her, but the first time I saw her undressed I thought I was losing my mind. Pictures everywhere – up her legs, between her thighs, over her belly, round her balloons and across her back. I felt her all over to make sure it was real, and that made me so excited that I jumped on her and banged away like a madman.'

'Through the front door, of course,' said Gerhart, smiling.

'To be frank,' said Heinz, lowering his voice to a whisper across the table, 'now that she knows me well enough, she lets me use both doors. It's a strange experience – have you tried it?'

'No, I told you that I'm boring. What sort of pictures does she have?'

'Oh, flowers, dragons – things like that.'

After lunch Gerhart firmly refused Heinz' well-meant offer to introduce him to Mina Bucholz. He strolled along the Kurfurstendam for a while, looking in shop-windows, and then took a taxi home, intending to work for the rest of the day to make up for lost time. He found it difficult to concentrate on *Venus in Furs*. Even though he thought Heinz' enthusiasm for his tattooed friend was ridiculous, he couldn't get out of his mind the idea of a woman's body covered in pictures of flowers and dragons. He drew a few pencil sketches of what such a woman might look like, they were not at all convincing.

It was with relief that he heard the apartment door open and Sieglinde's footsteps in the hall. He rushed out of his studio, threw his arms round her and hugged her tight.

'You can't have missed me that much,' she said, 'I've only been gone an hour or two.'

'I want to paint you.'

'For your book illustrations? Not me. You've got a model already.'

'I don't mean paint a picture of you,' he said, guiding her into his studio, 'I mean paint *you*. All over your body.'

'That's the craziest thing I've ever heard!'

'I know, but you'll like the result, I promise. Take your clothes off.'

'But will the paint come off afterwards?'

'It's only water-colour. I'll scrub you in the bath.'

She laughed and patted his face.

'I love it when you get one of your mad ideas,' she said, 'get your paints ready while I go and undress. I don't want anything to happen to this frock.'

Gerhart had not even noticed that she was wearing her newest and most elegant purchase – a summer frock of pale blue, the colour of her eyes – and a little matching jacket.

'You've been to lunch somewhere special,' he said.

'With Heinrich. He drove me home. I won't be a minute.'

In her absence Gerhart's thoughts ran uneasily on the friendship which had sprung up between Sieglinde and Heinrich Preuss. Yesterday it was tea with him, today lunch, tomorrow dinner perhaps. But on the other hand it was not much after three o'clock and there hadn't been much time, if any at all, for love-making with him after lunch. Did that mean that they were not such close friends after all? Or did it mean that they were such close friends that they were happy to meet and talk and nothing more?

That Sieglinde went to bed with men she went out with was no secret and did not worry Gerhart particularly. He would have been very surprised if she didn't. It didn't mean anything. But a really close friendship with a particular man instead of casual friendships with half a dozen – that would be a disturbing prospect. Friendships like that could lead to all sorts of things which were undesirable from Gerhart's point of view – love, for instance. Marriage perhaps.

His concern vanished when she returned, naked and smiling. She stood just inside the studio door, her arms by her sides, and Gerhart looked at her with warm admiration.

'You are so beautiful that there is no way to improve you,' he said thoughtfully. 'It was a silly idea to think of daubing paint on you.'

'It was not! I've taken to the idea. I want you to do it.'

'Are you sure?'

'Yes, no one has ever painted me before, and I don't suppose anyone will again. I want to know what it's like.'

Gerhart spread sheets of newspaper on the wooden floor for her to stand on.

'The paint might get splashed about,' he explained.

'Then you'd better take your clothes off and save me a trip to the dry cleaner tomorrow.'

He stripped to his striped underpants, took up a brush and stood uncertainly in front of Sieglinde, who was waiting impatiently for him to begin. Now that the moment had come, he had very little idea of what he wanted to achieve. What did a dragon look like? he wondered. Should it have a long tail wrapped round her waist, with its head between her breasts? His glance fell on the three flower pictures pinned to the wall, and they set his imagination running. He loaded his soft-haired brush with scarlet and began to turn her small, round right breast into a many-petalled rose, covering it completely. Sieglinde looked down to follow his progress and smiled encouragingly.

'Does the brush tickle?' he asked.

'It feels nice. Are you sure this will wash off.'

172

'It always washes off my hands.'

He took a step backwards to see the effect, liked it and made a start on her other breast.

'Lotte brought you roses when you were ill,' she remarked casually.

'Yes, perhaps that was all she could get. When you and I are very rich I shall order a thousand red roses and make the florist pull off all the petals and cover a bed with them, so you can lie naked on it. And I shall paint a picture of you that will stun the art-world when I exhibit it.'

'Oh, Gerhart – what a fantastic idea!'

'I shall be offered millions of Marks for it and millionaires will trip over each other in the rush to ask you to marry them. But I shall refuse to sell the picture, whatever is offered. It will hang in my bedroom for the rest of my life.'

'And I shall refuse to marry any of the millionaires, no matter how handsome they are. Not even if they are Grand Dukes or Princes.'

'Are you sure? Some of them will be as handsome as film-stars and far more intelligent.'

'Even so.'

He stepped back again to look at his handiwork with a critical eye. He had turned Sieglinde's breasts into two full-blossoming roses, though they were not as vivid as he intended, for her skin shining through the colour muted it. But the result was magnificent, he thought.

He changed brushes and colour, choosing a more delicate shade of red, and dropped to his knees in front of her.

'Stand with your legs just a little apart.'

'Like this?'

The blonde hair between Sieglinde's legs was so fine that the skin was hardly hidden at all. From a distance of two metres it was almost invisible, so that she presented the appearance of a naked young girl to the fortunate viewer. But with his face close to her thighs, Gerhart could distinguish each separate and soft curly hair on her fleshy little mound. He dabbed water-colour on it with care, right up to the pink lips.

'What are you painting on me down there?' she asked, craning her neck to see.

'A rose-bud, half-open and beautiful.'

'Like the picture on the wall behind you?' she asked.

'Something like it,' he admitted.

'I thought it must be me when I saw it. The brown one must be your model. Who's the other one – the mysterious Lotte who telephones you and visits you when I'm out?'

'Do you like them?' he asked softly.

'The one of me is wonderful. I'm not in a position to know whether the others are true likenesses or not.'

Gerhart became so absorbed in creating yet again the rose-bud of his flower picture that he forgot what it was that he was painting on and was startled when his living paper moved and almost spoiled everything. Sieglinde had moved her bare feet further apart, opening her legs wider.

'Gerhart,' she murmured.

'What is it?'

By way of answer she bent her legs and sank down until her knees touched the newspaper, outside his own knees.

'But I can't finish the painting like that,' he said.

She leaned forward to put her arms round his neck and press her mouth to his, making him understand her need. He dropped his brush and ran his hand along the inside of her thigh until his fingers touched wet paint on half-open lips. Sieglinde's mouth clung to his while he found her little bud and stroked it, and soon she was gasping into his open mouth and her tongue was licking at his tongue. Her arms about his neck held him so tightly that it was if she was taking possession of him.

To touch Sieglinde like this was the most exciting experience that Gerhart knew, and it had always been so, ever since the first time, years before, when they were growing up together. That was when they were still living with the General and Sieglinde was sixteen. Gerhart had gone to her room early one morning to wake her and, without knowing how it came about, he found himself sitting on her bed with his hands down her nightdress to feel her breasts. His trembling touch had

174

woken her quickly and there was a startled look in her pale blue eyes when they opened. He expected her to push him away angrily and he would be in terrible trouble with the General when she told him. But when she saw who was touching her, she only smiled and said *Gerhart*. He played with her little breasts until foot-steps outside the door frightened them both and he jumped up and left her.

Later in the day, when the General was out and the servants were nowhere to be seen, she came to his room, to interrupt his studies, and she kissed him and told him that he could play with her whenever he liked. What followed had been the most entrancing experience of Gerhart's life until then. And, though he did not realise it then or later, one of the most formative experiences. They sat squeezed together in an arm-chair, for they were frightened to lie on the bed together in case the maid came in and found them. She undid her blouse for him and he felt down the top of her slip to stroke her breasts with shaking hands, his tail so hot and hard in his trousers that he thought that he was going to squirt at any second. That moment came later, when Sieglinde put her hand down the front of his trousers and stroked his tail through his shirt.

In the years since then the bond between them had grown stronger and more permanent. Kneeling together on the studio floor, Sieglinde was shuddering and whimpering into his mouth, and Gerhart was beside himself with joy. For an instant her body went rigid, she sucked the breath from his mouth in a long inward gasp, and then she was shaking in spasms of release.

When she was tranquil again she sat upright opposite him, her hands on his shoulders, and he looked at her body. Her breasts still had their roses, but between her legs his hand had smeared the pink paint to a blur. Sieglinde looked down at herself and giggled.

'You've ruined my rose-bud,' she said, 'I wanted to see it in the mirror. Was it pretty?'

'I didn't have time to finish it properly.'

'Yes, you did. You finished it off very nicely. I like this

175

painting game of yours. Lie on the newspaper and let me paint you.'

Gerhart took off his underpants and stretched himself out on the floor. Sieglinde sat beside him, brush in hand, and he raised his head to see what she was doing. From the base of his hard stem she drew on his belly a representation of it, twice as thick and four times as long as the real thing, so that it reached up to his breast-bone.

'Tell me which flower is your favourite,' she said, 'there are three on the wall. That's not very flattering to any of us.'

The touch of the wet brush on Gerhart's belly was very exciting, and her choice of subject even more so.

'The rose-bud,' he said, 'you know that is my favourite flower. The others are only artistic exercises.'

'Is that so?' she said, filling in the outline she had drawn with the same pink he had used for her rose-bud 'I hope you mean that.'

'With all my heart,' he sighed.

She exchanged the pink paint for crimson and daubed a big oval head at the top of the stem she had drawn.

'It's almost impossible to get a good likeness if the model keeps on jumping about,' she complained. 'Shouldn't models keep still?'

'He's not a trained model,' Gerhart murmured, 'He's not used to holding still for an artist – especially an artist with two beautiful red roses where her little bundles should be.'

'Then it's time he *was* trained.'

'I don't think that's possible . . . certainly now now!'

'If he doesn't behave himself properly he'll be punished. Look at him – jerking about all over the place. Make him stop it at once.'

'He won't listen to me,' Gerhart gasped, 'he's uncontrollable.'

'Is he, indeed! Then I shall take him by the throat and shake some sense into him,' and she dropped the brush, seized Gerhart's twitching tail and shook it vigorously.

'Oh!' he wailed, as his belly clenched and he splashed the picture she had drawn on his belly.

176

'What a little coward!' said Sieglinde, her hand pumping up and down. 'He's burst into tears!'

'Oh, oh, oh . . .' Gerhart was gasping.

'He's cried all over my lovely painting and spoiled it!' said Sieglinde.

Chapter 16

Maximilian Glotz protests

Since the visit to Gerhart's studio and the episode in bed when he had fainted, Lotte had been telephoning twice every day. Her first call was in the morning, about nine o'clock, and the second in the evening about seven. The message was always the same – she wanted to see Gerhart and she hoped that he wasn't making himself ill again by working too hard. For three days Sieglinde kept her at bay, but that was obviously not going to serve for very much longer.

'She's very keen on you,' said Sieglinde on the morning of the fourth day. 'She almost wept when I told her you can't see her this evening because we're having dinner with the General. Why don't you ask her round this afternoon – I shall be at the hair-dresser.'

'I'd rather get on with my work.'

'I never thought I'd hear *you* say you'd rather work than take a girl to bed. Don't you like her at all?'

'That's not the point. I like her well enough, but she's very possessive, I think. If she gets a grip on me my life won't be my own any more. All these telephone calls – anyone else would have understood by now. But not Lotte! She'll keep on till she gets what she wants. And she's just the same in bed – totally possessive.'

'And suddenly you don't like that? You've always liked women who are enthusiastic in bed. What about your model friend Erna – I'm sure she gets very enthusiastic when you take her clothes off.'

'It's not the same. When Erna's had enough she gets up and goes. She keep things casual. Lotte forces the pace all the time – I'm sure that she wants to be here every day and every night and not give me a minute to myself.'

'Then she's in love with you. That makes it complicated. You'll have to talk to her and tell her. If you keep putting her off she'll get angry.'

'You're right,' said Gerhart with a sigh. 'The next time she telephones I'll speak to her myself. I'll invite her out for Saturday.'

Dinner with the General was not as bad as such occasions had been in the past. Ever since he had painted his parody of the picture of the old Kaiser's triumphal ride through the Brandenburg Gate Gerhart had ceased to regard the General as seriously as he once had. In consequence, the evening passed well and the General even congratulated him on getting the commission to illustrate a book. He asked what book it was, and when Gerhart told him, he laughed and said that he remembered reading it a good many years ago.

Gerhart and Sieglinde arrived back at Tauenzienstrasse soon after eleven, for the General did not keep late hours. They were talking cheerfully to each other and did not notice a man lurking in the shadows across the street. They heard footsteps behind them on the stairs and paid no attention, thinking that it was another tenant arriving home. Gerhart unlocked the apartment door and stood aside for Sieglinde to enter and was following her when a heavy hand fell on his shoulder and a voice behind him shouted *I want to talk to you!* He was pushed rudely into the apartment and turned to find himself confronting Maximilian Glotz, dressed in a dark suit and stiff-starched collar, his face pale and twitching.

'Herr Glotz – what on earth do you want at this time of night?'

Glotz slammed the door behind him with his foot.

'I'll tell you what I want!' he stormed.

Gerhart glanced over his shoulder at Sieglinde, who was looking frightened.

'It's all right,' he said, 'I know Herr Glotz. You go to bed while I talk to him.'

She raised her eyebrows in incomprehension and walked quietly away, leaving him to face the visitor.

179

'Come into the sitting-room,' said Gerhart, fairly sure that the visit was to do with Lotte. 'You seem to be angry with me, though there's no reason why you should be. What's the matter?'

'What's the matter!' said Glotz ominously. 'You have the effrontery to stand there and ask me that? I'll tell you what the matter is – you have callously seduced a young lady who is closely related to me. You have betrayed my trust and defiled my family honour. You are a degenerate and I shall see to it that you do not go unpunished for this flagrant act!'

'Heavens, what do you mean, Herr Glotz?' Gerhart asked, struggling not to laugh at this fine display of moral outrage.

'You know well enough what I mean, you swine! She has told me everything.'

'You mean Lotte, of course?'

'Who else should I mean, you pervert!'

'But Lotte is your sister-in-law, not your wife. Why are you so concerned about what she does? She is grown up and a free agent.'

Glotz' pallor had vanished and he was dark red in the face.

'You filthy degenerate!' he said furiously. 'While she lives under my roof she is my concern. She broke down and wept tears of shame when she told me the vile things you forced her to do!'

'Oh, this is too much,' said Gerhart, no longer amused, 'I didn't force her to do anything. I didn't even invite her to visit me. Anything that took place between us was with her full consent.'

'You are a liar!'

Glotz was working himself up into a paroxysm of rage. He jerked up and down on his toes as if he were a marionette controlled by strings from somewhere up near the ceiling. And Gerhart noticed that he was carrying a rolled-up black umbrella and was waving it about dangerously.

'Not only with her consent,' said Gerhart, to annoy him further, 'but with her whole-hearted co-operation. Off you go now – you've heard what you came to hear.'

'Where did it happen?' Glotz demanded, staring wildly

180

about the sitting-room, 'I intend to see the evidence for myself before I report this matter to the police!'

Gerhart was wondering whether to punch him or just throw him out of the apartment.

'I don't know what Lotte told you,' he said, treating Glotz to a thin smile, 'so I'm not sure which part of the apartment to show you. Give me a little description and I will lead you to the right spot.'

Glotz gave a hoarse bellow and ran out of the room, and Gerhart followed him at a more leisurely pace, wondering if the man was out of his mind. Glotz flung open the first door he came to and peered in, surprising Sieglinde sitting in pink silk pyjamas before her mirror to brush her golden hair before she got into bed. He dashed on until he found Gerhart's room and stood quivering on the threshold.

Sieglinde came to her door and stared.

'Is he drunk? Shall I call the police?' she asked.

'No, he's just an idiot. I can handle him.'

'What's his problem? Have you been up to something wicked with his daughter?'

'He's Lotte's brother-in-law and he's annoyed because she went to bed with me.'

'He must be mad to carry on like that. What are you going to do?'

'Throw him out. Lock your door and go to bed.'

Gerhart went to the open door of his own room and encountered an astonishing sight. Glotz was hunched over his bed, thrashing it with his umbrella and cursing under his breath – the sort of words which no respectable lawyer should know. He carried on until he ran out of steam, then dropped his broken umbrella and fell face down on the bed and wept loudly. Gerhart's annoyance was dissipated at once by this pitiful sight. He went back to the sitting-room and poured two glasses of brandy, waited a few minutes for Glotz to recover, and returned to his bedroom. Glotz had got over his fit of weeping and had turned over on to his back and was staring blankly at the ceiling with red-rimmed and swollen eyes. Gerhart sat on the bed and held out one of the glasses.

'Drink this, Herr Glotz, it will will make you feel better. And if there's anything I can tell you that will clear matters up, just ask.'

Glotz stared at him morosely for a few seconds before he sat up and took the glass.

'There's nothing you can tell me,' he said, 'I've been a fool.'

'We all make fools of ourselves at times over women. But we get over it.'

'It's easy for you to say that – you're young. But I'm almost forty. I should know better.'

'I don't think that age has much to do with it. If you meet a girl you like and everything goes well, then it's wonderful. And if it goes wrong, it's painful, whether you're twenty, forty or sixty.'

'I didn't know you were a philosopher,' said Glotz with heavy sarcasm.

'Will you tell me something which I don't understand,' said Gerhart, 'it might explain things.'

'I must be insane to sit here and talk to you!'

'Not really. Who else can you talk to about Lotte but me?'

'What have I come to that I should sit here and discuss my most personal concerns with a pervert!'

'That's a tricky word,' said Gerhart, grinning, 'it means someone who does something you don't do yourself.'

'It has a very precise meaning,' Glotz countered, 'it means a person who indulges in practices which right-minded people know to be wrong.'

'Then it means all of us at some time or other. Therefore it means nothing.'

'What was your question?' Glotz asked bleakly.

'My question . . . yes, you're a solid and respectable citizen. You have a charming wife and you have children. But as we both know, a man's fancy wanders a bit, however happily married he may be. So he has a woman friend in some part of Berlin that he can visit now and then to . . .'

'Certainly not!' Glotz interrupted him. 'How dare you suggest any such thing! Since the day I married my wife I have never even looked at another woman.'

'Until Lotte came to live with you.'

'What are you suggesting?'

'Only that if you did have a friend to visit from time to time, you would not have become so emotionally involved with Lotte.'

'That is the most immoral suggestion I have ever heard,' said Glotz, finishing his brandy. 'You are proposing organised infidelity as a support for marriage.'

'But Herr Glotz – you are a lawyer. You must be aware that many of your clients get themselves into difficulties by becoming attached to the wrong person. Then they come to you to help sort the mess out.'

'Yes, but I despise such people.'

'Maybe you do, but it's your job to help them out of their little troubles. I see your glass is empty – come into the other room and we'll have another drink. I have an idea that may be useful to you.'

Once he was settled into an armchair in the sitting-room and a glass of brandy in his hand, Glotz began to thaw a little, though he was still distant.

'What is this idea you spoke of?' he asked.

'I'll come to that in a minute. First of all, tell me what attracted you to Lotte.'

'The question is ridiculous. How can anyone say what it is about a woman that attracts him?'

'It's not ridiculous at all. Sometimes it's a girl's looks and sometimes it's her ways. One girl has beautiful hair, another has big bouncers, or is a good dancer or an amusing talker. It can be as simple as the shape of her bottom under a thin frock. Or it can be as complicated as a look in her eyes that tells you that she takes you seriously as a person.'

'Your conversation tends towards the vulgar,' said Glotz, finishing his second glass. 'Bouncers! What kind of language is that!'

'The words are not important. Bouncers, bundles – it means just the same as if you say breasts or bosom.'

'A sensible man does not fall in love with a woman because of her bosom,' said Glotz, 'perhaps a boy of your age might.'

183

Gerhart ignored the rudeness and leaned across to refill his visitor's glass.

'Sometimes a man is attracted to a woman for just that,' he said, 'and attraction sometimes leads on to other things.'

'Nonsense! You are talking about sex and I am talking about love,' Glotz insisted. 'You young people today do not understand the difference. Moral standards have collapsed since the War – there is promiscuity and perversion everywhere.'

'There always was. Before you married Lotte's sister you must have had girl-friends.'

'I was a student then. I had no time to waste on immoral pursuits.'

His words were beginning to slur a little as the third glass of brandy affected him. A silly smile flickered across his face and he ran a finger round the inside of his stiff collar as if it were getting too tight.

'I can't believe that a strong and healthy person like you didn't find just a little diversion away from his studies,' said Gerhart. 'After all, an acquaintance with women is a necessary part of a young man's education. I'm sure you studied them as conscientiously as you studied your law books.'

'Well . . . in confidence . . .' said Glotz, the foolish smile now firmly set on his face, 'I left no part of my education neglected. But that's a long time ago.'

'Not so very long. Let me fill your glass. Where did you go to meet girls in those days?'

'I have always been a very logical man. And a very practical one, of course. My friends wasted their time hanging about in dance-halls looking for girls. I went straight to the heart of the matter.'

'Naturally. What was it?'

'I am not going to tell *you*. It is a personal matter.'

Maximilian Glotz was lolling in his arm-chair, his legs out in front of him. He even went so far as to unbutton his tight-fitting dark jacket, to display an uncomfortable-looking dark waistcoat with a watch on a gold chain in one pocket.

'But you came here on a very personal matter in the first

place,' Gerhart pointed out, 'you might as well continue on the same line.'

'You are much younger than I am,' said Glotz in a meditative way, 'in fact, you are much the same age that I was when I was studying law. And yet I have no doubt that you are vastly more experienced than I am in the ways of decadence.'

'In the ways of women, I suppose you mean.'

'What else? The pursuit of women for immoral and base motives is itself decadent.'

'But not the study of them? Where was it that you did this branch of your studying?'

'At Frau Walser's brothel behind the Friedrichstrasse railway station,' Glotz confided, 'it was there that I had a woman for the first time. I was a regular client each Saturday.'

'A private university that awards no degrees to its students,' said Gerhart with a broad grin. 'I can't say that I've ever heard of Frau Walser. Is she still in business?'

'How should I know? I never went there again after I became engaged to Kathe. It would have been wrong.'

'Then consider this – just as a hypothesis – if after a year or two of marriage you had resumed your weekly visits to Frau Walser's establishment, you would have experienced such a variety of women and their ways that you would not have been so vulnerable to Lotte when she came to stay with you. Isn't that logical? Not to say practical, too.'

Glotz thought about it for a while and Gerhart took the opportunity to top up his half-empty glass.

'You may be right,' he conceded at last, 'much as I detest the thought. But that doesn't help me now. The truth is that I have fallen in love with Lotte and I am utterly miserable. It's too late now to go looking for Frau Walser and her girls.'

'That may be. What were they like, these girls? Pretty? Did you try all of them?'

'Naturally,' said Glotz, his mood becoming expansive under the influence of the brandy. 'She usually had four of them at a time and they changed about twice a year – not all at the same time, you understand.'

'Were they Berliners?'

'Some of them. Some were from other parts of Germany. Some were foreigners – there was a good variety.'

'Do you remember any of them in particular after so long?'

'I can remember every one of them,' Glotz claimed proudly, 'I have a remarkable memory, you know. I could tell you their names and what they looked like. The one I recall with most pleasure, if I allowed myself to think of such base things, was a wonderful big girl named Lou. She was from Leipzig.'

'A remarkable memory indeed,' said Gerhart. 'More brandy?'

'Just a drop, perhaps. Do you know, I can see Lou now in my mind's eye – she had long dark hair down below her shoulders. And such thighs! I was thinner in those days and each of her thighs was as round as my waist. She always wore a crucifix on a thin gold chain round her neck and when she was naked it dangled between her breasts. To make love to her was like rolling about on a big soft mattress stuffed with goose-down. And her *bouncers*, as you call them – words fail me!'

'Your studies were very thorough. I am surprised that you gave all that up so easily.'

'I can assure you that it was not easy. But when a man marries and enters an honourable profession, he acquires certain responsibilities. He is no longer free to indulge himself in frivolous pleasures.'

'I don't see why not.'

'You wouldn't. You are fundamentally frivolous and immoral, I am sorry to say.'

'At least I enjoy myself. Your upright life has not exactly made you happy, has it?'

'I was perfectly happy with my life and my family until Lotte came along. I am a sensible man – I cannot understand how my emotions could betray me so badly. I am bewildered.'

'There's no need to be,' Gerhart suggested, 'Lotte's a pretty girl and you want to get her on her back and see whether it's like rolling on goose-down again.'

'No, no, no,' said Glotz, 'that's too crude a way of looking at my plight. What I feel for Lotte goes far beyond the mere gratification of animal appetite.'

Gerhart considered this to be blatant hypocrisy, in the light of what Lotte had told him of Glotz creeping into her room with his tail in his hand and trying to jump on her.

'There's nothing wrong with animal appetite,' he said. 'Why pretend that you're not interested? You'd be happy to get your hands on Lotte's little bundles and your tail up between her legs.'

Glotz looked shocked for a moment to hear his beloved mentioned in such low terms. But the brandy had done its work and his expression mellowed to a smile.

'Oh, yes,' he answered, 'I'd give a great deal to be able to undress her and feel her all over. But now I never shall – you've come between us and ruined my hopes. I hated you when I found out, and I came here to do you harm. But I see that I've been a fool and that you are not to blame. I must learn to live with my misery as best I can.'

'You won't get Lotte into bed by hanging around her looking like a dog that's been beaten.'

'I'll never get her into bed at all.'

'What a pessimist! Lotte likes a roll on the bed and she can be persuaded. But your whole outlook would have to change first.'

'You think there might be hope for me still?' Glotz asked incredulously.

'I don't know. You'd have to go about it in a different way. Your attitude is wrong.'

'What do you suggest?'

'There is someone I know who is unlike any other woman you have ever met, even Frau Walser's girls. If you made love to her a couple of times your attitude to women would change. You might get Lotte to lie down for you – or you might stop hankering after her and enjoy yourself elsewhere.'

'Nonsense!' said Glotz, slurring the word badly. 'No woman can wipe away what I feel for Lotte. I'll tell you something very private – in the past week I have made love to my wife five times. And even while I was doing it I was thinking about Lotte. That's a terrible admission for a man to make about his own dear wife. I am ashamed of myself.'

'Then you should take my suggestion seriously.'

'Who is this person? Have you made love to her yourself? Stupid question – you probably make love to every woman you meet.'

'Not every one. But this one, yes. It was the strangest experience of my life.'

'But you still wanted Lotte afterwards,' Glotz pointed out with drunken logic, 'so it had little effect on you.'

'I had a pleasant afternoon with Lotte. I didn't fall in love with her.'

'That's true,' said Glotz, 'if you had been in love with her you wouldn't have done such vile things to her. You would have made love to her with respect and reverence.'

Gerhart was puzzled by the reference to vile things and wondered what Lotte could possibly have told her brother-in-law.

'You will never meet a more practical person than me,' Glotz declared, 'therefore I shall do as you propose. I shall be grateful if you will introduce me to this remarkable woman.'

'Now is as good a time as any,' said Gerhart, 'Come on.'

In the taxi Glotz was very talkative. He described for Gerhart's benefit five or six of the girls whom he had met and enjoyed at Frau Walser's in the days of his youth. He described their bodies in detail, their ways in bed, his rating of them, and much more. He was still deep in reminiscence when they arrived at the apartment building where Erna lived.

The time was about midnight and Gerhart was not sure of what reception he would get from the landlady. But it was Erna herself who opened the door, and she looked surprised when she saw him and another man.

'I thought it was someone else,' she said.

'Are you expecting Rudolf? If so, we'll go.'

'I'm not expecting anyone, but he does sometimes drop in late.'

'May we come in?'

'Don't make too much noise – I don't want to disturb Frau Leppman and her husband. They went to bed hours ago.'

Maximilian Glotz was swaying on his toes and heels as he stared at Erna. And she was a sight worth looking at. Evidently she had got out of bed to answer the door and she was barefoot and in white satin pyjamas. The trousers were very wide around the ankles and close-fitting round the thighs. The black-button jacket hung loosely to just above the join of her legs and the satin was thin enough for the points of her breasts to show through. Lower down, below the jacket, her brown patch of curls was faintly visible as a dark shadow through the white.

Gerhart steered Maximilian Glotz into Erna's vividly-coloured room and sat him down safely in one of the scarlet arm-chairs, where he gazed open-mouthed at the blue walls and ceiling. The divan had been turned into a bed by turning back the scarlet cover to reveal turquoise sheets, and Erna sat on it with her knees under her chin.

'Who's your friend?' she asked, staring at Glotz in a not very friendly way.

Gerhart sat on the bed facing her and took one of her hands in his.

'His name is Maximilian Glotz and he is seething with unrealised fantasies about women.'

'He's drunk. Why did you bring him here?'

'It's a long story and a sad case. He believes that he's in love with his sister-in-law and if she won't go to bed with him he's liable to hang himself.'

'What an idiot!'

Glotz paid no attention to the conversation at all. His long look round the room completed, he sat with a happy smile on his face and stared at Erna in her flimsy pyjamas.

'I know he's an idiot,' said Gerhart, 'even he knows that he's an idiot. I brought him here to save his sanity and his life. A few drops from your little bottle in a drink and he'll discover so much about himself and his lurking fantasies that he'll stop this silly moping about and start to enjoy himself. Just look at him – he's well-off and forty and the best time he's ever had in his life was in a whore-house twenty years ago.'

'But why bring him here instead of taking him to his sister-in-law, if that's his problem? She can solve his problem quicker than anyone else.'

189

'She doesn't want him. That's why he's in the state you see.'

'My God – I see it all now!' Erna exclaimed, 'You expect me to make love to him!'

'He's not so bad now that he's had a drink or two,' said Gerhart in a soothing voice. 'He's reasonably handsome for his age. And from what he's told me tonight, some of the stuff in his imagination is red-hot. You might be in for a surprise yourself.'

'I don't even know him. Why not take him back to his whore-house and let him try out his fantasies there?'

'He's too respectable to go there these days. And besides, they haven't got your special potion.'

'So you expect me to be a whore?'

'No, no! But you are a dear friend and you understand men like him and Rudolf.'

'And men like you,' said Erna with her sideways grin.

She pulled her hand away and unbuttoned her pyjama jacket to show her bare breasts to him.

'Send him away and you stay with me,' she suggested. 'I'll show you how well I understand what you want.'

Gerhart sighed deeply.

'I can't do that,' he said, 'this great fool would throw himself under a train or a tram or something equally stupid and I'll get the blame. You are the only one who can help him.'

Glotz was staring intently at Erna's breasts.

'Pretty little bundles,' he said, as if talking to himself, 'I want to put my tail between them.'

'Did you hear that?' Gerhart exclaimed. 'He's livening up already. If he says that now, what will he be like if you give him a taste of your special drops? He'll turn into a wild beast!'

'You can never tell in advance,' said Erna, 'but I don't see why I should let you drag any lost dog you find into my room. And that's all he is – a lost dog nobody wants.'

'You would be doing me a big favour.'

'I never do favours.'

'Not even for close friends?' he asked, stroking her breasts.

'Not even for you.'

'I want to nibble her bottom,' Glotz muttered, and Gerhart and Erna laughed together.

'I'll take him away and get him dead drunk,' said Gerhart, 'I should never have brought him here. I'm sorry, Erna, I didn't know what else to do. I went weak and silly when I saw him weeping.'

'I never do favours, but I make bargains,' said Erna.

'I'm listening.'

'I'll keep him here until the morning if you'll promise to come back before midday and stay for as long as I want you to.'

'You mean that you'll give him the full treatment?'

'I'll give him a night he'll never forget.'

'If he remembers it! You are having a day off tomorrow, are you?'

'Tomorrow is today by now, and it's a Saturday.'

'Damn!' said Gerhart, remembering his good intention to take Lotte out for dinner and dancing. 'There's something to do this evening.'

'I've offered you the bargain. I want you here for the whole weekend. Take it or leave it.'

'Are you sure you wouldn't prefer to have a day off for a rest between him and me? I could come back on Sunday about midday.'

'Why would I need a rest? That poor idiot's imagination will soon be drained dry, and mine will still be in full flight. Midday today or nothing.'

Gerhart thought it over for a moment and decided that Lotte would have to wait for another evening. It was more important to get Glotz loosened up so that he stopped being a nuisance.

'Agreed then,' he said, 'I'll be back before midday.'

'And stay all weekend?'

'Do you think either of us will last that long?'

'I want to find out. We might both die in the process, but it will be a fantastic way to die with your tail inside me.'

Glotz had closed his eyes and was asleep in his chair.

'I think the bargain's off,' said Gerhart doubtfully. 'By the look of him his big night is over before it's even begun.'

'Leave that to me. I've pulled Rudolf out of worse drunkenness than that and got him to perform. I'll wake him up with a cup of very strong coffee, black and bitter and laced with something he doesn't expect. He'll soon be thinking about bundles and bottoms again.'

She saw Gerhart out through the dark and silent apartment, her pyjama jacket still open. At the door he kissed her and clasped his hand over the curls beneath her satin trousers.

'Don't let your little chrysanthemum wilt,' he whispered, 'I don't want to come back and find you fast asleep.'

'No fear of that. You and I are going to do things to each other which you won't believe afterwards.'

'Now you've got me really interested! I've half a mind to throw Max out now and stay myself.'

His hand stroked over the smooth satin, feeling the warmth underneath.

'There's something else you can think about while you're away,' Erna said softly, undoing his trouser buttons, 'When you're with me later on and we're both so far gone that we're completely open to each other, you're going to tell me all about rose-buds. And I'll tell you my secrets, and then we shall be closer friends than you can imagine.'

'I don't know what you mean by rose-buds,' Gerhart sighed, slipping his hand down the front of her pyjama trousers to feel the soft flesh between her thighs.

'You'll tell me about the little pink rose-bud you painted a picture of. And you'll tell me what you do to it. You won't be able to help yourself.'

Her hand held his stiff tail and played with it.

'It's dangerous to tell secrets,' said Gerhart.

'Why?' she asked, her hand moving firmly up and down.

'When they're told they're not secrets any more.'

'They're safe enough between you and me,' Erna murmured soothingly, 'and it will be very exciting to tell them to each other, I promise. You must go home and sleep till midday – I want you to be strong and ready when you come back to me.'

'I shan't be able to sleep for thinking about what you've said,' he sighed, his tail quivering in her hand.

'Yes, you will,' she said, 'give me your handkerchief. You'll dream about what I'm doing to you now and you'll wake up with a stiff tail and come running round here to find out what fantastic things we can do to each other.'

'Oh!' Gerhart murmured as the familiar sensation rolled through his belly. 'Oh, Erna!'

Chapter 17

Women have important secrets no less than men

Lotte did not make her regular telephone call the next morning. Gerhart was surprised and relieved, because it made it unnecessary to put her off with another excuse. It also removed the need to explain to Sieglinde why he had changed his mind about taking Lotte out that evening. More than that, it meant that he would escape what he expected to be a long and awkward confession by Lotte that she had, for reasons best known to herself, said too much to Maximilian Glotz. It was awkward enough to answer Sieglinde's questions about their visitor of the night before. Without being sure why, Gerhart found himself reluctant to tell her too much about either Lotte or Erna Klemt.

In the past he had talked openly about his girl-friends if she asked, and this unusual reluctance made him uneasy with himself. He passed off the events of the previous night by saying that Glotz had been drunk and looking for somewhere to stay because he didn't want to go home in that condition. Sieglinde did not pursue the matter, but whether she believed him was another question.

All this feeling of relief was short-lived. Soon after ten o'clock in the morning Lotte arrived in person. Gerhart scrambled off the sitting-room sofa, where he had been lying and thinking about his forthcoming rendezvous with Erna, and braced himself for what he feared would be an embarrassing conversation. But Lotte took him by surprise.

'Gerhart!' she said in a distraught voice. 'You won't believe what's happened!'

'Come and sit down,' he said, and put an arm round her

194

shoulders to lead her to a seat. 'Tell me what's upset you.'

'I'll leave you alone together,' said Sieglinde tactfully.

'No, please stay,' Gerhart said quickly, unwilling to be left alone with Lotte in case she expected to be comforted in a way that would slow him down when he met Erna.

'It's Max,' said Lotte, 'he's been arrested!'

'Good God – what's he done?' asked Gerhart, thoroughly alarmed.

'The police found him wandering along Friedrichstrasse in the middle of the night – stark naked!'

Friedrichstrasse was some distance from where Erna lived. It passed through Gerhart's mind that Glotz had gone looking for Frau Walser's brothel to repeat the pleasures of his student days. But how could he have got that far with no clothes on – and why? Gerhart was worried about what might have happened to Erna.

'Where was he all night?' he asked.

'No one knows – he didn't come home. Kathe was worried out of her mind – and then the police arrived to tell her that they'd arrested him.'

'I don't know what to say,' Gerhart exclaimed, with complete truth.

'He went rushing out yesterday about five in the afternoon,' Lotte added, 'He didn't come back for dinner. I thought he might be on his way to see *you*.'

'We had an unexpected visitor late last night,' said Sieglinde, looking at Gerhart in an accusing way. 'He pushed his way in and started shouting when we arrived back about eleven.'

'So he was here!' said Lotte, staring at Gerhart. 'What did you do to him?'

'He was terribly upset. I gave him a drink and he calmed down after a while and we talked for half an hour.'

'And then?'

'The two of you went out together,' said Sieglinde, also staring at Gerhart in an unsympathetic manner. 'Where did you go?'

'We had another drink and then I left him and came home. Did you hear me come in?'

'No, I fell asleep after you'd gone.'

'He was all right when I left him about midnight,' Gerhart told

195

Lotte, stretching the truth a little. 'In fact, he seemed quite cheerful. Does he often stay out all night?'

'Never! That's why Kathe was so frantic. Where were you – in a bar?'

'More of a private club.'

'If it were any other man than Max I'd say he'd picked up a woman and been taken somewhere and robbed,' said Lotte, 'but not him – he'd never do anything like that.'

Gerhart was now seriously worried about Erna. He'd taken Glotz to her as a sort of well-meant joke to make him confront his own nature. Something had obviously gone very wrong.

'I'll go back to where I left him and see if they can tell me anything,' he said, getting quickly to his feet.

Sieglinde followed him into the hall.

'You know more than you're saying,' she said, smiling in a conspiratorial way. 'Where did you leave him? I won't tell Lotte.'

'With a woman, of course. That's what he wanted. With a glass or two of brandy inside him he told me that he wanted to nibble a girl's bottom. So I took him to a place where he could.'

'With a street-walker, you mean?'

'No, somewhere perfectly respectable. He must have caused trouble and got himself thrown out.'

'Naked?'

'I don't understand that at all. I'll go and find out.'

'What about Lotte? What do you want me to do?'

'Talk to her until she calms down and then send her home.'

'Will you be long?'

'I can't say. If it takes a long time to discover what went on last night I'll telephone you.'

Sieglinde kissed him on the cheek and returned to the sitting-room.

'Lotte, I'd like you to explain something to me. Why did your brother-in-law break in here last night in such a temper?'

Lotte blushed and explained the position between Maximilian and herself.

'But I still don't understand,' said Sieglinde. 'Why did you tell him that you'd been to bed with Gerhart if you knew it would make him furious?'

196

'I don't know why I did it,' Lotte sighed, 'Kathe was out and Max began to pester me. He had me trapped in an arm-chair and was groping under my clothes – and it made me so angry that I didn't know what I was saying.'

'But it stopped him?'

'He jumped up, white as a ghost, and started to ask me the most awful questions.'

'About what, Gerhart?'

'Yes – how many times had I been with him, when was the last, how did we do it – things like that. I made things up to annoy him.'

Sieglinde giggled and asked her what sort of things she had made up.

'I can't repeat them in cold blood,' said Lotte, smiling her-self, 'I just reeled out every perversion I'd ever heard about and told Max we'd done it all.'

'And your ridiculous brother-in-law believed you?'

'Every word! His face turned from white to crimson and he shouted *Whore*! at me and rushed out. I suppose it was wrong of me, but I'd had enough of his endless pestering.'

'And you were angry with Gerhart, so you were paying both of them back at the same time,' Sieglinde suggested.

'I suppose I was. Every time I phoned him, you told me that he was busy. All I wanted was to see him. He could have spared me half an hour, surely.'

'Seeing him was not all you wanted, Lotte.'

'Well . . . if he'd seen me he might have wanted more. Do you think he likes me? I thought he did, but now I'm not sure.'

'He's painted a picture of you. That must mean something,' said Sieglinde.

'Then he has been thinking about me, after all! Can I see it?'

Sieglinde took her to Gerhart's bedroom. He had moved the flower pictures there from his studio and, mounted on white board, they hung in a row across the wall. Lotte stared at them from across the room, not understanding what they were.

'They're very striking,' she said, her tone puzzled, 'But where's the picture of me?'

'You don't recognise yourself?'

197

'What do you mean? They're flowers, though not very realistic. I didn't know Gerhart went in for this modern style of painting.'

Sieglinde smiled and put her arm round Lotte's waist.

'Have a closer look,' she suggested. 'The one in the middle is me. The dark one on the right is you. The other is someone else.'

Together they moved across the room, nearer the paintings.

'Oh!' Lotte shrieked, her face turning bright red. 'Now I see!'

Sieglinde laughed and squeezed her affectionately.

'So you've learned something about Gerhart.'

'But . . . how could he! I mean, to paint pictures like that and put them where anyone can see them!'

'He's moved them out of his studio into this room, where no one can see them but himself.'

'You've seen them!'

'That's different. We don't keep secrets from each other.'

'That's obvious!' said Lotte, looking closely at the rose-bud picture. 'If he'd asked me to pose for a picture like that I'd have refused at once.'

'He doesn't ask anyone's permission for what he does. Why should he? And if you want to be on good terms with him, you won't make a fuss about what he does.'

Lotte was contemplating the blue-black flower on the wall.

'Is that how he sees me, do you think? Just that and nothing else?'

'It's a part of you he evidently likes, otherwise he wouldn't have painted it. And it's a very pretty picture, if you ask me. Have you noticed that all three are life-size?'

'Sieglinde – what a thing to say! But perhaps you're right, it is very pretty, the way he's painted it,' and now Lotte was smiling too, 'Who's the brown one?'

'I'm fairly sure it's the girl who comes here to pose for the book illustrations he's working on.'

'That explains how he saw her with her clothes off,' said Lotte. 'For a moment I thought she might be . . . you know, someone he's fond of. But you pose for him too, I see.'

'Sometimes, when he asks me.'

Her mind relieved on the question of rivals for Gerhart's affections, though mistakenly, Lotte resumed her study of the flower pictures.

'Why has he chosen a rose-bud to represent you, Sieglinde? I can see some sort of resemblance to me in the dark one, naughty as it is. But why a rose-bud like that?'

'I was about to say the same about the black peony. Your hair is very dark, but surely not that dark down there.'

'But it is! I know some people think I dye my hair black, but it's no more than a touch of tint to give it a glossy look. I am naturally jet-black.'

'Between your legs too?'

Lotte nodded and half-smiled, her cheeks a faint pink again.

'What a contrast between us,' said Sieglinde, 'I'm so fair that it looks as if I've got no hair at all down there until you look closely. That's why Gerhart painted a half-open rose-bud for me.'

'That's amazing! You don't bleach it or pluck it?'

'No, it's all natural, just like yours. We're such opposites, you and me.'

'Total opposites,' Lotte agreed, looking from one painting to the other.

'If we stood in front of a mirror together we could see the effect,' Sieglinde suggested.

'Have you got a big mirror?' Lotte asked, still blushing faintly.

Sieglinde led her to her own room, where a full-length mirror hung on the inside of the wardrobe door when she swung it open. Lotte glanced at it and then away, breaking into nervous chatter.

'You have a nice room – it's so light and pretty. And those lovely pillows with the broad lace edging – where did you get them? And I love your clothes – especially the electric-blue dance-frock here. Of course, you take a smaller size in everything than I do . . .'

To lessen the awkwardness of the moment Sieglinde crossed her arms and slid her apple-green pullover over her head, to reveal the silk slip she was wearing under it. She undid her skirt

199

and let it glide down her long legs to the floor. Suitably encouraged, Lotte put her gloves and hat on the bed and unbuttoned her jacket – she was wearing the same blue linen summer costume as the last time she had visited the apartment. Very soon both women were down to their stockings and knickers and, with a friendly smile, Sieglinde hooked her thumbs in the waistband of hers and bent forward to slide them down and off. After a momentary pause, Lotte found the courage to do the same, and the two of them stood side by side in front of the glass, looking at the reflection of each other's naked body.

'Beautiful,' said Sieglinde, 'the pink rose and the black peony.'

'What if Gerhart comes back and finds us like this?' said Lotte, sounding anxious.

'He won't be back for hours,' Sieglinde assured her. 'Don't you think we're beautiful together?'

'Oh, yes, very beautiful. You're so fair that your hair hardly shows and mine's so dark you could see it a kilometre off at night. And you're so slim that you make my hips look positively huge.'

They moved a little closer together until their thighs touched, and each put an arm round the other's waist.

'Your hips aren't huge,' said Sieglinde. 'Mine are too narrow. It's very attractive, the way your hips curve out from your waist like that.'

Her hand slipped down from Lotte's waist to her bottom and she stroked it.

'You've got more here than I have,' she said, 'men like that. I think that your figure's very nice.'

'At least my breasts aren't big and heavy,' said Lotte, 'I should hate that. They're no bigger than yours, I'd say.'

'About the same size. I've always thought that mine are very elegant.'

'Very,' Lotte agreed, a little breathlessly.

'Yours are slightly rounder than mine,' said Sieglinde. 'Mine are more pointed.'

'Yes, I see what you mean.'

As if by silent agreement, they turned slowly to face each

other. Sieglinde put her hands on Lotte's breasts and felt them gently.

'Your skin is like silk,' she murmured.

'So is yours!' Lotte sighed, her fingers brushing timidly over Sieglinde's belly, and then reaching down to touch the blonde floss between her thighs.

Under Sieglinde's fingers the pink buds of Lotte's breasts grew firm and pointed.

'Oh, Sieglinde . . . what are we doing?' she asked in a troubled voice.

'We are admiring each other, that's all.'

'But should we be doing it?'

'There's no one to say we shouldn't. Do you want to stop?'

'I don't know . . . it's so nice when you touch me.'

'Your breasts have been stroked hundreds and hundreds of times before today. Why are you nervous now?'

'I've never been touched by another woman,' Lotte whispered, her dark eyes downcast and her face flushed.

Sieglinde led her slowly to the bed, swept her hat and gloves off to the floor and pulled her gently down on to it.

'Close your eyes and don't talk,' she said.

They lay with their arms about each other, kissing and pressing their bodies together. After a while Sieglinde eased Lotte on to her back and spread her legs apart so that she could run her fingers through the black curls between them.

'Your wonderful black peony – it's even more beautiful than the painting.'

'Sieglinde – we ought to stop this,' Lotte whispered.

'Your curls are so strong and springy – I'm going to comb them.'

She was off the bed, across to her dressing-table and back in moments, bringing the long ivory comb she used for her hair. She sat cross-legged beside Lotte and ran the comb slowly through her curls, again and again, until the touch of the ivory teeth on Lotte's flesh made her tremble with pleasure.

'Does that feel nice?'

'You'll make me do it in a minute!' Lotte gasped.

She was already shaking all over as her easily aroused

passions took hold of her. A moan of protest escaped her when Sieglinde's fingers opened the petals of her dark flower, but the instant that its secret little stamen was touched, her long ecstasy was unleashed. Her back arched off the bed and her cries were shrill and sustained, surprising Sieglinde by how little had been necessary to bring on Lotte's climax. She thought it would be quickly over, and she learned what Gerhart had learned before her – that it lasted a very long time indeed. Her fingers played rhythmically between Lotte's thighs while she stared in delight at her squirming body and heard her wailing shrieks.

'Yes, Lotte!' she exclaimed, her other hand between her own slender thighs to touch her rose-bud, as Lotte's exceptional arousal carried her along with it.

Before Lotte's violent squealing began to slow down at last, Sieglinde moaned softly in her own self-induced release. Through it, and after it, she played expertly with Lotte, until the passionate storm eventually subsided and Lotte lay still and silent.

'That was incredible,' said Sieglinde, 'is it always like that?'

Lotte gave a long sigh of content and smiled shyly.

'I'm afraid so. Was it very boring for you?'

'Boring? My God – it was so exciting to watch that I had to play with myself.'

At that, Lotte forgot her embarrassment. She pulled Sieglinde down on top of her and hugged her close.

'My screaming excited you that much?' she asked, her hands sliding down to stroke Sieglinde's small and round bottom. 'What a pity that you've done something about it already. If you'd waited, I'd have done it for you.'

Sieglinde rolled off her and lay on her back.

'Then do it,' she whispered

Lotte climbed over her leg to kneel between her open thighs.

'You're beautiful,' she said, 'I never thought I'd play with another woman like this.'

Sieglinde's long legs were so widely spread that the pink lips between them were pulled open, and Lotte's fingers touched the smooth and slippery interior.

'Gerhart was right to choose a rose-bud for you! You feel as

202

soft and delicate as rose-petals. Tell me what to do – I haven't done this to a girl before.'

'You must have done it to yourself often enough,' Sieglinde sighed.

'Like this? It seems so strange to be touching you . . . I mean, it's not like having a man's big hard thing in your hand.'

Sieglinde's smooth belly was quivering and the tips of her breasts were standing up very hard.

'That feels so nice, Lotte,' she whispered.

'Am I doing it right for you?'

'Yes . . . kiss me there.'

After a moment or two's pause at the unexpected request, Lotte bent over, her bare bottom in the air, and kissed the skin of Sieglinde's belly.

'Lower down,' Sieglinde sighed.

Lotte trailed her tongue down Sieglinde's belly and kissed the silky blonde hair just above the open lips where her fingers were busy.

'Lower still!' Sieglinde shrieked faintly.

Hesitantly, Lotte moved her mouth downwards. Sieglinde reached forward with both hands to grasp her head and press her face down between her thighs, until her mouth was where she wanted it to be.

'Lotte, Lotte, kiss me!' she moaned.

Lotte was entirely without experience of this mode of love-making, no man ever having done it to her because of her extended climax. But instinct prevailed, and she thrust out her tongue and licked at Sieglinde's exposed little button. Almost at once, so great was her arousal, Sieglinde's bottom rose off the bed and climactic spasms shook her like a leaf.

After that they lay in each other's arms, caressing each other with tender affection. The first to speak was Lotte, her mind still slightly uneasy at what they had done together.

'I don't know what to say – I never expected anything like this to happen.'

'All that you need say is that you enjoyed it.'

'I did – but I feel as if I've done something wrong. Do you feel the same about it?'

'It's no more wrong than making love to a man. To me it's just as natural.'

'Oh, you've done it before with girls? I didn't realise . . . I thought it was the first time for you too. You must think I'm a fool.'

'There's a first time for everyone, and my first time was before yours, that's all.'

'But you do go to bed with men as well?' Lotte asked doubtfully.

'With beautiful men and with beautiful women,' said Sieglinde, caressing Lotte's round breasts, 'though it's much easier to find beautiful men than beautiful women. Most girls don't want to, and those that do are usually fat and middle-aged, and I don't want them. Only beautiful girls like you – girls as beautiful as I am.'

'How did you know that I would want to make love? What made you think you could talk me into undressing and standing by the mirror with you?'

'I didn't know. I wanted to see you naked, because you are beautiful. And I thought that if you saw me naked you might be interested.'

'You were right about that!' and Lotte rolled over on her back and giggled at the thought of what had happened.

'It's nice to hear you happy,' said Sieglinde, 'It would have been dreadful if you'd burst into tears afterwards and gone away feeling ashamed.'

'I'm not ashamed – I think I'm just surprised at myself. I never imagined I was capable of doing anything like that. But now I've got used to the idea I'm pleased that I did. Are you? I mean, you know more about it than I do – was it what you expected?'

'It was wonderful. You'll come here again and make love with me, won't you?'

'I don't know,' and Lotte frowned slightly, 'if Gerhart found out, he wouldn't want me again. And I'm very fond of him.'

'You're in love with him,' said Sieglinde, her hand roaming lightly over Lotte's warm belly.

'Yes, I am,' she admitted.

Tears welled up in her dark eyes and trickled down her cheeks. She sobbed and turned over, to hide her face in the pillow.

'What have I done!' she moaned. 'If you tell him about this he won't have anything to do with me again!'

'Don't cry,' said Sieglinde, stroking her back to calm her, 'Gerhart isn't like that at all. If you told him yourself that you and I had made love he'd only laugh and say he hoped that it was nice. It wouldn't make any difference to how he feels about you.'

'How can you say that!'

'I know him a lot better than you do, Lotte.'

'Then you know he doesn't love me.'

'You're frightening him away, if you want the truth.'

Lotte turned on her side and showed her tear-streaked face.

'Did he say that?' she asked miserably.

Sieglinde wiped away her tears with her fingers and then held the round breasts presented to her.

'He told me that he likes you. But you have to understand that he's afraid of being hemmed in and tied down to one person. It's not in his nature to give himself completely to one person – I saw that years ago. If you're there when he wants you and leave him alone when he doesn't, he'll become more fond of you and eventually start to rely on you.'

'That's fine for him – but what about me?' Lotte objected. 'What you're saying is that because I'm a woman I have to hide my feelings and wait for him. It isn't fair – and I don't know if I can do it. I want to be with him all the time.'

'If you let him see that, he'll run away from you. It may not be fair, but that's the way he is. You have to cool your feelings down and let him set the pace.'

'That's easy for you to say – but I need to be loved all the time, not just when he feels like it.'

'I'll love you when he doesn't,' said Sieglinde, her hands massaging Lotte's breasts steadily.

'But . . . that's the most immoral suggestion I've ever heard!'

'Why? I'm sure you've had two lovers at the same time in the past.'

'But they were both men,' said Lotte, breathing more quickly as Sieglinde's fondling reawakened her passions.

'As if that made any difference!' Sieglinde said softly. 'Two men, two women, one of each – as long as it pleases you, why bother with the distinction?'

'But suppose I fell in love with *you*!' Lotte murmured.

'Then you'd be in love with both of us at the same time,' Sieglinde answered with a giggle. 'We'd wear you out, between the two of us!'

'You make it sound so simple – if only it were!' Lotte sighed.

'It is simple, you'll see. You're ready again, aren't you?'

'I'm nearly there,' Lotte said in a quavering voice.

'Then it's my turn to kiss you – I hope my tongue doesn't get exhausted halfway through.'

Lotte rolled over on to her back and spread her legs wide, her knees up. Her own hands pulled open the petals of her dark peony. Sieglinde lay between her legs and touched her wet tongue to the exposed bud, and Lotte's climactic squealing started at once, this time interspersed with gasping words – '*I love you . . . Sieglinde . . . I love you!*'

Chapter 18

The appeal of film-stars

Erna's landlady opened the door to Gerhart and, in response to his request to see her, told him that she no longer lived there.

'That's ridiculous,' said Gerhart, 'I saw her here last night.'

'Were *you* here? You'd better come in.'

'Thank you, Frau . . . I have been here before but I'm afraid that I've forgotten your name.'

'Frau Leppman. And you are Herr Gerhart von Rautenberg. I haven't forgotten your name, you see.'

She took him into her sitting-room and pointed to a chair, her face serious and worried.

'Now tell me where Fraulein Klemt is if she's not here,' said Gerhart. 'Is anything wrong.'

'You're a friend of hers, so I'll tell you what I know, though I shouldn't. What time were you here last night?'

'About midnight. I came with a friend, but I didn't stay more than about twenty minutes.'

'But your friend stayed,' said Frau Leppman, 'was he drunk then?'

'We'd had a glass or two together, but he wasn't falling-down drunk,' Gerhart said hastily, 'I hope that he didn't cause any trouble.'

'Trouble! It was more like a riot, if you want to know! Look at this room – there's not a flower-vase or a picture left unbroken! And that little table propped against the wall – he smashed two of its legs off.'

'My God – he's usually such a quiet person! Why did he do that?'

'How do I know? We were woken up about four in the

morning by the most tremendous commotion in here. I thought burglars had broken in to rob us and I made my husband get out of bed to see. I was frightened, so I hid in the bed, but when I heard my husband shouting his head off I came in here – I thought he was being murdered!'

Gerhart stared at Frau Leppman, his mind in a whirl.

'I didn't even stop to put anything round me,' she said, caught up in the drama of her story, 'there I was, in bare feet and only a night-dress!'

She was a thin woman of about thirty-five, with dark brown and bushy hair. Gerhart wondered for a moment whether she would have been worth seeing in only her night-dress, but forgot the thought at once as she continued.

'There was a man in here,' she said, outrage in her voice, 'and he was stark naked! He was lurching round the room, laughing like a madman, knocking into the furniture and breaking things. He didn't seem to know what he was doing, so I thought he was blind drunk.'

'You must have been terrified, Frau Leppman,' said Gerhart, in as sympathetic a tone as he could manage.

'I was scared out of my wits! And to make it worse, his *thing* was sticking straight out like a broom-handle! I was sure that he was a rapist – and me with nothing on but a thin night-dress!'

Gerhart was trying very hard to stop himself from laughing at the ludicrous story of Maximilian Glotz's nocturnal misadventure. He put his hands over his face to hide the grin that threatened to turn into a guffaw.

'Well, what else was I to think in the middle of the night?' Frau Leppman demanded, 'but then I realised that he must be someone staying the night with Erna and when I told my husband, he grabbed the man and threw him out of the door.'

'Not by by his broom-handle!' Gerhart exclaimed, unable to suppress his laughter any longer.

Frau Leppman looked shocked for a moment, and then grinned.

'No, with a kick up the backside,' she said, 'I suppose there is a funny side to it when you think about it. But at the time my husband was furious – he told me to go and tell Erna he

208

wouldn't put up with any more of her visitors and she had to pack and clear out then and there. So I went into her room – and what a mess! The bed was tipped up by the wall and there were clothes and books thrown all round the room. And Erna – he'd tied her wrists together with a stocking and she was dangling naked from the wardrobe! I got her down and she was so limp and cold I thought she was dead. I ran and dragged my husband out of bed again and told him to go for the police.'

'He killed her!' Gerhart gasped in an agony of mind. 'Oh, my God!'

'Thank God she was still alive – Karl felt her heart beating and sent for an ambulance to take her to hospital. That's where she is now.'

'Is she all right?'

'I telephoned about nine after my husband had gone, and they said she was out of danger but still unconscious.'

Gerhart breathed a long sigh of relief.

'And the police – they are looking for the man? Or have they found him?' he asked cautiously.

'Karl wouldn't get the police when he saw that Erna was still alive. I told him the man should be arrested, but he said no.'

'He doesn't like dealings with the police, your husband?'

'You brought your friend here last night and left him with Erna,' said Frau Leppman pointedly, 'I don't care what games you get up to between yourselves, but surely you don't want him to be arrested, do you?'

Gerhart thought it better to say nothing about Glotz's encounter with the police in Friedrichstrasse.

'What is it you are suggesting?' he asked.

'I'm not suggesting anything at all. Karl said that if your friend was arrested it would be a police matter and we'd never get proper compensation for the damage he'd done. Just look at this room – that's all his work! And that's besides any compensation for the upset to my nerves and the disturbance he caused.'

'His clothes were still in Erna's room and you found his name and address in his papers, yes? You hid the clothes and said nothing. In due course Herr Leppman will go and see my friend to arrange financial compensation for keeping quiet. Have I got it right?'

'It wasn't my idea,' Frau Leppman protested..

Gerhart wondered how Maximilian would respond to blackmail after being arrested for public indecency. The little lawyer was experiencing some unusual adventures.

'Meanwhile, Fraulein Klemt is in the hospital,' he said, 'did he hurt her or was she just drugged?'

'There wasn't a mark on her body that I could see, except a bite on her backside. I'm sure it was no more than an overdose – God knows I've warned her enough times! You're a good friend of hers – tell me what to do. Karl won't have her back here, so I'm going to pack up her belongings for her. But there's nowhere I can send them except to the hospital, and I'd never be that unkind. We've been friends, Erna and me, while she's lived here. I don't want to annoy my husband, but I'd like to do what's best for her.'

'You are a good-hearted person, Frau Leppman. Get her things together and I'll talk to Herr Knuppel – the man she works for. He'll look after everything.'

'Are you sure? I wouldn't want her to lose her job.'

'There's no fear of that,' Gerhart said with a smile, 'she's on very close terms with him – he's been here often enough all night.'

Frau Leppman returned his smile and winked at him.

'She's a proper little alley-cat!' she said.

When she chuckled her big gold ear-rings shook and something stirred in the depths of Gerhart's memory. He couldn't recall it completely, but it seemed that there was a link between those golden hoops jangling and sensations of pleasure.

'Your name is Ruth, isn't it?' he asked, not sure of where that item of information had come from suddenly.

'You remember!'

'We met when I came here for a business discussion with Fraulein Klemt about pictures for a book.'

'A very long discussion,' said Frau Leppman with a knowing grin, 'it started at three in the afternoon and it was still going on

210

at nine that night. It must have been very important business.'

Gerhart grinned back at her.

'I know what you are thinking,' he said, 'you have the idea that after we'd finished talking about business we found something more interesting to do.'

'I know you did – I saw you at it,' and she rocked with laughter.

'Impossible!'

'You were in Erna's room for so long and everything had gone so quiet that I looked in just to make sure you were both all right. And there you were, Herr von Rautenberg, lying on your back with your pole standing up and Erna dead to the world across your legs.'

'I see that you are a kind and understanding woman,' said Gerhart, 'you didn't scream or call the police on that occasion either.'

'Not even the ambulance,' she said, chuckling again, 'you were both all right, I could see that. Erna was sleeping it off and you were half awake and half asleep. And you know what happened next.'

'To be truthful, no. What did happen?'

'Maybe this will jog your memory – your pole wasn't really standing up. You were wearing a pair of Erna's knickers.'

'I remember now! And you were wearing camiknickers – now how could I know that?'

'Because you saw them. Erna was out for the count and you asked me to lie down for you. It seemed a pity to waste what you'd got, so I climbed on top of you.'

'I was flying in a big red zeppelin!' Gerhart exclaimed. 'It was fantastic!'

That set her off laughing again. Gerhart reached out his hand and, when she took it, pulled her across to him and settled her on his lap. She cuddled against him, an arm round his neck.

'Your zeppelin was certainly flying high that day,' she said, 'You were so drugged that you lay still and let me take my time. I must have had a good twenty minutes of fun before I went off like a bomb.'

Gerhart had his hand up the skirt of her flower-patterned

frock to stroke her bare thigh above her stocking-top.

'Twenty minutes? That sounds very nice, Ruth. Did I go off like a bomb too?'

'Twice.'

'No! In twenty minutes?'

'And hard as iron the whole time! That's why Erna takes that drug – it keeps you going for hours. But it's dangerous.'

Gerhart had made an interesting discovery. Ruth Leppman was wearing no underwear and, when he touched the lips between her thighs, they were very moist.

'My dear Ruth,' he said, grinning at her, 'you've just been made love to. Have you got a boy-friend hidden in the bedroom?'

'No such luck!' she answered, her cheeks faintly pink.

'But this doesn't happen by itself,' he said, probing with an expert finger between the wet lips.

'If you must know, I was giving myself a little thrill when you rang the door-bell.'

'And you were doing it very well, by the feel of things. Do you do it often?'

'Every day,' she sighed, pressing herself close to him and sliding her legs further apart, 'I take my knickers off and sit in that chair when I'm alone. Well, if I don't give myself a feel, nobody else will. That's why I couldn't resist when I saw you lying on the bed with Erna. You're so good-looking and your body is so beautiful when you're undressed.'

'And today I arrived unexpectedly at your door and interrupted your pleasure. I must certainly make up for that, or you will think me most impolite.'

'You didn't interrupt me,' she sighed, wriggling her legs as wide apart on his lap as her frock would permit, 'It was all over and I was sitting there feeling content.'

Her face was fiery red from the sensations aroused by his busy fingers. She stroked his hair and breathed quickly.

'What do you think about when you play with yourself?' Gerhart asked.

'Film-stars, usually . . . Emil Jannings is my favourite.'

'And what does he do to you?'

'He hugs me and kisses me . . . and then he undresses me and feels me all over . . . I make it last for as long as I can.'

'As long as your twenty minutes with me?'

'Sometimes.'

'Does it last that long with your husband?' Gerhart asked out of curiosity.

'With Karl it's all over in thirty seconds.'

'That sounds disappointing.'

'Yes, I like a man to treat me gently till my blood is on fire and then make love to me till I'm really satisfied . . . does that sound silly to you?'

'It sounds very nice,' said Gerhart, his stiff tail flattened uncomfortably along his thigh by Ruth's bottom on his lap, 'haven't you got a boy-friend to visit you in the afternoons?'

'There's no one round here worth looking at,' she whispered, 'no one like you, that's certain. You know how to please a woman . . . I could sit on your knees all day and let you play with me.'

'Let's go to the bedroom and I'll give you the thrill of your life.'

She took him not to the bedroom she shared with her husband but into Erna's vividly-painted room. The divan had been set back on its feet and the wreckage of Glotz' rampage cleared up. Gerhart helped her out of her clothes and she lay on the scarlet divan watching him undress.

'I've seen *that* before,' she said, when he dropped his trousers and his hard pink staff stuck out.

'You've done more than just look at it,' he replied, grinning at her.

Ruth was narrow in the waist and hips, her breasts were small and flat, so that their brownish buds seemed large by contrast. The most striking feature of her body was an extensive mat of dark brown hair that spread into her groins and for some way down the insides of her thighs. Gerhart ran his fingers through it to feel its springy texture, then lay beside her and used his tongue on the tips of her little breasts.

'You were lying on this bed when I had you before,' she murmured.

'But this time I'm going to have you, Ruth – and remember it afterwards.'

'At least you're not wearing Erna's knickers.'

'Why do you think I was then?'

'I don't know what games you were playing with her. People do the strangest things when they're drugged.'

The points of her breasts were hard under Gerhart's fingers.

'Have you tried it yourself?' he asked.

'Only once . . . Karl was away and I let Erna give me a few drops in a glass of beer.'

'Do you remember what you did?'

'No . . . I woke up down there on the floor, stark naked and aching all over.'

'Perhaps you made love with Erna?'

He was stroking her flat belly, arousing her slow passions, his hand moving slowly towards her mat of brown hair.

'I don't know what we did,' Ruth whispered, 'I've been too frightened to try it again. Sometimes I have the strangest dreams and wake up wet between the legs and desperate to be made love to.'

Gerhart's fingers were inside her, teasing her slippery bud.

'Perhaps your dreams are memories. Tell me one of them.'

'You'll laugh at me,' she sighed, her thin body quivering as his busy fingers raised her sensations towards their limit.

'I won't laugh – it will make me excited too.'

'I'm riding on a tram at night,' she whispered, 'it's so crowded that we're all squeezed up together, and there are hands feeling me all over – dozens of hands . . . I want to get off the tram, and at the same time I want to stay on it . . .'

'Yes,' said Gerhart softly, 'yes, Ruth.'

'They pull all my clothes off and I'm naked in the crowd and they're all feeling me . . . I know I shouldn't let them, but I'm too excited to stop them.'

'Are they all men?'

'It's too dark to see . . . their hands are squeezing my breasts so tight that I can hardly breath – and they're gripping the cheeks of my bottom and stroking up inside my legs – and then there's a whole hand up inside me – right up to the wrist and the fingers are tickling inside my belly – oh my God, *put it in me!*'

Gerhart mounted her thin body and rode her firmly until she jerked beneath him in silent climactic spasms, and he stabbed hard and flooded her quickly.

She was so grateful for the pleasure he had given her that she wanted him to stay for the rest of the afternoon, saying that her husband wouldn't be back before six. But Gerhart was bored now that his emotions had been calmed and told her that he must go. She lay on the divan, hands behind her head and ankles crossed, while he started to put his clothes on.

'If you'd arrived ten minutes before you did,' she said suddenly, 'you'd have found me giving myself a thrill.'

'A pleasure I am sorry I missed – can we arrange it for another day?'

'What's wrong with today?' she asked. 'Or aren't you interested now you've had what you wanted?'

Gerhart paused, his trousers on but unbuttoned, about to pull his shirt over his head. Ruth uncrossed her ankles and ran her fingers through the dark brown mat of hair between her legs.

'Would you really show me?' he asked.

He dropped his shirt and sat on the bed near her, wearing only his trousers.

'Then you are still interested?' she said, 'I thought you were a one-shot man like my husband.'

'It's not that – I thought you might have had enough, Ruth.'

'Some days I play with myself three or four times,' she said.

She drew her knees up and spread them apart, to give him a full and unimpeded view of her bushy mound.

'Did you like being inside it?' she asked. 'You stayed there long enough.'

'It felt very nice – warm and clinging.'

She parted the wet lips under the brown hair and slid two fingers inside. Her eyes closed as she began to stroke herself in a short and rhythmic motion that quickly had Gerhart's stem standing upright in his trousers.

215

'You should know,' she sighed, 'I'm sure you've been inside plenty of them, young as you are. Tell me something exciting.'

Gerhart was entranced by the spectacle and very willing to oblige.

'You're on a tram at night,' he said, 'and it's very crowded – you're squeezed in tight between people you can't see properly and they're touching your little bundles and feeling your bottom.'

'Oh, yes!' Ruth said softly. 'They'll rip my clothes off in a minute.'

The tram dream was Erna's fantasy, Gerhart had realised, though not entirely a fantasy, as she sought out crowded trams wearing only a thin summer frock and nothing on under it. She must have related it to Ruth when they had been drugged together, or perhaps they had played out the fantasy together in this room, standing up in the dark.

'There are hands all over your body, Ruth – they've pulled your frock off and your knickers. They're feeling you between the thighs.'

He was very aroused himself. His spike thrust out of his unbuttoned trousers and quivered.

'My God – there's a hand right up inside me!' Ruth gasped. 'It's too much! It's going to make me . . .'

There was no question of taking twenty minutes to reach her goal this time. The evocation of her dream brought her to a quick climax and, while her belly was quaking and she was gasping out her passion, Gerhart was on her, still wearing his trousers. He pulled her flickering hand away and embedded himself in her very wet depths with a strong push. She squirmed under him as he pounded hard at her thin body and discharged his frantic emotions into her with a loud cry.

Later on he said again that he really must go now, and she nodded and smiled.

'But come back,' she said, 'I'm always at home in the afternoons during the week when Karl is at work.'

'I shan't forget,' he said, pulling his clothes on.

He thought it unlikely that he would see her again. A quick and unexpected roll on the bed was amusing, but more than that might become boring. Ruth was hardly his type, apart from being too old.

'And I shan't forget you in a hurry, Gerhart. Do you know why?'

'Tell me.'

'You've made me see that my tram dream is better than any film-star. The next time I give myself a thrill I shall be thinking about that.'

'So Emil Jannings has lost a fan!' said Gerhart, laughing.

Chapter 19

Gerhart visits a sick friend

They sat on opposite sides of the modernistic glass desk and looked at each other solemnly, Gerhart and Rudolf Knuppel. Rudolf was wearing a mauve tie with a grey suit, and it was tied badly, as if he had been thinking of something else when he dressed that morning. When he spoke, it was with an attempt at cheerfulness that failed to convince.

'I'm very grateful to you for what you did, Gerhart. Otherwise it might have been days before I found out what happened to Erna.'

'How is she now?'

'She came out of hospital yesterday and she is staying with me. She's still weak and confused, of course. It will be some time before she recovers fully.'

He paused for a moment or two and then thumped a fist down on to the glass desk-top, a gesture which looked painful to Gerhart.

'I blame myself,' Rudolf exclaimed.

'But why? You were not there. It was Erna's own decision.'

'I know that,' and Rudolf rumpled his sleeked back hair with a nervous hand, 'but I still feel responsible. Erna came here as a secretary a year or two ago – did you know that? Naturally, I soon saw that she was a woman of superior talent and promoted her.'

Her superior talent as a playmate, Gerhart thought.

'She and I work very closely together,' Rudolf continued. 'She understands my philosophy of freedom of self-expression and from the first she has been deeply interested in my dramas of the spirit.'

'To judge by the one I attended,' said Gerhart, 'her interest in your drama was phenomenal.'

'Yes, the night of the hyaena! That was truly extraordinary. I was most impressed by the enthusiasm you brought to the drama. I am certain that you experienced a total catharsis that night. It was my intention to invite you to be a permanent member of our little circle, but in the circumstances I cannot say when we shall resume.'

Catharsis – that's a new word for it, Gerhart thought, suppressing his amusement in case he offended Rudolf.

'Things have gone very wrong,' said Rudolf, lighting a sweet-smelling Turkish cigarette, 'I am forced to the conclusion that Erna does not really understand what I am trying to achieve.'

'I think she understands very well your aim,' said Gerhart, 'but perhaps she has got a step ahead of you.'

'No, that's not right. The fact is that Erna's education was neglected when she was young and therefore the subtleties of my philosophy have completely eluded her. She doesn't grasp the distinction between self-expression and self-annihilation. It is a mercy that she didn't accidently kill herself in her unguided experiments into new levels of awareness.'

'Thank God for that,' said Gerhart. 'What will you do now?'

'It is too early to say. I shall look after her until she is well again. After that I must talk to her and see what conclusions we reach.'

He was spilling cigarette ash over the glass top of his desk in an absent-minded way. Gerhart pushed a stainless-steel ash-tray towards him.

'Enough of that,' said Rudolf, 'I must not bore you with my problems. What progress are you making on the illustrations for *Venus in Furs*? Will the work come to a standstill now that Erna cannot pose for you?'

'No, I've enough pencil sketches of her face and body to complete the pictures without her. But as things are, do you still want your Wanda to look like Erna?'

'What a strange question! Of course Wanda must be Erna. Are you sure that you can continue?'

219

'Oh, yes, she came to my studio and I made a dozen or so little drawings to use as references.'

'Even so, I shall be surprised if you can produce what I am hoping for from you,' Rudolf said mournfully, 'sketches are useful, but they cannot give you the inner tensions your pictures should contain.'

'What do you mean by inner tensions?'

'As you know, Erna is a thin woman with smallish breasts and narrow hips. She is not beautiful, in the classic sense of the word. But she has an inner quality that transcends the merely physical. When she is naked I find her the most exciting woman I have ever known. Does that surprise you?'

'Not at all,' Gerhart answered, 'I've made love to really beautiful girls who turned out to be boring, and I was glad when it was over. Erna has a sensuality that is independent of her looks.'

'You do understand,' Rudolf said with a sigh, 'I hope fervently that she will recover that inner sensuality. At present she is like a sick old woman. It is essential that you immortalise her the way she used to be in your pictures, in case that glowing sexual spirituality has gone forever.'

'My God – is she that ill?' Gerhart exclaimed in dismay.

Rudolf shook his head to indicate that he feared the worst.

'I shall work very hard to make sure the pictures show her as we remember her,' Gerhart promised. 'Another ten days or two weeks and you shall have them.'

'I wish you had brought what you've done so far for me to see. Not that I doubt your ability, but just to make certain that we're thinking along the same lines.'

'That would be far from simple,' said Gerhart, not at all pleased by the suggestion, 'they're in different stages of progress. You could see all I've done so far at my studio.'

'Excellent! Would tomorrow at about five be convenient?'

'I shall expect you,' and Gerhart stood up to leave.

'One thing,' he added, 'is it possible to visit Erna? I'd like to take her some flowers and wish her well.'

'As long as you don't stay too long and tire her. I've engaged a house-keeper to look after her and cook meals for her while I'm out. I'll tell her to expect you. When do you want to go?'

'After lunch today is as good as any other time.'

'Her name is Frau Hollweg. I'll telephone her. Please don't say anything that will upset Erna – she needs absolute rest and calm.'

It was with some apprehension that Gerhart presented himself at Rudolf's apartment that afternoon. A middle-aged woman in a plain brown frock opened the door and admitted him when he told her his name. She led him to a bedroom he had seen before, the one with the sheepskin, now no longer on the bed but on the floor beside it as a rug.

Erna lay on the bed, her eyes open and staring at the ceiling. She was wearing black silk pyjamas, which emphasised the pallor of her cheeks, and her lack of make-up and missing eyebrows gave her face a naked appearance.

'Here's a visitor for you, Fraulein Erna,' the house-keeper said with great cheerfulness, 'and he's brought you these wonderful chrysanthemums. You must cover yourself up – you might catch cold like that.'

'Gerhart – I'm so pleased to see you!' said Erna, ignoring the other woman, 'bring a chair and sit down.'

'Let me put something over you,' Frau Hollweg suggested primly.

'No, it's very warm today.'

'Very well. I'll put the flowers in water and squeeze a lemon to make you a cold drink if you're so hot.'

Gerhart brought a chair close to the bed and, when the house-keeper had gone, kissed Erna on both cheeks. She was pale, but she did not look like the sick old lady of Rudolf's description.

'I thought you had one foot in the grave,' he said with a smile.

'I'm perfectly all right now, but Rudolf has made his mind up that I'm an invalid getting over a serious illness.'

'He's feeling guilty, that's why.'

'I know, and because of that I have to lie here all day and be bored out of my mind by that woman fussing over me. She means well, but she treats me like a sick child.'

'So make a dramatic recovery,' Gerhart suggested.

'I'm going to, believe me! But Rudolf has been so good to me that the least I can do for him is to act in his little game for a while, if it helps him to treat me as a dying swan.'

'That's not the usual way between you and him. I remember you in a shiny black top hat and red knickers and Rudolf down on his knees playing at being a leopard. That's what you both prefer, isn't it?'

'This sickness game isn't going to last much longer,' said Erna with a broad grin, 'I'll give it till tomorrow and that's all the guilt he's entitled to. I'll have Frau Hollweg out of the apartment and Rudolf stripped off with a pink ribbon tied in bow round his tail and licking my feet. That will get rid of his guilt.'

'Perhaps I should have a pink bow round my tail too,' said Gerhart. 'You see, I blame myself for what happened. If I hadn't brought that idiot Glotz to your apartment, none of this would have happened.'

'It wasn't your fault. I wanted to see how far I could go into hallucination and I overdid it and woke up in hospital. Guilt doesn't suit you – you're not Rudolf.'

Frau Hollweg came back with the flowers in a vase and set them on the cabinet beside the bed.

'Aren't they lovely?' she asked, 'I'll make your lemonade now if you're still hot.'

'Open the window – that will cool the room. You can leave the lemonade for later.'

When the house-keeper had gone, Erna gave Gerhart her sideways grin.

'Chrysanthemums! I knew you weren't feeling guilty.'

Gerhart laughed and patted her hand.

'By the way – what happened to your friend after I passed out?' she asked.

'The police found him strolling about with no clothes on and arrested him. Your former landlord is proposing to blackmail him for breaking up his furniture. From what I've heard elsewhere his wife is threatening to leave him. All things considered, his night of love turned out differently from what was expected.'

Erna laughed and said that she felt sorry for Maximilian.

'I don't!' said Gerhart, 'Frau Leppman found you tied up with a stocking – what on earth were you up to?'

'This will amuse you – I can't remember a thing! But it sounds as if we were having an interesting time when I passed out. I hope he did some wonderfully obscene things to me, so I've something to look forward to when I start remembering.'

'That's not the point, Erna. He didn't know what he was doing, any more than you did. He might have strung you up by the neck instead of the wrists.'

'Then I'd be dead and my troubles would be over.'

'That's a silly thing to say. You're young and attractive and clever – you have everything to live for.'

'But what a way to die!' she said, grinning at his disapproval. 'Strangled by a silk stocking while a stranger rams his spike up your behind!'

'Is that what he did?' Gerhart asked in disbelief.

'Now why did I say that?' she said thoughtfully. 'You jogged my memory for a second and that's what came into my mind. He must have been doing it when I blacked out. Well, well – a harmless little man like that! You never know what people are capable of until they let themselves go. Look at you, for instance – silky blonde hair and an innocent face – the sort of polite young man the most suspicious mother would trust to take her virgin daughter out for an evening. Yet every time you get your hands on me you turn into a violent rapist.'

'Because you want me to,' Gerhart countered. 'And the same with Rudolf – a plump middle-aged intellectual who turns into a leopard and ravishes helpless girls on his own sitting-room floor.'

'Damn Rudolf!' Erna said unexpectedly, 'I've been lying here since they let me out of hospital, day and night, and he's never touched me once.'

'But you've been ill.'

'As if that makes any difference! It's because when he feels guilty his tail won't stand up. Just wait till I get that top hat on and the whip in my hand – I'll make it stand up for him!'

She unbuttoned her black pyjama jacket and showed Gerhart her slack little breasts.

'Play with them a little,' she suggested.

223

'And have Frau Hollweg barging in with the lemonade?'

'Damn her too,' said Erna, tickling the buds of her breasts expertly, 'there'll be plenty of time to make myself decent when we hear the tray rattling outside.'

'Erna, is this sensible?' Gerhart asked, leaning forward to stroke her breasts.

'Yes, it's the only thing that will bring me back to life again. How would you like it if you had to lie in bed all day with no one to talk to and no one to play with? Your tail would be standing up like a tent-pole.'

'It's doing that now,' he said, delighted by the warm feel of her flesh.

'If you'd been lying here instead of me, you'd have jumped on Frau Hollweg long before now.'

'I might get desperate, but not that desperate. She must be fifty.'

'That's what you think because you haven't been deprived. If you were alone with her all day you'd drag her on to the bed and ravage her. I'm sure you noticed the size of her bouncers – that's the sort of thing you always notice.'

'Her hair's going grey,' said Gerhart.

His fingers were rolling the buds of Erna's breasts and he was thinking of how Frau Hollweg might look without her clothes on.

'What difference does that make?' Erna asked, 'I've seen you in action out there in the sitting-room and I know you're a rapist at heart.'

'I had a lot to drink that night – and you provoked me.'

'It was wonderful,' Erna whispered, 'you in that animal mask so I couldn't see your face – just the fangs and your tail. You raped me so furiously that I fell in love with you on the spot.'

'The first time or the second time?'

'Both times.'

The sound of foot-steps outside the door made Gerhart jerk his hands away from her. Erna had the three buttons of her jacket done up before Frau Hollweg came in with two glasses on a silver tray.

'There you are,' she said, 'fresh cold lemonade.'

224

She put the tray down and plumped up the pillows behind Erna's back.

'The colour's coming back to your cheeks,' she said, 'Herr Knuppel *will* be pleased! You'll be able to get up for an hour or two tomorrow.'

Gerhart and Erna grinned at each other as the house-keeper went out and closed the door behind her.

'Your face *is* a bit pink,' said Gerhart.

'And so it should be – you've got me excited. Put that glass down and get on the bed with me.'

'Too risky. If she sees anything and tells Rudolf, there'll be trouble.'

'I can't stop halfway – you'll have to do something.'

She pushed her pyjama trousers down to her ankles and smiled at him. Gerhart put his glass on the cabinet and leaned forward to stroke her soft belly and down towards the brown hair between her legs.

'What a pretty chrysanthemum,' he said softly, 'golden brown and beautiful!'

'You're the expert on flowers,' she answered, 'I've just remembered something – the last time we met and we were standing in the dark together in the Leppman's apartment, you promised to tell me about a certain rose-bud.'

'I don't remember any such thing,' Gerhart lied.

'Yes, you do. I was playing with your tail and you were feeling my chrysanthemum.'

'You mean the flower-painting you saw in my studio?'

'I mean your sister Sieglinde.'

Gerhart caressed the fleshy lips between Erna's thighs to distract her from this line of enquiry.

'Is that nice?' he asked.

'You know very well it's nice . . . listen, you don't have to be shy with me about Sieglinde. I grew up in a very poor family with three brothers and two sisters sleeping in the same room. The boys used to show us their little tails standing up, and we showed them our little slits, long before there was any hair on them.'

'What naughty children you were,' said Gerhart, and she

225

giggled and her hips squirmed on the bed as her excitement grew.

'How many girls do you know who've had three different tails in them night after night?' she whispered.

'What? You can't mean . . .'

'By the time I was sixteen my brothers were doing it to me every night of the week, and to Anni.'

'And did you enjoy it?' Gerhart asked in curiosity.

'I enjoyed it so much that I often wished I had six brothers,' she gasped.

'Dear Erna . . . I think you're about to go off like a little bomb.'

He was right about that. Her fists clenched and she writhed in a brief climax.

'You've saved my life, Gerhart,' she said slowly, grinning at him.

'That's what friends are for,' he answered lightly, hoping that she would not pursue her previous line of questioning. But in that he was too optimistic.

'Now you know my childhood secrets,' she said, stretching lazily. 'Did I shock you?'

'You surprised me. You ran a terrible risk – you might have become pregnant.'

'Of course I did – and so did Anni. It was a foregone conclusion, when you think about it.'

'Good God – what did your parents say?'

'They thought we'd been with boys outside, and we never told them different. The two of us got a hiding from father, and that was the end of it.'

'How could it be, if you were pregnant?'

'You really don't understand, do you? You grew up in a different world. Where we lived, girls got pregnant all the time. Nobody gave it a second thought. Anni and I had our babies about three weeks apart and they were just another part of the family.'

'Now you have surprised me! I had no idea these things could be so casual. With the people I grew up among, a young girl becoming pregnant would have been a catastrophe for her family. What happened to the baby?'

'He's nearly twelve now and he lives with my mother. He

thinks that she's his mother. So does Anni's boy.'

'That's amazing!'

'No, it's just part of life. You don't think Anni and I are the only ones, do you? It happens all the time – brothers and sisters, fathers and daughters – and nobody gives a damn if you're poor. It's different for your lot.'

'And in spite of this catastrophe as a child, you've climbed out of what sounds like a very depressing background. What about your sister?'

'She got married at eighteen and lives in the same old neighbourhood. She's got four children now, not counting the one with mother.'

'And your brothers?'

'All married and settled down. They're good-hearted, but a bit stupid.'

'You were the only one with ambition?'

'If that's what you want to call it,' she replied, grinning wryly. 'You don't have to be bashful when I ask you about the rose-bud, do you?'

'It's not a question of being bashful. Whatever you may think, the truth is that I've never made love to Sieglinde.'

'You expect me to believe that, after seeing your picture?'

Gerhart got up from his chair, very uneasy, and went to look out of the open window.

'I'm not saying there haven't been times when I wanted to,' he said, his back to Erna. 'But I never have.'

'You've done it to the other two flowers,' she insisted. 'Why is her picture there with them if you've not done it to her? Tell me that.'

'Erna, I must go. It's been nice to see you and I'm glad you're better.'

She was off the bed at once and across the room to stand beside him, her arm round his waist as they stared out of the window.

'I'm sorry, Gerhart,' she said hastily, 'I didn't mean to offend you – it was only teasing. Don't leave yet – I'm lonely here all day with only that woman to fuss round me. And your visit has done me so much good that tomorrow I'll be up and ready to

227

give Rudolf the surprise of his life when he gets back from his office.'

'You'll tie a pink ribbon round his clapper?'

'Yes, in a big bow, like a present. I'll make him lie on the floor while I walk bare-foot on him – that should get him going! I'll wear him out all night and he won't get to his office the next day – not that he'll get much rest here with me.'

Rudolf's apartment was in a quiet residential street, away from the main thoroughfare, and in mid-afternoon there were few people about. A man went past swinging a walking-stick in a jaunty fashion, and raised his hat to a woman walking slowly the other way, holding a little girl by the hand. A black car turned into the street and drove past to park some way down the road. A fat man got out and went into the next building. An old lady in a long shiny black summer-coat of the sort not seen for twenty years strolled along on the opposite side of the street with a dachshund on a leash. Erna's fingers had opened Gerhart's trouser-buttons and were fondling his stem.

'Do you know,' she said thoughtfully, 'we haven't known each other very long, but you're the only friend I can rely on.'

'But I'm not at all reliable, Erna!'

'But you are. Your tail stands up whenever I touch it – what could be more reliable than that?'

She had it out of his trousers and was stroking it.

'By the way,' she said, 'Ruth Leppman sent me a note with my clothes. She wants me to visit her when I get the chance, even though her husband threw me out. We're good friends, you know.'

'She seemed a very pleasant woman,' Gerhart murmured.

'She mentioned you in the note,' Erna informed him, grinning wickedly.

'What did she say?'

'She asked me to remind you when we met that she's home most afternoons. What was it like, making love to her?'

'Nothing out of the ordinary,' he sighed, his spike trembling in Erna's hand.

'This busy thing of yours did its business in Ruth and all you can say is that it was ordinary?'

228

'Perhaps not exactly ordinary . . . she told me about a dream she often has – she dreams she's on a tram and it's dark and there are dozens of hands feeling her . . .'

'Oh!' said Erna, as if remembering something unexpected.

'But all that Ruth does is lie on her back and wait for it to happen to her . . . I'm used to more excitement than that with you, Erna.'

'If it's excitement you want, you shall have it!' and she let go of him to slide her black pyjamas down her thighs and turn to lean forward with her fore-arms along the window-sill.

'Come on!' she said, 'if we hear the warder at the door there'll be time to do your trousers up.'

Gerhart was so aroused that the temptation overcame all apprehension of discovery. He stood close behind Erna and fondled the smooth cheeks of the bottom thrust towards him by her position. She turned her head to look at him over her shoulder.

'Put it in me,' she said, 'like your friend Max did.'

Gerhart's hand was between her open thighs to play with her chrysanthemum.

'This is good enough for me,' he gasped, and pushed his hard stem into her moist flower, 'you'll have to invite Max round if you want the other!'

'Oh, my God!' she exclaimed, 'I'd forgotten how nice it feels.'

He took her by the hips in a firm grasp and pressed himself to her bare bottom while he slide in and out, staring at the black silk that covered her back.

'You make it sound like years,' he sighed. 'It's only been a day or two.'

'Too long . . . even one day without is too long . . . you really enjoy doing it to me, don't you?'

Gerhart lay forward on her back and slipped his hands up inside her loose pyjama jacket to fondle her breasts.

'Yes, it's good with you, Erna – you don't pretend and I don't have to pretend.'

'I never pretend,' she murmured, her bottom making little jerking movements against him.

'I love you for that!'

'Then tell me the truth – have you done this to Sieglinde?'

229

He was too lost in sensation to be upset by the question.

'Never,' he murmured.

'Even though you want to?'

'Never!' he repeated, stabbing harder into her as his excitement rose towards its peak.

'But you've played with her – I can tell that from your painting.'

'Yes!' he gasped, his normal caution overwhelmed by his arousal.

'Gerhart!' she exclaimed, her voice high-pitched and strained, and her bottom thumped against him as she dissolved into ecstatic pleasure.

'Don't stop!' she gasped. 'Make me do it again!'

These frantic moments were brusquely interrupted by a sharp tap at the bedroom door. Gerhart pulled away from Erna and she, equally startled, stood upright and hauled up her pyjama trousers as she walked slowly towards the door to give him time to make himself decent. Gerhart stepped close to the window, fumbling to tuck his quivering pointer into his underwear and do up his buttons. His heart was pounding in his chest and there was a roaring in his ears, through which he heard Frau Hollweg's voice behind his back, sounding as if she were very far away. Then outraged nature asserted itself as he fastened the last button and his legs shook beneath him as he discharged his passion into his underwear.

He was leaning with both hands on the window-sill, breathing heavily, when Erna came back to him, grinning widely. She ran a hand over the bulge in his trousers.

'My poor Gerhart – I could hear you wheezing right across the room while I was talking to that silly woman and I guessed what was happening. It was all I could do to keep from laughing in her face.'

'I'd just got my buttons done up when I went off like a firework,' said Gerhart, surprise and regret in his voice. 'Did she suspect anything?'

'Who cares? She'll be gone tomorrow, I'll see to that.'

'What did she want?'

'That's the joke of it! She came to say that she was going for a walk in the sunshine because it was all right to leave me while I'd got a visitor to sit and talk to me.'

'Damn the woman!' said Gerhart. 'If she'd said that ten minutes ago I wouldn't have had an accident in my trousers. Has she gone? I must get my wet underwear off.'

Erna took her hand from his bulge and waved out of the open window.

'Is that her?' he asked, dropping his trousers.

'No – look across the street, on the third floor. You see that woman at the window? She's been watching us. I spotted her when I bent over for you. She's seen everything.'

'Why didn't you say something before?' Gerhart demanded in dismay.

'She's probably on her own too. I thought we'd give her a little treat. I'm sure she's got her hand up her skirt.'

Gerhart laughed and stepped out of his underpants.

'Come away from the window,' he said, 'I've been cheated by Frau Hollweg and I'm going to make up for it before she gets back.'

They stripped naked and lay on the bed together. Erna fondled his limp stem, waiting for it to regain its vigour.

'I've just had a very amusing idea,' she announced. 'Sit up.'

Gerhart sat up and she folded her black pyjama trousers into a long strip and tied it round his face to blindfold him.

'Can you see anything at all?' she whispered.

'Nothing.'

'Good – lie down on your back.'

He felt her finger-tips trailing over his body, from his chest down to his belly and then between his legs. His own groping hand found her breasts.

'How often have you played with the rose-bud?' she asked, so softly that he could only just hear her words through the black silk that covered his ears as well as his eyes.

'You tricked me into saying that,' he murmured.

'You wanted to tell me because you know I understand,' he heard, and he felt the sharp nip of her finger-nails on the flesh of his stem.

Her hand gripped his wrist and pulled his hand down between her thighs.

'You were cheated,' he heard, in a voice so indistinct that it could have been anybody's. 'You wanted to do it in there, but circumstances made you do it in your trousers. Just like you want to do it in Sieglinde.'

Gerhart's fingers moved ferveriously inside a warm and wet opening and his stem was up to full-stretch.

'Sieglinde is playing with your tail,' her voice murmured, 'and it's so hard and strong again.'

In his world of darkness Gerhart's senses were reeling.

'Put it inside her,' a voice whispered beside his ear, 'you know that you want to. I won't tell anyone.'

'I can't!' he moaned.

'You can do anything to it that you want.'

Gerhart pressed the warm body he was holding down on to the bed and scrambled on to it. A hand held his tail firmly and guided it to the right place, a shuddering push took it deep inside.

'That's it!' the voice by his ear whispered, with a little note of triumph that was lost on him. 'You're doing it to Sieglinde's rose-bud!'

He didn't hear her. Blindfolded and lost in his own world of wish-fulfilment, he was thrusting into her with an abandon that was almost hysterical in its intensity.

Chapter 20

Gerhart discovers the unusual arts of the Chinese

However ridiculous he thought Heinz's devotion to his tattooed friend, it was inevitable that Gerhart would want to view her himself after Heinz brought photographs to show him. Not that the photographs were at all appealing – they had been taken in poor light and were, to say the least of it, dark and shadowy.

One of them displayed the naked torso of a full-bodied woman from knees to shoulders, and she was sitting on what looked like the side of a bed, with her legs close together. She was wide of hip and full-bosomed, though her breasts were starting to droop. The whole front of her body was covered with markings, but the amateur photography lost all the detail and made her look merely blotchy. In the other picture she was standing with her back to the camera, again cut off at the level of knees and neck, and this was worse than the first photograph. Her broad back and the big fleshy cheeks of her bottom were covered in dark tracery, but it was impossible to make it out clearly.

Disappointing though the pictures were, and totally inadequate to explain Heinz's enthusiasm, they worked powerfully on Gerhart's imagination and he asked for her address. Without commitment, he told Heinz, who only laughed and said 'Maybe'.

Heinz had said that Frau Bucholz was twenty-eight and beautiful, but neither statement was, in Gerhart's opinion, true. She was five or six years older than that, and plain. She had a square face and a very broad mouth and her nondescript brown hair was pulled tight back over her head and held in a bun at the back. If any of that had been shown on the photographs, Gerhart doubted whether he would have troubled to visit her.

At the door she stared blankly at him until he raised his hat and told her his name.

'You're Heinz's friend – the one who's going to paint my picture?'

Gerhart confirmed that he was a friend of Heinz and was invited into her apartment. Somewhat to his surprise, after seeing the apartment of Lenchen and Gretchen, he saw that this one was clean and tidy, and the chair she offered him was comfortable. She sat down and crossed her legs, and he noticed that she wore thick beige stockings under her plain black skirt.

'When do you want to start?' she asked, unsmiling.

'You're going too fast, Frau Bucholz,' said Gerhart, by no means pleased by her attitude. 'As an artist I thought that I might find a certain interest in what Herr Graunach described to me as a fine example of tattooing. But to be frank with you, it is curiosity rather than artistic interest that has brought me to see you.'

'Will you sell the picture?' she asked, frowning at his words.

'If I ever paint it I shall give it to Herr Graunach in place of his terrible photographs of you.'

'As a present, you mean? But if you sold it we could both make money. It might be worth a lot, if you're any good as an artist.'

'I have enough work at present to keep me busy and I'm not looking for more. I came here out of regard for a friend.'

'Have you been friends for long?'

'Years.'

'Then you must know his other friends. Have you met Gretchen and Lenchen?'

'I have made their acquaintance,' he answered shortly.

'Too much for you, are they?' she said, smiling for the first time, 'They're big girls, those two. Still, Heinz likes them.'

Gerhart was struck by the absurdity of the conversation. For no reason at all he was excusing himself to a woman who took

234

money to go to bed with men – or at least with Heinz. To remain as polite as if he were talking to a young lady of good family was unnecessary and demeaning.

'He took me to their apartment once,' he said, grinning at Frau Bucholz in a familiar way, 'one of them mauled me about. It was no pleasure to meet them.'

'They've changed, you know,' she said thoughtfully. 'At one time they'd only go with heavy-weight boxers and circus strong-men. But since they've taken up with Heinz they're crazy about young men they can throw about. Did you have them both?'

'One of them had me – I think it was Lenchen. They look so much alike without their clothes that I couldn't be sure.'

'So they should. They're half-sisters. Their father was the Great Fritz, the world's strongest man – maybe you've heard of him.'

Gerhart shook his head, fascinated by what she was saying.

'Fritz was the greatest,' said Frau Bucholz, 'in his prime he could bend iron bars round his neck and lift ten men on a plank. He had every woman in the circus. You've met two of his daughters – he had eighteen children by at least a dozen women.'

From the affection in her voice Gerhart concluded that she too had been a recipient of the Great Fritz' favours at some time in the past.

'But Lenchen and Gretchen had different mothers?' he asked.

'That's right. One was a lion-tamer's wife and the other was a trapeze artist.'

'And now Heinz has transferred his affections to you while the girls are on tour.'

It was absurd to call Gretchen and Lenchen *girls* and he grinned as he said it. Frau Bucholz favoured him with a brief smile of her own.

'He comes round here for his fun,' she agreed, 'but I'm not a whore.'

'Certainly not. Heinz has always been attracted to rare and unusual women.'

'Rare and unusual – I like that, it's nice. Did he tell you how unusual I am?'

'Not in any detail.'

'You've seen the photographs he took of me, though, so you've got some idea.'

'They did not do you justice.'

The thought in his mind was that, wearing thick stockings and a high-necked blouse, Frau Bucholz was showing only her face and hands. Neither was worth a second look, her face being too square and her fingers stubby.

'I told him they wouldn't be any good when he took them,' she said, 'but his heart was set on it.'

She fiddled with the top button of her blouse, drawing Gerhart's attention to it and the heavy bosom lower down, but she didn't undo it.

'If you ask me,' she continued after a thoughtful pause, 'I'm the only one who gets nothing out of this painting you're going to do.'

'How do you mean?'

'Heinz gets the picture, you get the pleasure of studying me without my clothes on – and I get nothing. Even though I'm the one with something to show.'

'Put that way, it does sound unjust,' said Gerhart, smiling at her open greed, 'let me make a suggestion. So that I can decide whether I want to paint you or not, show me your wonderful pictures and I'll give you whatever you think is reasonable.'

'A hundred Marks,' she said, so rapidly that he could not help but laugh.

'Strip off,' he said, reaching for his money. 'Show me your marvels.'

Frau Bucholz took the money with a disappointed look, realising too late that she could have asked for more.

'I'll go and get myself ready,' she told him, 'stay here till I call you.'

Left to himself Gerhart wondered what Heinz found to like about this woman. Her manner was ungracious, her nature grasping, and by no stretch of imagination could she be thought physically appealing. But the same was true of the wrestling sisters, he thought. Heinz was perverse, there was no other explanation.

After a while he heard Frau Bucholz call 'You can come in now' and he found his way to the bedroom, leaving the door open in case it became prudent to make a fast retreat. He saw that she had undressed and dumped her clothes over a chair. At least she was standing up, which he considered a good sign, and she was wearing a long dressing-gown of dark green, holding it closely across her body with her folded arms.

'You can sit on the chair,' she said. 'No funny tricks now!'

'You need have no fear of that,' he answered tartly, 'I am an artist and I shall look at you as if you were a landscape.'

He sat on the chair over which her clothes were draped, there being no other, crossed his legs and leaned back with deliberate nonchalance. Frau Bucholz waited until he was settled and then turned her back to him. She shrugged her shoulders out of the dressing-gown and let it slide down her body to the floor. In the small room, much of which was taken up by a high, old-fashioned bed, she was close enough for Gerhart to reach out and touch, if he had been so minded.

His casual manner vanished at the sight of her back.

'My God!' he exclaimed. 'It's incredible!'

Her whole body was a colourful riot of reds, greens and blues. From each of her ankles the snake-like body of some fabulous monster wound its way up each leg, to vanish from sight at the level of her hips. Out of the crease between the cheeks of her rump the twisted trunk of a tree grew up her back, to spread out in a profusion of branches and foliage and clusters of little red fruit. Tiny coloured birds sat among the foliage with open beaks, as if singing. Her arms, hanging at her sides, had grape-vine tendrils and leaves spiralling down from her shoulders to her wrists.

'But this is a stupendous work of art!' said Gerhart, filled with admiration for the skill and precision – and the imagination – of the man who had created it. 'You are a living masterpiece, Frau Bucholz!'

'My friends call me Mina,' she said, sounding more friendly at his praise. 'Can you see the two little love-birds together under my right shoulder-blade?'

237

Gerhart scanned the vastly detailed picture until he found them.

'They're mating!' he said with a chuckle.

While he stared, Mina pressed her hands together in front of her and made her muscles ripple. It was as if a light breeze passed through the tree, shaking its green leaves and making the tiny birds' wings flutter.

'Fantastic!' said Gerhart, delighted by the effect.

'Shall I turn round now?'

'Do, please.'

She shuffled round on her bare feet until she faced him, and he was dumbfounded by what he saw. The scaly tails that spiralled up her legs belonged to two dragons, their spike-backed bodies shown upright on her belly, facing each other with clawed legs reaching out in menace towards each other. Their heads, with open jaws displaying needle-sharp fangs and pointed red tongues, were on her big and sagging breasts, so placed that each red-brown nipple formed the centre of the eye of the green and blue heads.

'What artistry!' Gerhart sighed.

'You like it then?'

'I'm speechless with admiration.'

'So you'll paint me?'

'That's another matter,' he said seriously, 'you're asking me to copy the work of a master. To be truthful, I'm not sure that I have the skill to do it.'

'If a little Chinese who couldn't speak four words of German could put this on me, it can't be much of a problem for a trained artist like you to copy it,' she retorted.

'Your little Chinese is a genius. Do you know where I can find him?'

'He drank himself to death years ago.'

Gerhart's intense admiration of Mina's tattooing had driven from his mind the interest that was usually uppermost when he contemplated a naked woman. But he remembered that Heinz had told him that she was tattooed everywhere, especially *there*, and he looked to see. Only then did he notice that she wore a small pouch of soft black leather between her legs, kept in place by a thin elastic string round her hips.

'I haven't yet seen the final master-piece,' he said, grinning at her.

'You have to be a very special friend before you see that,' she answered in a matter-of-fact tone.

'Like Heinz, you mean?'

'Are you going to paint me or not?'

'I would like nothing better, Mina, but I don't know if I dare even try.'

'Heinz took photographs of me – he didn't dither about like you.'

'They weren't very good,' he reminded her, 'the lighting was bad and the focus was wrong.'

'That doesn't matter. At least he got on with it.'

'But taking photographs is easy. You don't understand what you are asking from me.'

'Only a painting, that's all.'

'Weeks of work,' he said, gesturing at her body. 'First I would have to make detailed sketches of you, bit by bit, and then assemble them into the basis of a finished work. The colour-matching alone would take several days.'

'What you need is a bit of encouraging,' said Mina.

She turned away from him and he saw her beautiful bird-filled tree shake as she pushed the elastic down her legs and let her pouch fall to the floor. When she turned back to face him she had one open hand over whatever lay between her thighs.

'Only very special friends see this,' she told him, 'but I'm making an exception for you. You can think yourself lucky.'

'Perhaps I shall become a special friend,' he said, smiling now that events seemed to be progressing away from the question of painting her towards something less controversial.

'That's up to you,' she said, moving her feet apart.

She took her hand away and revealed another work of art which made Gerhart utter a long sigh. Between her legs she was smooth and hairless and on this interesting part of her body there was tattooed in exquisite detail a little Chinese pavilion. It had a red-tiled roof that turned up at the corners, set on tiny green and blue spiral pillars, above steps that led up to closed double doors.

'This is amazing!' he said, 'your Chinese friend was a true genius! What imagination – and what skill to carry out his design in so small a place!'

'It's nice, isn't it?' Mina said carelessly. 'Mind you, I went through agony while he was doing it. I was so swollen and sore between the legs that I couldn't walk for days. And I wouldn't let a man touch me for months afterwards.'

She sat on the side of the bed, her thighs together to hide her pavilion, in the pose Gerhart recalled from Heinz' photographs of her.

'You'll never guess what he called it, that Chang,' she said.

'He gave it a name?'

'He called it the Temple of the Six Harmonies. What do you think of that?'

'What did he mean?'

'I don't know – it's something Chinese. But it sounded nice and I've never forgotten it.'

'And did Herr Chang find the six harmonies in your little temple?'

'He used to go with boys,' she said. 'Want another look?'

She put her hands on the bed behind her and lowered herself backwards until she was lying flat, her legs dangling over the edge, her feet off the floor. Gerhart watched and was enchanted by the way she parted her thighs slowly to show him the colourful little pavilion again.

'Go on,' she said casually, 'have a good look.'

He got up from the chair and stood between her knees to stare down at Chang's work. Mina's legs slid further apart and the double doors of the pavilion opened a little to show a pink interior.

'Fantastic,' he said softly, 'utterly fantastic.'

'That's more like it,' Mina said, a note of satisfaction in her voice suddenly, 'I've opened the doors for you – I can't do more than that. Do you want to go in and try it, or not?'

As if, at such a moment, there could be any doubt as to what Gerhart wanted! His tail was hard in his trousers and, as he undid his buttons, he said with a broad grin that he knew very well what he would find in the pavilion.

'That's what you think,' she told him.

He stepped close to the high bed and brought his stem to the doors that were ajar for him, then pushed hard inside. Mina's legs clamped round his hips to hold him secure.

'Watch the dragons dance,' she said.

She clenched and unclenched the muscles of her broad belly, and the opposed dragons on it rippled with sudden movement, their claws seeming to reach towards each other.

'Do it again!' Gerhart exclaimed in delight.

'You can make them dance yourself – you know how to do it.'

He put his hands on her hips and plunged experimentally a few times. His thrusts made her belly wobble and set the dragons stirring.

'Wonderful, wonderful!' he gasped.

When he plunged harder and faster into her body, her big soft breasts rolled and shook, and the dragons' heads nodded at each other.

'Now you've got the idea,' said Mina. 'Do it faster and they'll fight each other.'

Gerhart slammed harder into her to keep the dragon bodies writhing and their open-jawed mouths swaying on her breasts, as if they were snarling and hissing at each other.

'They're fighting, Mina!'

The dragon-fight did not last very long. The vigour of Gerhart's attack soon brought on his paroxysm of delight and the battle reached its fierce climax when he spilled his rice-wine in her Chinese pavilion.

The moment that he was finished, Mina unclasped her legs from his waist and pushed herself into a sitting position, freeing herself from his spike. It was then that he understood that she had been entirely unmoved by what he had just done to her and that for her it was no more than a performance for a paying audience. The thought did not please him at all.

'You are going to paint me after that, aren't you?' she asked.

'I'll be back tomorrow to paint your Chinese pavilion,' he promised while he buttoned his trousers, 'Chang's miniature master-piece is worthy of a wider and more appreciative audience than it gets here.'

241

'I've never had one of my friends say he didn't appreciate it,' said Mina.

'I'm sure – but I meant appreciate it for its artistic qualities, not just its functional values.'

'I suppose you know what you're talking about, but it doesn't make sense to me,' she said, sliding off the bed.

She put on her black leather pouch, hiding her most important work of art from his eyes.

'Bring your paints round in the morning,' she said. 'Once you've copied my pavilion you won't be content until you've done all of me, you'll see.'

'I may need to enter the Temple of the Six Harmonies again to get myself in a suitable frame of mind,' said Gerhart, grinning at her.

'Very likely,' she agreed, showing no sign of interest, approval or dismay at his suggestion. 'It's always been a big attraction – that's why I've got so many friends. And you haven't seen my tree shaking in a storm yet?'

'That sounds interesting – how do you make it shake?'

'Use your imagination,' she answered, 'I lean forward over the bed and you provide the storm from behind to shake the branches.'

'Living art!' said Gerhart. 'Who would have thought it! How on earth would the art critics appraise it?'

Mina offered no thoughts on the subject. Before he left she drew his attention to some unexpected living expenses that were worrying her. Not that she took money from men for what they did to her, she assured him – after all, she was a respectable married woman, and not a whore, even though her husband had deserted her. But it was hard to live decently unless her special friends helped her out now and then. Gerhart smiled at her excuses and gave her five hundred Marks. It seemed to him little enough for the pleasure of watching the dragons fight.

Chapter 21

A surprise is in store for Maximilian Glotz

'You are wonderful, Gerhart,' said Lotte, when she was able to speak again after her long and noisy ecstasy.

Gerhart settled himself comfortably beside her on his bed and closed his eyes, his intention being to allow himself a rest before Lotte coaxed him into making love to her again.

'How are things at home?' he asked, to divert her thoughts for a while. 'Is Maximilian behaving himself after his trouble with the police?'

'He's behaving very strangely,' she said at once, 'I think he must have gone mad.'

'What's he been doing now?'

'He came into my room yesterday when I was dressing to go out, and I thought he'd try to grab me, as usual, but not a bit of it! He looked at me and he had tears in his eyes! He begged my forgiveness for the trouble he'd caused me – imagine that!'

'And did you forgive him?'

'I told him that he should be asking Kathe for forgiveness, not me, and he soon saw that I wasn't impressed by his performance. And then came the crazy part – he went down on his knees and said he was sorry for how badly he'd treated me and he was deeply ashamed of himself, but he couldn't help his feelings.'

'True,' said Gerhart, 'but he could control his actions if he wanted to.'

'Look who's talking!' said Lotte. 'When did you ever control yourself if your tail was standing up?'

'I don't have to – my advances are always welcome.'

'I've never heard anything so smug in my life!' Lotte

243

exclaimed, leaning over him to pinch his belly hard. 'Take that! And that!'

Gerhart laughed and seized her wrists before she made a start on his more vulnerable parts.

'So then you forgave Max,' he said, to get her back on to her story.

'I didn't have a chance! He ripped open his trousers and out flopped his tail – limp as a sausage – and he rambled on about this being the cause of all his problems.'

'You're making it up!' said Gerhart, laughing loudly.

'I swear I'm not. It sounds crazy but it's exactly what happened.'

'Your brother-in-law seems to have lost his wits after his drunken spree! What did you do?'

'I was dumbfounded! And I was blushing so furiously that I didn't know where to look.'

Well, well, Gerhart was thinking, a night with Erna has stirred up some fierce emotions in our little lawyer. Down on his knees with his dangler out begging Lotte to forgive him – it could almost be a scene from *Venus in Furs*, if it wasn't so ridiculous.

'Why were you blushing?' he asked, 'It wasn't the first tail you'd seen – not even the first time you'd seen his. You told me yourself that you'd had it in your hand often enough to stop him doing worse.'

'I was embarrassed by the way he was grovelling. What I ought to have done was kick him.'

'But you didn't?'

'I let him ramble on until it got to be too much, and then I just ran past him and out of the apartment. Do you think he's gone mad?'

'No madder than he was before. It's a change of approach, that's all. He's seen that he can't get his way by force, so now he's trying for pity. He thinks that if he abases himself enough, you'll feel sorry for him and let him have you.'

'What a pig!' said Lotte. 'If I'd known that I certainly would have kicked his sausage. Sorry for him, indeed! I'd like to give him a good thrashing!'

'There's something in my studio I want to show you,' said Gerhart, inspired by her words.

'Now, you mean?'

'This very minute. Come on.'

She reached for her knickers, but Gerhart took her hand and dragged her out of the bedroom, telling her that she didn't need clothes. That brought a gleam to her eye and she went along willingly.

On the studio wall was pinned a very large sheet of paper on which Gerhart had sketched, as a working drawing for his illustrations, the almost life-size outlines of a man and a woman. The man was naked and on his knees, his hands tied behind his back, and his disproportionately long and thick stem standing up boldly from between his thighs. The woman stood to one side of him, wearing a knee-length fur coat and high-heeled shoes. She was posed with one foot in front of the other, her knees slightly bent to give her balance, while she lashed at the man's unprotected back with a long thin whip. Her vigorous movement had swung the unfastened coat open to reveal the front of her body.

'Oh!' was Lotte's reaction to the picture.

She did not know that the woman's face was that of Erna Klemt, with her characteristic lop-sided grin. The breasts from which the fur coat had fallen away were also Erna's, but Gerhart had given his subject thighs a little more slender and sinewy than Erna's to improve his picture.

'What do you think of it?' he asked, slipping an arm round Lotte's naked waist.

'People don't really do things like that, do they?' she asked a little awkwardly.

'Some do.'

'But *you* wouldn't want to, Gerhart? Or would you?'

'I've never been tempted to try.'

While he was answering her question he pinned a sheet of white drawing paper over the victim's face and, after a moment or two's thought, sketched in another face.

'There,' he said, stepping back from his work, 'it's not much like him, but it will do for now.'

'That's Maximilian!' Lotte exclaimed, staring at the new face on the tormented man's body. 'You've turned him into Maximilian!'

'The original face was from imagination – and so it was nobody. But in the final illustrations the victim will be Max. I wonder if he will enjoy being famous.'

Lotte giggled and leaned against him.

'But why Max?' she asked.

'I don't know – it must be my intuition. I feel sure that your dear brother-in-law would enjoy being tied up like that and whipped by you.'

'That's silly,' said Lotte.

'What he did in your room yesterday was silly. And just consider – if you kept him under control like that, you'd have no more problems with him. He'd be your willing slave and you'd have the upper hand.'

'That's a monstrous suggestion! Do you seriously think that I'd have anything to do with such perversity?'

'That's just a word to shock church-goers with. The truth is that you would enjoy getting your own back on him with a few cuts of a riding-whip. He'd stop trying to get his hand up your clothes – and he'd get on with your legal business, because he'd be desperate to please you.'

'You're talking nonsense,' said Lotte.

'There is an easy way to find out. The next time he creeps into your room, stand up to him and tell him very sternly that you've decided that what he needs is discipline. Treat him like a dog, not like someone who makes you timid, and see how he responds. Order him down on his knees. He's done that once already, so it will be nothing new for him. Tell him that what he has done is beyond forgiveness and that only punishment can absolve him. Be harsh and cruel – let him see that you mean it. The moment he goes down on his knees, you've won and you can do what you like with him.'

'But I don't want to do anything with him!'

'Just hear me out – Max is kneeling in front of you, silent and ashamed. Now you say that he has hands that can't be trusted. Have a length of cord ready and tie his wrists behind his back – like the man in the picture.'

'My God, what are you suggesting?'

'If he lets you tie his hands, he's surrendered completely. Insult him – he'll love it. And while you're insulting him, take your clothes off slowly and let him see you naked. Has he ever seen you naked before?'

'Of course not.'

'Good – the sight will stun him. Run your hands over your body. Hold your little bundles and squeeze them. Touch your black fur – and while you're doing all this, tell Max that your beautiful body is far too good for a pig like him. Make him suffer by letting him see what he can never have – got the idea?'

'It's madness!' said Lotte, her cheeks flushed red.

'Maybe, but interesting, all the same.'

'What do I do next?' she asked, still looking at the picture on the wall. 'I haven't got a whip, even if I dared use one.'

'Let me think. There's Max on his knees with his hands tied and you standing over him naked. He'll have a very hard tail by then. I know – make him kiss your feet. In fact, make him lick them. That will fix in his mind that he has to obey you.'

'And then?'

'Put your clothes on, slowly, letting him see everything you do. Then untie his hands and tell him to go away.'

'But he'll be so excited by then that he'll try to rape me!'

'Not if you've established very clearly that he is your slave and has to do what you say. He won't dare touch you.'

'And that's all there is to it?'

'That's only the beginning. At the next opportunity you take the game a stage further. Order him to strip naked before he goes down on his knees and you tie his hands. Buy a riding-crop before then and use it on his back – just a few flicks to let him know who's in charge. And make him thank you for the privilege of being whipped by someone as beautiful as you.'

'If only I dared!' Lotte breathed. 'You make it sound so simple, but I'm sure it's not.'

'If Max is that way inclined, you'll be surprised at how simple it is. And from what you've said about his little performance yesterday, I think he is crying out to be humiliated by you. Why else would he flop his tail out and burst into tears?'

'There's one thing wrong with your picture,' said Lotte, 'I hope you don't mind if I point it out to you?'

'I know – it's the way the fur coat is swirling about the woman. I haven't got it right yet.'

'That's not what I meant. It's the man's tail sticking up there – Max' isn't nearly as big and bold as the one you've drawn.'

Gerhart laughed and said that he'd drawn it from imagination.

'Or looking at your own in a mirror,' said Lotte. 'But the thing is – I can't do all that to Max in the apartment. There's nearly always somebody about, even if it's only the maid.'

'Then what you must do is to order Max to find a place where he can receive his punishment and training. A cheap hotel room will do. But be sure not to go there with him.'

'Why not?'

'Because that suggests a degree of complicity. You must be aloof and distant. Tell him to be there promptly at whatever time you arrange, and then turn up a good twenty minutes late, to make him uncertain.'

'I can't arrive at a hotel with a riding-crop in my hand,' Lotte objected.

'No, you make Max take it there. Better still, make him go and buy it himself.'

'It's all a dream. I could never whip Max. That's not to say I wouldn't like to, after the trouble he's caused me. Not to mention the anxiety he's given Kathe by getting himself arrested naked in the street.'

'Yes,' said Gerhart, grinning to himself, 'you owe it to Kathe as much as to yourself. Max deserves to be taught a very sharp lesson. For his own good, of course.'

'That's true. But I'd feel such a fool . . . unless . . .'

'Unless what?'

'It's only a thought – why don't we have a rehearsal, so that I'd know how to go about it.'

'You want me to be Max for you to practise on – is that it?'

'No, that wouldn't work at all. I'll be Max and you show me what to do,' she replied, to his surprise.

Gerhart took her back to his bedroom, thinking over the possibilities. She stood watching him as he put on his dressing-gown and pulled a leather belt from the trousers he had discarded earlier.

'You're not going to beat me with that?' Lotte asked in alarm.

'Shut up!' said Gerhart harshly, 'I've had enough of your whining and creeping in here when I've got better things to do. It's time you were taught a lesson. Get down on your knees and beg my forgiveness for being such a nuisance.'

Lotte blushed pink and sank to her knees.

'You're forever trying to touch me,' said Gerhart, 'you can't keep your hands to yourself! Well, I know how to deal with that – put them behind your back at once!'

When she obeyed he walked round her, pulled the cord from his dressing-gown, and used it to bind her wrists together.

'Gerhart – I don't like this game,' she said, 'let's stop.'

'I don't give a damn what you like and don't like. You're going to listen to me for once, without trying any of your tricks. Where did you get this stupid idea that I want to make love to you?'

'But I love you, Gerhart,' she said plaintively.

'Love me! All you want is my body! What gives you the right to maul me about?'

He opened his dressing-gown and displayd his body to her, from blonde-haired chest to dangling tail.

'Look at me,' he sneered, 'because that's all you'll ever do. Tell me that I'm beautiful.'

'You are beautiful, Gerhart,' Lotte murmured, adoration in her dark brown eyes.

'Yes, I am – far too beautiful for you to touch. Get that into your thick head and remember it – or I'll make you sorry you ever met me.'

'I don't care what you do to me,' she said softly, 'I still love you.'

'You can keep your love. I've no use for it.'

'Please . . . don't be cruel to me, Gerhart . . .'

'Cruel, you say? I'll show you what cruelty means,' and he flicked lightly at her back and breasts with the end of his leather belt.

Lotte's face was bright red, though hardly from pain, for the whipping was purely symbolic.

'You can howl all you want!' said Gerhart, though she had not uttered a sound, 'now you know what I think of you and your love. Kiss my feet, you miserable creature!'

She bent over awkwardly, her bare bottom in the air, to press her mouth to his foot. Gerhart trapped her neck between his legs and lashed at her exposed rump with his belt.

'This is what you'll get from me from now on!' he said fiercely. 'You'll be here waiting for me whenever I order you, understand? And I'm going to make you scream, make no mistake about that!'

He reached over her bowed back to pull loose the cord that held her wrists, then stepped back. Lotte's dark head came up slowly, her cheeks crimson.

'That's how to do it,' he said, smiling at her, 'can you manage that?'

She reached out to clasp his bare legs just above the knees.

'It's very exciting, Gerhart! I had no idea!' she breathed.

'A few cuts of the whip across Max' bottom, the way I showed you, and he'll be squirting on the carpet before you release him.'

Lotte's hands slid up his thighs, parting his untied dressing-gown to look at him.

'It was exciting for you too,' she said, when she uncovered his hard stem.

'When I saw your bare bottom sticking up and flicked it with the belt I was almost carried away,' he murmured, 'I had to stop myself from really thrashing you.'

'Suppose Max doesn't squirt on the floor when I whip him,' said Lotte, kissing his belly. 'Suppose he gets so excited that when I untie him he grabs me.'

'After a good whipping he'll be completely under your control. He'll want you to dominate him. If he hasn't done it by then, order him to use his hand while he's still down on his knees.'

'Gerhart! That's terrible – I wouldn't dare!'

'Ah, but you'll be excited yourself by then – you'll enjoy ordering him to do it to himself.'

'You are terrible,' Lotte sighed, her hands stroking the cheeks

250

of his bottom under his dressing-gown, 'you're putting perverse thoughts into my head. I can just see Max on his knees in
front of me playing with himself after I've whipped him . . .
but would he do it?'

'It will be the high point of his life,' Gerhart sighed as she
fondled his stiff tail. 'Once he's done it for you like that, he'll be
your slave for life.'

'Perhaps you're right . . . but I'd rather have you as my slave.
Better still, I'd like to be your slave.'

She took his quivering stem in her wet mouth and her tongue
sent little spasms of delight through him.

'I'm nobody's slave,' he sighed.

Lotte said nothing, her pretty mouth being too occupied to
speak. Gerhart put his hands on her bare shoulders to steady
himself on legs that trembled.

Chapter 22

Confessions at an engagement party

There were two parties to celebrate the engagement of Bertolt
and Clara. The first was given by Clara's parents at their home
in Bellevue-strasse and was very formal. All the von Nimitz
family was present, aunts, uncles, cousins and even a grand-
mother. Bertolt's parents came from Frankfurt for the occasion,
bringing his younger brother and sister with them and seem-
ingly pleased with the alliance.

Only a few of Bertolt's and Clara's own friends were
invited – the presentable ones, of course – including Gerhart
and Sieglinde, Heinrich Preuss, Roma von Gloeden and half a
dozen others. All things considered, it was a boring event,
though the champagne was of the best. By ten-thirty in the
evening it was all over, the speeches made, the hands shaken,
the bottles emptied. So that the evening should not be a total
disaster, Gerhart and Sieglinde took themselves off to the most
disreputable night-club they knew and drank and danced and
laughed at the cabaret until the place finally closed in the early
hours.

The real party was the next day, at Bertolt's apartment, and
to this all his friends and Clara's friends were invited. By ten in
the evening his sitting-room was packed with couples cavorting
to American jazz from the gramophone, the popping of corks
was almost continuous, and everyone was in the best of moods.
Bertolt lurched about, his bow-tie crooked and a half-drunken
grin on his face, as everyone told him what a lucky fellow he was
to be marrying Clara. Considering the size of her family's
wealth and influence, and her own good nature, perhaps he
was.

Sieglinde, looking particularly beautiful after a day sleeping off the ravages of the night-club outing, was sitting on Heinrich's lap in a corner, laughing and putting her glass to his lips to let him sip at her champagne. The sight did not please Gerhart. The thought in his mind was that if Heinrich became overwhelmed by drink and romantic emotion on this happy occasion, he might be stupid enough to suggest to Sieglinde that another engagement was in order. It was while he was pondering what action to take to put a stop to any such nonsense that a hand slapped Gerhart's back so heartily that he staggered two steps forward and spilled most of his drink.

Naturally, it was Bertolt. The grin had gone from his face and he looked almost solemn as he informed Gerhart that he wanted to speak to him in private.

'In private? At a party?' said Gerhart, wondering what it could be about.

Until this moment he had been convinced that all the foolishness of who Clara belonged to had been settled, but the look on Bertolt's face made him wonder if some other curious notion had lodged itself in his befuddled brain on the occasion of his engagement.

'It won't take long,' Bertolt assured him.

With Bertolt's arm round his shoulders there was little Gerhart could do except go with him.

'In here,' said Bertolt, opening a door. 'No, we can't go in there.'

Gerhart looked over his shoulder and saw Roma stretched on a bed, her evening frock up round her waist, and someone he didn't recognise from behind lying on her. The other bedroom was also unavailable – two girls were using the dressing-table mirror to repair their make-up.

'I know – the bathroom!' said Bertolt, until Gerhart pointed out that with so much drinking going on it was probable that the bathroom would be in constant use.

They tried the dining-room, but several people were there already, helping themselves to the cold buffet. In the kitchen there were two more people – Heinz and a girl Gerhart didn't know – boiling eggs. It seemed a most odd thing to be doing, but Gerhart was never surprised by anything Heinz did.

'I've got an idea!' Bertolt exclaimed, leading Gerhart back to the crowded sitting-room.

Like all the apartments on this side of the building, it had a stone balcony overlooking the street below. Bertolt closed the glass doors that led from the sitting-room and cut off some of the noise of the jazz and the laughter.

'So after all that, what do you want to talk about?' Gerhart asked, looking down at the traffic passing two floors below.

'It's a bit awkward,' said Bertolt, sounding embarrassed. 'It's a matter of honour, you see. You're about the only person I know who understands these things.'

'Matter of honour,' Gerhart sighed, almost afraid of what he would hear next.

'To be frank with you,' said Bertolt unhappily, 'I've done a terrible thing.'

'Who hasn't?'

'But this is serious. I know you'll think me an awful swine, but I've been thinking about calling off the engagement. I don't think I should marry Clara, after what's happened.'

'But I thought you were in love with her? That's what you told me.'

'I am! I really do want to marry her. And she wants to marry me.'

'Then what's bothering you?'

'The thing is,' said Bertolt, speaking in a low voice and with evident embarrassment, 'I've made love to Frau von Nimitz.'

'Clara's mother? Surely not!'

'It's true,' said Bertolt, sounding thoroughly miserable.

'But she must be fifty!'

'I know.'

Gerhart was afraid to laugh in case he offended Bertolt, but it was an effort not to.

'She's got bouncers as big as those women wrestlers we went to see,' he said. 'They must fall down to her waist when she takes her corset off.'

'She is a well-built lady,' Bertolt conceded.

'How in heaven's name did this come about?' Gerhart asked, astounded at the absurdity of it.

254

'It was like this – she came round here to talk about who should be invited to the official engagement party. Clara was shopping that day – in fact she's done nothing but buy clothes ever since we decided to get married. And with my family in Frankfurt, there was only me to look after my side of the arrangements.'

'Forget the details – what happened?'

'I'm not sure – and that's the honest truth. We had a bottle of champagne while Frau von Nimitz made lists of people to be invited, and all of a sudden we were in a clinch on the sofa, me squeezing her bundles and her hand down my trousers.'

'Unbelievable!' said Gerhart, grinning at the thought. 'Who started it – you or her?'

There was a louder burst of laughter from the other side of the glass door and Bertolt pulled Gerhart by the arm into the corner of the balcony, anxious not to be overheard.

'It just happened,' he said, 'it was just as if lightning struck us both at the same moment.'

'That's very poetical. So you took her to bed?'

'There wasn't time for that. Down came her knickers and I was on top of her on the sofa.'

'The sofa where Clara passed out naked that night you and I had the dispute over her?'

'Unfortunately, yes,' Bertolt agreed, sounding slightly shamefaced.

'The self-same sofa where you jumped on Clara when you woke up and found my carnation between her legs,' Gerhart persisted, determined to extract as much amusement as possible from Bertolt's confession.

'I know it sounds dreadful, but it's the only sofa in the room and things do seem to happen on it. Do you think I should get rid of it?'

'Too late for that. Besides, it seems to be the most useful piece of furniture you've got. What did Frau von Nimitz have to say after this demonstration of your virility?'

'Nothing, really. I was embarrassed, but she behaved very correctly. She went to the bathroom to tidy herself up and then came back and carried on discussing the guest-list as if nothing at all had happened. I was very grateful for that. And very impressed too.'

'I've heard of volcanoes erupting when nobody expects it, but Frau von Nimitz exploding on your sofa! Are you sure it really happened, Bertolt? You didn't get drunk and dream the whole thing?'

'It's extraordinary you should say that!' said Bertolt earnestly. 'That's exactly what I thought myself after she'd gone. Some sort of hallucination – it does happen to people, you know. A friend of mine once imagined . . .'

'Leave your friend out of this – was it a dream?'

'She came back the next day to show me the final list and I thought that would settle it for me. But we did it again. It was only about nine in the morning and I wasn't dressed – she caught me in my dressing-gown and pyjamas.'

'And the lightning struck you both again?'

'Not exactly.'

'What does that mean?'

Down in the street a passing car hooted as if in derision.

'She had her hand in my pyjamas before I got the door shut,' said Bertolt, 'I was a bit hung-over from the night before with Clara, and that always makes me easily excitable. I pushed her up against the wall and did it to her standing up. I must have been a bit rough, because her hat fell off while we were doing it.'

'Her hat fell off!' Gerhart howled, unable to control himself any longer. 'You are priceless, Bertolt!'

'What's so funny about that? It was one of those big summer hats with flowers on it.'

'A flowered hat! How wonderful! What did she have to say about that?'

'Nothing at all. We drank coffee together and she read the list to me to make sure no one had been left out.'

'Just like that? No comments, no endearments, no regrets?'

'Not a word. I was a bit ashamed and didn't want to make things worse.'

'But not too ashamed to spike her up against the wall?'

'You know how it is when your tail stands up,' said Bertolt,

256

gripping the balcony with both hands as if about to leap over it and put an end to his confusion, 'you don't stop to ask questions or think about consequences. It's only afterwards that you begin to wonder if you did the right thing. You're a man of honour, Gerhart – advise me what I should do.'

'Do? There's nothing you can do but forget it. I'm sure it's no more than a little lapse on the part of Frau von Nimitz because she's excited over the prospect of her daughter marrying a strong and worthy fellow like you. Women get carried away when there's a wedding in the offing – even the most staid of them.'

'You don't understand at all – she's been here every day. I've done it to her seven days in a row, leaving out Sunday, when she goes to church with the family.'

'Oh,' said Gerhart, 'that puts it in a different light. Was she here today?'

'About five o'clock, while Clara was having her hair done for this evening.'

'Not up against the wall this time, I hope!' Gerhart asked, trying to keep a straight face.

'Certainly not! That's only happened a couple of times when she's come early, before I've been dressed.'

'So it was back to the faithful old sofa again?'

'Not today, no. I took her straight into the bedroom and she undressed. That's the first time she's done that for me.'

'Why did you drag her into the bedroom if you find it embarrassing to make love to her? You really are strange, Bertolt.'

'In confidence, between you and me, I wanted to have a look at her bouncers. You said yourself that they're big – I mean, they stick out under her clothes like a shelf. I was curious.'

'Was it worth it?'

'My God, yes! They really are tremendous when she takes her corset off and lets them dangle. It was like lying on a couple of pillows.'

'In effect, you have progresed from the silent stab against the wall to full-scale love-making in bed.'

'I don't think so,' Bertolt said. 'The thing is, she didn't say a word the whole time. She just lay there panting and moaning.

257

And when she was dressing she started to talk about the engagement party last night and how well it went. Then we shook hands and she left.'

'You shook hands!' Gerhart said in disbelief, choking back his laughter.

'She couldn't have been here more than twenty minutes altogether,' said Bertolt. 'To tell you the truth, I'm worried about her state of mind, if you see what I mean.'

'Her state of mind seems obvious enough to me.'

'I'm glad you agree with me. She doesn't know what she's doing – it's some sort of mental breakdown, like loss of memory. She does things without knowing what she's doing and she doesn't remember afterwards. There's no other explanation, is there? There's sure to be a fancy medical name for her disorder. Much as I dislike the idea, I'm beginning to think that it's my duty to speak in confidence to her family doctor.'

'Are you mad? It's your duty to keep your mouth shut!' Gerhart exclaimed.

'But there may be treatment for her affliction.'

'There certainly is – and you're providing it.'

'What do you mean?' Bertolt asked blankly.

'Bertolt – sometimes I think that the reason I like you is because you are an idiot. The treatment for what ails Frau von Nimitz is a quick stab a day. No doctor's going to prescribe that. You are co-operating in a work of mercy and you need feel no embarrassment.'

'How can you be so sure?'

'Ladies of her age often suffer from this affliction. Evidently Herr von Nimitz is unable to provide the remedy – or unwilling, perhaps. And so she turns to you, as one about to become a member of the family circle, for assistance in her hour of need.'

'Good Lord – I never guessed!'

'You are bound by the Hippocratic oath of confidentiality as much as if you were a doctor in circumstances like these,' said Gerhart, piling it on thickly.

'Thank heaven I asked for your advice, or I might have behaved incorrectly.'

'Not only that, but it would be dishonourable to breach the confidence Frau von Nimitz has shown she has in you. Despicable, even.'

Bertolt pulled himself upright and slapped Gerhart's shoulder briskly.

'Thank you,' he said, in heart-felt gratitude, 'you've made me understand the delicacy of the situation.'

'How are you coping with Clara while you are giving this healing treatment daily to her mother?'

'No problem there. A bottle or two of champagne and I'm ready for her. But one thing, Gerhart – how long do you think this treatment will have to go on?'

'Until you take Clara on honeymoon. Make it a long one – six or eight weeks. By the time you get back to Berlin Frau von Nimitz will have found someone else to assist her with her problem.'

'Do you think so?' Bertolt asked, a doubtful note in his voice.

'Well, well!' said Gerhart, grinning widely. 'You haven't been telling me the truth. At least, not all the truth. Admit it – you enjoy these little consultations with your future mother-in-law. It's those big bouncers of hers!'

'Today was the first time I've seen them, but I can't say that I don't like the feel of them.'

'What else, then?'

'I like her correct behaviour when she's with me. There's no chatting or wasting time – she takes her knickers off and I'm straight into her. She doesn't want love-talk while we're doing it, or afterwards. She puts her clothes to rights and sits up straight and talks about ordinary, sensible things, like the wedding arrangements. There's no fuss, you see – just simple and straight-forward love-making.'

'I can see that you have a busy and satisfying married life ahead of you,' said Gerhart. 'There's no reason why you can't share yourself out between the two women.'

'Do you think that's possible?' Bertolt asked.

'Love will find a way! But you must eat heartily every day to keep your strength up.'

Bertolt seized Gerhart's hand and shook it warmly.

259

'If there's ever anything I can do for you . . .' he burbled.
Gerhart laughed.

'Don't confuse the two and shake hands with Clara after you make love to her, or she'll wonder what's going on,' he said. 'There is one little thing you can do for me, Bertolt.'

'Anything! Anything at all!'

Gerhart explained in very simple words, hoping that Bertolt would grasp the idea. He was not over-confident of his friend's power of understanding, especially when he was half-drunk, but the plan was one which required no great level of intellectual ability to carry through.

'But I don't understand why,' said Bertolt.

'It's only a joke,' said Gerhart, 'you like jokes, don't you?'

'A joke!' Bertolt echoed, very seriously. 'Now I understand. Leave it to me.'

Back in the sitting-room Gerhart made straight for the corner where Heinrich and Sieglinde were sitting together. Heinrich had a hand on her knee and was stroking it in a way that suggested that he would like to stroke a little higher, up above her stocking-top. Sieglinde had an arm round his neck and was doing nothing to discourage his advances.

'Heinrich – this is my favourite song,' said Gerhart loudly, to make himself heard over the music from the gramophone, 'do you mind if I borrow my sister for a dance?'

'Nobody dances with his own sister,' said Heinrich, 'Find somebody else's sister.'

'But it's Sieglinde's favourite song too,' said Gerhart, smiling pleasantly as he took Sieglinde's hand and pulled her upright off Heinrich's lap. 'I'll bring her back.'

On the small area of floor that had been cleared of furniture they danced energetically to the music and the negro voice that sang to it.

'If this is my favourite tune, what's it called?' Sieglinde asked, her little breasts bouncing up and down inside her blue frock.

'I don't know. I just wanted to dance with you.'

'I believe you're jealous!'

'A little.'

'Since when have you and I been jealous of each other?' she asked, evidently puzzled.

'I'm being silly,' he said, grinning at her in his most charming manner, 'you're by far the most beautiful girl here and it's not right that I should be left with second-best all evening.'

When the record ended he suggested that they should eat and steered her to the dining-room and filled plates for them both from the array of cold food laid out on the long table. Clara, less restrained than the previous evening, threw her arms round his neck and kissed him loudly on the cheek, almost sending his plate of food to the floor.

'Darling Gerhart, I'm so happy!' she exclaimed. 'And it's all because of you!'

'What did she mean?' Sieglinde asked when Clara rambled away to find more champagne. 'What did you have to do with her engagement to Bertolt?'

'Nothing at all – I was an innocent by-stander on the fringe of their complicated affair. Bertolt wouldn't ask Clara to marry him because he thought that I'd made love to her. Then she told him that I hadn't, and he did.'

'But you have made love to her,' said Sieglinde, none the wiser for his explanation. 'You went out with her quite a lot at one time.'

'Yes, but we didn't make love on the occasion when Bertolt thought we did.'

'What occasion was that?'

Gerhart wondered if it would have been better not to begin this exposition of the complications that had arisen.

'It was one night when Bertolt was dead drunk,' he said, 'so was Clara, as a matter of fact.'

'But *you* were sober?'

'Semi-sober. At least I was sober enough to know that I didn't want to make love to Clara while she was unconscious.'

'But if she was unconscious,' said Sieglinde thoughtfully, 'she wouldn't know whether you had or not. So how could she tell Bertolt that you didn't?'

'Because I told her that we didn't.'

'And naturally she believed you?'

'It was the sacred truth!' Gerhart protested, and Sieglinde looked at him with open scepticism in her pale blue eyes.

'It can't be very interesting to make love to an unconscious girl,' she said, 'why did you do it?'

'But I didn't! I may have given her bundles a quick feel, but that was all.'

'Then why did Bertolt think that you did? He must have had some reason.'

Gerhart sighed. It had been a mistake to start the explanation, but now he was committed.

'The thing is,' he said, 'Clara was naked at the time and I left a carnation between her legs.'

'It gets stranger and stranger! Why was Clara naked?'

Gerhart began the story from the beginning and soon had Sieglinde in helpless laughter.

'You're crazy, Gerhart,' she said, 'and I love you for it! I'd have adored seeing Bertolt's renunciation scene in the bar.'

Gerhart glanced secretly at his wrist-watch and decided that Bertolt had by now had time enough to get their little *joke* under way. He took Sieglinde back to the sitting-room, where she at once glanced around to find Heinrich. He was nowhere to be seen, and another couple were occupying the arm-chair he had been sitting on, their mouths pressed together in a kiss so avid that it was clear that their next stop would be one of the bedrooms.

'It's very hot in here,' said Gerhart, 'let's get a breath of fresh air.'

He guided Sieglinde through the gyrating dancers, opened the curtained door to the balcony and followed her out into the warm evening air.

'That's better,' he said cheerfully.

At the end of the balcony a couple were pressed tightly together, the girl's back against the stone face of the building.

'Sorry!' Gerhart called out, 'We didn't mean to disturb you.'

The man pulled sharply away from the girl, his stiff tail plainly visible as it poked out of his trousers. The girl's frock slid down from her waist to conceal her pale thighs.

'Heinrich!' Sieglinde exclaimed.

262

It was indeed Heinrich, staring foolishly at her and fumbling with his trouser buttons.

'Heinrich?' Gerhart exclaimed, trying to sound surprised.

'Heinrich!' said the abandoned girl, 'What's the matter? I was nearly there!'

'Good Lord! Is that you, Roma?' Gerhart asked, 'I'm sorry if we've put Heinrich off his stroke – we came out for a breath of air.'

'Another few seconds and it wouldn't have mattered,' said Roma, 'Now look what you've done – Heinrich is having some sort of attack!'

Heinrich's embarrassment at being discovered by Sieglinde in the very act was either pitiful or comical to behold, according to the viewer's frame of mind. He was making gobbling noises and waving his arms about.

'Heinrich – there's a policeman down there!' said Gerhart quickly. 'On the other side of the street – he must have been watching you.'

Heinrich uttered a hoarse cry, grabbed Roma's arm and dragged her towards the door to the sitting-room.

'Well, really!' she said as she was pulled past Gerhart and Sieglinde. 'First he couldn't wait to get me out here, and now he can't wait to get me back inside!'

Sieglinde had her back to the embarrassing scene and was looking over the balcony rail. Roma's hand brushed lightly over the front of Gerhart's trousers as she went past him and in the semi-darkness he saw the white gleam of her grin.

'I can't see anyone down there,' said Sieglinde, 'where do you mean?'

'Over there in that door-way,' Gerhart answered innocently, 'I'm sure I saw a uniform. Has he gone?'

They heard a roar of laughter through the half-open glass door behind them and went in to find the cause. Clara had vanished and Heinrich, his face crimson, was shouting abuse at Bertolt over the raucous music, while a circle of friends stood round and laughed.

'What's going on?' Sieglinde asked the girl nearest her.

'Clara came in with Heinrich and her knickers were hanging

263

out of his pocket,' the girl said between giggles, 'Bertolt pulled them out and held them up for everyone to see.'

'I've had enough of this party,' Sieglinde said to Gerhart, 'will you take me home?'

'We could go and dance somewhere,' he suggested, 'It's early still.'

'I'd rather go home.'

Chapter 23

Gerhart becomes interested in the work of a great poet

Gerhart was a little surprised to receive an invitation from Rudolf Knuppel to bring his three flower paintings to his apartment on Sunday afternoon, since Rudolf had expressed no interest in them when he had seen them in the studio. Nevertheless, the publisher sounded on the telephone as if he had a specific idea in mind, and there was nothing to be lost by accepting. He found Rudolf dressed very casually, in an open-necked blue shirt and yellow trousers, a colour combination not wholly in keeping with the black and white furnishings of his sitting-room.

Erna was still living with Rudolf and she was stretched out on one of the white satin sofas, her clothes casual to the point of being bizarre. She was in an off-the-shoulder gypsy blouse in white, tucked into close-fitting shorts of soft grey leather that exposed her bare thighs completely.

'I'm glad you could come,' said Rudolf, taking the portfolio of water-colours from Gerhart, 'sit down and have a glass of wine. Erna and I have been discussing our future publication list and she's had a wonderful idea.'

Without moving from her sofa, Erna raised a bare arm and Gerhart kissed her hand. She winked at him and grinned and he took a seat opposite her. By then Rudolf had arranged the paintings in a row across the back of the other sofa.

'Fantastic,' he said, looking at them with his round and sleek head cocked to one side, 'the pink rose, the black peony and the golden chrysanthemum – how could I have missed their significance! You are right, my dear Erna, the book will be a publishing sensation.'

'Excuse me,' said Gerhart, 'what book are we talking about – *Venus in Furs*? These are not for that book.'

'No, no! That will be a great success too, but I'm talking about the book after that.'

'But I haven't finished illustrating the first one yet. I need another week or ten days.'

'Certainly,' said Rudolf, 'take all the time you want – the sketches I saw in your studio promise great things – in particular the one of Severin on his knees with his tail in his hand and Wanda whipping him while he pleasures himself. That was a stroke of genius.'

Gerhart glanced across at Erna, who grinned at him and said she was astonished that he hadn't required a male model for that particular scene and that if he had asked, she might have been able to suggest someone. Rudolf's attention was still centred on the flower pictures and he missed the innuendo in her tone.

'Tell me one thing,' he said, 'are you enjoying doing the illustrations for *Venus in Furs*?'

'Of course he is,' Erna answered for him, 'the pictures I've seen are alive with strong emotion. He couldn't produce work like that if he wasn't personally involved to an exceptional degree.'

'That's true,' said Gerhart, 'some of the sketches have had so powerful an influence on friends who have seen them that unusual events have taken place.'

'Ah!' said Rudolf, turning to face him. 'That sounds as if it might be amusing. You must tell me about these unusual events later on. First of all, though, we must discuss your flower pictures.'

'What do you have in mind?' Gerhart asked cautiously, 'I didn't paint them with the intention of selling them. They were done for my own satisfaction.'

'Naturally! Merely to look at them is to understand that they are from a private world of your own – a world of deep and overpowering passion. They speak without words of an intense relation with three particular women. In short, they are superb.'

'He knows all that,' said Erna, 'get to the point, Rudolf.'

266

'You are so impatient! Very well then, have you read the works of Charles Baudelaire, Gerhart?'

'The name seems familiar, but that's all.'

'He was a great French poet,' said Rudolf. 'He died young about seventy years ago, just before we marched into France and captured Paris.'

That was something which Gerhart did know about, thanks to the General's professional pride in German military history.

'That was when we took Alsace-Lorraine from them,' he said.

'And now they've got it back,' Rudolf answered dismissively. 'The point is that Baudelaire's poems were published under the general title of *Les Fleurs du Mal* – the Flowers of Evil. Now do you understand the relevance of your water-colours?'

'Only if his poems had the same subject as my paintings,' Gerhart said with a grin.

'But of course they did – that's the point! Erna, read a verse or two to our non-poetical friend.'

Erna fished a thin book out from behind her, where it had slid down between the sofa cushions, and opened it at random.

'This one is called *The promises of a face*,' she said, 'and he's describing a mulatto woman he's been making love to. He starts off with her black hair and works his way down her body till he gets to this bit –

You will find at the tips of two beautiful and heavy breasts
Two ample bronze-coloured medallions
And beneath a smooth and velvet belly
As tawny as the skin of a Buddhist priest
A rich fleece which is truly the sister
Of your enormous head of hair
Supple and curly, as thick and black as a starless night'

'Magnificent,' said Rudolf, 'Even in translation it has a languorous passion that excites the imagination.'

'Are all his poems like that?' Gerhart asked.

'Not all of them, but a lot are. Read him the one about the Jewish whore, Erna, where she lies alongside him naked and he kisses her feet.'

267

'He can read them all for himself,' said Erna. 'If he's interested, that is. Are you interested, Gerhart?'

There was a certain ambiguity in her question. She was holding out the book to him and in some inexplicable manner her gypsy blouse had fallen off one shoulder to expose, as if casually or unknowingly, one of her breasts.

'Your medallions are not bronze-coloured,' said Gerhart, 'but I am interested. What are you proposing?'

'Erna, you are distracting him,' Rudolf complained.

'No, encouraging him,' she answered. 'He needs to be encouraged to produce really exciting pictures. You've seen what he's made of me as Wanda. And that golden chrysanthemum over there was inspired by me, as you very well know.'

'Six flower paintings,' said Rudolf, 'for a new German edition of *Les Fleurs du Mal*, that's what I want from you, Gerhart, and I'm willing to pay well for them. You've done three already and they're perfect. Can you do three more as good?'

Gerhart thought it over for a moment or two.

'Erna was right when she said that my inspiration comes from personal involvement. And you said much the same thing yourself about my flower paintings.'

'So have short and intense affairs with three more women,' Rudolf suggested with a brief smile, 'that can't be much of a problem for a handsome young man like you.'

Gerhart was wondering whether he could produce similar water-colours based on his intimacies with Clara, Roma and Ruth Leppman, without the trouble of involving himself with more women. It seemed to him that the three he was already involved with were enough for one man to handle.

'It's not that easy,' he said, 'I can't see every woman in terms of a particular flower. The three you have there suggested themselves – there was a natural resemblance of some sort, however distant, that led to the choice of specific flowers.'

'Yes, yes,' said Rudolf, slightly impatient with what he obviously regarded as unnecessary artistic quibbling, 'but now that the concept is firmly established in your mind, it cannot be impossible to choose three more *flowers* from the many you are acquainted with. There are so many to choose from – tulips, lilies, orchids, carnations, poppies – do you know any red-headed girls?'

'No, but I have an idea about a carnation, now that you mention it.'

'Good! You see how simple it is really, if you put your mind to it. How did you get the idea in the first place?'

'He got it from me,' said Erna, 'he looked between my legs and saw a chrysanthemum. That's how it started.'

'Really?' said Rudolf. 'Was it a flash of inspiration then and there, or did you think about it for some time before you drew this delightfully ambiguous picture of Erna's most precious part?'

Erna swung her legs up in the air and, lying on her back on the white sofa, wriggled out of her leather shorts. She turned to pose on her side, propped on an elbow, the position she had assumed on the glass top of Rudolf's office desk.

'It was instant inspiration,' she said, running her fingers through the golden-brown curls between her thighs.

'I can understand that,' Rudolf said in a strained voice, staring at her chrysanthemum. 'It has a fascination all its own – a fascination which I feel strongly. No wonder Gerhart felt the same and translated it into art.'

'The creative process is not easy to describe,' said Gerhart, also staring at what fascinated Rudolf. 'Art transcends nature.'

'Yes,' Rudolf agreed, 'you have captured in your painting some of the quality that exudes from Erna. Look at the state I'm in! She has only to show me her body naked and I start to tremble like a sixteen year old boy! My hands shake and my tail stands up at once.'

'I know what you mean,' Gerhart sighed, his eyes on Erna's stroking hand.

'Of course you know what I mean. Do you think I don't know you made love to her every time she posed for you? Isn't that so, Erna?'

Erna smiled enigmatically and said nothing.

'Not that I blame you,' he continued, 'you can't help yourself any more than I can when she takes her clothes off. I can see that from your flower pictures. You are an artist of exceptional talent.'

269

'Art changes the way we see reality,' said Gerhart, pleased by the praise and very willing to expound his theories of aesthetics, 'when you look now at the very ordinary tuft of hair between Erna's legs, you see it differently because of my picture. The reality has not changed, but in your mind you see a golden-brown chrysanthemum.'

'Very ordinary, is it?' said Erna. 'We'll see about that! Come here and kiss it.'

Gerhart stayed in his seat, though his stem was fiercely hard. Not so Rudolf – he threw himself on his knees by the sofa and kissed Erna's chrysanthemum.

'The picture has increased her hold over me,' he mumbled.

'You can free yourself if you want to,' said Gerhart, winking at Erna over Rudolf's bowed head.

'But how? Even if I could bring myself to tear up your painting, the image will remain in my mind when I look at her.'

'When you kiss Erna between the legs you see a tuft of light-brown curls, that's all. In your mind you superimpose the image of the flower on it. Since you cannot change the image in your mind, you must change the reality.'

'What do you mean?' Rudolf gasped, his head down between Erna's parted thighs.

'Remove the curls and the chrysanthemum will no longer fit what you see.'

'My God, I never thought of that!'

'What a pair of idiots you are,' said Erna, grinning her sideways grin at Gerhart, 'it wouldn't make the least difference. I had you both sweating to get your hands on me long before the flower picture was painted.'

'She's right,' said Gerhart, smiling back at her.

'No, I'm sure that you're right,' Rudolf contradicted him. 'We'll do it! Into the bedroom, Erna – and you keep an eye on her, Gerhart. I'll be with you right away.'

Rudolf's bedroom was decorated in shades of restful green, with a broad and low bed. Erna stripped off her gypsy blouse and pressed her naked body against Gerhart, her arms round his neck.

'Now you've started something,' she said, 'whatever gave you an idea like that?'

Gerhart stroked the cheeks of her bottom, his upright tail squeezed against him inside his clothes by the pressure of her belly.

'I don't know. I thought it might be an amusing way of passing a Sunday afternoon. Do you mind if he shaves you? It will keep him happy.'

'It's important to you to keep Rudolf happy, isn't it?' she asked.

'It's important to both of us. Where would you be without him?'

'Yes, but I've got something he can't do without. He can find a hundred artists tomorrow to draw pictures for him, but he can't find a woman who understands his little needs like I do.'

'You're very sure of yourself, Erna.'

'With every reason. I can make him crawl naked across the floor to kiss my feet.'

'Just like Baudelaire in his poem?'

'Do I hear a note of doubt in your voice, dear Gerhart? You're going to see just how far I can go with him. And with you.'

Rudolf came into the bedroom, a towel over his arm, carrying a bowl of water carefully with both hands. He looked at Gerhart and Erna in their close embrace.

'You are as susceptible to her as I am,' he said to Gerhart. 'Here – take this.'

Gerhart freed himself from Erna's arms and took the bowl of warm water and set it on the dark green carpet. Rudolf spread his towel over one side of the bed.

'Now, Fraulein Erna,' he said momentously, 'the time has come for you to submit to an experiment that will determine a point of the utmost importance. You remember the story of Samson and Delilah, I hope? We are about to reverse it. This time it is Delilah who loses the hair in which her power resides.'

Erna's smile was cruel as she sat on the side of the bed, her bottom on the towel and her legs splayed wide to display her golden-brown flower.

'Very well, my Samson,' she said, 'since it pleases you – but you will not be able to chain me up afterwards, as they did the bald-headed hero.'

271

'Lie back,' Rudolf murmured thickly, 'open your legs wider! Gerhart – go round the other side of the bed and hold her firmly for me.'

Erna lay back and stretched herself out in apparent submission. Gerhart knelt on the bed behind her head and put his hands on her bare shoulders, to find that she was smiling at him upside-down. Plump Rudolf was on his knees between her feet, a pair of curved manicure scissors in his hand. He snipped carefully at the curls between her legs, his face red and his breathing loud and irregular.

'When Samson's hair was cut off he became weak and powerless,' he mumbled. 'He was a slave of others.'

'It wasn't the hair round his tail that Delilah cut off,' said Erna.

She pulled Gerhart's hands from her shoulders to her soft breasts and he clasped them eagerly. Rudolf looked up from his task and saw what Gerhart was doing.

'Hold her tight,' he said, his voice strained, 'her power will soon be gone.'

'Yes, hold me tight while Rudolf plucks my chrysanthemum,' she said to Gerhart.

Her hands reached up above her head and she unbuttoned Gerhart's trousers.

'There's a good, strong tail,' she said, tugging it out, 'I know what it wants. But whether it gets what it wants – that's another question.'

Rudolf had finished his shearing. He dipped a shaving-brush in the warm water, worked up a lather from a stick of shaving-soap, and spread it thickly between Erna's legs, his breath rasping loudly. He glanced up to see Erna playing with Gerhart's exposed stem.

'Make the most of your final moments of power, Erna! In a minute you will be as smooth as an egg and you will have no more attraction than a little girl. See this?'

He held up a safety-razor and she raised her head briefly to smile at him.

'Poor Rudolf,' she said, 'he understand nothing. Smooth or curly, you'll still be desperate for what I've got between my legs. There isn't another one like it in the whole of Berlin – you've tried enough others to know that. And so has Gerhart – am I speaking the truth?'

'There isn't another like yours in the whole of Berlin,' Gerhart agreed, squeezing her breasts, 'it has a sensual and degenerate quality that makes it unique.'

'Is that meant to be a compliment?' she asked softly, her hands moving feverishly over his hard spike.

'Oh yes, it's a compliment,' he said.

Rudolf was sitting back on his haunches, gripping his right wrist with his left hand.

'My hands are shaking!' he sighed. 'I can't do it! Gerhart – come here and finish it for me.'

Gerhart was highly aroused himself, but he took Rudolf's place between Erna's legs, dipped the razor in the bowl of water and, with great care, started to shave away the thick creamy lather and the short stubble beneath it. Erna giggled and her legs opened as far as they could. Rudolf was sitting on the edge of the bed, staring down at every stroke of the razor, one hand flat on Erna's belly and the other clutching at his yellow trousers.

'Is it done?' he asked heavily.

Gerhart put the razor down and wiped between Erna's legs with a corner of the big towel she lay on.

'Ready,' he answered, staring at his handiwork.

With her curls gone, it was no featureless little slit that Erna presented to view. The bare and fleshy folds between her legs rolled outwards slightly from where they joined at the top, in a way that enchanted Gerhart. The removal of the chrysanthemum petals had uncovered something of great fascination.

'Let me see!' and Rudolf was off the bed and pushing Gerhart aside.

He stared fixedly, his breath rasping in his throat.

'We have brought about a transformation,' Gerhart told him, 'instead of a golden chrysanthemum we now have a pale and fleshy orchid.'

Rudolf moaned loudly and bowed his head to press a long

273

kiss on the bare-shaven lips that confronted him. Gerhart retreated round the bed and sat by Erna's head, his spike still sticking out of his trousers.

'Well?' Erna asked, not bothering to raise her head to look at Rudolf. 'Has it lost its interest for you, Rudolf? Are you glad that it's not dangerous any more?'

He moaned again as he showered kisses on her nakedness.

'Answer me!' she said sharply.

'It's more beautiful than ever,' he gasped, 'an orchid – so smooth and so sinister!'

He wrenched open his trousers to pull out his thick and swollen tail and would have mounted her with no more ado, but Erna put the sole of her foot against his face and pushed him back on his haunches.

'Not so fast, little Samson,' she sneered, 'I'm not your slave after all. What a disappointment for you!'

'Not a disappointment,' he groaned, ' a wonderful revelation!'

'And it's mine, not yours,' she told him, 'did you hear me say anything about you jumping on top of me?'

'Erna – please!'

'I'll let you know when. Stay down there and look at my orchid. Gerhart, kiss my bundles.'

Gerhart slid round on the satin bed-cover and gladly kissed her breasts and licked their buds.

'That's nice,' she said, 'do you want to make love to me?'

'Oh, yes Erna!'

'Maybe I'll let you, when I'm ready, but I'm making no promises.'

He used his tongue and hands on her breasts to excite her as quickly as he could, desperate to get his stem into her. She sighed and trembled as she became aroused, her buds firm as berries.

'No, you don't!' she cried out suddenly, and her body heaved as she brought her legs up fast.

Gerhart looked up to see Rudolf crouching half over her, in the very act of throwing himself upon her, his hand clasping his tail and rubbing it hard. Erna's feet thudding into his belly

274

made him grunt and stopped his forward movement, but she had reckoned without the ingenuity and determination of a man in his extremity. Before she could push him away with her legs, his arm swept up under her calves and her heels went over his shoulders. Instantly, half standing and half crouching, he jammed his spike into the bare lips exposed between the backs of her thighs.

'Stop it!' she screamed.

It was much too late to stop anything. Rudolf was so far gone that he cried out in relief and discharged his pent-up passion at once as he slid into her. Then Erna had her knees doubled back to her breasts and kicked out again with all her strength against his chest and he fell over backwards, his twitching tail still spouting. He landed on his back on the carpet, one blue-shirted elbow in the bowl of soapy water, and lay gasping. Erna twisted round on the bed and lay face-down, her chin on the towel, and glared at him as his throes subsided.

'I'll make you sorry for that,' she said with soft menace.

For Gerhart all this comedy was too much. He flung himself on Erna's bare back, determined to have her whether she struggled or not, so acute was his need. But there was no struggle. His hands slid under her hips to lift them off the bed and she at once raised her bottom in the air for him to get at the fleshy lips Rudolf had parted.

'Yes!' she squealed as he slid deep into her. 'Watch this, Rudolf! Gerhart's doing what you tried to do to me!'

Rudolf stared weakly up from the floor at her flushed face and at Gerhart's face over her shoulder.

'You whore,' he whispered harshly.

Gerhart paid no attention to this family squabble. He drove hard and fast into Erna, frantic with desire, until he went off like a firework inside her.

'He's done it!' Erna cried out to Rudolf, her voice shrill with emotion, and an instant later she was squirming under Gerhart in her own climactic release. When she calmed down, Gerhart saw with some trepidation that Rudolf was sitting up on the carpet, his legs crossed, removing the blue shirt he had splashed with his misdirected passion. But then he smiled up at the two of them and suggested that they should open a bottle of wine and talk about the arrangements for the book of poems.

'Not for long,' said Erna, stretching lazily under Gerhart, 'I want to play another game.'

Chapter 24

Gerhart and Sieglinde make plans for a party

The General was so old that his death could hardly be said to be unexpected, although the manner of it was. He dined out one evening with old army friends, ate and drank well, and discussed the glories of the past and the degeneracy of the present with men who fully sympathised with his point of view. Soon after eleven o'clock he was home again, well pleased with his evening, and his manservant brought him a glass of brandy before he went to bed, which was his normal routine. Sitting comfortably beneath his painting of lost Imperial triumph, glass in hand, the old man closed his eyes and died quietly.

There was nothing quiet about his funeral, of course. It was on a very large scale, as befitted a national hero, even one in retirement and forgotten for so long. There were a great many elderly and retired army officers in uniform, with their stately wives, hundreds of friends from years past, a distant cousin or two, all looking as if their time was short, though they were ten or fifteen years younger than the deceased, the newspaper reporters and photographers – and any number of middle-aged men who had once served in the army and remembered with nostalgic pride what the General had represented. Gerhart and Sieglinde, the nearest family the old man had, were the only civilians of any importance present.

It was after five in the afternoon before they got back to their apartment. They sat down facing each other in the sitting-room and Sieglinde took off her plain black shoes and rubbed one heel.

'Are you all right, Gerhart? You haven't spoken a word for the last hour. Did the funeral depress you?'

'It's not that. I'm just beginning to realise that we're free and it's a strange feeling. We're not responsible to anyone now.'

'We haven't been for years. What's different now?'

'The shadow was always there,' he said, 'now it's gone.'

Sieglinde hitched up her black frock on one side to slide a blue garter over her knee and roll her stocking down.

'These new shoes have rubbed my heels,' she said. 'Look – this one is red and sore. I'll go back to the shop tomorrow and complain.'

'I feel that I should be jumping up and down and shouting,' said Gerhart, 'but it's a different sort of elation I feel.'

'You don't care whether I've got blisters on my heels or not!'

'Yes, I do. Let me see it,' and he knelt before her to raise her bare foot in his hand and examine the chafed spot.

'There's a mark, but the skin isn't broken. If you soak it in cold salt water the redness will be gone by tomorrow.'

Sieglinde wriggled her toes in his hand and he tickled the sole of her foot, so that her leg jerked back and showed him the smooth underside of her thigh to her lace-edged underwear.

'Black knickers too!' he said, his eyebrows rising. 'Aren't you taking the mourning too far?'

'A small token of respect for the deceased,' she answered with a broad smile, 'he liked me in black underwear. Besides, it looks good against my skin.'

'We've paid our respects today and we're finished with mourning, you and I,' said Gerhart, sounding angry. 'We're done with the past – do you understand me?'

Sieglinde looked at him in mild alarm.

'I'll go and change my clothes,' she said.

'No! The new life is starting for us and I won't let the old life hang in your wardrobe like a ghost!'

His hand went up her frock to take hold of her black knickers and drag them down her legs. When he had them off, he tried to wrench the flimsy silk with both hands to tear it.

'Gerhart – do you know what I paid for those knickers!'

'I don't care. We're free! Take that funeral frock off before I rip it off.'

Thoroughly alarmed now at his mood, she scrambled up and

278

did as he said, pulling the frock off and throwing it behind the chair and out of sight. All that she now wore was a black brassiere and one black stocking.

'Get rid of all of it!' Gerhart muttered fiercely.

Still on his knees, he pressed his cheek against her bare belly, an arm round her thighs. When he looked up again, the brassiere was gone.

'Is that better?' Sieglinde asked cautiously.

'I'm going to open a bottle of champagne so we can drink to our future,' he said. 'Stay here.'

'We haven't got any champagne.'

'Brandy, then. Just don't move.'

But when he came back with the bottle and two large balloon glasses, she had moved sufficiently to remove her final black silk stocking. He sat on the sofa, a glass in each hand, and she sat down naked on his lap and took one of the glasses from him.

'To us,' he said, his arm round her waist. 'To freedom. To wealth.'

He emptied his glass while she was sipping at hers, and hurled it across the room. It smashed against the far wall and rained down in shards of broken glass to the floor.

'That was one of our best glasses,' Sieglinde said mildly.

'So?'

'You're right,' and she emptied her own glass and threw it after his.

'We can afford to do anything we like now,' he said, stroking her flat belly as she cuddled against him. 'We can buy all the glasses, clothes, furniture, apartments and anything else we want.'

'I still can't get used to the idea.'

'You will – tomorrow we'll have our first wonderful shopping trip together. Anything we see that we like – we'll buy it.'

'Anything at all?'

His hand was between her thighs, caressing the sparse and straw-coloured tuft where they joined. She put an arm round his neck and kissed his ear.

'Our new life will be wonderful,' he said. 'There's so much to do and see.'

279

Sieglinde took off his black tie and unbuttoned his shirt so that she could put her palm on his chest and rub it slowly. His fingers had found her secret bud.

'Now that you can do anything you want, promise me that you won't fall in love with someone else and leave me,' she sighed.

'Never.'

'Never, never?'

'Never, never, never,' he assured her.

'Oh, Gerhart . . . you want me to tell you my Little Secret, don't you?'

'After all that we have been through today, I need to hear it, to know that you love me,' he murmured. 'You are the only person I love – I have to be sure that you love me.'

'And how about Lotte – don't you love her a little?'

'No, not even a little.'

'But you play with her a lot,' Sieglinde sighed, her open thighs quivering.

'I've played with a lot of girls, but you are the only one I love.'

'Then I'll let you hear my Little Secret . . .'

'Oh, yes – but don't be in a hurry – all our time is our own now.'

'I can't wait . . .' she gasped, 'I've got to tell you now!'

Her naked body shook against him in a long and gentle release of passion.

'So beautiful,' he said, kissing her face repeatedly, 'I love to watch you when you tell me your Secret.'

Sieglinde, still breathing quickly, unbuttoned his trousers and eased his hard stem out through the slit in his underpants.

'How do I look when I do it?' she asked.

'Your eyelids come slowly down, as if in modesty, and your mouth opens in a sort of half-smile that shows the tip of your tongue. Your cheeks flush pink – and then a look that could almost be surprise appears on your face and you do it.'

'Surprise?' she said, fondling his stiff tail with a practised hand. 'Yes, you're right – I feel an instant of surprise that any-thing could be so wonderful just as it starts to happen to me. Is it the same for you?'

She turned on his lap to straddle his legs and face him, her bare

280

feet on the sofa at his sides. Gerhart put his hands on her breasts and played with them.

'Yes, though *surprise* is not the right word when I'm with you,' he said, 'There is a moment of amazement that it feels so good just as I do it.'

'I shall watch your face for your look of amazement when you tell me your Little Secret,' she said, her hand busy with his upstanding part.

'But I have a Big Secret to tell you,' he said slowly.

'Do you mean it?' she gasped.

He held her by the hips and pulled her forward along his black-trousered thighs until she was close enough for his purpose.

'I mean it, Sieglinde. Do you want to hear my Big Secret?'

She nodded, her face flushed pink, though not with modesty. Her hand trembled a little as she guided his tail to the soft folds between her legs and he sank it into her with a long and steady push.

'Oh my God!' she exclaimed. 'Gerhart!'

'Stay absolutely still and let me kiss you,' he whispered. 'This is a moment we shall remember forever.'

Her arms were round his neck, pressing his mouth to hers, while he stroked her long back with hands he tried to control, but which were shaking. Nor was it only his hands that shook – his penetrating stem was shaking of its own volition. Sieglinde's loins and belly were quivering in response, adding to the fast-growing sensations.

'Gerhart!' she moaned, 'I can't stop myself!'

'Nor can I!' he gasped, his hands clenched on her bottom to pull her tighter to him.

Without assistance from either of them, the golden moments arrived. Gerhart and Sieglinde cried out together as his essence fountained into her and they clung together in their long and ecstatic spasms. All too soon for them, the delight faded, and they sat still and silent, dazed by the intensity of what they had felt.

It was Sieglinde who recovered first. She stroked his face and smiled at him.

'That was a Very Big Secret you told me,' she said softly, 'I never guessed it would be like that.'

'Nor did I. I thought it would be fantastic, but not an earthquake.'

'Yes, an earthquake – a soulquake,' she said, still slightly dazed.

'And now we know each other's Big Secret – you're not sorry, are you?'

'Silly question! I adore you, Gerhart.'

'Good – that was the overture to what we shall do together. Let's go to bed and I'll get these ridiculous clothes off.'

They went to Sieglinde's room and she lay face-down on the bed, her chin on her hands, as she watched him undress. When he was naked he lay beside her to kiss the satin-skinned cheeks of her bottom and trail his fingers along her spine, until she was trembling with pleasure. She rolled over and folded her arms beneath her head while he kissed her straw-blonde tuft.

'This beautiful rose-bud,' he sighed, 'It will be world-famous when Rudolf publishes his book of French poems with my pictures.'

'And so will the other flowers be,' she said, 'mine will be only one of six.'

Gerhart noticed a fading bite-mark on the inside of her thigh and kissed it.

'Some men have gone crazy over it already, even before the book comes out,' he said. 'Who bit you – Heinrich?'

'Did someone bite me? I can't remember,' she answered lightly.

Gerhart punished her by tickling her sides until she giggled and begged him to stop.

'Then tell me who bit you,' he insisted. 'Was it Heinrich?'

'It might have been him in the past – but you turned me off him.'

'Me?'

'It was no accident that I saw him with Roma on the balcony of Bertolt's apartment. I thought so at first, but then I realised that you had arranged the whole thing. You were jealous of him – admit it!'

'Perhaps I was. So who was it that bit you?'

'Lotte, I suppose.'

'Lotte?' he said, thunderstruck.

The humour of the confession dawned on him and he laughed and asked how long this had been going on.

'Not very long. It started that day she came here to tell you that her stupid brother-in-law had been arrested. After you'd rushed off to look for that brown-haired whore of yours I showed Lotte your flower pictures and then we compared the real things in the mirror.'

'You didn't!' Gerhart exclaimed, grinning all over his face.

'We stripped off and stood together in front of my mirror. Then we lay down and made love to each other.'

'Here on this bed we're on now?' Gerhart asked, excited by the thought, 'Was she very noisy?'

'She screeched like a cat on a roof-top at night. And her climax lasted forever.'

'I know – she's like that toy soldier I had once! You wound him up and he beat his little drum and kept on beating it till the spring ran down, and then he got slower and stopped.'

'Yes,' Sieglinde giggled, 'just like that.'

'Did she do this to you?' he asked, his fingers stroking inside the pink petals of her rose-bud. 'Of course she did – anyone you show this little flower to finds it impossible not to kiss it and play with it.'

'You did more than kiss it and play with it a little while ago,' Sieglinde murmured, her blue eyes half-closed.

'Are you ready for Big Secrets again?' he asked, and when she nodded and spread her legs wide, he mounted her and settled his belly comfortably on hers.

Her knees came up at his sides and he pushed into her blonde-fuzzed split peach deftly.

'Not so fast this time,' she pleaded, her hands stroking his face. 'It was wonderful before, but it was over too soon.'

'I didn't move at all,' he sighed, 'the thought of being inside you was enough. It won't be like that this time.'

'How *will* it be, Gerhart?'

There was no need to answer. His long and slow thrusts

assured her that it was going to be very satisfactory indeed. He looked at her face with affectionate attention, familiar with her changing expressions as her excitement grew. A flutter of her closed eye-lids warned him that she was nearing her peak of sensation, and he paused for a moment or two, to let her calm down a little. Three times he took her to the brink, and then retreated, and she was squirming under him and clawing at his back with her finger-nails. The fourth time was more than he could bear himself. His own long crescendo of passion carried him on to a searing explosion of delight. Sieglinde's back arched off the bed and she cried out at the same moment as he did.

They slept in each other's arms for an hour or two after that and when they woke up it was dark outside and they were both hungry. Sieglinde put on a pair of lacy white silk knickers and Gerhart, grinning, pulled on his striped underpants and, lightly attired in this way, they went together to the kitchen.

'There's nothing to eat,' she said, 'it never occurred to me that we'd be dining in today. I thought you'd be taking me to a quiet and expensive restaurant.'

'That was exactly what I planned. In fact, I even reserved a table for eight o'clock. But that was before we made such astounding discoveries about each other. We can still go if you want to – we'll only be an hour late.'

'Not tonight,' she said. 'Tomorrow, after a day's shopping, I want to be taken to the most expensive restaurant in Berlin.'

Though she had claimed that there was nothing to eat, she made an omelette with a dozen eggs and chopped herbs into it, and Gerhart found a bottle of wine to go with it. They sat at the kitchen table, Gerhart's eyes hardly ever away from her soft little breasts as they bobbed about to her movements as she ate, and her eyes on his face in silent worship.

'I've had a wonderful idea!' Gerhart announced, banging his fist on the table. 'A party such as there has never been before!'

'Yes, we must give a big celebration party,' she agreed, 'but is the apartment big enough for all the people we know?'

'Listen to my idea and tell me what you think. Instead of the usual sort of party where everyone turns up in evening clothes and there's dancing and drinking and taking girls into the

284

bedrooms and people falling down drunk and being sick in the bathroom – we'll have a very special kind of party for only about twenty people.'

'What about all our other friends?'

'We can invite them later to the sort of party they expect when we move into a bigger apartment.'

'So what is this wonderful idea of yours?'

'The banquet of the gods,' he said, 'ten or a dozen men and the same number of girls. A long wooden table loaded with food and drink – wild boar ham and haunches of venison, things like that. Wagner's music non-stop on the gramophone. The men dressed as Gods, in helmets and animal-skins and with swords.'

'Yes! And the girls?'

'They will all be Valkyries. We must find the right place – somewhere old with stone walls and wooden beams, that we can hire for the party, where they won't mind what we get up to.'

'The Valkyries I've seen at the opera wear white sheets draped round them,' Sieglinde objected, 'that's not very flattering.'

'Not our Valkyries. They'll be naked, with long blonde wigs and spears.'

'Another of your crazy ideas!'

'Do you like it?'

'I think it's fantastic. I've never been to a party naked before.'

'This won't be a party – this will be the banquet of the gods. We shall all be gods, and gods can do anything they like. By the time everyone is half-drunk it will be uproarious.'

'And who's going to be your Valkyrie at this banquet – Lotte, I suppose?'

'No,' Gerhart answered, reaching across the table to take her hand, 'You.'

'But we can't! Not in front of other people!'

'We can do anything we like.'

'But isn't there a law against it?'

'Laws for other people don't concern us now. We can get on a train for Paris or Rome at any time we want to. But no one will take the least notice of what we do. We're rich and that makes us important.'

'I'm blonde already,' Sieglinde said thoughtfully, 'I don't need a wig, even though my hair isn't very long.'

'Just the long braids to hang down to your little bundles,' Gerhart agreed.

'When shall we give the banquet?'

'One day next week – to give time to find the right place and make the arrangements.'

When they had finished eating they went back to Sieglinde's room and stood together before the long mirror, she in front of him and his arms round her waist, so that he could see the reflection of her face and slender body over her shoulder.

'This has been a day to remember,' she said, smiling at Gerhart's face in the mirror.

'The first day of our new life,' he said, kissing the back of her neck.

Her round little bottom was pressed against his loins and he could feel her warmth through the thin silk of her knickers and his own underwear. His hanging tail twitched and began to harden in response to her pressure and he cupped her soft breasts in his hands.

'It was nice that day you painted roses on them,' she said, 'will you do it for me again sometime?'

'Gladly – and try to paint the rose-bud between your legs. Though I doubt if I'll succeed with that any better than last time.'

'You will if you make love to me first, so that the paint-brush doesn't drive me into a frenzy.'

'If I make love to you first, I might not want to paint you.'

'You will – I'll make sure of that.'

Gerhart slid her white knickers down over her narrow hips to uncover her blonde tuft.

'The Temple of the Harmonies,' he said, remembering what Heinz' tattooed friend had said to him, though whether it was six or seven harmonies to be found in her Chinese pavilion he could no longer be sure.

'The what?' Sieglinde asked.

'Nothing – just a phrase from somewhere,' he said, his fingers playing with the delicate lips beneath the straw-coloured hair.

'Are you happy now?' she asked.

'Happier than I've ever been in my life.'

She turned in his arms to face him and his stem, protruding through his striped underpants, was squeezed between their bellies.

'I want it to be like the first time,' he whispered, 'I want to see.'

They stripped off their underwear and Sieglinde sat on the side of her bed, her feet on the floor and her knees wide apart. Gerhart knelt between her thighs and positioned his tail at the open rose presented to him.

'I want to see what I'm doing to you, Sieglinde,' he breathed.

He took hold of her slender thighs and eased himself forward very slowly, staring the whole time at the gradual insertion of his long spike into her, until he was completely embedded in her warmth. He hardly dared move, so intense were his emotions, that he was afraid of bringing on an instant climax of sensation.

'Oh Gerhart,' Sieglinde sighed. 'It feels so wonderful! You could have had this anytime in the last five years.'

'Do you remember the first time I touched you?' he gasped, 'I woke you up by feeling your little bundles – and I was terrified when you opened your eyes.'

Her hands stroked his shoulders as she looked into his flushed face.

'You weren't terrified when I put my hand down your trousers and held your tail later that day,' she said, giggling at the memory.

Her giggle undid him. He cried out wordlessly and stabbed hard and fast into the blonde-flossed pink lips that held his stem as he discharged his passion into her in a furious outburst.

'Sieglinde!' he moaned, still staring down at the soft folds of flesh into which he was pouring his sap, the *rose-bud* that had become the centre of his world.